The Last Revolution

W.O. Joseph

Greenstone Creative Inc.

Bigfork, Montana

Greenstone Creative Inc.
Bigfork, Montana
www.wojoseph.com

Publisher's Note: This is a work of fiction. Names, characters, places, and incidents are a product of the author's imagination. Locales and public names are sometimes used for atmospheric purposes. Any resemblance to actual people, living or dead, or to businesses, companies, events, institutions, or locales is completely coincidental.

The Last Revolution by W.O. Joseph. -- 1st ed.
ISBN 978-0-578-63868-3

For all of the grand children: Waiting to fully appreciate our liberty, until after it has been taken away, will be the biggest mistake humanity has ever made.

Part 1: The Legend

CHAPTER ONE

11,501 BCE   The Village of Vandalay

The air outside was crisp and cool, the sky a deep cerulean blue. Pearl white cumulus clouds billowed over the valley as they often did. Though it was early winter, the warmth emanating from the ground made it seem almost balmy. Despite the beauty of the day, Sanjay was feeling slightly anxious. This morning he would be making his carefully crafted presentation to the Council of Regents. He couldn't remember the last time he'd felt this anxious. It had been decades ago.

From the window of his study, he could see the mists rising and furling off the surface of the great steaming lake. The warm water of the lake was heated by the presence of molten lava in a volcanic chimney, that rose up from the planet's core, near the bottom of the body of water. If he listened carefully, he could just hear the muted roar of the waterfall cascading down from the mountains above the north end of the valley. A slight breeze caused the reflection of the stone façade of the great council hall to ripple across the surface of the hot water. The meeting hall had been carved out of a solid rock face next to a small bay at the edge of the lake millennia ago. The grand fluted stone columns of the portico rose into the sky above a broad stone terrace with stairs that went down into the waters of the bay. On celebration days, the people would gather there to bathe in the hot water and to discuss philosophy and art.

The hot water that poured out of the south end of the lake was distributed by an elaborate system of fired clay pipes throughout the entire village. The ceramic piping was made by the master potters from clays that were the same color as the local limestone. The piping was laid to all homes and shops as well as through the streets and plazas and on down to the greenhouses, pastures, and cropland below the village in a curious herringbone pattern.

The result was that the valley, surrounded by the dark green conifers of a boreal forest, enjoyed a very mild climate in a location that would otherwise have proven to be quite inhospitable. The valley stayed green year-round and was one of a very few places at this latitude where fruit trees and grape vines grew.

The village, elegantly situated at the head of the valley, just below the bay and the great hall, was built of a buff-colored limestone. The stones were set so closely and in so exact a manner that no bed of mortar was needed to keep out the wind. The stone cutting technology had been developed centuries ago, and now only one extended family was in charge of the quarries and met all the needs of the village and the region. The roofs of dark grey slate were likewise cut and installed so precisely they were known to have lasted for many generations. The built environment had been mastered long ago and didn't require a great deal of effort to maintain.

Sanjay, a tall, thin man of timid disposition, was the last in the long line of historians. He preferred the company of his books and archives to the hustle of the marketplace or the burdens of government. He was the keeper of the story of the Ularian people. In times past, the historians studied the great conflicts of history to achieve some perspective on how current discontent might be alleviated. But this was an age when the crimes of humanity against itself had long since been buried under the sands of time. No conflict existed in the land. It was an age when what used to be known as the rule of law was no longer written but carried spiritually in the hearts and minds of humankind, as it was in the beginning. An age when the veil between the worlds grows thin and permeable. The Golden Age. Sanjay understood, however, that change was imminent.

There was a knock at the door of his study. A page, from the Council of Regents, cracked the door open far enough to stick his head through.

"Honored sir, they are ready for you now."

Sanjay stood and straightened his purple velvet robes. He gathered up some papers from the top of his desk, inserted them into a well-used folio, and tucked it under his arm. He left his study. The cobblestone streets were alive with villagers hurrying to and fro. They were all preparing for the coming Grand Solstice. Everything had to be left just so.

Sanjay was greeted by many who knew him, as he made his way to the council hall. "Good morning Master Historian. Blessings be upon you, sir."

He took the 108 steps of the grand portico without becoming winded. Even at his advanced age, he still enjoyed the body of a much younger man. He entered the building, his footsteps echoing through the great stone foyer. Rays of sunlight angled through high clerestory windows, illuminating the two thirty-foot high cast bronze doors of the council chamber that bore the double oval symbol of Ularian society. Two men stood at attention, one in front of each door. They were clad in the elaborately colored silk uniforms of the ceremonial guard.

Sanjay paused in front of the doors, awaiting permission to enter. Without any visible or audible signal, the two guards turned and with some effort pushed the great doors open. Standing to both sides, neither man uttered a word, but with a sweep of their arms bade him enter.

Sanjay strode up the finely tiled aisle. The wooden pews on either side of the aisle were densely populated with lesser officials from all levels of regional government. They were all here to finalize preparations for the coming Grand Solstice. As the custom of government officials had been, time out of mind, the twelve Regents sat behind an imposing semi-circular edifice that was elevated above the floor of the hall. So long ago, it hardly bore remembering, the Regents debated whether or not the elevated dais symbolized a latent desire of the Regents to raise themselves above the people. After a detailed review of the issue, it was decided that the high platform was necessary in order to be heard throughout the chamber without amplification.

As a result of that debate, the edifice hadn't been changed. If one were so inclined, one could have wondered if there wasn't still the smallest smidgeon of ego left in the political mind even in this age of enlightenment.

Marina, the Planetary Governor, sat in the middle, flanked by six Regents on either side. Sanjay arranged his papers on the lectern and stepping aside made the traditional bow to the panel, the sleeves of his robe gently brushing the floor. He straightened and stepping back to the podium, he locked eyes with Marina. As well as being the Planetary Governor, she was also his maternal grandmother, though the distinction blurred somewhat when you were several hundred years old. Sanjay's eyes gave off the slightest twinkle, and he could see the corners of her mouth crack just a little. He knew he had at least one supporter on the Council.

Sanjay began. "Members of the Council, I give you greetings and thank you for allowing me to make this presentation today. For those in the hall who do not know me, my name is Sanjay; I am the Royal Historian to the Council of Regents and keeper of the Ularian Archives. The term "Royal," of course, no longer refers to being in the service of a monarch, as in past millenniums, but like some things in this chamber, it has remained unchanged as a matter of tradition."

A ripple of laughter swept through the crowd. Some of the Regents smiled knowingly.

Sanjay continued, "On the eve of the Grand Solstice, you have before you a draft proposal that could be considered somewhat unusual, in that we have no record of such a suggestion ever having been made before. It has been my privilege for these many years to be the keeper of the story of the Ularian people." Sanjay reached into a pocket in his robes, extracted a round palm-sized silver storage device, and held it up.

"In addition to keeping the written and recorded evidence of our history, I have attempted to chronicle the feelings and perceptions of our people as we progressed through the four stages in the development of human intellect, both ascending and descending. This history, which would have otherwise gone unrecorded, has been the subject of my efforts for quite some time now. Many of you are familiar with the library of knowledge which I have compiled on behalf of the Ularian People.

"In the many years I have been collecting and recording this information, it could be said, I have assembled a holographic awareness of the trials, tribulations, and triumphs our culture has endured during our sojourn on the planet. Most people are loathed to exhume the squalor of the lower ages, preferring to inhabit the present age of enlightenment, for which no explanation is necessary. Therefore, an in-depth appreciation of our history and the future plight of the next class of planetary inhabitants has, in my view, been under-appreciated.

"In the process of recording the thoughts and impressions of our people, I have developed a deep sense of compassion for the pain and suffering that is a normal aspect of human existence during the lower ages. I have taken the liberty of providing a detailed reminder of the nature of that pain and suffering in my proposal, which you have all had a chance to review.

"So, without belaboring the point, I wish to state before this council my sincere desire to do something to help alleviate at least some of the suffering of the next class of incarnates to inhabit our blessed planet. I am proposing that we leave behind an artifact outlining a detailed explanation of the nature of the Ularian orbital system for the use of future generations. It is my desire they be able to use this information to accelerate their journey through the four developmental stages of the human intellect and to avoid what we could decide today, is unnecessary pain and suffering."

There was a murmur of conversation in the crowded hall. Some people came specifically to hear this debate. Sanjay paused and took a drink of water from the glass, which was placed on the podium for him.

He continued. "So, it is with great humility, I formally put this proposal before the Council and ask for your approval. I apologize for not presenting this issue long ago, but the truth is, I only received the inspiration recently."

The crowd giggled again.

"As there is little time left to act before the Grand Solstice, I hope we can reach an accommodation today. I will be happy to entertain your questions."

Marina leaned over slightly, smiled at Sanjay, and addressed the panel. "Thank you, Sanjay, for your eloquent words. Members of the Council, you all have a copy of the Royal Historian's proposal before you, which I have no doubt you have each reviewed in detail. Do you have any questions?"

"Madam Governor," said Keturah, the minister from the 12th Regency. "I have questions for the Royal Historian."

"Please proceed," said the Governor.

"Master Historian, we all know the specifications for the Ularian system are not intended to be eternal. The fossil record tells us there was a time before humans walked the planet. It was a time when the members of the natural kingdom, which is ruled by instinct, were its sole inhabitants and the planetary free will experiment had not yet commenced.

"There may well be a time when the planet is, once again, no long-er the home of beings capable of exercising free will. There is nothing written by Aeon Manu, I am aware of, suggesting that the Planetary Free Will Experiment cannot be changed.

"However, as you know, the criteria have remained constant for a very large number of cycles. I do not know the number. My question is this: How can we leave this artifact you are proposing and not vio-late the covenants of the primary directive which prohibits us from interfering with the evolution of coming cultures?"

Sanjay reflected for a moment. "I congratulate the Regent for hom-ing in on the weakest aspect of my proposal without delay."

Another murmur of laughter made its way through the spectators.

"I believe, if it is done correctly, the dissemination of the truth re-garding our system will not serve to manipulate or influence the development of a new culture in a specific manner but would only accelerate their perception of our ancient galactic wisdom. One of the central questions I wish to answer today is: If you approve this pro-posal, at which point in the procession of the next orbit would it be appropriate to release this information?"

"Madam Governor, if I may?" It was Rinnah, the minister from the 7th Regency.

Marina invited him to speak. "Please, Minister."

"Master Historian, I sympathize with your intent to lessen the suf-fering of the coming class of incarnates. However, the descent into the density of the lower ages has always been a feature of the Ularian Mystery School and is, in my view, a critical part of the curriculum.

It provides a contrast with the culture's memories of a higher state of awareness and encourages the inhabitants to improve themselves during the ascending ages. I know from your writings that you under-stand the experiences of density are ultimately an illusion. Before we debate at which point it would be appropriate to reveal your artifact, I would like to hear more about why we would consider doing this in the first place."

Sanjay had studied this issue and was ready for the question.

"Minister, with all due respect, it is very easy for us to discount the intensity of the suffering that occurs during the lower ages from our lofty viewpoint here at the apogee of the golden age. You have the benefit of wisdom and access to the genetic memories for your comfort. You know how it all comes out.

"But I assure you, the inhabitants of the lower ages do not have the benefit of that wisdom and do not know how it comes out. They feel great pain and great fear that they may cease to exist. Their concerns are not unfounded. Such a thing is difficult to access if you are not in the middle of it, and we are not.

"I agree, in the context of eternity, their pain and suffering are illusory and will pass. Perhaps the better question is, why wouldn't we want to help alleviate their suffering? I have studied this question at length and believe we should take steps to increase the ability of our solar system to reflect the divine wisdom of galactic center."

Rinnah retorted, "An admirable undertaking I'm sure. However, it is clear to me, and I suspect other members of the Council agree that the release of the knowledge during the descending ages would be quite useless since it would be lost by the end of the Kali Yuga."

Some of the other ministers nodded.

Sanjay saw the opening. "I quite agree, Minister; you are correct. Perhaps we could take a different approach. Every culture comes to a point in its evolution where they have developed the technology to destroy themselves. It is at that point the question is called. Do they have the will to continue to exist, or do they not? All cultures must pass through that initiation. In our history, this phenomenon occurred during the middle of the ascending Dwapara Yuga.

"We exhibited the will to adapt and survive. Not all classes are so fortunate, and we know some have perished from the planet. When this had occurred in the past, the planet laid fallow until the passing of the next Satya Yuga. I suggest we fashion a method whereby the development of the technology that could be used to destroy themselves would be the same level of technology required to discover the artifact and learn the ancient galactic wisdom."

That statement received nods from several of the ministers. Tamar, the Minister of the 5th Regency, motioned to the Governor who nodded her assent.

"Master Historian, you no doubt are aware, Gaia, the spirit commonly referred to as "nature," causes the planet to be vigorously scrubbed at the end of each orbital cycle. Immediately after the grand solstice, there will be a thousand-year ice age when the oceans will recede, and the ice caps will form. Then, as the ice begins to melt, there will be a great deluge. Almost all traces of previous civilizations will be removed in preparation for the introduction of the new class of incarnates. Where are you proposing such an artifact be placed to avoid the great deluge?"

Now Sanjay hoped the last piece of the puzzle would fall into place. He outlined in detail how and where the artifact would be placed. When he was finished, he paused.

Marina asked, "Are there any more questions for the Royal Historian?" There were none.

"Then, thank you for your presentation, Sanjay. You will be notified of the Council's decision."

Sanjay made his bow, picked up his notes, and worked his way back down the aisle. As he went by, many of the spectators showed their approval, and some reached out to shake his hand. When he drew near the doors, one of the guards took him aside and asked him to wait a moment. A few minutes later, a page came up to him and handed him a note. It was from Marina and said, "Come to my hearth tonight. I may have consensus by then."

Later that evening, Marina sat gazing serenely out over the lights of the village from the beveled glass windows in her study. The stars twinkled overhead in a crystal sky. The yellow and orange flickerings of the night fire spilled out over the stone hearth and across a hand-woven rug. The shadows danced gently across the dark wooden bookshelves that housed her collection of hand-bound books, many written by Sanjay himself.

She did so love a fire. It was entirely ceremonial these days since the waters of the lake heated all buildings. Her reverie was interrupted by a knock at the door. "It's open," she said.

The door creaked slightly as Sanjay opened it wide. "Marina, may I come in?"

"Please, Sanjay, come and sit with me by the fire." He came in and sat on the hearth next to her rocker.

"Were you able to come to a conclusion?" he asked.

Marina adjusted herself in her chair. "We stayed late, continued the debate, and were able to come to an agreement."

Sanjay was aware that the decisions of the council were usually handed down in the form of a scroll. He looked over her shoulder apprehensively at a very nicely made gold bound scroll, tied with a green ribbon, laying on Marina's desk. She could see he was about to burst and decided not to torture him any further.

"They honored your intent not to affect the evolution of new societies, but to help alleviate the suffering inherent in the lower ages. At first, there was a lively debate about whether our star system had reached a level of maturity appropriate for such a move.

Then there was more conversation about how this could be done without violating the prime directive not to interfere directly in the evolution of the new society. At long last, a consensus was reached, and they gave me the scroll. Your scroll, I believe."

She reached around, picked it up from her desk, and handed it across to Sanjay. His hand trembled just a little as he took the scroll from his grandmother. He hastily untied the ribbon and read.

The Honorable Sanjay,
Royal Historian to the Council of Regents,

We are pleased to have considered your proposal at the Council of Regents and have discussed its merits in detail. We are aware of the many years you have studied the history of the Ularian System. We feel we owe you a great debt of gratitude on behalf of the Ularian People for the work you have done.

Your eloquently expressed compassion for the ordeal humanity must endure during the lower ages has caused us to reconsider some of the specifications for the Ularian Planetary Free Will Experiment. The question we have undertaken to answer is, whether we should allow a graduating class to have contact with an incoming wave of incarnates by virtue of an artifact capable of surviving the great deluge. In a length of time that is difficult to comprehend, this has not been permitted. Each new wave of humanity has been left to make their way unaided, except for the assistance of the Guardians. Historically, this has been one of the central features of the free will experiment.

However, we have been moved by the depth of your compassion and the love you show for humanity and have reached consensus. It might now be appropriate to alter the specifications of the Ularian System to see if this form of contact will inspire the next new population to rise somewhat more into the light at an earlier stage in the great cycle than has been prevalent in the past.

Your proposal has been approved by the Council of Regents, and you are directed to proceed with the project subject to the following considerations:

It is granted: You will develop an artifact that depicts the orbital nature of the Ularian System and the resulting effect it has on the development of human consciousness.

It is granted: You will situate the artifact in such a way that it will survive the coming period of cleansing.

It is granted: You will situate the artifact in such a way that it will not become accessible to the population until that point in the development of their technology where they have acquired the ability to destroy themselves. All societies must pass through the initiation and answer the question:

Do we have the will to recognize ourselves as a species connected by spirit, and will we take the steps necessary to survive the negative aspects of our technology so that we may thrive and prosper?

If their evolution parallels our own, we would expect the question to be called sometime toward the middle of the ascending Dwapara Yuga. We recognize that this approval will not alleviate suffering during the dark ages. The presence of the dark ages in our system is a structural matter that is not currently a subject for review. Those hav-

ing no need to endure the entire spectrum of experience in our world are adorning some other.

However, introducing the galactic truths near the beginning of the ascending cycle may serve to accelerate the development of higher awareness, and by so doing we may help to alleviate at least some of the overall suffering experienced by the inhabitants during the course of the great cycle.

We leave the rest of the details to you and to Governor Marina and know that the intent of the Council will be honored.

Blessings be upon you.

The Council of Regents

Sanjay sat back with the most beatific smile on his face. Of course, the artifact couldn't be allowed to be discovered during the descending ages, a time when humanity would gradually forget the ancient wisdom. If revealed during that period, the great truths would be lost or used for manipulation. Of course, the divine knowledge must remain hidden until the dawn of the ascending cycle, a time when humanity could make the best use of it.

He looked at the bottom of the scroll. "It even has the stamp and seal of Aeon Manu! How did you get that so quickly?"

"My dear, Manu has been watching the proceedings of the Regents with great interest for some time now," Marina said softly.

A tear of joy made its way down Marina's cheek; she could see by the look on Sanjay's face that this project was going to be the culmination of his life's work to this point.

Marina had one more question. "Do you plan to inform the Guardians about what you are doing?"

Sanjay knew that memory loss during the descending ages was a part of the Guardian experience and he had given the matter a great deal of thought.

"It is true that the Guardians will lose their memory of the Ularian People and our civilization as a natural part of the Grand Solstice process. So, we will download the memories of our history into their cellular structure. They will be able to access the ancient wisdom as a matter of instinct instead of intellect. The information regarding the artifact will be included, if for no other reason than they might have intense feelings of familiarity when they discover it several thousand years from now. Will you be present at the Guardian ceremony?"

Marina thought for a moment. "Why yes, I think I will join you," she said.

Sanjay rose, and grasping Marina's hand, kissed it gently. "Thank you, Grandmother. Time is short; I'd best be about my task." He slipped out the door and was on his way. Marina sat back in her rocker and let out a sigh of deep satisfaction.

Sanjay returned to his study and summoned his assistant, Aadesh. The young man appeared at the door moments later.

"Aadesh, meet me at the archives this afternoon at the normal time, please. We have some last-minute work to do prior to the grand solstice."

Later that afternoon, Sanjay strode through the doors of the archive which consisted of one large room and a horizontal tunnel leading to two smaller rooms deep in the mountain. The inside of the archive was finished in a blinding white material that seemed to glow from within whenever a person walked by. The three rooms and the tunnel had been carved out of the solid rock under the base of the cliffs at the north end of the valley.

Many such rooms throughout had been created when the stone was removed to build the village. The room immediately inside the entry doors to the archive was used as the curator's workshop and storage facility. Several worktables filled the center of the space. Tools were kept in cabinets under each table, where the objects of antiquity were restored and cataloged.

Rows and rows of shelving ran across the back of the archive. In between the shelves at the center of the back wall, a very heavily constructed bronze door, with a small window, led to the tunnel that ran deep into the mountain. Aadesh had never been allowed to see past the tunnel into the second and third rooms. Sanjay and Aadesh began to move items about on the archive's shelves.

"Aadesh, I am looking for a specific container dating back to the early Treta Yuga." Sanjay explained in detail.

The two men spent the next couple of hours searching for what Sanjay wanted. Finally, behind some crates, they found a smooth white container with rounded edges. They hauled it out from the very back of the room and placed it on the table in the center of the workshop. Sanjay pressed a latch on the side of the box. The lid popped open with a hiss, revealing a relatively small machine that was clearly very old. The machine's case was made of a highly decorated bronze-colored metal and had seen better days. A large crystal was visible inside of the metal enclosure under a clear glass bubble.

Aadesh asked, "What, exactly, is that?"

Sanjay dusted the artifact off with a brush and placed a hand on top of a handprint on the front of the device's case. The crystal began to emit a piercing violet-white light that lit up the ceiling and caused the entire room to glow more intensely.

"Hah!" he said. "It still works! This device will represent a giant leap forward to the next class of incarnates. It was used thousands of years ago when we still relied on external power to do things. As you can see, it continues to work after all of these years of sitting in the archive."

Aadesh found the demonstration of antique technology a little boring. "Okay, but why do you want to leave it here? We don't even know if this room or anything in it will survive the great cleansing!"

"Oh, let's just say it's a sentimental gesture for whoever might come here next, if it does manage to survive," Sanjay sighed. "Let's leave it in that storage niche inside the tunnel."

Aadesh entered a code into a keypad with nine Ularian symbols on it. Silently, the heavy bronze door to the tunnel swung open on oiled hinges. They closed the container and together carried it fifty feet into the tunnel. Sanjay placed his hand over another handprint on the side wall. A hidden door slid open, revealing a small storage space. Aadesh slid the box into the space, and Sanjay closed the door. Aadesh knew not to ask what was at the other end of the tunnel.

"That will do for now," Sanjay said. "Thank you for assisting me for the last few years Aadesh. I will see you on the other side."

CHAPTER TWO

Vandalay

Once again, the page from the Council of Regents knocked and stuck his head through the door of Sanjay's study.

"Master Historian, it is time for the Guardian Ceremony. Are you ready to proceed?"

Sanjay looked up from his desk. "Be there in a moment," he sighed.

He'd been working non-stop for the past few days and was tired. He needed to summon the energy for just the one more thing left to do. Pocketing the silver disc from the top of his desk, he left the study. It was early in the day as he strolled across the empty plaza to the archive. The double entry doors slid back into the carved facade of the building as he approached. Sanjay made his way to the back of the room and opened the bronze door to the tunnel. The walls emitted a glow that followed him deep into the mountain. At the end of the tunnel, a second door automatically slid open to let him pass. The area, consisting of two rooms, was also made of the glowing white material. The back room was separated from the entry by a curved glass wall with a control panel just below the windows. The control panel was very simple with only an access port, two buttons, a dial, and a curious indicator in the shape of the double oval Ularian symbol. At the moment the glass wall was an opaque dark gray color.

Sanjay turned to his right. Marina, dressed in the saffron robes of her office, sat directly across from him in a semi-circular arrangement of chairs. She seemed to have aged slightly since he had last seen her. The six members of the Guardians sat on both sides of her with three women on the left and three men on the right. Sanjay bowed and pulled over a chair for himself.

He nodded toward Marina and said somewhat formally to mark the occasion, "Madam Governor, how nice to see you again."

He greeted the six Guardians. He hadn't known any of them in this life, but he was very well acquainted with their individual stories, having been responsible for choosing them from a planet-wide pool of candidates. They had all undergone years of training. They were young, fit, and in the prime of life. They had been selected for beauty, strength, dexterity, intelligence, and the ability to procreate.

He addressed the group as if they had known each other for years. "The material I am about to cover is well known to you. However, as a part of this ceremony, I am required to state the facts one final time. This will be your last opportunity to decline to participate. If you choose to decline, you will be replaced by one of the six alternates that are waiting here in the capital.

"The Ularian solar system is a member of what is known as a binary orbit. Our star system takes a partially overlapping elliptical orbit around a sister star system which takes approximately 24,000 of our solar years. While we refer to our planet and solar system as Ularia, the correct designation for our solar system is Ularia Two. Our sister solar system is known as Ularia Prime. Ularia Prime won its designation because its elliptical orbit is closer to galactic center than ours. Subsequently, its habitable planet is much more evolved than ours.

"Every 24,000 years, we come to that point in our binary orbit where the two solar systems are closest to each other. This event is known as the Grand Solstice. The proximity of the two solar systems makes it possible for the planetary population to migrate to Ularia Prime en masse. Having participated in the previous 24,000 years of the Ularian Mystery School, the inhabitants of Ularia Two will have an opportunity to move into a higher dimension.

"As you know from the training you undertook to become a Guardian, you will be placed under stasis for an undetermined length of time until the great planetary cleanse is completed. When your life support systems detect that certain parameters have been met on the surface, you will be released to commence your tasks during what remains of the new orbital cycle.

"A side effect of the process of stasis is that, upon awakening, you will have no memories of Ularian civilization. The planet will have been vigorously scrubbed. Almost no remnants of our culture will be visible. This feature of the transition from old culture to new is by design so that the new culture may form itself independently from the biases and perceptual limitations of the past. It is Aeon Manu's desire that each new class of incarnates make their own way in the world and create whatever they see fit to manifest in accordance with the terms of the Planetary Free Will Experiment.

"Your mission is twofold. First, you will procreate and begin to re-populate the planet. Secondly, you will do what can be done behind the scenes, without violating the prime directive, to prevent humanity from destroying itself and bringing an end to the Planetary Free Will Experiment. You will, in fact, become the Guardians of Humanity. The future potential of the human race on Ularia Two will primarily be determined by you. Do any of you wish to decline?"

Sanjay paused and took turns locking eyes with each Guardian in succession. In turn, they each indicated that they did not wish to decline. He addressed Marina, "Madam Governor, shall we proceed?"

Marina addressed the group, "Being chosen to be a Guardian of Humanity for the next cycle is of the highest honor. You will be operating in the shadows behind all of the significant events in the coming cycle of human history. I am satisfied that your hearts are true. Let us proceed."

They all stood and walked over to the control panel against the glass wall. Sanjay pressed a button, and the door to the next room slid open. The curved glass wall became transparent revealing six luminous white life-support pods with glass covers, arranged in a semi-circle around a slim pedestal at the focal point. The Guardians entered the room, each taking a pre-assigned pod. They sat on the edge of their beds, swung their legs in and laid down. Marina and Sanjay stood next to each other at the control panel. Sanjay pressed a button, and the door to the inner room slid shut. At the same time, the glass covers on each pod closed.

Sanjay pulled the silver disc from the pocket of his robe and held it up. He addressed the Guardians one final time.

"This device contains the entire history of the Ularian People during the last orbital cycle. Since you will have no conscious memory of the ancient wisdom it contains, we will download the history into your

genetic structure where it will be available to you as a matter of instinct. When the question is called, you will experience a higher level
of synchronicity in your affairs compared to the general population.
While you will not be able to access the visual images from our history, you will have an innate understanding of the principles of your
mission. Best of luck to you all."

The Royal Historian plugged the disc into a slot on the control
panel, and the download began its high-speed playback. Using the
knob on the control panel, Sanjay turned the speed down so he could
follow it for a while. It was, after all, the culmination of his work on
Ularia Two. The pedestal at the focal point of the pods emitted a hologram directly above it. The first image was of an incredibly beautiful
spiral galaxy floating in space.

The holographic images changed to follow the narration, "There
are several types of galaxies in the universe...our home is a spiral galaxy with a luminous center...Ularia Two is a member of a binary
orbital system in which our planetary system orbits around another
solar system known as Ularia Prime...the long axis of our elliptical
orbit points toward galactic center...the length of our orbit is 24.000
years...our solar system approaches galactic center for 12,000 years,
during which time the human intellect evolves...rounding the closest
point to galactic center our solar system travels away from it for
12,000 years, whereupon the ancient wisdom is gradually forgotten...this movement through space relative to the center of our galaxy
causes the rise and fall of human intelligence and the subsequent rise
and fall of civilizations...Galactic center is inhabited by spiritual beings, known as the Aeons, who project the power of creation into our
galaxy...the Aeons are entirely non-physical and are the most highly
aware of all forms of intelligent life in our galaxy. They create and
energetically project throughout the galaxy, the archetypes that form
what we refer to as the natural world..."

Marina tugged at Sanjay's sleeve startling him from his concentration, "Will you come to my hearth tonight for the Grand Solstice?"

"Yes, of course," he replied. "There is nowhere else I'd rather be.
I'd like to stay here for a while, just to make sure the download is pro-
ceeding correctly."

Marina kissed him on the cheek and took her leave, making her way back through the tunnel and the archive to the village plaza.

Sanjay looked at the double oval indicator on the control panel. The double ellipses represented the respective orbits of Ularia Prime and Ularia Two during the 24,000-year cycle. Two small round green lights indicated the position of the two solar systems as they made their way along the outer ellipses. The images projected by the hologram matched each particular point in Ularian history. As the indicator moved, so the images changed, telling the story of the Ularian people for the last 24,000 years.

The narration continued, "There are four ages in the development of the human intellect...from the most developed to the least; they are known as Satya Yuga, the age of enlightenment; Treta Yuga, the age of mental power; Dwapara Yuga, the age of energy; and Kali Yuga, the age of materialism...the closest point to galactic center is known as the Satya Yuga or the golden age...a time when the common people fully understand their nature as spiritual beings...the furthest point from galactic center is known as the Kali Yuga...a time of strife on the planet, during which the strong enslave the weak, and the human intellect can only understand the gross material world...the Ularian Mystery School, otherwise known as the Planetary Free Will Experiment, has been in place for thousands of orbital cycles...humanity is much older than the physical evidence would indicate..."

Having been the curator of this information, Sanjay had seen it all before. He was satisfied that the system was running properly. He twisted the dial to bring the speed of the transmission up to a level that couldn't be followed by the naked eye. He pressed the last button, and the curved glass wall became opaque once again. Sealing the outer door, Sanjay slowly made his way back through the tunnel and into the archive. He gazed fondly at his workshop for the last time before making his way home.

That evening, at the zenith of the full moon, some of the villagers sat calmly around the pool while some strolled the streets of the village holding hands. Marina sat entranced by her hearth watching the flames of her fire dance within the fireplace. Again, Sanjay knocked at her door and was admitted.

Marina looked up, "The Guardians are sleeping peacefully?"

Sanjay nodded, "All is well."

"The artifact is in place?"

"Yes, Grandmother, it is done, and rather elegantly, if I do say so myself."

"Well then, come sit by the fire; it's almost time."

Sanjay sat at her feet and laid his head in her lap while she stroked his hair. They sat for a long while, motionless, staring into the fire, enjoying the deep peace and the love they felt for each other and the Ularian people.

By and by, a great flash of violet-white light, so intense yet so soothing, erupted from a single point in the heavens above, engulfing the entire planet. In one fleeting moment, except for the six guardians sleeping peacefully in their pods, the streets, the plazas, and the homes that had been occupied continuously for thousands of years, were entirely empty of human beings.

A soft rumbling noise arose from deep in the earth, and the waters of the lake—the life source of the village of Vandalay—flowed backward into the earth. The lake was no more. The stillness was intense and complete. There was no sound except the whisper of falling snow.

Part 2: The Space Race

Lunokhod 1

CHAPTER THREE

Mission Control, Houston, July 20th, 1969

They all knew Armstrong would say something profound. Anyone who'd been training for an event of this significance would've had plenty of time to think about how he'd like to go down in history.

Tom Parish was sitting at the master communications console at mission control in Houston when Neil Armstrong let go with "One small step for man, one giant leap for mankind," followed by the first human footprints in the lunar dust.

Talk about goosebumps. It blew them all away. As the world watched, the entire mission control team sat there in stunned silence for just a moment, the essence of a turning point in history washing over them. Then the big room fairly exploded. Cigars were passed out, but not lit in deference to the sensitive equipment in the room. The backslapping went on for a few minutes until Chris Taft reminded them that they still had men out there on the surface.

Tom Parish sat back down at his console amidst the rows of technicians and refocused on his control board. Tom was the radio telemetry specialist who had designed the Unified S-Band system used to communicate with the Apollo spacecraft.

The system combined crew medical telemetry, spacecraft systems telemetry, television images, and audio communications into one signal stream. Tom's current job was to maintain the overview of the entire piggybacked signal system and make the adjustments required to keep all the data flowing into mission control from monitoring stations located around the world.

Tom had been a Ham radio nut since his early teens. Growing up on his dad's farm in rural Ohio, he'd had plenty of room to play with Heathkit radio components and fabricate antenna towers from scrap. He erected and experimented with all types of ground plane and dipole antennas. He dearly loved to bounce a signal off the ionosphere and talk to someone in Asia or Australia. It gave him such a sense of power. He loved the fact that a 14-year-old kid could build his own equipment and talk to another human who was 8,000 miles away.

Now, fifteen years later, he had designed and was responsible for the equipment used to speak to astronauts who were 240,000 miles away.

It was twenty minutes to nine p.m. in Houston when Armstrong stepped onto the surface. The first moon walk lasted two hours and twenty minutes, during which the astronauts collected forty pounds of moon rocks, set up several experiments, and placed the first lunar laser retro-reflector on the lunar surface.

The Russians would place two of the devices, used to reflect laser beams to Earth, and two more would arrive aboard Apollo 14 and 15. Four out of the five retro-reflectors would still be in use, measuring the distance from the earth to the moon to the nearest millimeter, some forty years later.

Just after eleven p.m., the astronauts returned to the Eagle. The shift change at mission control had been held off so that the green team could complete the EVA. Tom was a member of both the green team and the black team and would need to be back in the morning for liftoff from the lunar surface.

After the astronauts went to sleep, Tony Vicente, a New Yorker, slapped Tom on the back. Tony worked in the Spacecraft Guidance, or GUIDO section, two stations down the row of technicians from Tom. "Whadda ya say we go have a drink buddy? Doreen is waiting for me over at the Planet. She has a friend with her who might interest you."

Tom was exhausted, but who could go home to bed after an experience like this? He looked up at Tony. "Hell of a good idea, Tony; let's go meet the ladies!"

They pushed through the double doors of the Planet Bar and Grill and found to their surprise that the place was packed. The bar was paneled in knotty pine that had yellowed from contact with clouds of cigarette smoke over the years. The booths were lined in red vinyl, and the walls were plastered with autographed pictures of all the astronauts and spacecraft covering the entire history of the Mercury, Gemini, and now the Apollo programs.

The bar had standing room only. All of the TVs were on with continuing coverage of Armstrong and Aldrin capering around on the lunar surface. This was a favorite haunt of NASA staff, and the French fries were to die for. Tom and Tony were well known in the bar, and the first of the control room staff to arrive. As they strode into the room, the hubbub ceased for a second, and then the applause broke out, accompanied by more back-slapping and offers to be the first to buy a round for the tired technicians. Tom and Tony looked at each other grinning from ear-to-ear. The din resumed.

They collected a couple of drinks from their well-wishers and, looking around, Tony spied Doreen and her friend in a booth nearby. They elbowed their way through the crowd, finally shoe-horning themselves into the booth next to the ladies.

"Hi, Tom," Doreen shouted.

"Hey, Doreen," he replied in kind, pecking her on the cheek as he sat down.

She pointed to the young lady sitting next to him, "This is my friend, Rachael Deneuve"

Tom extended his hand, "Nice to meet you Rachael." His eyes never left her face. The handshake was firm, and she held on for just a moment longer than was necessary.

He detected a slight French accent in her response, "I am most pleased to meet you as well, Tom."

In contrast to Tom's buzz cut, starched short sleeve white shirt, pocket protector and tie, Rachael wore a much more casual outfit. An off-white peasant blouse complemented an ample bosom. A long flowing skirt and sandals indicated her disdain for formality. Her shoulder length, straight black hair radiated the glow of good health. As she spoke, a wisp of hair kept falling over one eye. She had the alluring habit of tossing her head, just so, to flick the hair off to one side. She wore no makeup, and none was needed.

Most of the women who frequented the Planet sported the heavily made-up "Go Go" look. Tom was frankly surprised to find such a naturally pretty and unpretentious woman in Doreen's company. As they talked, she reached over and began to undo his tie. She pulled it away, draping it over the back of the booth, stirring Tom's loins at the same time.

"There," she said, "that will be more comfortable."

Rachael, he learned, was the daughter of high-level diplomats attached to the French Embassy in Quebec. She grew up in the midst of the aristocracy of Canadian politics. She despised the politicians and their culture of dealmaking and trickery. She'd made it her business to investigate what were beginning to be known as alternative lifestyles. Upon her twenty-first birthday, Rachael received a small inheritance from her maternal grandmother. With her parent's blessing, she outfitted herself to travel North America by camper van, and so far, had made her way from Quebec down the eastern seaboard of the United States. She hopped from artist colony to commune, even dropping in on a cult or two, arriving in Cape Kennedy just in time for the launch of Apollo 11.

Rachael had joined the thousands of people who witnessed the historic launch across the water from the Kennedy Space Center four days earlier. She'd taken two more days to drive to Houston specifically to indulge her interest in the astronauts and to see her friend Doreen. She was a believer in extraterrestrial life and was very happy to meet one of the heroes responsible for putting the first men on the moon.

One of the skills that helped Tom become the inventor of Unified S-Band technology at the age of twenty-nine was an ability to focus his laser-like concentration on anything that held his interest—often to the exclusion of whatever was happening around him. It was like a state of altered consciousness. All around him went silent as he gazed into Rachael's heart-shaped face. All he could see was her, and all he could hear was the lovely French Canadian accent as she told her story.

Tom's friends thought that maybe he was just one of those absent-minded professor types. He possessed the ability to become so lost in a sequence of thoughts that he would frequently return to a conversation having missed much of what had been said. As a young man, he'd emerge from his reverie not remembering where he'd been or what he'd been thinking about.

Over time he learned how to record in his mind not only where he'd been, but also parts of the conversation that took place while he was lost in thought. He stored what was happening around him in a sort of organic random access memory, so he could play it back in his head and thus regain a foothold in the conversation as if he'd never left. It was a clever way to cover the fact that he always had multiple conversations going on in his head.

Rachael leaned over again and unbuttoned his collar. Tom was captivated by her. He'd never thought of himself as a hero. But if she wanted him to be a hero, tonight a hero he would be. What could be the harm?

Rachael kept up her end of the conversation, "Tony tells me you are a pilot? I so love to fly; can we maybe, fly together sometime?"

"I love to fly, too," he said. "I have a four-seat Piper Arrow, and we can definitely fly together."

They enjoyed some burgers, the legendary french fries, and a couple more hours of conversation with Tony and Doreen.

Draining her last drink, Rachael leaned over and whispered into his ear, "Would you like to get out of here? It's too noisy."

He nodded. "Where to?" he asked.

"Come, I'll show you," she said.

They said their goodbyes to Tony and Doreen who gave them knowing looks. She grabbed him by the hand and led him out to the large gravel parking lot behind the bar. In a dimly lit back corner of the lot, stood a brand new, dark blue 1969 Chevy van. Rachael reached into a pocket in her skirt and pulled out the keys. She opened the side door. The van had been converted with a bed in the back and a small kitchenette. The windows all had red gingham curtains, and the interior smelled faintly like she did, of perfumed soap.

A dream catcher hung from the rear view mirror. Tom entered and took a seat on the bed. Rachael slid the door shut and sat in the passenger seat, switching on the eight track stereo. Johnny Mathis crooned "Chances Are" softly while she fumbled about in the glove box. She swiveled around in the captain's chair, holding a small pipe and some matches. Without a word, she lit the pipe and took a long pull on it. She held it out to Tom. Tom Parish was as straitlaced as they come and more than a little naïve regarding the ways of the world outside NASA.

He was vaguely aware of the hippie lifestyle but had never smoked any grass or done any kind of illegal drugs in his life. He was also a bit drunk. He looked at her and looked at the pipe. Discipline won the argument in his head.

"I can't," he said. "If I got caught, they would take my security clearance away, and then my job. But you go ahead."

All of his attention was riveted on Rachael, who was busy unbuttoning his shirt. He'd never been more attracted to any woman in his life than he was right now. There had been references to free love in the media for several years.

He thought, *"This sort of thing never really happens, does it?"*

He didn't care what you called it; he hadn't been this excited by a woman in quite a while. They shucked their clothing in a hurry and slid beneath the covers. She was soft, wet, and ready. He had taken pains to hide his arousal with his blazer as they came out of the bar. Now there was no need to be bashful. As they came together, he was nearly overwhelmed by her scent and the feeling of her skin against his. He promptly lost all sense of being Tom Parish and lost himself in Rachael Deneuve.

CHAPTER FOUR

The Lavochkin Design Bureau, Moscow Nov. 19th, 1969

Anatoly Barsukov stuck his head around the corner where Nikolai was standing at the grungy row of wall-mounted sinks in the communal bathroom of his apartment building.

"Niki, they've called a meeting this morning at the Bureau. The Americans have landed on the moon again. I think there are some big changes afoot. We need to go, or we'll miss the tram."

Nikolai grumbled in response, "The fucking Americans. They're such Cowboys. They always go for the maximum gee whiz factor in everything they do. The next thing you know they'll be driving around the moon in cars!"

Anatoly Barsukov was Niki's roommate and a payload specialist at the newly reorganized Lavochkin Design Bureau, the Soviet version of NASA. Both Niki and Toly worked in the lunar robotics section of the Bureau. It was Toly's job to calculate the weight of all components that were to ride in the payload bay for any Luna project launch to the moon. Niki was now in charge of the fabrication and assembly of robotic spacecraft. They had worked together on Luna missions 9 through 15, but the glory to come was still in the hands of the manned lunar program.

There had been a lot of talk in the hallways. Since the Americans had surged so far ahead in landing men on the moon, the Soviet government might actually be considering postponing its manned lunar program. Since it was clear they couldn't beat the Americans to the moon, they might regain leadership in the space race by having the first long term presence in orbit aboard the Salyut Space Station. In truth, the Central Committee was much more interested in weaponizing LEO (low earth orbit) than in lunar exploration. The fact that the Americans had spent all of their money on this lunar stunt and were lagging far behind in space station development would give the Soviet Union a considerable advantage in asserting control from low earth orbit.

Nikolai hiked up the collar of his overcoat as he and Toly came out the front doors of worker's paradise housing into the crisp November morning. It was bitter cold, the snow blasting by almost horizontally. The Moscow electric tram rattled up to the stop, the doors hissing open. It would take them downtown to NPO Lavochkin.

Nikolai Chubukin tramped up to the third floor, threaded his way between his comrades, and plopped down in the seat next to Anatoly at the conference room table. The third-floor conference room at NPO Lavochkin looked like it had been decorated by a turnkey from the basement of the Lubyanka Prison. In classic Soviet military style, the floor was polished concrete, the walls were painted a dark semi-gloss green up to a parting line at eye level, above which, they were a lighter version of the same hideous color, as was the concrete ceiling. A long, much worn, and peeling birch veneer conference table sat in the middle of the room surrounded by a dozen terribly uncomfortable bent plywood chairs with aluminum legs.

Nikolai nudged Toly in the ribs with his elbow. They exchanged knowing glances. They all had an idea of what was coming. The room was filled to capacity by the various members of the Lunar Rover Design Team who were lounging around the table and leaning against the chalkboards. The word had gone out early this morning to gather here for an important announcement, and the room was buzzing with anticipation. Suddenly the background noise ceased as if on command. Everybody straightened up.

The sea of bodies parted and Dmitri Arturovich Koslov, section chief of the Lunar Rover Project, strode to the one vacant seat at the head of the table. He dumped an armload of files on the table and, grasping his military tunic with both hands just below the belt, gave it an audible snap before seating himself.

Dmitri may have been a small round man who smelled of stale tobacco, but he had huge ambitions. He learned at an early age that short people needed to bring something else to the table besides stature, to be taken seriously. Dmitri brought fear. Ruthless to a fault when it came to getting what he wanted, he made it his business to give the impression of toeing the party line at all times, at least when his superiors were present.

Not well liked by his subordinates, he knew he was feared, and that was fine with him. He fancied himself to be on the fast track to the very top of the management structure within NPO Lavochkin, and he was willing to take the necessary risks to get there. After that, who knew? An appointment to the Central Committee? Dmitri sat and took his time gazing around the room. All murmuring ceased, and the silence began to get heavy.

"Comrades, as you know by now, the Americans have landed Apollo 12, a second manned mission, on the moon. While we, the Supreme Soviet Union, were the first to place a satellite in orbit. While we were the first to put a man and a woman into space, and while this division's Luna 9 mission accomplished the first soft landing of a spacecraft on the moon, we have now decisively lost the race to put the first men on the lunar surface."

He banged his fist on the table. "Now the Americans have done it twice!"

The room buzzed again, each man whispering to his neighbor. Dmitri cleared his throat. "Comrade Reshetnev and I met last night with General Secretary Brezhnev and various members of the Central Committee. Secretary Brezhnev questioned me about the status of our program. As you know, until now our division has been considered to be a back up to the more attractive prospect of placing our own men on the moon."

Everyone sat up straight anticipating what might be coming next.

Dmitri went on, "I told the General Secretary that due to the constraints of supporting human life in the hostile lunar environment, the American astronauts, Armstrong and Aldrin, had been able to spend only two and a half hours on the surface. I don't expect the current mission to do much better. That isn't much time on the surface to perform the critical science that will help us determine what materials are present that we could use to build a colony on the moon.

I pointed out to the General Secretary that we could study critical life-support issues much more easily in low earth orbit as part of our developing space station project. Our Lunokhod 1 robot doesn't suffer from the limitations of supporting life in the lunar environment and will be able to operate more or less continuously during lunar daylight for three to six months.

"I also told him we could execute many more experiments during that time than the American missions and do any science just as well or better by remote control from our Deep Space Center here in Moscow."

The staff all began talking excitedly. Dmitri attempted to suppress an all too rare grin. He raised his hands to quiet the room.

"The General Secretary took my testimony under advisement. This morning I have been informed that since we are substantially behind the United States in the manned lunar effort, we are officially putting our own manned program on hold.

"The committee ordered that the Lunokhod 1 mission proceed full speed, without delay, to a launch and landing of our Lunokhod lunar rover on the moon, and that we have eight months from today's date to accomplish our objective!"

The room erupted, everybody talking loudly at once.

Koslov paused, allowing them their moment. "Comrades, please quiet down."

The staff members were all nodding their heads and elbowing each other. They, of course, had been wondering about most of this for some time. The grapevine had been crackling all night. Dmitri tried to stifle the very smallest self-satisfied grin.

Toly slapped Nikolai on the back, "This is it! This is what we've been waiting for!" He whispered into Niki's ear, "At last we're going for a drive on the moon!"

Dmitri allowed the men a few moments to jabber at each other. "Comrades," he began again. "As you now know, this places our division at the forefront of the Soviet Space Program. This is the moment in history we have all been waiting for. I trust you will execute your duties with the utmost dedication.

Failure in this mission will not be tolerated. I expect nothing less than your best work at all times. You will receive your tasking through the usual channels. Please return to your workstations. I want an update from all project leaders on my desk by 8:00 AM tomorrow. You are dismissed! Comrade Chubukin and Comrade Barsukov, please remain."

Everyone else filed out.

CHAPTER FIVE

Houston: July 21st, 1969

The first sound to enter his consciousness was the early morning chirping of birds. Tom cracked one eye open. For a time, he lay slightly confused as to just where he might be. The fog finally cleared, and he realized that he was still in Rachael's van in the parking lot behind the Planet Bar & Grill. The events of the previous evening came back into focus. He smiled to himself.

The morning sun cast a subdued red glow inside the van through the gingham curtains. He rolled his head to the left. Rachael lay on her side, her bare back to him. The sheet and the blanket draped, just so, across her hip—her luxurious black hair cascading across the bed linen. He could see by the shape of her back that she was well-built, not overweight at all and yet not skinny either. He liked that, a lot.

Nothing like this had ever happened to him. Every woman he'd ever pursued had to be wooed at length. Only after the obligatory dinners and movie dates did he ever feel confident enough to move on to physical intimacy. Mostly it had been awkward and hadn't lasted very long. The truth was that so far, his lady friends couldn't keep up with him intellectually. He had kept losing interest. He was still single at twenty-nine.

Rachael was so easy to be with. They lost themselves in conversation. Her interest in the details of the space program was refreshing. She understood his explanation of Unified S-Band theory and his obsession with long-range communications. That was much more than could be said about any of his previous girlfriends. She was beautiful in a very natural way, not all made up like most of the wives and women who hung around the Mission Control staff.

He had a headache from the previous night's festivities, but overall, he felt good. Damn good. He reached over her back and cupped a breast, pulling her into him. She placed her hand on top of his, holding it in place, and gave a contented sigh, wiggling her butt into his groin. He held her tight, and the arousal returned. Afterward, they fell back into a deep sleep.

Tom sat up with a start. Rachael stirred, softly mumbling, *"Qu'est que c'est, cherie?"*

Tom spoke no French and didn't understand the question. "What time is it?" He asked.

She reached out and pulled some clothing off the bedside clock. "It's seven o'clock," she said. "Do you have to go so soon?"

"Yeah, we're going to lift off from the moon late this morning. I need to get back. Do you have a shower in this thing?"

"Oh, yes, of course, it's in the drawer under the stove," she quipped. "We could use the restrooms in the bar, maybe?"

He grabbed up a small mirror that sat on the sideboard and looked into it. "It's gonna take more than a sink to get through this," he said. "Let's go to my place, take a shower, and have something to eat." Then an idea came to him, "how would you like to see the lift off from the moon at Mission Control? I can get you into the visitor's gallery!"

She raised up on one elbow, her face brightening, and let the sheet fall away. She wasn't self-conscious in the least. "Yes, please, I would so love to see it all up close!"

Tom paused for a good long look. Then they threw on their clothes, and she handed him the keys. "I'll bring you back for your car later," she said.

Tom drove the three miles to his apartment on the second floor of a vintage 50's complex. He parked the van in the space with his apartment number on it. Rachael grabbed an armload of clean clothing, and they skipped up the concrete steps to the second-floor balcony. Tom unlocked the door, and they went in.

"So this is how the communications genius of NASA lives?" Rachel stood with her hands on her hips and surveyed his domain somewhat critically. The furnishings were sparse: a sofa, a recliner, a system of shelving made of 2x12's and cinder blocks, with a Hi-Fi and TV set. The carpet was a green shag. The countertops and the kitchen cabinets, a dark, walnut-colored Formica. Tom looked around; he never really considered what his home might look like to a woman. He suddenly felt a little self-conscious.

"It's not as nice as your van, is it?" he frowned. "Maybe you could help me fix it up?"

She made no response, leaving him with the feeling it was way too soon to be discussing such a commitment.

She began to undo the buttons on her blouse. "Where is the bathroom, please?"

He took her by the hand, and they walked down the hall to the bathroom, leaving a trail of clothing behind. She scrubbed him from

head to toe with a washcloth and soap. He was A solidly built 5'10",
with brown hair and brown eyes; she liked what she saw.

Wearing his robe, she went into the kitchen and rummaged around
for something to eat. They sat at the breakfast bar together exchanging
smiles and comments in between bites of scrambled eggs and bacon.
Rachael asked what would be happening on the moon today.

Tom took time to explain, "Armstrong and Aldrin spent the night,
our night that is, getting some rest. This morning, they'll do some
housekeeping and stowing of the samples they took yesterday. Then
there's a lengthy countdown during which we'll run through all the
spacecraft systems to make sure everything checks out. Then they'll
lift off from the surface."

"I can see all of this happening from the visitor's gallery?"

"I don't see why not. They let some of the guy's wives in. Maybe
you can meet some of them. Doreen might be there, too."

That afternoon, Rachael, sitting next to Doreen, watched from the
visitor's gallery as Armstrong and Aldrin lifted off from the lunar surface and rocketed away into lunar orbit to dock with the command
module and begin the long journey home to Earth.

Occasionally, Tom looked up from his console and gave her the
thumbs up sign. Rachael Deneuve was smitten with his boyish good
looks and especially his attitude toward his work. He was highly intelligent and was considered to be on a par with the men who were in
charge of America's space program. Men who were twice his age.
Doreen and many of the dignitaries present left just after the liftoff.
Rachael fell asleep sitting in the visitor's gallery during the last hour
of Tom's shift.

He shook her gently. "Hi sleepy," he said, "would you like to get
something to eat?"

She rubbed her eyes. "Yes, please, I am quite hungry."

"And then if I feed you, will you come home with me?"

She looked up at him feigning consternation. "If I say no, will you
kidnap me?"

He gave her a grin. "I might have to," he said.

"Oh, alright, if you insist." She stood, put her arms around his
neck, and gave him a long, deep kiss. Applause broke out in the control room. They forgot they were standing in front of a large plate
glass window.

CHAPTER SIX

Tyuratam, Kazakhstan October 1965

Responding to a tap on his left shoulder, Niki raised one gloved hand to signal, "Just a minute until I finish this pass."

The cross slide on his engine lathe was dialed into a .05 millimeter cut, making a smooth and shiny finish on the aluminum pivot shaft he was machining. As the tool carriage neared the end of its travel, he disengaged the automatic feed and finished the last bit of the cut by hand. He punched the red stop button and turned as the lathe wound down to greet Bohdan, the shop manager, who had been standing behind him with a stranger.

"Nikolai," Bohdan said. "This is Comrade Koslov, who is here from Moscow to inspect our work."

Niki removed his gloves, set his plastic face shield aside, and shook hands with the man, "A pleasure to meet you, comrade," he said.

"And I you," Koslov replied, though his face showed no emotion. He gestured to a roll-around toolbox that displayed twenty or so gleaming aluminum parts, laying on its top on a shop towel.

"This is your work, Nikolai?"

Niki narrowed his eyes just a bit. He could tell from the air of self-righteousness emanating from Koslov, that he was a man of some importance. He cast a quizzical glance at Bohdan, who was not only the shop manager but also his father.

"Yes, sir, this is my work," he pointed out humbly.

"Very good, Comrade, very good." The bureaucrat wasted no words.

Koslov stood only 5'6" tall with slicked-back black hair, a round face, yellow teeth, and a substantial five o'clock shadow though it was only late morning. His belly protruded slightly from his grey wool overcoat. A powerful mid-level bureaucrat, he was quite used to obtaining anything he wanted that would further first his career goals, and secondarily, of course, the goals of the Soviet Space Program.

What he wanted was Nikolai Chubukin. Niki looked down at the man, waiting for him to take the lead.

"Comrade," Koslov began, "I am the section chief for Lunar Robotics at the NPO Lavochkin Design Bureau in Moscow. I am in charge of the design and construction of all remotely operated spacecraft that are a part of the new Luna Program. I have discussed the matter with Comrade Bohdan, and you are to be transferred to Moscow immediately to a position in the Luna machine shop to assist me in the upcoming Luna 9 mission to the moon."

Niki let out an involuntary gasp of surprise. This was roughly the equivalent of a coach from Moscow coming to a small pond in the country and informing one of the locals he was now the newest member of the Russian Hockey Team!

"I am honored, Comrade," Niki stammered. "When will I need to come?"

"Next week will be suitable," Koslov muttered, "Railway passes will be provided to you." Koslov started to turn away.

Niki was taken aback. In the last sixty seconds, his whole life had changed. This was exciting but also scary as hell. He knew he shouldn't question the man, but he felt he had to. "And what of my new wife, who is pregnant?"

Koslov turned back to face him, "I didn't know you were married," he frowned slightly. "You will come and get settled, and we'll send for your wife as soon as it is practical." Koslov turned and walked away, Bohdan in tow.

"Thank you, Comrade, thank you very much," Niki said to the man's retreating back. Koslov waived one hand in dismissal.

Niki had been ten years old in 1956 when his parents were transferred to the squalid little frontier town of Tyuratam in Kazakhstan. Many of the streets were still unpaved, and the mud was legendary. New, gray and soulless concrete housing blocks, that were the signature of the Soviet regime, were springing up everywhere. Niki's papa had been reassigned to manage one of the machine shops being opened in Tyuratam.

The sleepy little one-horse town on the Kazakh steppes was exploding in all directions since the Central Committee decided to locate the new Baikonur Cosmodrome nearby. Construction of the new launch facility required hundreds of thousands of custom made parts to be built in a hurry. After Niki's parents, Bohdan and Irina settled into the three-room gray concrete supervisor's flat, Bohdan set about the task of assembling his new machine shop. Niki showed an interest in his father's work, and once the shop was up and running, Bohdan took Niki to work with him.

He told the boy, "Nikolai, you will sweep the floors and bring materials to the machinists, and in time, I will train you to become one."

Niki had never been intimidated by work in his life. He was elated; he loved the big machines. As the '50s came to a close, Nikolai was showing a surprising level of aptitude on the machine tools. He was given simple tasks to learn at first but had soon graduated to the more complicated procedures. Bohdan tried not to show it, but Irina could tell he was very proud of his boy. Nikolai became adept at reading technical drawings and was soon making corrections not spotted by the part designers themselves. He was fast gaining a reputation as the local child prodigy of machine tools.

By early 1963, a tall, well-built, and good looking young Niki was being seriously considered for a full-time position as senior machinist on his 18th birthday. Nikolai's work at the machine shop took a great deal of concentration, which would occasionally result in a deep ache between his shoulder blades. If he didn't pay attention, it soon escalated into a migraine headache.

As yet, he was still an unofficial employee and could take some time to himself. So, he took to going on short walks out on the steppes, just outside of town, both to exercise his body and give his mind a break. It also helped lessen the effect of the migraines. It was on one of these afternoon walks out on the plains south of town that he first saw her.

She was watching over a herd of goats, clothed in the traditional Kazakhi dress of a nomad herder. Nikolai ambled up to her. She stood her ground, gazing at him impassively. He could see from a distance that she was strikingly beautiful.

Her smooth skin was darker than his; she had jet black hair and black almond shaped eyes. No wrinkle or crease crossed her face. Her look was of an unspoiled princess of the natural world. He was drawn to her immediately.

"Hello," he said, "my name is Niki. Will you tell me yours?"

She continued to stare at him. "Do you speak Russian?" he asked.

The corners of her mouth crinkled slightly, "Da, a little," she said."

"Can you tell me your name?"

"I am Jumaana." She smiled up at him.

"These are your animals?"

"These are my father's animals. We give our goat milk to the commissary. Do you live in the new town?"

Niki said that he did and found out from her that during the summer she lived in a hide-covered yurt with her parents, who were devout Muslims. They moved around the rolling plains seeking fresh grass for their herd. During the winter, they moved back into their sod-roofed home and kept a close eye on their flock. They'd been camping around the outskirts of town for the last two years since the Russians were willing to trade for the milk and the meat.

Nikolai began to see Jumaana whenever he could. She would tell him if they were moving camp, and Niki would seek her out on the plains whenever he had a chance. He took the tram or the bus to the edge of town and became quite the hiker in order to be with her. Jumaana was unsure how her parents would react if they saw them together. During that summer of 1963, the two young lovers lay on their blanket together and watched Valentina Tereshkova blast into the deep blue morning sky, atop a contrail of orange fire, on her way to becoming the first woman in space.

On Niki's 18th birthday, he became the youngest man in the short history of Baikonur to attain the rank of senior machinist. Bohdan was well pleased with his boy. The salary was pathetic by western standards, but Niki was thrilled to the core. He actually had his own money!

He would still have to keep living with his parents in the three-room flat consisting of one bedroom, one bathroom, and a kitchen-living room. He slept at night in the living room and folded up his bed in the morning. But he could now chip into the family budget, raise the standard of living for all, and still have a few rubles in his pocket to do with as he pleased. Niki took it upon himself to buy Jumaana some clothes. While he was conflicted about taking the initiative to make changes in her life, he knew she'd have to look more Russian if Bohdan and Irina were to approve of her. As yet, there was no place to go shopping in Tyuratam. So he bartered and dickered with some of the machinist's wives to get secondhand clothing for her.

One day, early in his 19th year, Jumaana took his hand and put it on her breast. "Do you feel that?" she asked. Her Russian had improved markedly over the last year.

"Yes, of course I feel it," he leered at her.

She laughed. "No silly, they're getting bigger. What do you think it means?" She smiled up at him.

"Bigger is good." Niki grinned and took hold with both hands.

"It means Niki that I'm pregnant!"

Niki let go as if he had touched a hot stove. He stood there with a dumb look on his face. "You mean *you* are going to have a baby?" he stammered.

"No, Niki, it is *we* who are going to have a baby," she said.

"I'm going to be a father?" he stammered, a note of wonder in his voice. "I think it's time for you to meet my parents!"

Bohdan was not happy. Surely, the girl was very pleasing to look at, and he could understand his son's attraction to her. But her family was devout Muslim, while his family was Russian Orthodox, and her skin was of a slightly darker cast than was acceptable.

Irina, while wary of Bohdan's lack of approval, was swayed immediately upon learning that Jumaana was pregnant. Her parents were completely intimidated by Bohdan, who was known to be a very important man locally, and they kept to the background. Niki and Jumaana were married by the local magistrate during the summer of 1965 and moved into the flat with Irina and Bohdan.

Toward the end of the summer, Niki burst through the apartment door. Jumaana was sitting by the third-floor window looking out over the town. "Jumaana!" he cried, "I am to be promoted to the Lavochkin Design Bureau in Moscow!" He stopped dead in his tracks as he noticed that her eyes were red. She'd been crying.

"I already know that Niki; Irina told me." She looked mournful.

"But why are you crying? I am to be promoted!" Nikolai was bewildered.

"I'm afraid, Niki," she moaned, "I've never been to a big city. I'm not sure I could live there."

Niki was taken aback. It hadn't crossed his mind that she might not want to go. It made no difference in the long run. He was being transferred, and that was that. He knew he couldn't whine about his wife's feelings to a man like Koslov.

He held both of her hands and gazed into her eyes. "I'll be a very important man like Bohdan is here," he said. "We'll have lots of money, and we can buy whatever we want! You'll see; you'll love it. And besides, I don't have a choice. I have to go next week, but as soon as I get settled, Comrade Koslov says I can send for you."

She clung to him, "Oh Niki, if it's what we have to do, then I'll make the best of it."

His enthusiasm fell like a birch tree with shallow roots, the fear of uncertainty beginning to possess him. He held her against his chest. Slowly, a tear made its way down her cheek and dripped onto Niki's shirt.

CHAPTER SEVEN

Moscow, November 20th, 1969

The plan, for the Lunokhod 1 remote-controlled lunar rover called for a bathtub-like pressure vessel with a large convex lid. The lid contained an array of solar cells that would charge the internal batteries when opened. The vehicle had eight independently driven wheels, each with its own electric motor and brake. The rover was designed to let the operators drive around exploring the lunar surface in real time using its four TV cameras as windows onto the new world. The device would be operated by joystick from Bear Lake Deep Space Center near Moscow.

The only catch in the control sequence was a slight five-second delay between control input and response due to the time it takes for a radio signal to reach the moon. The mission plan called for the rover to operate for a maximum of 168 earth days or six lunar days. During the lunar nights, it would sleep warmed by its radio-active polonium 210 isotopic heat source.

In addition to its TV cameras, it carried two types of communication antennas, several scientific experiments, a soil sampling and analyzing capability and a lunar laser retro-reflector for bouncing laser beams back to earth. All systems had been tested extensively by driving mock-ups around in the Soviet desert.

When the Americans built a spacecraft, every piece was custom designed for its purpose, ultra-lightweight, and hideously expensive. Instead of spending millions of rubles emulating the American method, the Russians took a different approach. In keeping with certain aspects of the Russian national character, both the booster that would send the robot into space and the rover itself were built like the proverbial brick shithouse.

The Soviets would integrate more off-the-shelf components that were heavier, but hopefully more reliable, and enclose them all in a very heavy-duty pressure vessel. They would ship the entire package into space using the Proton K, the world's largest heavy-lift booster. The Lunokhod 1 rover, weighing in at nearly two thousand pounds, was no exception to the rule. Even at that, there was still some pay-load capacity left.

"Comrade Chubukin, we are close to freezing the specs for the Lunokhod 1 rover," Dimitri said. "Comrade Barsukov has just completed the final weight and balance calculations. He tells me that we have an additional available payload capacity of ninety-five kilos."

Anatoly nodded, "I've had all my calculations verified. We have room for more equipment."

Nikolai Chubukin was one of the designers and the machinist in charge of the fabrication and final assembly of the rover. Anatoly was the payload specialist whose job it was to make sure the damn thing would fly. Of course, Niki already knew there was excess payload capacity. He and Toly roomed together. But he kept silent knowing that pricks like Dmitri needed to hear themselves wax away ad nauseam on subjects that were already common knowledge.

Dimitri droned on, "So now that we have a mandate to proceed with the launch of our spacecraft, I want to add a small project to your work list."

Nikolai's eyebrows shot up. There was something new here.

Dmitri continued, "I want you to develop what I'm going to call an autonomous mission extender module for the rover. We're going to take advantage of our additional ninety-five kilos of payload capacity. The purpose of this module will be two-fold. First, the module will be capable of extending the mission by at least one lunar day, and second, we are going to use this opportunity to integrate our very latest experimental technologies.

"The module should be designed in such a way that if it fails to come online, the mission will not be compromised at all. It will have its own solar array and storage batteries. It will have its own TV camera and should be accessed by a discreet S-Band frequency that I will provide to you. I want you to use some of the technologies we have been experimenting with that are not yet proven. The module will mount just under the pressure vessel above the suspension system. It must integrate with all of our control systems, but it must be a completely separate entity and not interfere with the operation of any of the existing systems.

"The idea is that when the rover has come to the end of its main battery bank capacity, we can deploy the module and extend the mission for one more month. This will also serve as a practical test of some of our newest technologies."

Dmitri slid a printed list across the table. "You are to contact these departments for the latest technical information on the new lithium battery bank and the latest developments in solar cells and miniature TV cameras."

Nikolai's jaw dropped just a little. Dmitri was talking like a scientist for once, instead of a political bureaucrat. He had no doubt that this was one of Dimitri's carefully planned career enhancing moves, but it wasn't a bad idea. In fact, it actually had merit.

Nikolai brightened, "I understand the concept, comrade. Will the unit need to be pressurized?"

Anatoly broke in, "If we plan not to integrate with the existing experiments package and leave those instruments in the main pressure vessel, I don't believe the module needs to be either pressurized or heated. It should live longer that way."

"I agree," said Dimitri as he passed two large manila envelopes across the table. "Here are some preliminary specs I've drawn up for you, Comrade Chubukin. Once the drawings are complete, I want you to personally machine most of the parts. Any parts you farm out to the shop staff will have no reference on the drawings as to where they are going or to what assembly they belong.

"The battery and camera technologies we will employ in constructing this module are as yet unknown in the western world. Any leak of what we are doing could give the Americans an advantage that would be catastrophic to our efforts to regain the lead in the race to colonize the moon. This project is to be considered top secret. You are to tell no one, not even your wives."

Koslov had been informed, since the beginning, that Anatoly was not married, but remembering such things was apparently beneath his station.

Toly sighed, "What about the approval tracking? Do we have enough time to fold all the approval sequences into our schedule prior to the launch date?"

Dmitri's eyes took on a slightly menacing look, "Approvals are not your concern, comrades. Due to the highly secret nature of this endeavor, I will personally walk the project through the approval sequence. I want a preliminary design on my desk within thirty days."

Toly and Nikolai left the conference room smiling. Nikolai knew he could put away the disappointment of his wife's absence for a time. After all, this is what they had come here for in the first place. Once they had completed this mission, he was sure he would finally be allowed to bring his family to Moscow.

CHAPTER EIGHT

Seattle

Tom Parish and Rachael Deneuve went shopping for wedding rings. They couldn't seem to find anything pre-made that they liked. Rachael thought diamonds were too common. She believed that certain gems gave off different energy frequencies and favored stones of color. Shopping together, they found an unmounted emerald of very high quality and had two matching stones cut from it. The stones were mounted in sculptural gold settings custom made by a well-known jeweler. They were simple yet elegant at the same time.

Rachael insisted, "I will pay for yours, and you will pay for mine. We'll take a bundle of cash from you and a bundle of cash from me and we'll bind the two bundles together with a ribbon. We'll have a little ceremony of blessing when we exchange the cash for the rings." She told Tom, "We'll both be wearing the same frequency, and that will keep us attuned to each other forever."

Tom smiled; that was his girl. She always surprised him with the depth of her thinking in ways that would never have occurred to him. Tom and Rachael were married, in January of 1970, after a whirlwind six-month courtship. The wedding was held in Ottawa at the request of Rachael's parents. They wholeheartedly approved of the communications wonder boy from NASA and wanted to show him off in diplomatic circles. Tom's parents took to Rachael right away, as well.

How different Tom and Rachael were from each other was a topic of conversation amongst their friends. Tom was absolutely scientific in his focus. He believed in what you could assemble with your hands and what you could prove with your calculations. When he was concentrating on a problem, he would become absent-minded to a fault, almost as if a part of him had left the planet.

On his own, he never thought about religion or spiritual issues, unless Rachael brought those topics up. He allowed her to engage him in conversation about any subject she wanted and knew she was widening his focus. He liked that about her. Since he was so busy with his work, he relied on her to keep him informed on what was transpiring outside of his area of expertise.

Rachael was ever the earth mother; she was into herbs, natural healing, the paranormal, and looking after those less fortunate than herself. While Tom managed his affairs with schedules and lists, Rachael flowed through life like the wind through a wheat field. Tom found her lack of methodology both unsettling and refreshing at the same time. She gave birth, in him, to the possibility of inner freedom. Together they were the essence of opposites attracting one another.

After the first landing of men on the moon, Tom participated in the Apollo 12 mission and had sweated through Apollo 13 with all the members of mission control. He continued to create innovations in Unified S-Band technology in missions 14 through 16. There is a certain mindset that one must adopt in order to withstand the bureaucratic culture of any government agency. NASA had its own particular version of bureaucratic hell, and Tom was beginning to fade under the weight of it. His colleagues noticed more and more grumbling every time Tom had to bow under the senseless demands of the bureaucracy.

He stayed on at NASA through the Apollo 17 mission. In May of 1973, when the Apollo program was wrapping up, he was called into Chris Taft's office. The venerable head of the Johnson Space Center looked him up and down.

"Tom, you've performed a great service to your country, and to the effort to put men on the moon. I've been watching you very closely since the day you came under my wing. Now that we've been to the moon and learned what we'll have to deal with to inhabit the place, the powers that be have decided that we're going to spend the next couple of decades working in low earth orbit. The space shuttle will be our focus in the foreseeable future.

"It won't take people of your caliber to adapt what you've already done in communications for that work, and I don't want to see you languish in some program that doesn't challenge you. That would be a gross waste of God-given talent. It's time for you to take your high energy brand of creativity and apply it to the private sector. So, in the nicest possible way, you're fired."

Tom was stupefied for a minute, but he knew deep inside, that the boss was right. He knew he'd been chafing at the bit and had wanted to embark on something new for a while now.

Mr. Taft went on. "I've sent a letter of introduction for you to a friend of mine over at Motorola. He's very interested in seeing you. I want you to meet with him and take a look at the project he's working on. It's called cellular telephone technology.

Dr. Cooper is going to revolutionize earthbound communications. Last month he demonstrated a telephone that you can carry with you wherever you go. He calls it the DynaTac. In the future, you won't be calling a person's location; you will be calling his body! I want you to go over there and see what you can do to help Martin; he's expecting your call."

Tom stood and offered his hand. "Thank you, sir. It's been a privilege and a pleasure to work with you over the years. I'll never forget what we accomplished here together."

"Nor will I, Tom, nor will I."

Uncharacteristically, the tough old space program manager teared up just a little. So, Tom Parish's career at NASA came to an abrupt close. Over the next couple of days, he cleaned out his office and said his goodbyes.

The developmental work for the cell phone at Motorola took ten years, far longer than it had taken Tom to implement Unified S-Band Communications at NASA. But he already had some practice at seeing into the technological future, and knew he was about to be at the right place at the right time.

In 1979, prior to the end of his stint with Motorola, Tom could clearly see the massive need for infrastructure that the cell phone would generate. He identified Seattle as the best place for him to embark on his new business venture. With a series of loans from Rachael's parents and all of his and Rachael's assets, he founded Parish Communications Inc. When Motorola introduced the first practical cell phone to the public in 1983, Tom was ready. He already owned the cell towers and switching equipment that provided cell phone coverage to the Seattle area. The foundations for a massive personal fortune had been laid.

PCI flourished in Seattle, and Tom began to expand to other cities around the country. He found that his involvement in the Apollo program opened a lot of doors for him in business. When the prestigious Columbia Center, the tallest building in Seattle, opened in 1985, PCI took a suite of offices on the 65th floor.

When prospective customers came to call and were ushered into the inner sanctum, they were suitably impressed by the photo gallery on the walls showing all the various Apollo spacecraft: Tom at his control station and Tom shaking hands with Neil Armstrong, Gordon Cooper, Buzz Aldrin and President Nixon. Tom's history with NASA would open up a lot of opportunities for him.

Being the free spirit that she was, Rachael had declined to have a child during the early years of PCI. With the hand of her biological clock sweeping across the thirty-three mark, she realized the time to consider having a family was running out. In 1985, Rachael gave birth to their only child, a son. The labor was quick and satisfying. Rachael had just finished reading an autobiography of some Indian Guru, and there was a character in the story named Amar. She loved the name and so Amar James Parish came into the world. James was after Tom's father.

When Tom Parish signed his first contract to provide cell phone infrastructure overseas, he changed the company's name from Parish Communications Incorporated to Parish Communications International. The acronym remained PCI. At forty-four, Tom Parish was well on his way to becoming the first telecommunications billionaire.

CHAPTER NINE

Moscow 1970

Nikolai applied himself to the design and construction of the mission extender module with renewed enthusiasm. He machined the case for the module out of a solid slab of aluminum. Before final assembly, the case would be gold plated to guard against corrosion. He consulted with each department head for the latest developments in cameras, solar cells, batteries, and all the other components that would be needed. He selected only the highest quality parts and materials.

Niki kept the drawings to himself and compartmentalized the acquisition of components. Each of the department heads knew only the specs for the equipment they were providing. None of them understood how their piece of the puzzle fit into a final project or even what that project might be. All they could deduce was that it had something to do with lunar robotics. Everyone who knew anything was sworn to secrecy on the grounds of national security.

Dmitri met with Toly and Nikolai regularly and indicated that the approval sequence was progressing. The launch was scheduled for mid-November 1970. If they were going to be ready on time, they had to hurry. Dmitri absolutely would not stand for a launch delay. He didn't care if they had to work double shifts and stay on top of their other duties to get it done.

Finally, in late October, the module was finished. Niki had mocked up each component and tested it vigorously as he was building the module. Dmitri called for a final meeting in complete secrecy. Niki and Toly didn't really understand what all the fuss was about. After all, the module was basically a sophisticated battery pack with cameras. But Dmitri was the boss, so they did what he ordered them to do.

Dmitri came into Niki's studio and admired the gleaming polished gold module, which was sitting in the middle of his worktable. He closed and locked the door behind him.

Koslov was complimentary, "Chubukin, you have outdone yourself this time. It is a thing of true beauty! You shall have your reward. I'm looking for a flat so you can bring your family to Moscow."

Nikolai hadn't felt this good in a long time. "Thank you, sir, thank you very much! Do we have clearance to mate it with the spacecraft?"

"Yes, please do so, but remember security is to be kept extremely tight on this. I want you to do the installation this evening. Can you do it by yourself?"

"No sir, but Toly can help. He's all I'll need."

"Then please proceed. We're less than three weeks from launch. We have other issues to attend to."

"Yes, comrade, I will get this done, and thank you, sir."

Dmitri narrowed his eyes. "Thanks for what?"

"Why, for allowing me to finally bring my family to Moscow!"

Dmitri looked relieved. "Oh, right, that. It won't be until after the launch. You do know that?"

"Yes, comrade, I understand."

"Good, let's get on with it."

That night Niki sent a letter to Jumaana, who was eight months pregnant, with the good news.

The module itself was relatively slim and fit under the pressure vessel of the rover, just above the eight-wheeled suspension system. The installation went according to plan, and everything checked out. The module was so unobtrusive that unless a crew member knew what to look for, none of them would have noticed it. If anybody had seen it, they were smart enough not to ask.

Nikolai, Toly, and the final assembly crew were all in the clean room where the final packaging of the rover was taking place prior to shipping the spacecraft to Baikonur. The module had been installed but was no longer visible due to the protective wrapping that had been applied to the rover for shipping.

The door banged open, and their boss's supervisor, Comrade Reshetnev, strode in wearing his uniform instead of clean room garb. He looked like he was ready to kill. He called the staff to order. "Comrades, it has come to my attention that Dmitri Koslov has been doing work outside of approval channels. This unfortunate fact has come to light during our investigation of the causes of the crash of Luna 15."

The crew members stiffened. There had been some sort of malfunction aboard Luna 15, and they lost control approaching the surface of the moon. The spacecraft had crashed, destroying itself and wasting millions of rubles. Now, it seemed they knew what had caused the crash, and apparently it was Koslov's fault. When the hammer came down from the Soviet hierarchy, collateral damage was expected by anyone unlucky enough to be in the vicinity. Everyone was well aware of that fact. They all took refuge in silence.

Reshetnev went on. "Some of you worked on that project. Is there anything you want to tell me?"

Nikolai looked at Toly out of the corner of his eye. He had a sick feeling in the pit of his stomach. Toly elbowed him in the ribs and said out of the side of his mouth.

"Keep quiet Niki, or we'll all end up in the gulag."

Niki took his friend's advice and said nothing. No one else came forward.

Reshetnev waited. You could hear a pin drop in the uncomfortable silence.

"All right," Reshetnev said. "I better not find out that there is anything I need to know that you haven't told me, or you might find yourselves joining Koslov in Siberia. Good day, comrades."

Reshetnev turned and went out, slamming the door behind him. Everybody looked at Nikolai expectantly. They knew he'd been working on something covert. Niki shook his head to dismiss the incident. "All right comrades, let's get back to work."

At the end of the day, Toly came by Nikolai's office and closed the door softly behind him. He was carrying a black leather briefcase.

"Quick, Niki, before anyone comes looking, give me all your files on the mission extender module. I'll destroy them and no one will be the wiser."

Niki was sitting at his desk, deep in depression over Koslov's dismissal. The man had just told him he could now bring his family to Moscow. But Dmitri had been hauled off, and he'd have to start all over again with Reshetnev. The guy hardly knew Niki existed. It could be years.

"Uh, yeah," he said. "They're all in the top drawer of that file cabinet. Take them. We're all probably screwed anyway."

Toly crossed the room and heaped the files into his briefcase. Snapping it shut, he turned to Nikolai.

"I'll take care of this. You keep your mouth shut, Niki. Don't go getting a conscience on me, or we'll both be stamping out hubcaps."

"Yeah, sure, fine, whatever," Niki said. He really didn't care anymore as he sat down to write yet another letter home with the bad news.

Two days later Niki received a telegram from home. Jumaana had gone into labor early, and the baby had been stillborn. Niki was granted two weeks leave to go home and bury his son. Jumaana was physically damaged and deeply disturbed by the experience. Her doctor told her that a second pregnancy would be unlikely. But she was young and otherwise healthy; maybe time would heal her wounds.

Lunokhod 1 was shipped to the Baikonur Spaceport to be installed atop its Proton K Booster. No one ever said another word about Dmitri Koslov. On November 10th, the crew was invited to the third-floor conference room to watch the launch on closed-circuit TV. Despite the Koslov debacle, they all felt a great deal of pride for what they'd built as the Proton K thundered into space. They just hoped everything would go as planned.

Luna 17, as the mission was known, went much better than anyone expected. The Luna module entered lunar orbit on November 15th, 1970 and made a successful soft landing in the Mare Imbrium on November 17th. After a day of housekeeping, system, and software checks, the access ramps were unfolded, and Lunokhod 1 drove down a ramp from its landing module onto the surface of the moon.

Koslov was never replaced. Reshetnev himself assumed the supervisor's duties. Nobody at Lavochkin knew what went on above his pay grade. When Lunokhod 1 began to perform flawlessly, he became much easier to live with. While the operators at Bear Lake Deep Space Center put the rover through its paces, Niki, Toly, and the crew started work on Lunokhod 2.

Lunokhod 1 exceeded all expectations. It had been designed to operate in the lunar environment for 168 days. It ran for 322 days. The rover took more than 20,000 TV images, 208 panoramas, performed twenty-five soil tests, and penetrated the lunar surface at five-hundred different locations. The spacecraft could have gone on, but its batteries were finally losing their ability to recharge. After traveling 10.5 kilometers, the end was near.

No one ever mentioned the mission extender module again, nor would they. Anatoly had destroyed the plans and the operational specs. Like a whale sounding and diving, the mission extender module slid gracefully into the depths of history.

Bear Lake Deep Space Center, Moscow, Sept. 1971

Reshetnev was a proud papa. His division had performed like heroes of the Soviet Union. The staff at Bear Lake finally reported that Sept. 14th, 1971 would likely be the last day of operations for Lunokhod 1. Reshetnev was unable to attend the gathering that typically took place at the end of a mission, and he sent Nikolai Chubukin and Anatoly Barsukov in his stead.

Niki and Toly traveled out to the Space Center and were invited to take seats in the control room just behind the operator's console. The atmosphere was festive. Everyone in the control room had a glass of vodka in hand. In the history of lunar exploration, the Luna 17 mission had been the most successful at seeing the surface of the moon and reporting back the composition of its soil and rocks. The Soviets had outdone all of the American Apollo missions for the sheer volume of testing that had been accomplished. The celebrations commenced, and the vodka began to flow a little early.

None of the Soviet mission staff were aware that the American public had never heard of their triumph and probably never would. Despite what the American party line said, reverse propaganda was a real thing. Evginy was the operator that day. Looking over his shoulder, he explained to Niki that the rover had been a bit erratic for the last two days. It had been jumping around a little, spurting forward, and responding erratically to control inputs.

The battery charge indicator told the story; the battery bank was dying. Most everything else was still operating quite well. Evginy was switching back and forth from the one kph traveling speed to the two kph traveling speed to coax a little more distance from the machine. For some unknown reason, the camera recorders shut down every time he switched between the two speeds. To make matters a little more complicated, there was a five-second control delay due to the time it took for a signal to reach the moon. Evginy had been resetting the damn recorders all day.

It didn't really matter; there wasn't enough power left to make any additional tests. He would drive it until it quit, taking the last few photos. In the late afternoon, Evginy made a long forward motion control input and then leaned over to fiddle with the recorder reset. The damn thing still wasn't working right.

He straightened up, and to his horror, the sharp edge of a crater appeared directly in front of the rover. The control input had been made and couldn't be recalled. As the rover drove over the crusty edge, it gave way, and the front camera swept wildly across the adjacent landscape as Lunokhod 1 tipped violently nose down and came to rest on a ten percent slope.

The rest of the crew had been filling their glasses and slapping backs. Only Nikolai and Evginy saw a large black mass with straight edges that swept past the camera for a split second, the picture coming to rest on a patch of lunar dust. Both Niki and the operator jumped up. There were no straight lines or hard edges on the moon!

They cried out in unison, "What the hell was that?"

Everyone crowded around the console, wanting to know what they had seen.

"Play that back!" Niki shouted.

Evginy fiddled around with the recorder. "I can't play it back; the damn thing was offline again."

"Then back the rover up so we can see what that was!"

The operator made the control input. There was no response. He tried again; still no response. Lunokhod 1 had finally died. The rest of the staff wanted to know what Niki was shouting about. He thought hard before replying. He wasn't sure what he'd seen. Maybe there was some sort of interference and in its death throes, the rover had picked some part of a domestic broadcast out of the airwaves. There couldn't be anything manmade out there. There was nothing to be done, and Niki decided to keep his mouth shut.

They tried for a while to revive the spacecraft, but it was over. The last reading they received from the instrument package showed that the rover was resting nose down on an incline. That meant they couldn't orient the solar cells to the sun. The rover's laser retroreflector lay at such an angle that no laser beam measurements would be taken from Earth. There'd be a flap about that. But what the hell, it wasn't Niki or Toly's fault, was it?

Toly asked for permission to take a picture of the control room crew to mark the moment in time. The slightly inebriated crew chief was in a celebratory mood and despite all regulations to the contrary posed with Niki and his crewmates while Toly snapped the shutter.

The final resting place of Lunokhod 1 had been its only mission failure. For all intents and purposes, the spacecraft and Nikolai Chubukin's relationship with Lunokhod 1 had just disappeared into the gray dust of the moon forever.

In 1973, after the Lunokhod 2 mission was completed, both Nikolai and Anatoly were reassigned to less glamorous positions. Niki was put to work at an aircraft factory in Moscow developing engine mounts. He always wondered if Reshetnev had somehow been responsible for the move. Anatoly was shuttled off to some bureaucratic downtown hellhole to push paper.

Housing continued to be a problem, and after all of these years, Niki and Toly still shared a room at the dormitory in Moscow. Both were incensed and disillusioned with life under the Soviets. They had given the best years of their lives to Mother Russia and had not been rewarded in kind for their efforts. Anyone who lived under the notion that there was justice for working people in the Soviet Union was sadly mistaken. However, they both knew to keep their mouths shut lest they disappear on permanent reassignment to Siberia as Koslov had.

Nikolai had been unable to see Jumaana with any greater frequency during his years as an aircraft mechanic than he had while working in the rover program. After the death of their stillborn son in 1965, he began to drink in earnest to dull his pain. Niki and Jumaana made the best of each vacation he was allowed. After thirteen years of trying, Jumaana finally conceived again in 1978, and a healthy daughter was born the following year. They named her Katya. Jumaana and Katya continued to live with Niki's parents in Tyuratam, where the young girl went to school.

As a teenager, Katya was well known to her friends for being an unusually beautiful as well as exotic-looking creature. She was a blend of white Russian and dark Kazakhi. She had almond shaped eyes and cafe au lait skin. Her breasts were beginning to show. All of her friends knew she was going to be a stunner. One of the local apparatchiks also knew it and sent a picture of her to a KGB contact in Moscow. Two months later, at fourteen years of age, she was conscripted to attend a KGB sponsored school for young women in the capital city.

Jumaana was told it was a great honor for Katya to be selected to go to this school. But she had heard all of that before and was distraught over her daughter's absence. The damn Russians were just robbing her of her family. Niki felt bad for her, but he also felt hope for the first time in years. Katya was nearby, and he would be able to see her more frequently.

By 1991, the Soviet Union was beginning to fall apart. The signs were starting to become apparent. The citizenry had lived under the constant weight of Soviet centralized rule for several generations. Most people in the USSR couldn't entertain the idea that the giant would ever fall to its knees. The Russian people figured they were just seeing another typical downturn. They had seen it all before. There would be another five-year plan, and the cycle would start all over again.

Niki and Toly made a habit of drinking together each night after work. Toly, ever the researcher, whispered into Niki's ear just in case someone was within earshot. "The Soviet Union is going to collapse, Niki. It is going to die from its own obesity."

Niki shook his head. "Such a thing is not possible, Toly. We're too big; we are a superpower."

"If we are such a superpower, Niki, how come life here is so shitty? In America everyone gets to do just what they want, and they are all rich. Perhaps someday, Niki, when the Soviet Union falls apart, we will go to America."

Nikolai chuckled and patronized his friend. "Oh, yes, Toly, perhaps someday we will go to America." That turned out to only be half true. Toly would go; Niki would not.

CHAPTER TEN

Seattle

First and foremost, Tom Parish was a scientist. His forte was to find a technological thread into the future and to doggedly follow that thread to see where it led. In addition to designing NASA's early spacecraft communications systems, he also held nineteen patents for cellular telephone switching systems and related equipment. He had built out northern Washington's first cellular network. He'd landed one contract after another to do the same in several other states and had begun to tap foreign markets, as well.

Tom Parish understood that the growth rate of his business was due in part to the unstoppable march of cell phone technology. He also understood that his reputation as the wunderkind of NASA spacecraft communications gave his cell phone infrastructure clients a sense of confidence. He wasn't blatantly egotistical but didn't shy away from polishing his own image either. During 1990, in an effort to make his brand more visible, he decided to open a museum dedicated to the history of communications around the world, culminating in his personal work in long-distance spacecraft communications and cell phone technology. He would place himself alongside Morse, Marconi, Bell, Edison and Tesla. That should be good for business.

The intercom buzzed, and Tom picked up. "Mr. Guilford is here to see you." Jan Meyer, his executive assistant, said.

"Send him in," Tom replied. "Trevor, nice to finally meet you. Jan, bring us some coffee, will you please?" Tom motioned for him to take a seat on the sofa.

Trevor Guilford was a Brit. Having been warned by Jan that Tom Parish disdained suits, he was dressed casually in khaki pants and a nicely tailored long sleeve shirt, no tie. Recently arrived from London, he could not be described as having a nice tan. Guilford had answered a headhunter's ad for a professional curator, and due to a favorable reaction to his resume, had been invited to come to PCI in person to interview for the position. He'd been vetted by the staff prior to this audience with the chairman.

"Very nice to meet you as well, Mr. Parish," he said as they shook hands.

"Call me Tom, please. I don't like to waste time, Trevor, so let's get right to it, shall we? I want to open a museum dedicated to the history of communications. I'd like to start with Samuel Morse and the development of the telegraph in 1844. It could be an interactive display where people can play with the telegraph key to compose a message. From there, I'd like to progress to Bell's work on the telephone and Edison's phonograph and maybe even his early work on movie cameras. I want to move on to Marconi and his invention of the radio. We'll touch on some of the less controversial parts of Tesla's work. Then, we'll trace the development of the wireless through Bill Lear's invention of the car radio.

I might even want to create a section on two-way radio communications and possibly include the development of radar during World War II. Then we'll move on to the space race. I have commitments to receive tons of historical equipment from NASA, including old control room equipment, space suits, and even a mock-up of an Apollo capsule. When we can't acquire original equipment for a display, we can have replicas made. I've purchased a suitable building across the road from the Seattle Air and Space Museum at Boeing Field. I'm down there a lot since that's where my plane is hangared, so it's a convenient location for me. I think this will be a lot of fun, and I think that based upon your experience, you are the right man for the job. What do you say?"

Trevor liked Tom's no bullshit attitude already. He was almost taken aback by the man's energy. He was interested in moving on from his assistant curator position at the British National Maritime Museum, which was quite static compared to what Tom Parish was proposing. Tom could tell the deal was already done and proceeded to outline his vision in more detail. "We'll call it the Parish Museum of Communications. I'd also like to feature my work on the both the Apollo program and cell phone technology. I'm even thinking about a Soviet display.

"We could contrast their work against what we did during the early space race. It really was an amazing competition. We would produce an innovation; they would react with one of their own; then we would bring out another innovation in reaction to what they had done. It was a form of technological ping-pong. I suppose you had to be there, but that story isn't well known, and I'd like to tell it in some detail. We'll finish up with my latest work on satellite phone technology. That work will provide a steady stream of new information with some rich visual content for the future."

Guilford was grinning. Tom Parish's enthusiasm was intoxicating. Being associated with this level of creativity was a dream come true. Apparently, Mr. Parish had the financial clout to make his vision materialize.

With Trevor on board, Tom took advantage of old contacts from his NASA days to help with the acquisition of artifacts for the museum. Chris Taft and the old guard of the space program scoured every warehouse and scrap pile for equipment that could be useful to the museum. Tom was deluged with offers of original space race gadgets for the museum's displays.

When the Soviet Union fell in 1991, the oligarchs who took over began selling everything that wasn't nailed down. Surplus materials started to become available from the Russian Space Program. In 1993, Tom was contacted by a representative from Sotheby's in New York. The Russians were going to auction off the rights to one of the lunar rovers they had landed on the moon in 1970. Would he be interested in it for his museum? He would.

Tom and his curator traveled to New York to view and possibly bid on the rover. The title was just a piece of paper that conferred ownership of the Russian rover Lunokhod 1 where it lay on the moon, not that you could do anything with it. It would give its owner the dubious distinction of being the only private person to own a spacecraft on another planet. However, the transaction came with a full-scale mock-up of the spacecraft that had been constructed prior to the launch of the real Lunokhod 1. That had Tom's interest. It could be the centerpiece of the new Soviet wing that Tom had been daydreaming about.

The mock-up, which matched the real machine in almost every detail, had been in storage for twenty-two years and was covered in some sort of Cosmoline-type preservative. Tom had to look hard to see its potential. When the bidding was over, Tom Parish paid 68,500 dollars to add the artifact to his displays. Though he didn't fully understand it at the time, he would be spending much more on related Soviet equipment from the Cold War era in the near future.

Trevor Guilford had his hands full acquiring equipment and creating the displays according to his employer's vision. Every day was filled with new logistical challenges. Tom had the foresight to buy a building with a loading dock and a small warehouse in addition to the floor space dedicated to a world-class museum. Truck deliveries were arriving every day. The curator put together a workshop, stocked it with all of the relevant tools, and brought in two restoration techies to run the operation. When the Lunokhod 1 mock-up arrived from New York, the look on their faces was less than inspiring.

They photographed and disassembled the machine part by part. The Cosmoline was removed. Any part that was corroded was thoroughly cleaned, repaired and re-plated for display. Some of the plating was gold, which was commonly used on most spacecrafts to combat any form of corrosion. The model would turn out to be much prettier than the real rover ever was. When the process was complete, the boss was summoned to come and see it.

As it happened, the chairman of PCI was returning from a business trip and would be landing at Boeing Field that afternoon. It would be a short hop across the street to the museum. Tom came into the workshop through the back door. Trevor was standing in front of a large lump under a white drop cloth with some sort of clipboard in hand. Tom walked up and tapped him on the shoulder.

Trevor jumped, "Good heavens boss; you startled me!"

"Sorry about that; I didn't mean to sneak up on you. But, hey, I'm a sneaky guy. What do you have to show me?"

The curator smiled, he was really proud of what they had accomplished and anxious for Tom's approval. He grabbed an edge of the drop cloth and pulled it away, then he pushed a button on a pedestal attached to the display.

Tom gasped. "Oh my god! It's amazing!" he stammered.

Trevor had set up the rover on a turntable. The surface of the platform was done in an authentic representation of grey lunar dust, complete with tire tracks behind it. The rover had been more than lovingly restored. The polished aluminum surfaces, engine turned steel parts and gold plated fittings gleamed and sparkled as it rotated under the workshop lights.

"Trevor, you've really outdone yourself this time! I'm very impressed. Thank you!"

"Thank you, sir. I appreciate your feedback," Trevor said.

"Please put it out on the museum floor. How soon can we schedule our grand opening?"

The grand opening of the Parish Museum of Communications took place on March 1st, 1995. Amar, who was ten years old, and Rachael, who both referred to dad's hobby as playing with his "space junk," attended the celebration. The museum opened to rave reviews in the Seattle press and was featured on every local TV talk show as well as some national programs.

Anatoly Barsukov emigrated to the United States from Russia in 1995 to work as a payload specialist for a think tank that ultimately became SpaceX in Hawthorne, California. He was fifty years old, suffering from prostate cancer, and the medical bills were piling up. Barsukov was unaware of the sale of Lunokhod 1 until he watched a national news show featuring the opening of a new communications museum in Seattle by billionaire entrepreneur, Tom Parish. Immediately, he went to his storage unit and spent several hours looking for an old leather briefcase. The call came into Jan Meyer's desk.

"My name is Anatoly Barsukov. I would like to speak with Mr. Parish, please."

Jan replied, "What is the nature of your business Mr. Barsukov?"

"I was the payload specialist on the launch of Lunokhod 1 in 1970, and I have some information about the rover that I'm sure would interest Mr. Parish," he said in a heavy Russian accent.

"Hold, please." Jan punched a button, "Tom, I have a Russian gentleman on the phone who claims he was the payload specialist on the launch of Lunokhod 1. He says he has information that you will interest you. Do you wish to speak with him?"

"Absolutely, put him through."

"Mr. Parish, my name is Anatoly Barsukov."

Characteristically impatient, Tom cut him off, "Mr. Barsukov, my secretary tells me you were the payload specialist on the launch of Lunokhod 1, Is that correct?"

"Yes sir, I was responsible for all of the weight and balance calculations."

"And you have some information that I might be interested in?"

"I do sir. I know where all of the original control room equipment is located in a warehouse in Moscow. I believe I can broker the sale of that equipment to you at a very reasonable price if you are interested. In addition, I have information about a device that was attached to the rover which is not a part of the mock-up you bought. If we can meet, I will be happy to review the specifications for that attachment and its purpose with you."

Tom thought for a moment. An entire authentic control room to go with the rover display would probably be an unprecedented achievement in the world of space museums.

"When can you get here?" He asked.

"I am not in good health, sir. Is there any way you can come to me here in Hawthorne?"

Tom checked his book. "As a matter of fact, there is. I'll be in Los Angeles next Monday."

"That will work for me, Mr. Parish."

"Mr. Barsukov, I will need some sort of evidence that you have access to what you have to sell. Can you fax me any paperwork describing the equipment?"

"Yes sir, I can make that happen right away."

"Very well, hold for my secretary, she will take your information and set up the appointment."

That afternoon Tom received a three-page fax. The first page was a photograph of five men standing behind a row of analog control consoles, each holding up a cocktail as if they were toasting an achievement, which they actually were. The second page contained a schematic for some sort of device. The third page showed the location of the device affixed to Lunokhod 1, which Tom easily recognized. All of the text was in Russian, but Barsukov had handwritten the words—Mission Extender Module—in the margin.

Barsukov's word was good, mostly. The original analog control room equipment that had been in use on the final day of Lunokhod 1's travels across the lunar surface had been stored many years ago in the back of a leaky old warehouse in Moscow. Buying the equipment was substantially easier than getting it out of the country. Some oligarch by the name of Reshetnev had received the payment, but once the check had been cashed, he was less than motivated to cut through the red tape required to actually ship the stuff from Moscow to Seattle. When the shipment finally arrived in 1998, it proved to be incomplete.

Tom Parish had been intrigued by Barsukov's description of the Mission Extender Module. He daydreamed about actually restoring the control room, waking up the rover and driving around on the moon. What foolishness, he knew. There was no possibility that the spacecraft would respond after four decades of 300-degree temperature swings on the lunar surface. Russian engineering was good, but it couldn't be that good.

Nevertheless, Tom insisted on authenticity and encouraged Guilford to keep looking for the missing pieces. Guilford's task was made even more difficult when Barsukov succumbed to cancer early in 2008. Tom Parish was busy building his empire. The crates containing the Russian control room sat neglected under a tarp in a back corner museum's warehouse for another decade. Tom still intended to complete the display, but for now, he was engrossed in rolling out his next technological achievement.

CHAPTER ELEVEN

Seattle

Tom Parish easily fell into the role of wealthy entrepreneur. As his fortune grew, so did his appetite for material possessions. He and Rachael purchased a lovely six-bedroom waterfront home on Mercer Island. Next, came a fifty-foot Viking yacht. Every rich mover and shaker he knew had a yacht. Though modest by the standards of the rich and famous, Tom bought it as a symbol of his membership in the upper tenth of the top one percent of society. Somehow, cruising around in a boat felt so two dimensional compared to flying. He'd moved up from the Piper Arrow to a Cessna 340 some years ago and found himself neglecting the yacht. Based upon the amount of time he spent cruising, the old saying that a boat was "a hole in the water into which you pour money," definitely applied to him.

It wasn't until he passed the five-hundred million mark in net worth in 2002 that he felt he could satisfy his heart's desire with a brand new, gleaming white, Cessna Citation X. The Citation X was capable of cruising at seven hundred miles per hour, just below the sound barrier, making it the fastest private business jet in the world. It turned out to be a wise purchase for PCI, enabling the chairman to extend his reach into the international business world. The Citation required two pilots to be on board. Without a second thought, Tom hired Ted Lockhart, an experienced Citation pilot. He then went back to flight school and upgraded his rating so he could fly as co-pilot when he was on board.

In the summer of 2002, Amar received a brand new Land Rover Defender 110 for a graduation present and appreciated the gift. However, his enthusiasm for the SUV paled in the presence of the jet. With his father's approval, he started flight training in the venerable Cessna 172 that summer. Amar was a handsome young man and being the only son of a famous entrepreneur was a bit of a chick magnet. He loved a pretty girl, and was never without a date. He was far too young to get serious about any one woman and enjoyed spreading his affections among several young ladies. The press was always hovering around his dad and once they realized that the great man's son had come of age, Amar began to be plagued by the paparazzi.

He didn't know how they knew. Every time he took a date on his father's plane, with or without Tom and Rachael, a photo of him and his girlfriend on the stairs of the jet would appear in the tabloids the next day. Amar used the boat more than his father did, and the same result occurred on the water. Without any input from him, the media created, "Amar Parish, rich playboy," the most eligible bachelor in Seattle, blah blah blah. It was a reputation that was wholly divorced from reality. Well, almost.

In truth, Amar was cut much more from Rachael's cloth than from his father's. Rachael was ever the earth mother and environmental activist. She was involved in saving the whales hugging the trees, and global warming. She was concerned about the state of human consciousness. Having grown up in a prosperous family, she was no stranger to the trappings of wealth. She was grateful for the comforts her life afforded but flaunting the outward symbols of wealth were not her reason for being.

On the other hand, while Tom Parish enjoyed his role as a creative technological genius, he was also a hardnosed businessman. He placed a high value on the trappings of great wealth, particularly the wealth of a self-made man. He relished his informal membership in the club of fledgling billionaires, who made it the old fashioned way, by producing products and services that were on the cutting edge of technological development. Products that society, in general, wanted to own next. He revered the symbols of his success. The house, the boat, the PCI office at Columbia Tower, the jet, the museum, and his plans for the future all shouted that Tom Parish was someone to be admired.

Strangely enough, Amar had been a history buff since he was old enough to speak. Rachael had said that he brought it into this life, maybe from a previous incarnation. So, when the young man announced that he wanted to major in anthropology at the University of Washington in the fall, Tom called a family meeting.

"Amar, your mother has informed me that you want to go into anthropology. Why would you want to do that? There's no money in anthropology. I had hoped you would prepare to take the reins at PCI and follow me as the chairman. For that, you'll need a business education. I really want you to reconsider."

"Dad, I do appreciate everything you've accomplished. I really do. You've made a very comfortable life for us, and I'm grateful for that. I've never really wanted for anything, but isn't the objective of wealth to be free? I know you place a high value on the freedom your fortune has given you. So do I. I'm just not attracted to modern technology the way you are. I never have been, so far anyway. I'm interested in the history of humanity. I'd like to understand the forces that have made our species what it is today. Frankly, I'm interested in the current state of human consciousness. I want to know why the world is so fucked up and what we can do to make it better."

Tom turned to Rachael with both arms outstretched as if to say, "help me out here?"

Rachael cut in, "Tom, one of the things that has helped you to get where you are is that you have allowed yourself to follow your interests all of these years. You know that. Why can't we allow Amar to follow his? You can always hire people to run PCI. Let him pursue this thread. He's still young. If it doesn't hold his interest, maybe then you two can talk about his future with the company."

Great men who control who is allowed to enter their presence and what roles they will be cast in when they do, can still be heavily influenced by the desires of wives and children. Sometimes to their own consternation.

Tom stammered, "I haven't even told you what's on the drawing board at PCI. It's all top secret, and I've been waiting until we're a little farther along to tell you."

"To tell us what?" Amar and Rachael asked simultaneously.

Tom pulled a file from his briefcase, "I'm just about to launch the next evolutionary step in telephone technology, literally. We've been so successful with our cell phone investments that I intend to move into the next technological wave which will be in satellite phone systems. In the very same way that we created the wireless cell phone network using land-based cell phone towers, we're now going to create a satellite-based wireless network.

"It'll be amazing. No more dropped calls, no more weak signals. You'll be able to use your sat-phone anywhere on earth. Robby Harris and I have designed an integrated system that relies on a high number of tiny communications satellites in medium earth orbit. They are in the form of cubes that are only twenty-four inches on each side. Initially, one hundred of the cubes will be spread around the earth and will act cooperatively serving five larger com-sats that will be placed in geosynchronous orbit.

"The thing about the smaller birds is they are relatively cheap to manufacture and launch, and we can vary the number of satellites in the system as usage increases. I have acquired a building in Everett where we will establish both a satellite communications facility along with a robotic plant to manufacture them at the rate of one satellite every two weeks. We're talking with France, Space X, and NASA about piggybacking batches of ten satellites per payload on launches they're already planning. Selling extra payload capacity has started to become a normal part of the commercial launch business.

Each of the cubes will act as a fraction of the total processing capacity and available memory in the system. It will be a kind of intelligent electronic necklace surrounding the earth. On top of that, each of the smaller satellites has a high tech camera, and there will be an additional lucrative profit center in the mapping and surveillance markets."

Rachael was not inexperienced at hearing these kinds of pronouncements from her husband. They usually came unexpectedly when he could no longer keep his next innovation a secret and was about to burst.

"It sounds like the satellite phones will be very expensive," she said.

"Honey, you may remember that cell phones were expensive in the beginning, as well. This development will follow the same path. Satellite phone service will have to be expensive in the beginning to help amortize the cost of the system. Then the cost will come down over time as usage increases. We're going to beta test the system by introducing it as a service to the executive class."

Tom opened the file and took out a picture of the new phone. The artist's rendering showed a sparkling phone made of green carbon fiber with silver titanium trim.

"Isn't that a thing of beauty? Now, Amar doesn't this project get your creative juices flowing?"

Amar threw up his hands and addressed both of his parents. "It does; I'll admit that. You are nothing less than amazing. I believe you'll never quit before you die. In fact, I think if you did quit, you would die. That doesn't change the fact that I've decided what I want to do with my life. It's going to take a couple of years for you to get the satellite plant and communications system set up, right?"

Tom nodded, "Yeah, it will take a little while."

"Alright then," Amar said. "let me pursue anthropology for a while, and we'll see how things go."

Tom looked a little dejected. He sighed, "Okay, we'll see how it goes. But I'm not giving up, you know."

"Frankly, I wouldn't expect you to," Amar countered. "What are you going to call your new system?"

Tom held up his left hand showing his emerald wedding ring, grinning at Rachael he said, "We're going to call it the Greenstone Satellite System."

Part 3: An Ancient Discovery

CHAPTER TWELVE

The ruins of the ancient city of Persepolis, Iran

The ancient Persian city of Persepolis was built by Darius the Great and his son King Xerxes starting around 518 BCE and grew into a regional center of wealth, political influence, and power. Enough of the architecture remains to allow modern historians to digitally reconstruct the city. We know what it looked like and how truly magnificent the megalithic stone architecture was. The ruins of the gray limestone city consist of an elevated stone and dirt plateau of 125,000 square meters, upon which was built a council hall, a throne hall, living quarters, and several palaces. One of the most notable structures is the Apadana Palace, which served as the seat of government for both Darius the Great and his son King Xerxes.

The city was destroyed by Alexander the Great in 330 BCE in revenge for the burning of Athens by the Persians that had taken place one hundred and twenty-four years before his birth, the need for revenge having crossed generational lines. Plutarch wrote that the great treasures of Persepolis were carried away on the backs of twenty-thousand mules and five-thousand camels. The ruins of the city had been covered by the sands of time until The Oriental Institute of the University of Chicago began excavations in 1931. The building known as the Queen's Quarters is now restored and houses a museum dedicated to the history of the archaeological site and early Persian culture.

Nasrollah Brahoui, the museum's curator, thought that all significant excavations had been completed at the site decades earlier, and there was nothing left to discover. Then, one of Brahoui's work crews excavated along the northwest wall of the Apadana Palace in order to reinforce a portion of its stone foundation that was deteriorating. In so doing, they discovered the first few steps of a previously unknown stairway leading to a hallway directly underneath the palace.

The walls surrounding the stairway were relief carved in a manner similar to the Grand Staircase in front of the Gate of All Nations to the north of the Apadana Palace. The walls of the Gate of All Nations displayed panels of carved inscriptions, but in the ancient cuneiform language. That was where the similarity ended. In addition to the relief carvings, the underground stairway also had a few small carved inscriptions. The problem was, they were in a language unknown to Brahoui and all of the scholars of ancient Persia that he consulted.

Not sure where to turn, Brahoui contacted his old friend Dr. Evan Chatterjee, who was universally acknowledged as the foremost translator and expert on ancient languages and hieroglyphs in the world. Obtaining a visa for Chatterjee, who was a Muslim and a British citizen, had been relatively simple. Acquiring a visa for his American assistant, Amar Parish had been more difficult, requiring the intervention of the Governor of Fars province. The governor insisted that Amar's identity be kept under wraps to avoid a conflict with any of the local hardliners who hated the United States.

Amar, the only son of well-known telecommunications billionaire, Tom Parish, was an anthropologist by education, on his way to becoming an archeologist in action. He was passionate about the study of ancient civilizations around the world. Two questions had come to dominate his attention. First, is it possible that some ancient civilizations may have been more advanced than what sadly passed for civilization in the modern world? Secondly, why had the great civilizations of the past perished from the world stage?

Three years had passed since Amar had declared to his parents his intention to pursue a career in anthropology. He had quickly tired of the slow pace of formal education and threw himself into a passionate personal quest, traveling all over the world to sites like Machu Picchu, Easter Island, and Ankor Wat in Cambodia. He made in-depth studies of the Aztec, Mayan, and Inca ruins in Latin America focusing on Sacsayhuaman in Peru. There he found fifty-ton stones that looked as if they had been heated and stuck together like giant marshmallows. The seams between the stones were so tight you couldn't stick a thin knife blade between them. No evidence survived to tell how the stones had been cut, much less how a so-called primitive civilization could have placed them in such an articulate manner.

At Gobekli Tepe, in southern Turkey, he visited a megalithic site with sophisticated carved stonework. Organic material used by humans at the site had been carbon dated as being over 12,000 years old. This dig alone had overturned the notion that only primitive cavemen existed that far back in human history. There Amar discovered evidence of submersion, indicating the site may have been under water at the end of the last ice age around 10,700 BCE.

Site after site after site declared to him that we didn't really know much about how the pyramids and the other examples of megalithic stone architecture had been built. There was a growing school of thought in engineering circles saying the idea that the pyramids had been built by thousands of slaves was simply physically impossible. The volume of stone moved would be a challenge beyond even the capabilities of today's modern equipment.

The technology that produced a type of nearly seamless stone cutting evident in some ancient sites is not known to us today. No evidence of the widespread use of the wheel was found in the older sites. Amar wondered if maybe they hadn't relied on the wheel to do their large scale stonework because they had other non-mechanical means of moving heavy weights. Amar had no answer to the question—why had such sophisticated societies simply vanished? Why couldn't we go to Egypt and meet the descendents of the people who built the pyramids? A people still in place who remembered their own history. He knew deep in his soul that significant pieces of human history were missing. He was beginning to conclude that the real story of humanity must be more fantastic than modern science had revealed.

Amar had recently discovered the transcript of a meeting of the annual Congress of the American Association for the Advancement of Science, that had taken place in the fifties. Unbeknownst to each other, two scholars attending the conference presented separate papers, one in biology and one in anthropology. The anthropological paper reviewed the histories of human tribal cultures that had become extinct. The biological paper investigated the histories of biological species that had become extinct.

Unaware of the other's efforts, each scholar had come to the same conclusion. The common cause of extinction for both biological species and human tribal cultures was a phenomenon known as **overspecialization**.

The biologist told about a species of bird that fed only on a select variety of micro-marine life. As these birds flew around searching for sustenance, they gradually discovered certain marshes and shores in which that particular marine life thrived. Instead of migrating endlessly in search of food, they gathered where it was most abundant in bayside marshes. After a while, the water started to recede in the marshes because the Earth's polar ice caps were beginning to increase, and sea level was going down. As the water in the marshes receded, only the birds with the longest beaks could reach deeply enough into the mud to get at the marine life. Over time, the unfed short-billed birds died off. Only the long-beakers remained.

As successive generations of the birds mated, only other long-beakers survived with whom to breed. So, with continually receding waters and generation after generation of inbreeding, longer and longer beaked birds were produced. The birds seemed to be thriving when suddenly there was a huge fire in the marshes. Because their beaks had become so heavy, these birds couldn't escape the flames by flying away. They were trapped in the marsh and perished. This is typical of the way in which the extinction of species occurs—through overspecialization.

The anthropologist reported that tribes which had experienced extinction became so invested in doing things only one way, they lost the ability to adapt to changing circumstances. When unforeseen changes occurred, the people were unable to react, and they had also perished. One of Amar's biggest hits regarding overspecialization came on Easter Island.

The small, well-forested, Pacific island enjoyed a thriving eco-system based upon fishing and agriculture. Sometime in its history, the priesthood decided extraordinary measures had to be taken to scare away the island's enemies. This could be accomplished, they told the people, by erecting giant stone heads on the hillsides just above the beaches ringing the island.

The people, wishing to stop the periodic pillaging of the island by pirate voyagers, agreed to the belief system. The carving and erection of the first few stone heads took an enormous toll on the island's economy. The activity required huge investments in labor and timber from the forests to quarry, carve, transport, and install the effigies. However, when next the pirates came, they turned away and sailed off into the sunset, fearing the island was now inhabited by giants they would have no hope of overcoming.

The priests and the people, noting the success of their endeavor, felt the gods had smiled upon them and set about the task of carving and erecting more and more of the giant stone heads. Over the years, the activity became a normal part of the island's economy. Generation after successive generation of islanders learned that carving the stone heads was simply what they did to protect themselves.

In the process of creating and maintaining their defenses, the people of the island cut down their precious forests to build the wooden scaffolds and equipment used to transport and erect the statues. Eventually they overstressed the forest's ability to recover. After a time, they discovered they had created serious erosion, and there wasn't enough timber left to build their houses and keep their fires.

Ultimately, without knowing exactly when they had crossed the point of no return, the civilization died out. Their extinction was a direct result of the intellectual overspecialization encouraged by their leaders and the economic overspecialization of the use of their natural resources. All that remains of their belief system are rows of giant stone heads looking out to sea.

Acquiring this knowledge had completely revamped Amar's approach to his inquiry. He wrote several papers on the subject. He didn't want to know only why the ancient cultures he was studying had failed, he wanted to know if the study of their respective extinctions would tell us anything about the future of modern civilization. Will humanity prosper, or will we ultimately fail as a species?

Amar knew that the development of technology was always accompanied by a certain amount of risk. One of the conversations he had with his father centered around the exponential increase in the worldwide broadcast of RF signals of all kinds. The presence of electro-magnetic fields in our environment had increased by many orders of magnitude over just the last twenty years. We're literally bathing humanity in unprecedented levels of electronic frequencies from telephone, radio, television, radar, and even satellite signals. The average suburban dweller could click on Wi-Fi settings on any laptop and see that it was receiving signals from a dozen or more routers in the local neighborhood. No one really understood the long-range biological implications of such a development.

Most of the more ancient archaeological sites Amar studied offered up no evidence of the widespread use of the wheel. No gadgets were found in the ancient ruins. The prevailing feeling in the twenty-first century was that an abundance of electronic and mechanical gadgets was evidence of the historical superiority of our civilization. Amar wasn't so sure.

Amar Parish was deeply worried by the implications of his research. He felt the looming end of the fossil fuel supply, the gradual melting of the great ice sheets, which was now accelerating, and the rate at which we were polluting the planet, surely were indicators that modern civilization may have already crossed an unseen point of no return. Amar had jumped at the chance to accompany Dr. Chatterjee on this dig. Maybe there was something here that would support his intuition regarding the ancient history of humanity.

CHAPTER THIRTEEN

Persepolis, Iran

If it hadn't been for the purple bandana he'd tucked under his Colorado Rockies ball cap, the back of his neck would have been scorched raw by the late afternoon sun. Flouting the unfortunate current fashion trend of the dirty beard, he was clean shaven and wore Kuhl cargo pants and hiking boots. Amar Parish stood at the bottom of the recently excavated stone staircase, dusting brush in hand. In his father's image—he was a solidly built six feet tall with brown hair and brown eyes—he had a slim waist, the muscles of his arms and chest well-defined, the skin deeply tanned from many years of working out-of-doors. He could pass for a handsome dark-skinned Persian in a pinch.

Further up the stairway, Amar's mentor and colleague, Dr. Evan Chatterjee, was dressed in the epitome of British khaki expedition wear, complete with a broad-brimmed straw hat. He was using a fancy new high tech Greenstone satellite phone to photograph a series of recently excavated relief carvings on the stone walls of the stairwell. In his fastidious way, Evan had erected a sunshade out of a blue plastic tarp and took the time to seat himself on a folding chair, with a drink by his side, before beginning his task.

Amar wasn't half as careful. Evan, noting the sweat staining the back of his protégé's t-shirt, chuckled to himself. The young man, nearing his thirty-third birthday, was prone to leap before he looked. He couldn't fault him for his enthusiasm, though. Now, he was so focused on uncovering the doorway, he was unaware that he was literally frying himself in the late afternoon desert sun. He swept the last of the dirt away from the upper surface of the doorway revealing a strange double oval symbol that looked very much like the one commonly used for the concept of infinity.

"Evan, look at this, will you? Have you ever seen this symbol before? I've got that feeling in my bones," Amar said. "This could be significant. This could be the find that will prove once and for all that human civilization is much older than we think!"

Evan Chatterjee was dark-skinned with jet black hair, graying only slightly at the temples. At 5' 8" he was smaller and more wiry in build. Evan was twenty-one years older than Amar. He'd been born into a Muslim family and had grown up in Pondicherry, India. He excelled in his early scholastic studies and emigrated to England when his parents relocated their textile business to London in 1979. Evan went on to earn two doctorates from Cambridge University, one in ancient languages and one in world history, along with a master's degree in astronomy.

Foremost among his talents was an innate ability to absorb and become fluent in foreign languages. His colleagues all swore they had never met anyone else who could travel to a foreign country and within a week be conversing casually with the locals in their own dialect. Evan was fluent in twenty-three languages and had grown his natural talent into a thriving international translation business. His company was known by the acronym, TAI, which stood for Translation Associates International. TAI was in demand in both the business and political realms providing document and transcript translation services across international borders. TAI had made Evan wealthy enough to be able to pursue his hobby translating ancient manuscripts, hieroglyphic engravings, and relief carvings. When introduced to each other by Rachael Parish, Amar and Evan found they had a lot in common.

Evan looked up from his phone, "Now, that's a symbol I've never seen before! Stand aside and let me photograph it." Every time Evan punched the shutter button, the high tech phone automatically downloaded the image to a server at Evan's office without leaving a trace of the picture on the phone itself. He'd been told that such a feature was desired by corporate executives, or maybe even spies, who had occasion to do business in the third world. If the phone's user ever came under the scrutiny of local authorities, there would be nothing in its memory to expose his or her activities.

Having removed the last few shovels full of dirt from the front of the bricked up doorway, Amar stepped aside so Chatterjee could take the photo. The young man picked up a nearby sledgehammer that he'd left sitting on the stairs. "Let's open it, shall we?"

"Amar, you know the rules. Nasrollah has gone into Kenareh on business. We are not supposed to open something like this without him being here to observe."

Disappointed, Amar dropped the sledgehammer on the stairs with a resounding thud. One second later, the ancient mud bricks that were blocking the doorway and which had been supported by the surrounding dirt for millenniums, collapsed in a billowing cloud of dust.

Grinning mischievously Amar declared, "I think that's a sign from God, don't you, Evan?"

Overcome with curiosity, Evan replied, "I suppose it could be. It can't hurt if we just take a look."

Evan reached into his duffle and pulled out two one thousand lumen flashlights. He handed one to Amar and gestured toward the door.

"After you, colleague," he said.

The two men shone their lights into the dimly lit space consisting of a single round room twenty-five feet in diameter. Both men gasped at the same time. The floor, walls, and ceiling were completely covered with a mural constructed of tiny but very colorful mosaic tiles. The floor depicted the surface of a lake that appeared to be so real the two men felt anxious about stepping into the room lest they disappear beneath the waves. The strange elliptical symbol Amar had uncovered on the door seemed to float just under the surface of the water in the center of the lake.

Amar swept his flashlight around the room. "Oh my god Evan, I've never seen anything like this before!"

Evan was nearly struck dumb. His eyes were tearing up.

"Neither have I, neither have I," he mumbled.

The circular walls of the room showed a stone city built around a lake in an alpine cirque. The stone architecture rose gracefully up the sides of the valley on a series of lushly landscaped terraces. Different parts of the city were connected by beautifully crafted stone bridges with relief carved arches and balustrades. The buildings were also decorated with carvings and looked as if they had organically grown out of the surrounding alpine forests.

Misty waterfalls cascaded down the walls of the valley. Terraces of fruit trees in bloom were interlaced between the buildings on the lower slopes. The scene was illuminated by a full moon hovering just over the rim of the valley. The color, detail, and use of light and shadow were incredible. The two men felt as if they were standing on a balcony looking across the lake at a magical city.

Scenes depicting idyllic mountain villages reminiscent of a Maxfield Parrish painting are not unheard of in the world. Scenes crafted from mosaic tile at this level of mastery are very rare. As they stood gawking at the room, one more detail catapulted the work into an absolutely unique category, making both men's pulses race. Entering the diorama at the left side of the village was a flying machine. It was easily identifiable as a flying machine since it had windows framing the faces of its passengers.

"It's a Vimana," Evan was nearly breathless.

"What's a Vimana? Amar was keen to know.

"Vimanas are flying machines that are depicted in many ancient Sanskrit texts."

At the top of the walls just below the night sky, a thin band of script circled the room.

Amar ran both hands through his hair. "Is there any way to tell how old this is? Do you recognize the language?"

The crow's feet at the corners of Evan's eyes deepened as he squinted at the writing. "It looks like it might be a very early form of Indo-Iranian Sanskrit. The first references to Vimanas that I know of are in the Ramayana from around 7,000 BCE. Judging by its location under the ruins of Persepolis, this room could be as much as nine to twelve thousand years old."

Amar shone his light on the ceiling. The stars of the night sky blinked back at him. There was something in the pigment of the tiles that made the stars seem to generate their own light. When he moved his flashlight away, they still glowed with a celestial presence.

"Who could have built this?" Amar asked.

"The only word that comes to mind is the ancients," Evan said in reply.

Evan immediately recognized some of the constellations visible in the night sky of the northern hemisphere. He was struck with inspiration.

"If I can translate the text, it may give us an idea as to the age of this room. If it's more than a few thousand years old, the builders would have no knowledge of our modern calendar, which is based upon the birth of Christ. They would have marked time in a totally different way than we do. On the other hand, if this is an accurate portrayal of the night sky at the time this room was built, we might be able to use the stars to pinpoint the date that this scene represents."

Amar asked, "They left the configuration of the night sky as a calendar so we could tell when this room was built? How can you use the stars to pinpoint a date?"

"There is something called the precession of the equinoxes that may allow us to calculate the date. Are you familiar with that concept?"

The expression on Amar's face revealed his puzzlement. "Uh, no, I've never heard of it."

"We'll come back to that later," Evan said, panning his light slowly across the walls from left to right.

Goosebumps rose on Amar's arms. "Can you translate it?"

"I'll need to study it at length. It will be easier once I have the images back at the office where all of my reference material is located."

Amar pointed to the lower right side of the image, which showed a stone building under construction.

"Evan, look at that!"

In front of the building stood a single man holding a small handle in one hand that was attached to a giant piece of cut stone which appeared to be hovering in the air.

Evan gaped at the image. "You've always said, there must have been some technology used by the ancients to build megalithic architecture that we're not aware of. Now, here it is in living color! This is extraordinary!"

The two colleagues stood side by side, playing their lights back and forth over the mural. Amar noticed a white zigzag pattern of some sort emanating from the edge of the lake and disappearing beneath their feet.

Pointing to it, he asked Evan, "What do you think this represents?"

"I don't know; maybe it's some sort of irrigation system," Evan guessed.

The two men stood enraptured by the most beautiful artifact they had ever encountered. Their reverie was interrupted by hasty footfalls on the steps outside.

Nasrollah Brahoui, the curator, burst into the room and stopped dead in his tracks. His jaw dropped as he took in the scene. His gaze settled on the Vimana and hovered there.

After a moment he stuttered, "You can't be in here! This violates every agreement clearly specified in your visas! You were only supposed to uncover the stairway and help me translate the script outside. Are you trying to create an international incident? You must leave at once!"

Evan turned and looked at Brahoui. He could see fear emanating from the curator's eyes.

"You would deprive us of viewing the greatest archaeological discovery in history, even for a few minutes?" Evan said dryly.

Without a word, Brahoui turned and ran back up the steps.

Amar faced Evan, "That didn't go well. Maybe we should get as many photographs as we can."

For the next hour Amar held the light as Evan shot picture after picture, all downloaded via satellite directly to the TAI office in New York.

CHAPTER FOURTEEN

Persepolis, Iran

The men were finishing up the last of the photographs when Amar's head came up. He thought he heard sirens in the distance.

He spoke to Evan over his shoulder. "I'll be right back," he said, leaving Evan in the room as he bounded up the stairs.

The limestone colonnades of the nearby Throne Hall cast long shadows away to the east. Amar ran across the front of the Gate of All Nations and skidded to a stop at the top of the grand staircase. He squinted through the heat waves pouring off the dirty pavement of the access road leading directly toward his position.

He could just make out a three-vehicle convoy, traveling at high speed, leaving a rooster tail of dust behind them, light bars shimmering in the late afternoon light. He ran back to the excavation and yelled down the stairs.

"Uh, hey, Evan. I think you might want to come up here and look at this," he said, the concern evident in his voice.

Evan consulted the cheap black plastic watch he had recently acquired. It showed that the time was just before 7:30 p.m.. He came up the stairs, stood by his friend, and stared at the approaching convoy.

"Oh dear, they look serious, don't they?"

Amar glanced at his colleague. "Evan, is there anything we need to discuss? Anything I should know about the locals?"

"Give me a minute, dear boy." Evan pulled back the flap on his left shirt pocket and extracted the high-tech satellite phone. He thought for a moment, and then grabbing his phone with both hands, pressed and held two small orange buttons that were recessed into the bottom corners of the phone. He returned the phone to his pocket.

The three desert-colored Land Rovers skidded to a halt at the bottom of the grand staircase, spraying gravel and dust in every direction. Five men wearing identical tan uniforms with black kepis got out of the two rear vehicles. They all wore side arms in black leather holsters. The policemen ran up the stairs and took positions on either side of both Amar and Evan standing at attention. The fifth man took a position off to the side, as if he was about to make a presentation to a superior.

The passenger door of the middle vehicle opened, and a rather skeletal, dark-skinned, and slightly hook-nosed policeman, in a similar but more opulent uniform, got out. The man strode around the vehicle and casually made his way up the stairs stopping directly in front of Evan. His face was pockmarked, his black hair somewhat greasy. The man's driver exited the vehicle and stood behind his master.

"You are Dr. Chatterjee, a British citizen?" he asked in Farsi, which Evan understood but Amar did not.

Amar stood still while Evan replied in kind. "Yes, I am, and who might you be?"

The sinister looking officer sneered back at him, "I am Colonel Tarik Golzar of the Provincial Religious Police, I wish to see your papers and those of your American lapdog."

Evan took a deep breath and doing everything in his power to contain his concern, pointed to his blue tarp over by the excavated stairway. "Both of our passports and visas are in that duffle bag over by my sunshade."

The colonel gestured to his driver, who ran over, snatched the satchel off the ground next to Evan's folding chair, and handed it to his superior. The Colonel rummaged around in the bag and came up with the papers and passports. He unceremoniously dropped the duffle in the dirt and rifled through the documents. He drew his arm across his body and knocking Evan's hat off his head with the back of his hand, held the passport up next to his face comparing the photo. Evan's eyes took on a steely resolve.

Apparently satisfied, he stiffly repositioned himself in front of Amar. He drew his hand back to knock Amar's hat off. Amar wasn't going to put up with such an affront and started to make a move to defend himself. Both soldiers were too quick for him and grabbed him by each arm, preventing any further movement.

The Colonel, grinning maliciously, reached out at arm's length and gently removed the purple and black ball cap by the bill. He dropped it onto the ground. Then taking one step forward, he stepped on the hat, grinding it into the dirt as he held the passport next to Amar's face.

Satisfied that he had the right people he sneered, "Dr. Chattejee and Mr. Parish, you are under arrest for crimes committed against Holy Islam."

Having witnessed the arrival of the Religious Police from behind one of the nearby stone columns of the Gate of all Nations, Nasrollah Brahoui hurried across the plateau, his robes flapping in the light evening breeze. He arrived at Evan's side just as the colonel announced their impending incarceration.

"Colonel Golzar, crimes against Holy Islam is a little strong, is it not? These are not capital crimes; this is a simple visa violation, no more. These men are here by permission of the provincial government!"

Evan could tell that Brahoui had called the police out of fear of what might happen to him if he had not.

"Ah, Nasrollah, how nice to see you again," Golzar said curtly. "Show me the dig in question, please."

The two men strode away toward the excavation and returned in a few minutes. Golzar was on his phone.

"I have been instructed by the Mullahs to take these men into custody until such time as their fate can be decided," Golzar pronounced to all present, sliding his phone into its holster.

Nasrollah began to protest, but the colonel pushed him back none too gently. He stooped over, put his face only three inches from the old man's and hissed, "If I were you, old man, I would go back into your museum and keep your mouth shut!"

The old curate knew this man and realized that if he kept protesting, bodily harm would likely be the result. He was much too old for that. Reluctantly, he turned away, walking slowly and dejectedly back to his office. He would, however, get on the phone and protest to the provincial government.

Golzar gestured to his troops, they picked up Evan's duffle, stuffed the hats inside, and roughly hustled Amar and Evan down the stairs, throwing them both up against the side of one of the Land Rovers. The policemen frisked each of them to determine if they had any weapons. Finding none, they cinched their hands behind their backs with flexi-cuffs and shoved them into the back seat of the middle Land Rover. In a spray of gravel and dust, the line of vehicles turned in a circle and went back the way they had come.

CHAPTER FIFTEEN

Shiraz, Iran

It was difficult for the two colleagues to remain upright, trying to sit on the edge of their seats with their hands tied behind them, as the Land Rover sped toward the capital city of Shiraz.

Amar leaned close to his friend and asked in a low voice, "Evan, what the hell just happened?"

Evan began to explain but was cut short by the colonel in the front seat.

"Silence!" he roared. "You will not speak unless I command you to do so!"

Evan leaned forward and explained to Golzar in Farsi, "He doesn't understand your language. I will explain what you have said."

The colonel nodded in assent. "Do so but be quick about it and then keep your mouths shut."

He turned to Amar and spoke softly in English. "The fascist pig has told us there will be no talking unless we are commanded to speak. We should probably keep quiet until we get to wherever we're going; then I'll tell you what I think we're up against."

Amar's eyes narrowed. "He stepped on my hat, Evan. He shouldn't have done that. Nobody steps on my hat."

Evan shushed him, and just as the Colonel began to turn in his seat, he said in Farsi, "He understands, and will do as you wish."

Nearly an hour later, the convoy exited the highway and took a series of surface streets, finally pulling into a walled compound on the northern outskirts of the capital city of Shiraz. The three-vehicle convoy entered the gated compound and pulled to a stop in a large, dirt and gravel courtyard that must have measured one hundred meters on each side. The dimly lit courtyard was surrounded by heavily fortified buildings on three of its four sides. On the fourth side was a thick, bullet-ridden masonry wall.

One of the buildings had bars on its small windows, and Evan assumed this must be the local headquarters of the Religious Police. As Amar and Evan were dragged from the rear seat of the Land Rover into the darkness, they both looked back in response to the sound of steel grating against steel. The two huge iron gates of the compound squealed and clanged shut as the prisoners were pushed and prodded into the police station's receiving room.

Lacking any sort of traditional judiciary, as is prevalent in the west, many Islamic countries are ruled by decree of the clergy. The mandate of the Religious Police is to enforce the decrees of the Mullahs as to what constitutes proper Islamic dress and behavior under Sharia Law

Colonel Tarik Golzar was in charge of the Provincial Religious Police both in Fars Province and in the city of Shiraz. He ruled over a force of 120 officers who operated out of this central station as well as a number of satellite stations scattered around the province. He was a self-important prick of colossal proportions.

The Religious Police consisted of both men and women. The female officers patrolled the city streets in black burkas, detaining women who didn't have their hair appropriately covered, whose coats were too short, or pants too tight. The male force concentrated on the more serious offenders, those who committed adultery or allowed the unlawful mixing of the sexes.

The result of the high level of restriction imposed upon the people by the Religious Police was that vast numbers of ordinary Iranian citizens lived double lives. The citizenry observed more strict standards in public and were much more permissive behind closed doors. Because of their continued harassment of the populace, the Religious Police were generally despised in private, by all but the most devout Muslims.

A personal visit from the Religious Police was received with as much enthusiasm as a personal visit from the local tax collector. A great many of the officers relished their positions of power. Others were squeamish about persecuting friends, relatives, and neighbors, and still more squeamish about some of the punishments that were handed down.

Evan and Amar were jerked to a halt in front of a large wooden desk on a raised platform above the floor. Behind the desk, a burly jailer frowned down upon them. Evan's satchel was dumped on the desk. Two other jailers appeared and began to turn the prisoner's pockets inside out, while the Colonel stood by, a sour look of reproach on his face. One of the policemen plucked the satellite phone from Evan's shirt pocket and held it out to the Colonel.

Golzar took the phone and examined it. It was a beautiful piece of technology. Emerald green in color, with silver titanium trim, a stylish logo with the word "Greenstone" was engraved on the back. He had never seen anything quite like it, a thing of beauty. He pocketed the phone. He would bring it to the electronic tech who worked on the third floor to see if it could be made to work with the local phone system. Perhaps he would keep it for himself.

Once all of Amar and Evan's belongings had been processed, the Colonel gave orders that they were to be taken to a holding cell. They were frog-marched in single file by the two jailers down a set of stone stairs and through a gloomy flagstone paved hallway. The exposed light bulbs mounted to the arched stone ceiling, cast eerie shadows all around.

They stumbled past a series of cell doors until they came to the last thick wooden door on the right. The hefty iron bolt was drawn back with a screech, and the door creaked open. One of the jailers cut the flexicuffs off of each man with a pair of wire cutters, and without a further word, they were shoved into the cell.

The detention cell had a rough cobblestone floor. Two steel bunks with thin fabric mattresses were suspended by rusty iron chains from the masonry walls. At the far corner of the cell was a beat-up combination toilet and sink made of stainless steel. The only window, placed high on the wall next to the ceiling was twelve inches square. The place smelled like rat piss.

Evan asked, "Which bunk do you want?"

Amar quipped, "After you, old chap, after you," as he climbed up on the toilet to look out the high barred window.

Evan sat on one of the bunks. "What can you see?" he asked.

"This window faces the courtyard we just came through."

Amar jumped down, walked to the other end of the cell, and threw his weight against the heavy wooden door. It didn't budge. He sat down on the other bunk and faced his friend.

"So, Evan, tell me; what the hell just happened to us?"

"I think I know," Evan said. "based upon what we saw at Persepolis, I believe that your mission to find evidence of an ancient civilization more advanced than our own may have been fulfilled."

Amar's eyebrows shot up, but he didn't say a word.

Evan continued, "The problem with our discovery is that it will contradict not only the fundamental Islamic version of human history but also the fundamental Christian version, as well. I don't believe they want this discovery to see the light of day."

Parish grinned, remembering the capabilities of the Greenstone phone.

"Too late, the cat is out of the bag! All the pictures have been sent," Amar said. "Is that one of my dad's new satellite phones? I haven't paid much attention to the new product line."

"Yes, it is. You saw me press those two little orange buttons?"

"Yeah, I saw it. What do they do?" Amar asked.

"I didn't make a call; I sent a distress signal. Your dad will be sending some kind of a team to pull us out of here," Evan declared. "He wouldn't have allowed you to come here unless I brought the phone with me."

Amar was angered. "Yeah, I've been one of his test subjects all my life. I refuse to carry one of the damn things. Will I never escape the long arm of my father? I can't go anywhere on this earth that he hasn't pulled some strings to pave the way for me. I'm really getting tired of this bullshit!"

Evan replied, "In this case, you may eventually be grateful for what will happen here."

"Why, do you think we're in a lot of trouble?"

"If the provincial police have researched me by looking at my website, they will no doubt object to what they see on my blog."

"But you're a Muslim yourself, aren't you? What could you have said that would offend other Muslims?

Evan sighed. " I was raised as a Muslim, but I gave all of that up years ago. I have written extensively on the fundamental misconceptions both Islam and Christianity harbor regarding the nature of God. These people will see me as an apostate. The penalty for apostasy in Islamic countries is death."

Just then, the metallic grating noise of the bolt being withdrawn echoed through the cell. The door swung open, and Colonel Golzar strode in with two of his jailers. All wore sidearms. Amar jumped up as if to defend himself and his colleague. Evan remained seated.

The colonel pointed to Amar. "Restrain him," he said in Farsi.

The two men grabbed Amar by the arms, jerked him off of the floor, and dragged him over to the stone wall next to the toilet, where they slammed him against the wall and held him tightly.

"When your pre-approved visa came across my desk, I took the liberty of checking up on you my friend, and guess what I found?" Golzar sneered.

He didn't wait for an answer. "I found that you are a writer of filthy lies against Holy Islam! You thought that the backward Iranians wouldn't have access to the Internet. You thought we would never find out who you really are and would never know about the lies you've been printing? You have the gall to write these lies and then come here to my country to spread your filth, thinking we would never be the wiser?

"We had a great civilization here in Persia when your countrymen were still trying to figure out how to rub two sticks together and light a fire! You are the enemies of Allah, and we are instructed by the Quran to send you from this world that it may be purified for the coming golden age of Islam!"

Evan saw the futility of trying to explain himself to this man and responded with a question. "Is Allah not the supreme creator and ruler of all the universe?"

A momentary look of confusion flitted across the colonel's face. He wasn't expecting this infidel to acknowledge the power and glory of Allah.

"Yes," Golzar replied. "God is great, and he has mandated the removal of his enemies by the true believers."

"How can Allah, who has the supreme power to create and to destroy anything he chooses, have enemies? And even if he did have enemies, why would Allah need to you to fight his battles? Is not Allah sufficient unto himself? Allah fears no man. Allah can have the world any way he wants. If Allah wished for the world to be inhabited only by Muslims, why is it not already so?"

Golzar's eyes burned into Evan's, "You are an infidel and therefore incapable of understanding the true wisdom. We are the holy warriors of Allah. We have been chosen by Allah to rid the world of unbelievers. It is written in the Quran, the Holy Word, given directly to Mohammed by Allah."

Evan, at long last, and despite the risks involved, was starting to lose his temper.

"That's what all the religious exclusionists say. The holy scriptures were indeed written by the prophets. They actually do contain the holy word, in a symbolic form. But you and I both know that over the centuries the word has been re-interpreted by you, the so-called 'chosen ones.' You use the holy books to suit your own misguided purposes. In your case, to indulge your own cultural blood lust! I categorically reject the idea that God or Allah, however you want to identify him, wishes for his finest creation, human beings, to be destroyed by you or anyone else!"

Golzar's eyes bulged. So quickly that Evan never saw it coming, Golzar drew his arm back and slapped him hard across the mouth, splitting his lip.

"Silence, you impudent pig!"

He put his pockmarked face inches from Evan's, and whispered hoarsely, so as to not be heard by his henchmen. He didn't want what he was about to say to leak out to his staff just yet. The spittle flew from his greasy lips onto Evan's face as he hissed, "You are guilty of crimes against Holy Islam, and both you and your arrogant young American will pay for those crimes in the morning!"

He held his face there, his eyes searching Chatterjee's for signs of fear. Satisfied that he had seen it, he motioned to his men, who slammed Amar up against the wall and then dropped his arms. The three left the cell, and the bolt shot home with a loud thump.

CHAPTER SIXTEEN

Shiraz, Iran

Amar rubbed his biceps, which were slightly bruised from the thug's grip. He looked somewhat droll. "I take it that was about your website?"

Evan felt a little sheepish as he dabbed at his lip with a handkerchief. "Yeah, that was about the website."

Amar, not having understood a word of the conversation, crossed his arms across his chest.

"So what did you say about their glorious belief system that pisses them off so much?"

Evan managed a little bit of a smile. "I said, that in the near future, any religion that condones the taking of human life for trumped-up religious reasons should be outlawed by the World Court and condemned by public opinion.

"Every major religion has followers who claim that the rewards of the hereafter are denied to all who don't believe as they do. The concept of the "chosen ones" was conceived thousands of years ago during the dark ages. They can't all be right and still claim to be the chosen ones. I think people who promote such viewpoints today are pretty much out-of-date.

"At a time when we should be coming together to recognize our common humanity, these people are still laying the groundwork for dissention and violence. I gave hints on my blog, in no uncertain terms, who I think the worst offenders are."

Amar cocked his head to one side. "Yep, that oughta do it. Let me guess, radical Muslims topped the chart?"

"Something like that." Evan was debating within himself whether or not to reveal his complete opinion of the colonel's threat to Amar. He thought it would be good if at least one of them could get some sleep tonight.

"I thought you told me you grew up as a Muslim?" Amar asked.

Evan replied, "I was born into a Muslim household, but gave up the religion when I went away to Cambridge. I decided as a very young man I needed to form my own opinions about what's real in the world. There's a great deal of difference in being born into a faith and being a committed member of its belief system. I guess that's the rub for me. I view most religions as circular belief systems. When you question the membership, they have a first tier round of explanations as to what they believe. That's usually followed by what will happen to you if you don't believe, too. When you get into a lot of detail in your inquiry, the discussion starts to break down. Eventually, the conversation always comes back to 'It is written.'

"When you question the veracity of their holy scripture, you find out whatever interpretation of the writings that group favors was given to the prophet directly by God. Just like here. They use that mechanism to justify anything they want to do, like kill all the infidels. So much death and destruction could be avoided if people would just change their minds!"

"Geez, Evan, are we in real trouble here?"

"I don't know, Amar. Since neither of our respective countries has diplomatic relations here, I don't know where else we can turn. I've already sent a signal to Greenstone Security."

"Are you suggesting that our lives could be on the line?"

Evan paused thoughtfully. "I don't know yet. I suspect we'll know shortly."

"If God were truly judgmental, he would have wiped this planet clean and started over long ago. Truth be told, from my study of extinctions, we seem to be doing an adequate job of wiping ourselves out on a regular basis with no outside assistance." Amar said.

"Too true, Amar, too true," Evan replied.

"We're all trying to figure out what's real. From my point of view, a more appropriate question might be, 'What the hell would have to be true in order for this world with all its flaws, to be considered in balance by a supreme being, if he exists?' I haven't figured that one out yet."

Evan contemplated that statement for a moment. "I haven't either, come to a conclusion that is, though I've been working on the question in earnest. I am a fervent believer in intelligent design, though."

"I know you are, and you're doing more with it than most, too. Do you think they'll ever let us out of here?" Amar asked.

"I don't know, Amar. They have no concept of human rights the way we do in the West. I hope it won't be long."

On the third floor of the police station, the colonel entered a large room with one wall of windows that overlooked the courtyard. The other three walls were covered by a system of cheap modular steel shelving that contained a series of wire baskets. Each basket bore the name and contained the personal effects of someone doing time in the cells below.

Hadi Mirza, the property master, as well as the Colonel's electronic surveillance tech, sat at a wooden bench just inside the door, the pieces of a cell phone arrayed in front of him. Colonel Golzar made it a regular practice to bug the cell phones of detainees who were prosperous enough to own one. Then he might better find out what they were up to after they had served their punishments.

Golzar put Evan's satchel on the desk and handed Hadi the paperwork.

"Hadi, this belongs to the Brit and the American we just brought in. You can put it all in one basket. Whose phone is that?"

"It belongs to Aban Hosseini, the merchant. He is suspected of hosting parties in the rooms behind his store where unmarried men and women mix unlawfully. Once I install this chip, we'll be able to monitor his communications, and then we'll see what he is really up to."

"Good, very good, Hadi." The colonel reached into the large pocket of his tunic and handed over Evan's satellite phone.

"I want you to look this over. I've never seen one quite like this. Are there any pictures on it?"

Hadi brought up the home screen and pecked away for a minute. "It must be new, Colonel. There are no photos that I can see."

"Good, find out if it will work with our local network and tell me in the morning. I might want to keep it for myself. I'm going home."

CHAPTER SEVENTEEN

Seattle

Tom Parish, Chairman of Parish Communications International, sat down at his high tech, black glass and burl wood desk to start his day. He looked down over the city of Seattle from his corporate offices on the 65th floor of Columbia Tower. It was one of those rare clear Seattle mornings, with only a smattering of cloud cover on the northern horizon and unlimited visibility. He was turning over the details of the acquisition of a South Korean telecommunications company in his mind when the intercom buzzed.

Jan Mayer, his long-time executive assistant, came over the intercom, "Mr. Parish, we've just received an extraction signal from the Greenstone network!"

Tom shot up in his chair. Extraction signals were relatively rare. "Put it on screen and come in here, please."

He swiveled around as a part of the cherrywood paneling behind his desk slid up into the ceiling, revealing a seventy-two-inch high definition flat screen monitor. Jan ran in from the outer office, carrying an electronic datapad, just as the screen came alive displaying client information and GPS coordinates along with a private authentication code.

PCI was one of the world's leading providers of cell phone and broadband technology along with the associated infrastructure. They also owned a division with a presence in the field of corporate security. They had recently introduced a line of highly sophisticated personal security devices to the executive protection market.

The units were comprised of a satellite phone with GPS reporting capability and all of the bells and whistles of the most advanced Blackberry. The phones were built of an emerald green carbon fiber with titanium trim and hardened to withstand extended use in the field. They were small enough to fit in a shirt pocket and could communicate via dedicated satellites from anywhere in the world.

Each unit bore a PCI Greenstone logo and was available with a subscription to Greenstone Executive Security services. Occasionally, a unit was provided to the purchasers of major infrastructure contracts as a perk, though usually without the security services bundle.

Greenstone Executive Security, a subsidiary of PCI, provided security services to the top echelon of corporate execs who conducted business all over the world. The Greenstone units were obscenely expensive and had one unusual feature—two little orange buttons both marked EXT. The little buttons were mounted on each lower corner of the unit and recessed in such a way that they couldn't be pressed by mistake at the same time. Holding the unit with both hands and pressing the buttons simultaneously sent a message by satellite, along with GPS coordinates and medical data, directly to GES requesting extraction from wherever one might be, anywhere on the planet.

Receipt of an EXT signal triggered the deployment of a team of former Army and Navy black ops commandos to the precise location from which the signal was sent. Each team was prepared to extract the sender from whatever pickle they found themselves in. Depending on the circumstances, the team might arrive in business suits, local peasant garb, or full combat regalia, ready to use whatever means necessary, from posting bail to lethal force, to rescue a subscriber. One extraction was included in the cost of the GES subscription. Additional rescues were charged to the client's account and could be quite pricey, discouraging reckless behavior.

The system had been up and running for two years and had a devoted following amongst the world's financial elite. Whenever Tom introduced a new feature, he would set up a beta test in the field with half a dozen of his subscribers. When he found out that Evan and Amar would be working together in third world locations, he set Evan up with a free subscription. He knew Amar wouldn't have accepted the gift.

Jan came to rest behind Tom's chair; the info came up on her datapad first. "It's Evan Chatterjee, sir."

"Christ, the extraction code says there are two people. Is my son with him?"

Jan consulted her datapad. "Probably sir; Amar was scheduled to be at this location with Evan on an archaeological dig."

"Where are they?" asked Tom.

"Iran, sir."

"For the love of God," he was about to say, "What the hell are they doing in Iran?" Then he remembered pulling some strings with the local governor to set up the dig. That was some time ago, and he'd forgotten about it. "Do we have an overhead?"

Jan pressed a button on her datapad. "Yes, sir, one of our comsats was re-tasked automatically as soon as we received the EXT signal. Satellite image coming up now, sir."

The flat screen switched from the client dossier to a satellite image of the entire country. As the picture zoomed from low earth orbit down through the broken cloud deck, a blinking cursor appeared over the GPS coordinates. Once an EXT signal was sent, the unit would keep on transmitting, even if it appeared to be turned off.

The zoom continued until the picture showed an adobe-style compound, with a courtyard and three vehicles parked in it. The courtyard was surrounded by a large building on three sides. A green cursor was blinking over one section of the roof.

Each Greenstone was paired with what looked like a wristwatch. There were two versions of the watch available. One of the watches was designed to look cheap for use in the third world, so an adversary would think it had little value and wouldn't confiscate it. Evan had one of those.

The second type of watch was very stylish and expensive-looking for use in the business environment. In addition to telling the time, each of the watches also transmitted the wearer's medical data to the Greenstone unit from up to a mile away. The watch also had a back-up GPS capability, should the subscriber become separated from his phone.

Tom stared at the overhead shot. "Bring up the medical data."

Jan punched a couple more keys on her datapad, and Evan's vital signs came up on the display.

"Blood pressure is good, body temp is within limits for the location, pulse is a bit high, which is to be expected from someone requesting extraction," she said.

Tom was more than a little tense, "Get Gary Renfro on the phone, now."

Gary was president of GES.

Jan pressed a speed dial number and the CONF button on her datapad activating Tom's speakerphone. "He's on his cell, sir."

"Renfro here," Gary said.

"Gary, do you have the EXT data?" Tom asked.

"Hi, Tom, yeah I just got it; Evan Chatterjee, huh? I guessed it was only a matter of time before we had to go in and rescue that bloke from hostiles somewhere."

Tom ignored the remark. "Gary, this is a code red. Amar is with him. I want a complete breakdown on the location and who likely has them in custody. Where's our closest team?"

"Team six is currently in Djibouti. We have a C-130 on site. It's late there, but I can have them activated in a couple of hours, and if we can get permission from the Saudis to overfly, we can be close to a drop zone four-to-six hours later. I'll need to study the incoming data for a bit to determine the preferred method of extraction."

"Okay, Gary, make it so. I want all telemetry routed to my screen real-time as the mission unfolds. Meanwhile, we'll work the business side and see if we have any contracts with the locals that we can use to make a point. Keep me posted on your progress."

"Yes, sir, Renfro out."

Just as he clicked off, the cursor showing Evan's location in the Iranian building split into two and one cursor began to migrate to a different location in the building.

Jan pointed at the screen. "It appears they have confiscated his Greenstone, sir."

Tom looked up. "He still has his watch on, so we'll continue to know if he's in good health. I wish to hell I could convince Amar to carry a unit since he travels so much, but he won't have it. He doesn't like me in his business, or so he says. For the moment, we'll have to assume he's healthy, too. Jan, get me Alistair Pembroke at PCI in Mumbai, will you?"

Jan made a couple of strokes on the screen of her datapad with her finger. "Coming up now, sir."

She looked at the display of clocks on Tom's office wall, showing the local time all over the world.

"Good evening, this is Jan Meyer at PCI Seattle. I have Chairman Parish on the line for Mr. Pembroke."

Pembroke picked up, well aware of the time difference. "Good morning, Mr. Chairman, I was just preparing to leave for the day. What can I do for you?"

"Hi Alistair, I need to know if we have any contracts either being negotiated or in force in, where is it, Jan?"

Jan consulted her datapad. "The city of Shiraz in Fars Province, Iran, sir."

"Did you hear that, Alistair?"

"Yes, sir, I'm pulling it up now." There was the sound of computer keystrokes.

"Ah, here it is. We've just negotiated and signed a contract with the Governor of Fars Province, a man named Mahmoud Khani."

"What's the scope of the contract work?" asked Tom.

"Let's see; this contract is for a complete new infrastructure system including servers, towers, and switching stations for both broadband

and cell communications. You can access the contact information from your computer."

"Okay, Alistair, how much is it worth?"

"Looks like 143 million, give or take," Alistair replied.

"All right, good, that's good. I'll review the file from this end. Thanks, Alistair."

"Any time, Tom, any time at all. Will there be anything else?"

"Not at the moment. Goodbye, Alistair."

"Cheers, Mr. Chairman." Pembroke hung up.

Tom turned to Jan. "Let's have a look at the contract data."

Jan made a couple of keystrokes on her datapad. "The contract file will come up on your screen in a moment."

Tom scrolled through the contract. "I see we have given Mr. Khani a Greenstone of his own."

"So it would seem, sir."

Tom turned to Jan. "Let's get Mr. Khani on his unit and see how much he wants his new phone system."

"Yes, sir. I'll see if I can raise him from my workstation."

"Thanks, Jan." Tom turned back to the credenza and began to review the contract file in more detail.

After a few minutes, Jan buzzed him again. "Yes, Jan."

"Gary Renfro for you sir; he's on video in his office."

"On screen, please."

The contract file reduced to a smaller window off to one side of the display as Gary Renfro's face appeared on the screen.

"Here's the update, Tom. Team six is loading and will be ready to take off in approximately one hour. They have a full suite of identity documents showing them as contract workers for the new phone system in Shiraz and are prepared for either a covert or combat extraction."

Tom, an experienced pilot, asked, "What's the weather look like?"

"We checked the local weather conditions, and the winds aloft are right for a HAHO (high altitude high opening) jump under the cover of darkness. The team will exit the plane over the Persian Gulf approximately thirty-eight miles off the west coast of the Iran, near the 29th parallel, and glide into the beach."

"Can we get the team in without radar detection?"

"The C-130 will probably get a scramble out of the Iranian Air Force but will turn and hightail it out of there before it becomes a problem. Since the individual jumpers create no significant radar signature, the whole thing will look like an offshore aerial recon. PCI already has a two-man team on the ground in Shiraz doing the front work for the infrastructure contract. You are no doubt aware of their presence?"

"Yeah, I was just looking at the contract."

Renfro continued. "Our two-man advance team will set up a GPS beacon on the beach for our jumpers to home in on. Once they rendezvous, the five-man force will return to Shiraz by car. We'll also be standing by to learn the results of your negotiations with the government. Have you made contact yet?"

"Not yet, we're working on it, though. The contact for the infrastructure deal is the Governor of Fars Province, a man by the name of Mahmoud Khani. We gave him a Greenstone phone as part of his contract package. Jan is trying to reach him now. What about the method of extraction?"

"The plan is still being worked on, but most likely it will be by car back to the beach and by boat from there. We're inventing as we go."

"Okay, Gary, keep me informed."

"Yes, sir, Renfro out."

CHAPTER EIGHTEEN

Seattle

The screen went blank. Tom rubbed his temples with both hands. This was the last thing he needed in the middle of the South Korean deal. He hit a key, and the contract info came back up. He pressed his intercom switch. "Jan, anything on Khani yet?"

"Yes, sir, his unit is forwarded to his office. I'm told he's been tied up in a meeting with the national finance minister in Tehran. It's believed he's forgotten to take his unit off forwarding and is currently en route to Shiraz by helicopter.

He may be a couple of hours yet. I understand that he speaks passable English; so when we finally get him, you can talk with him directly. "All right. I'm not going anywhere until this is resolved. Please stay on top of it."

Fifteen minutes later, Jan buzzed. "Sir, I have a video call from Terrance Van Zant, Evan's second in command at TAI in New York."

"We've met before; he's listed in Evan's file as a need to know. Onscreen, please."

Van Zant's face came up on Parish's screen. He was fully aware of the contract that Chatterjee had with Greenstone Security. "Mr. Parish, you are no doubt aware of the abduction of Evan Chatterjee and your son?"

"Yes, Terrance, we received the extraction signal early this morning. Do you have any information to add?"

"Yes, I believe I may. Just a few minutes ago, I received a phone call from a man named Nasrollah Brahoui in Iran. He's the Curator at Persepolis. He told me Evan and Amar have been arrested by the Religious Police and most likely have been taken to their station in Shiraz approximately one hour away from Persepolis, where they were working."

"Terrance, tell me what they were arrested for and what the hell they're doing in Iran in the first place?"

Terrance explained the unique nature of the excavation and its requirements for a translator of Evan's qualifications.

"If I remember correctly, they were invited into the country."

"Yes, I have a file of the correspondence which I can e-mail to you for your review."

"Thank you, Terrance; please do so. We have their location under satellite surveillance, and the medical telemetry is good. We don't know for sure how or why they were taken, but your call confirms where they are now. I thank you for the information."

"You are very welcome, sir."

"I'm going to pass you back to Jan, and she'll establish a link to your computer so you can stay informed as we proceed with the mission. If you come across any additional information, no matter how insignificant, please forward it to us by phone or e-mail."

"Thank you, Mr. Parish, I'll be sure to do that. Do you think this is serious?"

"I have little personal knowledge of the political situation over there, except to say they don't like Americans, or the British either for that matter. However, our cultural desk is preparing a threat assessment, and that report should be available shortly. I'll see you are kept in the loop, Terrance. Not to worry; we'll bring them home."

"Thank you again, Mr. Parish. Goodbye."

Tom's screen returned to the satellite image with a sidebar on medical telemetry and an icon for the contract.

Another half hour passed during which he tried to concentrate on other work, largely to no avail. Finally, Jan buzzed.

"Sir, I have Governor Mahmoud Khani on the line for you. He made a fuel stop at the airport in Esfahan on his way back to Shiraz and is catching up on his calls. Just so you know, it's about eleven o'clock at night over there."

Tom punched the speaker button, "Governor Khani, this is Tom Parish, CEO of Parish Communications International."

Khani, a handsome 6'2" example of Persian heritage, replied somewhat tentatively, "Mr. Parish, how very nice to hear from the Chairman of PCI. To what do I owe this honor so late at night?"

"First, I'm calling to see if you're satisfied with the efforts of Mr. Pembroke, of our India Division, in the execution of your contract?"

"Why, yes, we are. But as you know, the contract is in its infancy, and at this stage, we're only setting up logistics for the move in of your construction crews and equipment."

"I am aware of that Governor. I wanted to establish whether or not, in your view, we have performed to the letter of the contract thus far?"

"Yes, of course, we are quite satisfied at this stage."

"Good, that's very good. The second purpose of my call is to ask if you are aware that your provincial government arranged to have a British translator of ancient languages and his American colleague visit an excavation at Persepolis to assist your scholars in translating a new archaeological find?"

"Indeed, I am; I approved their visa applications personally. It was my staff that requested their assistance here in Iran. Why do you ask?"

"It seems they were arrested earlier today by your Religious Police and taken to some sort of compound in Shiraz. Would you know anything about that?"

The Governor swore in Farsi, which Tom didn't understand. "I was not aware this had taken place, Mr. Parish. I'll look into it first thing in the morning."

"Governor Khani, let me make myself perfectly clear, in the nicest possible way. One of those men is a dear friend of mine, and one of them is my son. Your people invited them to come into your country to help with something you couldn't handle on your own. Then you arrested them and incarcerated them for who knows what reason."

"I assure you, Mr. Parish, I had no knowledge of this event. You should be aware there is a disconnect between the civil and religious governments in my country."

"I don't doubt that Mr. Khani, but I assure you if one hair on either of their heads is harmed, your contract with Parish Communications International will be canceled. I will go so far as to say that any other contract we have anywhere else in your country, regardless of its stage of completion, or its cost to my company, will be canceled as well. If I were you, I wouldn't wait until morning to sort this out. I'd look into it right now."

Governor Khani was above all a pragmatist. His job as governor of Fars Province was to make sure the roads were repaired, the electricity flowed, the sewage didn't back up, that there were jobs for his constituents, and above all, that the telephone system worked.

"Of course, Mr. Parish, you are quite right. There are those in the government of my country who understand we must get along in the world, that we must be able to do business with other countries. There are also those who would waste all of the progress we have made in our trading relationships in a quest for the dominance of Islam. The Religious Police in my country are afforded wide latitude to act upon their own authority."

"Do you know who's behind this?"

"I suspect there is one man, a certain colonel, a complete thorn in my side, who is behind this. He and I have clashed on this type of situation before. I will find out what has transpired immediately. You do realize it is nearly the middle of the night here and communications may be difficult?"

Tom felt this wouldn't be the right time to inform the governor, if he didn't get off his ass, Greenstone Security was about to invade his country's sovereign territory.

"Yes, I do realize that, Governor Khani. Let's stay in touch over the next few hours."

"Yes, you can be assured that we will. Goodbye, Mr. Parish." The Governor attempted to sign off first, but Tom Parish had already hung up.

CHAPTER NINETEEN

Shiraz, Iran

Evan and Amar lay in their fetid bunks. The compound was asleep, and the night was quiet. The dim light that filtered its way into their cell came through the small window from the area lights in the courtyard. They had each slept fitfully, the sleep of the newly incarcerated.

Amar wondered if the Religious Police would really stoop to bodily harm to make their point. In any case, he would do whatever he had to do to protect the doctor. The older man wasn't really capable of defending himself physically.

"Evan, are you awake?"

"Indeed, though I'm sorry to say it."

"I was thinking about our trip in here in the Land Rover. I saw some of the common people on the streets. What do you think about their lives?"

"What did you see?" Evan asked.

"I saw regular people going about their daily business, just like people do everywhere. Except for the fact that most of the women are all covered in black, which has to be terribly uncomfortable, they all seemed like regular people to me. People like Nasrollah, good family people. The Religious Police, on the other hand, appear to be cut from different cloth."

"You know who they are, Amar. Whether they wrap themselves in religion, economics or power, they're still the politicians. In modern day Iran, they want to tell the population what to think, what to wear, what customs they can engage in, and what they cannot. They even go so far as to prescribe how and when to pray."

"I can't imagine being told how I have to pray!"

"Ah, but you're from the West, where freedom of religion is a sacred part of your culture. Here it isn't. The hardliners over here believe they're preparing the way for the golden age of Islam. When finally, everyone is of like mind and all are marching in formation, the dawn of utopia will come. Everyone left on the planet will be a devout

Muslim, there will be only one religion and our hardliner friends will conveniently be the ones in charge."

Amar scoffed, "Don't they know that kind of philosophy has never worked in all the annals of history? There are countless examples: Genghis Khan, Hitler, Alexander the Great! Hell, Alexander the Great conquered the entire known world. He only lasted twelve years. That's not much of a golden age is it?"

"The radical Muslims have become wed to a fictitious ideal and don't seem to understand that a healthy society is not a monoculture but one of great diversity. As you've uncovered in your research, monocultures are the epitome of overspecialization. They're unstable and doomed to eventual extinction," Evan said.

"That's a recorded fact. Every time a population is fooled into accepting some form of overspecialization, they end up perishing," Amar replied.

"Nevertheless, the conquerors go about their business with the conquest as their only focus. They're so wrapped up in the mechanics of winning, they give little thought to what it will take to manage the great new society once the carnage is over. Centralized economic control, no matter how ideally inspired, doesn't work. The Soviets demonstrated that for all to see, and China is about to demonstrate it once again."

Evan went on, "it's rather like the dog who barks and chases cars. He's a really good barker and everyone fears him. He demonstrates incredible prowess in pursuing the car. Then one day, through supreme exertion, he catches the car, and now with it in his teeth, he finds that he is totally unprepared to deal with the new reality, dog in possession of car."

Amar laughed, "That's funny, can I use that?"

"Are you planning to write a book?"

"I just might," Amar said, "I know someone who can advise me on how to do it. Though if it gets us in this much trouble it might not be worth it."

Persian Gulf

The Hercules C-130 skirted Yemen due to reports of insurgents in possession of SAM missiles on the ground and was flying up the centerline of the Red Sea. Once past the northern Yemeni border, it would turn to a heading of 30 degrees and due to a contact Chairman Parish had in the Royal Kingdom, would be permitted to overfly the Empty Quarter of Saudi Arabia.

The plane would go feet wet, over the Persian Gulf, just to the north of Bahrain. From there it would approach the west coast of Iran at 33,000 feet above sea level at roughly the same latitude as Houston, Texas. The three-man extraction crew was geared up and ready to jump at the end of their eighteen hundred mile flight.

Greenstone Executive Security owned a fleet of three of the old transports. Including the engines and airframes, they had all been brought up to zero time specs as they had been acquired. Each plane was outfitted specifically for cargo and crew transport and evacuation.

In the late nineties, Gary Renfro, an ex-Navy Seal, and the owner of a small privately held security company, approached Tom Parish with a unique marketing plan. He suggested to Chairman Parish that there was a very large, potentially lucrative, untapped market for cell phone technology in third world countries that had oil or other types of natural resource income.

Many third world countries had no diplomatic relations with the West, and an inadequate judiciary, which made doing business with them a risky proposition. If, for instance, there was no court system, it would be difficult to sue a client for breach of contract.

Most western countries had gone through several stages in the development of communications technology, starting with the advent of the telegraph during the mid-nineteenth century. As the telephone gained acceptance at the turn of the twentieth century, the United States, in particular, led the way with the installation of an enormously expensive nationwide copper-wired landline telephone system. When cell phone technology became available in the eighties, the American phone companies just piggybacked it onto the existing landline system.

The growing trend in third world countries, wishing to enter the 21st century, was often to go from stone-age communications directly to a fully integrated wireless infrastructure, bypassing the enormous cost of landlines altogether. Many families, and in some cases whole villages, might share one or two cell phones the way family members in the West shared a car.

Renfro had convinced Tom Parish that these third world markets could be tapped by modifying his business model only slightly. The key was to train ex-military operatives to become cell phone technology contractors, capable of operating in less than stable environments. Renfro, being an ex-Navy Seal, knew the right people and could recruit the best of the black ops warriors who were about to retire from active service.

By military standards, the pay was fabulous, and the company provided the training to teach new telecommunication skills to complement the operator's military training. Once the word got out, Renfro had a steady stream of applicants, and Tom Parish had places to put them.

Doing business in countries often controlled by dictators was difficult at first. Renfro took the brunt of the learning curve upon himself. It had taken Parish and Renfro a few years to polish up the operational philosophy. Several contractual devices needed to be invented to ensure payment of the contract sums in countries with no judiciary system. Funds had to be placed in escrow, out of country, according to very stringent terms for their disbursal. Once the funds were in place, an advance team consisting of trained paramilitary contractors entered the country in question. The team would make arrangements for the arrival of equipment. They secured housing for the construction staff that would follow.

The advance team monitored the progress of the ongoing construction contract and continued to provide security for the endeavor as the work progressed. All of the contract work would be performed from the point of view of protecting the workers and providing for their emergency evacuation in the event of a local political meltdown.

The fleet of three C-130s was instrumental in delivering crews and supplies to accomplish the contract work, and on several occasions had been used to pull crews out to safety. The plan worked pretty well, and despite the fact that he was only an employee, it had made Gary Renfro a millionaire in his own right.

When Tom Parish began dabbling in satellite phone technology, Gary felt that their business model could now be exported to other types of businesses, and Greenstone Executive Security was born. They equipped themselves to perform both SWAT and military type hostage rescues and had demonstrated their prowess by bringing several well-heeled executives home from dicey situations around the world.

Now they were going to test their skills in the Muslim world and see if they could get the Chairman's son out without creating an international incident.

CHAPTER TWENTY

Tehran, Iran

Governor Mahmoud Khani and key members of his staff departed Tehran around nine o'clock in the evening. The governor was at the controls of his Shabaviz 2-75 helicoptor which was a pirated Iranian version of the Augusta Bell 214C built illegally in Iran and otherwise known around the world as the venerable Huey helicopter. Khani could have taken the much more comfortable Boeing 727, but he was ex-Iranian Air Force and liked to keep his proficiency in the helicopter up to standards. They landed at Shahid Beheshti Airport near Esfahan two hours later to refuel and enjoy a late dinner.

His personal secretary, Jalal, remembered to take the governor's Greenstone phone off of forwarding and checked his messages. He discovered an urgent call from the chairman of Parish Communications and relayed the information to the governor.

Khani understood that it was the middle of the business day on the west coast of the United States and was curious to know why the chairman of PCI was trying to contact him so late in the evening, here in Iran.

He made the call to PCI, spent twenty minutes on the phone with Chairman Parish, and upon hanging up turned to his secretary. "Jalal, do you remember the visas we issued to two translators who were going to Persepolis?"

"Yes, Governor, I do. They were going to assist Nasrollah Brahoui at the Apadana Palace in Persepolis."

"Ah, yes, I remember now; Nasrollah is a fine old gentleman. It seems that idiot, Colonel Golzar, is at it again. Apparently, he went down there, arrested the two men, and now has them in custody at his station in Shiraz."

"He arrested them on what charge, sir?"

"It seems that the two archaeologists have made a discovery that Colonel Golzar believes is a threat to the existence of Islam. Just between you and me, the man is slightly off his nut and well on his way to creating an international incident. I don't know why he can't stick to flogging adulterers or enforcing the dress code." Khani heaved a sigh.

"What do you wish me to do, Governor?" asked Jalal.

"Call the station and find out where he is. Then get him on the phone for me. But be quick about it, we still have a two-hour flight ahead of us, and I'd like to sleep in my own bed tonight."

Jalal made the call only to find out from Hafez, the night duty sergeant, that Colonel Golzar had gone home where he kept no phone and had turned his radio off. Jalal inquired if someone could be sent to the colonel's home and rouse him to talk with the governor.

Hafez had observed the cruelty of his superior firsthand and did not wish to be the object of it. He made a lame excuse, saying he was the only one on duty, and could not abandon his post. Just prior to climbing up into the cockpit of the chopper, Jalal, still unaware of the Colonel's intent regarding the prisoners, relayed the information from the call to his boss.

"Governor, the colonel is at home with no phone, and there is no one at the station who can go get him at this late hour. According to Hafez, the duty sergeant, the prisoners are fine and will still be in good health in the morning. I don't see how we can accomplish anything further tonight."

"No, I don't either. Let's complete the last leg of our flight, and we'll call Mr. Parish from Shiraz."

Khani settled himself into the pilot's seat, went through his checklist, and pressed the starter on engine number one. The turbine spun up and ignited with a muffled "whoof." As the engine came up to rpm, Khani noticed he had an oil pressure indicator light in the red, even though the gauge still showed adequate oil pressure. He cursed and shut down the turbine.

"Damn, I guess we're going to be here for a while. Let's go over to air force headquarters and see about having this repaired."

"Would you rather drive down from here, sir?"

"No, I need the bird tomorrow morning for some VIPs who will be visiting. Jalal, I want to leave here no later than four in the morning if it can be fixed by then. That way we can be in the office by six and deal with the colonel before we start our day."

They inquired with the duty officer at the front desk of the air force crew quarters, and the governor was assured that they had a mechanic on the field working the second shift. He was an expert on the Pratt & Whitney turboshaft engine variant and was in fact, working on one of the air force Hueys at this very moment. He was summoned and appeared at the front desk.

"Good evening, Governor, how may I be of service?" the mechanic asked.

Khani explained the problem with the oil pressure indicator light.

"I'm familiar with this problem, sir. Usually, this is a result of a failure of the indicator light sensor and doesn't mean an actual loss of oil pressure. I can replace the sensor, and we'll start the engine again. If the light doesn't come on, and the gauge reads within the pressure range, we can assume the problem has been fixed."

"And how long do you expect these repairs to take?" asked Khani.

"If all goes well, and I don't encounter any other issues, no more than three hours, sir. We'll want to take the time to check all your fluid levels, as well. I can't comment as to how long the aircraft will remain out of service, should we find other problems."

"Okay, Sergeant, please get started," the governor ordered. He asked the duty officer where they might wait and was offered the pilot lounge and the on-call crew bunk room, which was currently vacant. Some of the staff members arranged themselves in the pilot's lounge and watched TV. The governor picked out a bunk in the crew quarters and lay down for a snooze.

Three hours later, Jalal shook Khani by the shoulder. "Governor, the aircraft is ready to depart.

Khani came awake with a little start. "What time is it?"

"It's about 3:30, sir. The staff are gathering up their belongings; no doubt they will nap during the flight."

"Give me just a minute to throw some water on my face, and we'll go.

After performing his ablutions, Khani strolled out onto the ramp and climbed up into the cockpit. Jalal took the left seat, and the staff loaded themselves into the passenger compartment in the back of the helicopter. All donned headsets to defeat the noise of the rotor.

Khani fished around in the console and produced a small cable. He reached into his coat pocket, found the Greenstone phone, and turned it on checking for messages. There were none. He gave the cable and the satellite phone to Jalal.

"Here Jalal, plug this into the radio stack so we can stay in touch if anything else happens."

The Governor brought the engines up to rpm, pulled up on the collective, and the chopper rose gently but noisily into the pre-dawn night. He leveled off at 1,000 feet AGL and they flew south toward Shiraz at 130 mph.

Geneveh, Iran

The two-man Greenstone advance team had driven to Genaveh, on the coast of the Persian Gulf north of Bushehr, several hours earlier. Both men had arrived in country months before, to begin the front-end work on the new PCI cell phone system for Fars Province. They were, at Renfro's directive, the type of men that were "mission ready" at all times. The drive down from Shiraz in their Nissan Patrol took two hours in the dark of night.

Upon arriving in the country, they purchased two of the yellow and white vehicles. They were the most common type of SUV in Iran and would attract little attention. The men made sure to give the heavily fortified and patrolled nuclear facilities at Bushehr a wide berth since they had no good reason for being in the area.

After performing a quick recon of the beaches north of the small town of Genaveh, they selected two isolated landing zones, about a mile apart, that would minimize the possible detection of the jump team. One would function as the primary landing zone, and one would be designated as the alternate, in the event of trouble or detection. Working quickly in the dark, they set up a small GPS based transmitter in the sand at each location.

The three-man jump team got to their feet in the cargo hold of the C-130 and began to make the final check of each other's equipment. They were extensively trained to make high altitude, high opening parachute jumps with covert insertion into enemy territory. Clad in well-insulated jumpsuits, they also wore special insulated gloves and boots to withstand the extremely cold temperatures of the atmosphere at 33,000 feet.

Each jumper's parachute pack contained a highly sophisticated Hi-Glide canopy with a 6-to-1 sink rate allowing them to depart the aircraft and make an unpowered descent to a landing zone on the beach nearly forty miles away. The parachute packs also contained special oxygen bottles that fed custom-fitted helmets with full face shields. The helmets were equipped with a scrambled radio intercom so the team members could communicate during their descent without being monitored by anyone else.

Each helmet also had a heads up display that projected an artificial image of the terrain and the landing zone they were approaching, as well as giving the critical data of altitude, outside temperature, sink rate, and distance to the LZ. A knob on the side of the jumper's helmet could turn the display down so the image was just a ghost overlaying what the jumper was actually seeing. Or the image could be turned up to obscure the actual view, to look like what one would see if jumping into a video game. This feature was particularly useful in low visibility, but tonight conditions were CAVU (Ceiling And Visibility Unlimited).

The ground team could project information directly onto the jumper's displays to direct them to the alternate LZ if their position had been compromised. The jumpers also carried an Airborne Systems CSPEP cargo pack that contained emergency rations, ID papers crafted specifically for the mission, and clothing that would help them blend in with the local populace.

When the jumpers approached the LZ, their packs would be dropped and suspended from a nylon strap below them. That would remove the weight of the pack from the jumper's bodies and help prevent injuries upon landing.

Each parachutist carried a silenced 9mm Beretta 92FS in a thigh holster, and a Heckler and Koch MP5 9mm submachine gun with two extra 30 round clips in his pack. Each man was also outfitted with a Taser X26 Electronic Control Device which could instantly, but non-lethally, incapacitate an adversary from a distance of thirty-five feet.

The mission-prep computer geniuses at Greenstone Security in Seattle identified a regular cargo flight, from Bahrain to Abadan, Iran, that had been temporarily delayed, and their C-130 would be taking its place tonight. Once the mission was completed, the real flight would probably appear and create some confusion, but the Greenstone airplane would be long gone by then.

The Hercules C-130 went "feet wet" over the Persian Gulf just north of Bahrain and intercepted the flight path of the delayed cargo plane. The pilots flew up the center of the gulf slowly drifting toward the coast of Iran. They passed Khark Island on a direct line to Abadan just forty miles off the beach when the jumpmaster gave the order to lower the rear cargo door.

A violent wind buffeted the operators as they stood poised at the threshold. The jump light turned from red to green, and the jumpmaster yelled, "Go! Go! Go!" into the intercom.

The three operatives walked like penguins to the end of the airplane's tailgate and threw themselves out into the inky black slipstream. Their equipment was carefully engineered to create no radar cross-section. Once their canopies opened, they arranged themselves in flight formation. They flew in a skewed line like geese, the two wingmen to the right and slightly behind Mr. White, the team leader.

Mr. White asked for a sit-rep from both of the other jumpers on the intercom. After a positive response, the operatives maintained radio silence during the descent to the beach, which lasted thirty-five minutes in a very light headwind.

One-by-one they flared their para-wings and landed gently on the deserted stretch of sandy beach, directly in front of the GPS transmitter. The jump team leader hit his quick release buckle and jettisoned his chute.

He shook hands with his hosts and then whispered, "Gentlemen, I'm Mr. White; no other names, please." The two advance men nodded silently. They knew the drill.

Quickly, the other two jumpers shucked their harnesses and rounded up their packs in silence. The two advance men gathered in the team's chutes to bury them in the sand. One of them picked up the GPS transmitter and pulled a small remote out of his pocket. He pressed a red button, and the other GPS transmitter, a mile away, quietly incinerated itself. The leftover black plastic blob would wash out to sea with the tide.

Once the jumpers re-clothed themselves in what would pass for local dress, the five men shouldered their equipment packs and made their way up the bluff behind the beach to their waiting SUV. They were still two hours away from Shiraz.

CHAPTER TWENTY-ONE

Shiraz, Iran

Colonel Tarik Golzar woke long before dawn and went into the living room to perform his morning prayers. He then dressed in his best uniform, downed a cup of tea, and kissed his wife, who had risen early to serve him.

He left his modest home and got in his Land Rover for the short drive to the station. He felt good and rested. This morning he would rid the world of two more troublesome infidels. It was one thing to overlook a simple unbeliever, but quite another to let one live who was capable of swaying public opinion and subverting the emergence of the golden age of Islam.

He had contacted an influential friend, Parvaiz Zehadi, who held a supporting position with the Imams in Tehran and asked for a Fatwa to be issued against both Evan Chatterjee and Amar Parish. The Fatwa was essentially a license to kill. He switched his radio on and almost immediately received a call from the night duty officer, Hafez.

"Colonel, I've been trying to contact you for some time. While you were asleep, I took a call from the governor. He's very interested in the status of the Brit and the American."

"He is, is he? Well, I'll be sorry to report to the Governor that the prisoners were punished before I was able to return his call. I'll be at the station in a few minutes. We'll be having an execution at first light!"

Hafez was stunned; he put down his radio. There hadn't been an execution of foreigners in the province in years. Yes, they had harassed foreign nationals and even detained them. But this, this was something else entirely. He feared his superior officer had finally gone over the edge.

It was one thing to execute Iranian citizens for crimes against Islam, but quite another to involve the international community. Hafez feared opposing the colonel might cost him his job, possibly even his life, depending on Golzar's mood. He also feared that not opposing the colonel might land him in prison for failing to avert an international incident. After a few moments of thought, he decided to call his old friend, Nasrollah Brahoui, to ask his counsel, even if he had to get him out of bed. Nasrollah would know what to do.

The Colonel pulled into the courtyard through the iron gate, parked his Land Rover, and went into the administration building. The cell blocks for men and women were separate. The bulk of the female inmates that were housed here were women who had not worn proper Islamic dress in public or unmarried women caught in the presence of a man who was not part of her immediate family.

The male population was being detained for adultery and blasphemy, the more serious criminals among them having been accused of apostasy, the crime of abandoning the Islamic religion.

Golzar greeted the duty officer. "Good morning, Hafez, all is well this morning?"

Hafez wondered whether the treachery he had just committed could be seen on his face.

He greeted Golzar nervously. "Good morning, my Colonel. All is quiet. There have been no outbursts from the prisoners."

"Good, may they go quietly into their eternal night. I would like a cup of fresh coffee, Hafez. I'll be in my office."

Hafez brewed a fresh pot and took a cup into the Colonel's office. Golzar was sitting at his desk, a small towel spread across it. He had disassembled his CZ-75B semi-automatic pistol and was cleaning it thoroughly.

Terrance Van Zant stayed at work late and had takeout delivered to the TAI conference room in downtown Manhattan. He was eating his dinner, waiting for any development in the situation when the second call came in from Nasrollah Brahoui.

The news was bad. The Iranians were planning to execute Evan and Amar at daylight. He kept Nasrollah on the line and conferenced in Tom Parish and Gary Renfro in Seattle where the business day was just ending.

Brahoui told them that the sun would rise in Fars Province within the hour. The curator was asked to give a description of Colonel Golzar. Renfro thanked him, copied down his number, and warned him he probably didn't want to know what would transpire from here. Brahoui agreed and disconnected.

Renfro and Chairman Parish checked in with their team and found them to be only twenty minutes away from the station in Shiraz. They had informed the team leader, Mr. White, that he and his men would be walking into a hostile extraction. He was to understand Amar and

Evan's lives were at stake, and the gloves were off. Tom Parish then called Rachael at home, explained the situation, and asked her to come to the office.

Jan Mayer called Governor Khani on his Greenstone. She then linked all the Greenstone units into a conference call. She zoomed the satellite image back slightly so Tom and Gary could see the cursors of all the Greenstone units converging on the target, even though it was still slightly before sunrise in Iran.

Tom Parish knew when to let Gary Renfro take over, and that time was now. When Rachael arrived, Tom remained in the background, trying to comfort her. Renfro asked Governor Khani what his ETA was and whether he could bring force with him. The Governor scanned his dimly glowing instruments and reported on his tactical situation.

"Mr. Renfro, I am inbound to Golzar's compound at a ground speed of 130 miles per hour. We are cruising at 1,000 feet AGL. I have a passenger load of seven people, and one pistol on board. I can call for backup, but I will most certainly arrive at the scene before any military team can respond."

"This situation is unfolding much too fast. I don't want to make this event public. We could be on the verge of a major international incident. If Golzar has completely lost his mind, I'll have some difficulty stopping him."

"Governor Khani, you will recall that I have an advance team in the area per the terms of our contract?"

The governor indicated that he did remember that.

"The force consists of two men whose visas were approved by you and three additional men who are, shall we say, recent arrivals,"

The governor concealed his surprise. "I see," he said.

"My team leader, Mr. White, and his men are highly experienced in this type of extraction. Do you have GPS capability on board?"

"Yes, Mr. Renfro, I do."

"Can you take down these coordinates while you are flying?"

Khani nodded toward Jalal, who had his headset on, and was a party to the conversation.

"Go ahead, Mr. Renfro," Jalal said.

"Standby." Renfro checked with his team to see if they were in a suitable location for a pickup. They were. The SUV skidded to a halt by the side of the road so that Renfro could get a read on their GPS coordinates. They were located just north of the city, passing through the countryside on their way to Golzar's compound.

"Governor, here are my team's coordinates."

Jalal wrote them down.

"Do you copy their location, sir?"

The Governor responded, "Jalal, my secretary, has entered their coordinates into the flight director as a waypoint."

"Good. They appear to be almost in a direct line between you and the objective."

"You can see this from Seattle?" asked Khani.

"Yes, sir, we can," Renfro said.

"Amazing!" Khani replied.

"Governor, here's what I suggest you do. Land at the team's coordinates and discharge your passengers. They can continue into the city in my team's vehicle, pick up my men, and proceed directly to the compound.

They are highly experienced in non-lethal tactics. It may be of great benefit to have you at the location, in case this guy doesn't want to listen. If you want to keep this quiet, as we prefer to do, your authority over him may be critical to the success of this mission."

"I agree, Mr. Renfro. I'm approaching your team's coordinates. Have them turn their flashers on so I'm sure to identify the correct vehicle."

Renfro inquired, "Mr. White, can you comply?"

"Copy that, sir." He could hear the "whump whump whump" of the Huey's rotor as it approached.

Khani spoke directly to the team leader. "Mr. White, I have the landing zone in sight."

A few moments later, Khani turned on his landing lights, verified the area was clear, flared the helicopter, and touched down in the field just behind the team's SUV. The team ran up and slid open the crew compartment door while Khani kept the rotor turning. White held out his car keys.

Khani had kept his staff's headsets switched off during the flight, and they came awake in the sudden breeze, thinking they had completed their flight and were at Shiraz International Airport.

Jalal switched on the crew compartment intercom. "Please exit the helicopter. Take this man's vehicle and drive to the office. No questions, please."

The staff did as they were told and scrambled out into the cool morning air. White and his four-man crew, who appeared to be ordinary Iranian citizens, though somewhat heavyset, threw their equipment bags in the back and jumped in.

White donned one of the headsets. "Governor Khani, I'm Mr. White, team leader for Greenstone Security."

The Governor leaned around. "Mr. White, it is a pleasure to meet you. I have been briefed on your team's capabilities. It is my desire that we go in, make this rescue using non-lethal means, and get you and your friends out of the country as soon as possible so I can begin to attend to the fallout that will surely come."

"I agree, Governor. Let's get this bird over to our objective. Can you land it in the courtyard?"

Khani smiled, though he knew Mr. White couldn't see it in the darkened cockpit. "You can rest assured I will do so, Mr. White. ETA is fifteen minutes."

Khani revved the engines, made a jump take off, and sped away into the coming light of dawn.

CHAPTER TWENTY-TWO

Shiraz, Iran

Colonel Tarik Golzar reassembled his semi-automatic pistol, inserted the nine-round clip into the butt, and shoved it home with a thunk. He holstered the weapon, got up from his desk, and went over to the fax machine that sat on a small table under the window that overlooked the courtyard of the police station. He glanced casually out the window and noticed that his electronic tech, Hadi, had just arrived and was entering the building.

Good, he thought, *maybe he'll have figured out how to use Chatterjee's phone. It's such a pretty thing, such impressive technology.*

Golzar took a piece of paper out of the fax machine. It was the Fatwa against the infidels he'd asked for. He read it through. Satisfied with the language, he folded it twice and placed it in the inner breast pocket of his tunic.

He looked at his watch, 7:15. Might as well get the business done before the day shift arrives.

He picked up the phone and buzzed Hafez at the front desk. "Hafez, bring the American and the Brit out to the courtyard."

Hafez grew nauseous with fear, "Yes, Colonel, right away." He went to the crew room and turned out the two jailers who were napping. The three of them went into the cell block.

"Jalal," the governor said. "See if you can raise the colonel on the phone."

Jalal made the call but got no answer. "They're not picking up, sir."

The governor looked in the overhead rearview mirror to see what was going on in the passenger compartment. Mr. White and his team were pulling black balaclavas over their heads.

He hit the push-to-talk button. "Mr. White, is that entirely necessary?"

"I am afraid it is, Governor."

"You did say you would employ non-lethal means, did you not?"

"Yes, Governor, I did, and every effort will be made to ensure no one is injured. But if it comes down to my principals or your misguided policemen, I will have to side with the lives of my principals."

The governor finally lost his patience. "If that bastard Golzar harms those men, I'll string him up by his balls. I don't care if Hassan Rouhani himself told him he could do this!"

The Huey thundered over the dusty desert landscape, closing in on Golzar's compound. Amar and Evan came awake at the sound of the bolt being slid back. The door scraped open, and the two policemen who had abused Amar the previous night came in. The desk sergeant stood in the doorway, his hand on the flap of his holster as the jailers roughly yanked both Evan and Amar to their feet.

Both were groggy, their clothes completely rumpled, having slept only for the last two hours of the early morning. The jailers spun each man around and roughly installed another set of flexicuffs while grunting at them in Farsi.

Amar could smell coffee brewing somewhere in the jail. He looked over at Evan who appeared to be alarmed. "So, what do you suppose is for breakfast in this dump?"

Evan felt slightly nauseous. "I'd give my left arm for a cup of coffee, but I don't think breakfast is what they have in mind."

They were hustled out into the hallway, up the stone stairs, through the reception area where the phone was ringing unattended, and out into the courtyard. It was a warm morning, the early light casting long shadows across the compound. They were pushed and shoved over to where Colonel Golzar was standing in the northeast corner of the courtyard.

"On your knees," Golzar ordered.

Evan understood the command in Farsi and started to feel faint just as the jailer kicked him hard in the back of one knee. Amar put up a fight and had to be subdued before sinking to his knees. They both squinted up into Golzar's pockmarked face which was backlit by the rising sun.

Evan turned his head and began to apologize to Amar when he heard and felt the heavy thumping sound of a big helicopter approaching.

Golzar looked up at the noise, then ignored the sound of the approaching aircraft. He took the Fatwa out of his pocket, unfolded the document, and began to read.

"Evan Chatterjee and Amar Parish, you have been tried by the Guardian Council, found guilty of crimes against Holy Islam and are sentenced to death!"

Evan looked wretched. He couldn't believe he was about to die for something he'd written. Amar suddenly woke up to the fact that they weren't just being abused; this guy intended to execute them.

Golzar pulled the pistol out of his holster and jacked the slide back, chambering a round. He walked around behind Evan and pointed the pistol at the back of his head.

The Huey rocked back on its rotor, thundering and clattering over the compound wall as the governor flared it, sending clouds of dust and debris into the faces and eyes of the small group gathered across the yard. As the governor put the ship into a hover and swiftly set it down, White came over the loudspeaker in Farsi.

"This is the Governor of Fars Province. Put down your weapons and stand down."

Golzar had kept his eyes open a little too long, and they had filled with dust. He momentarily lowered his gun and turned away from the blast. Khani, noticing the effect of the rotor wash, lowered the collective slowly, letting the engines spool gradually down to idle so the whirlwind continued. "Go now, Mr. White," he said through the intercom.

White, seeing that his two charges were in danger, but that the rotor wash had created a momentary advantage, hollered, "Pistols, lethal force on my command."

He and his crew tore off their headsets, jumped from the chopper and ran toward the three men holding Amar and Evan captive, their silenced pistols at the ready.

Hafez's arms shot up immediately. The two jailers, slow to clear the grit from their eyes, were only thinking about drawing their guns when two of the Greenstone crew were on them. They were knocked to the ground and immediately disarmed. The two Greenstone operatives remained with their knees in the middle of each man's back, cocked pistols shoved against their heads while they were cuffed.

As the rotor blast subsided, Golzar began to pivot back toward Evan, his gun hand leading with the CZ. White drew his X26 Taser and shot the colonel under his left arm, immediately hitting the button. The two barbed projectiles penetrated through the colonel's uniform and into the skin over his ribs, each trailing a thin wire from the taser. When White hit the button, 50,000 volts traversed up the wires and into the Colonel's body for a fraction of a second.

Golzar's body gave a hideous spasm; he dropped his pistol and went down in a heap. The other two Greenstone team members were on him in a flash, grabbed him by both arms, and pulled him to his feet, quite dazed. Then White cut the cuffs off Amar and Evan and helped them to stand.

Amar gave Evan a hug and a pat on the back. "Now maybe we can get a decent breakfast," he said. "The food around here sucks!" He turned to Mr. White and asked, "Who are you guys?"

White, not without a little pride said under his breath, "Greetings from Seattle."

Amar nodded and smiled. For once he was glad to have his father messing around in his business. He faced Mr. White and held out his hand.

Mr. White understood and handed the taser to him.

"This isn't lethal, is that correct?"

White replied in the affirmative.

Amar turned and nodded to the two crewmen who were holding Golzar up. Understanding his intent, they released the colonel like a hot potato. Amar hit the button again.

Golzar collapsed like he'd taken a headshot and lay shaking in the dirt.

Amar stood over him. "That's for the doctor, Colonel."

Mr. White's men waited until he stopped vibrating and dragged him to his feet again. He was completely disheveled, his fine uniform covered in dirt.

Amar put his hand on Evan's shoulder. "I probably shouldn't have done that."

"Probably not," Evan grinned.

"I probably shouldn't do this either."

Amar walked over to Golzar, who still had the Taser probes stuck in his side. The colonel stood weakly leaning on his captors for support. Amar reached up, gently removed the colonel's kepi by the bill and dropped it on the ground. He stepped on it, grinding it back and forth into the dirt and put his face in front of Golzar's.

"That's for me, Colonel. Never step on a man's hat!"

The governor, having witnessed the entire encounter, walked up. He understood that a little subterfuge was called for as he addressed Mr. White.

"Thank you, Farshid. That was very well done."

Mr. White nodded his approval and said in Farsi, "We should leave now, Governor."

The governor replied, "Yes, we will, in just one minute."

He towered over Golzar, "I requested that these men come here to help us translate our own ancient heritage, possibly to help us make an unprecedented discovery. Then you try to execute them? Have you gone mad, Colonel? Are you trying to start World War III all by your-self?"

Golzar nodded weakly toward the crumpled piece of paper laying on the ground next to him.

His voice came out in a hoarse whisper, "I have a Fatwa from the Imams. You have no jurisdiction here. This is a matter for the Imams and the Religious Police!"

The Governor retorted, "I don't care if Ayatollah Khomeni climbed out of his grave and told you to do this. If I ever hear of you threatening anyone to whom I have personally given a visa, I will shoot you myself. Are we clear, Colonel?"

Golzar was fuming inside, but only nodded; he was still weak and could barely stand.

"Now, Colonel, do you have personal possessions to return to these men?"

Golzar mumbled to his duty officer. "Hafez, fetch their belongings. Make sure Hadi includes the telephone." Hafez took off at a trot, completely relieved at not having been implicated in the rescue.

CHAPTER TWENTY-THREE

Shiraz, Iran

At the sound of the helicopter arriving, Hadi was drawn to the window and observed the entire altercation from the property room on the third floor. He went to the shelving unit and got down the prisoner's basket. He took everything out and put it back into Evan's duffle. Then he went to work on the phone.

Hafez came into the room. "Did you see it, Hadi, did you see it all?"

"Yes, I did. I took the liberty of pulling out their property, Hafez. Here it is."

Hadi gave him the duffel bag. Hafez ran down the stairs and back out into the yard. He handed the duffle to Evan.

The Governor approached Amar and Evan and shook their hands. "Gentlemen, my name is Mahmoud Khani. I am Governor of Fars Province. Allow me to extend an apology to you on behalf of my country. I am deeply disturbed that you have been treated so unjustly."

Both Evan and Amar thanked him.

The Governor gestured toward the duffle, "Mr. Chatterjee, would you please verify that all of your belongings are there?"

Chatterjee rummaged through the duffel, verifying that their passports and his satellite phone were still in it. He handed Amar his cap and put on his own hat. "Everything is here, Governor, except for what was left behind in Persepolis."

"I think we can count on Nasrollah to return your other belongings to you. At the moment, I suggest that we get you out of the country." Khani extended his arm toward the chopper, inviting them to climb in.

Amar turned to Evan. He could see that the older man had been severely shaken by his close brush with death. He grabbed Evan under the arm and gestured toward the helicopter.

"Shall we, Doctor?"

Evan, feeling quite a bit better, nodded, "We shall," he said, and arm-in-arm they sauntered off toward the Huey.

Khani, remembering the floor of the helicopter was littered with machine guns and equipment, took White aside and asked. "Farshid, will you be needing a vehicle?"

White, understanding that it might be awkward to leave the governor in possession of so much firepower, picked up his drift. "Why, yes, Governor, that would be kind of you."

The Governor spoke to Golzar, making it clear by his tone that "no" would not be the correct answer.

"Colonel, I will be borrowing one of your vehicles for a few hours. I suspect it will be left at a location where you can find it easily." White nodded his approval of the plan.

Golzar fished around in the pocket of his tunic and handed over his keys. He pointed to his Land Rover.

"That one," he grumbled

Mr. White handed the keys to his advance men, who would remain in Shiraz, their identities having been protected. Still in their masks, the two men jumped in the vehicle and drove it around to the back side of the Huey.

Once Evan and Amar were in, they closed the sliding door nearest to the courtyard and began loading the arms and equipment into the colonel's vehicle from the other side of the chopper.

From his location, Golzar couldn't see what they were loading, but he could guess. When everything was transferred, they backed the heavily armed Land Rover up and pulled over in front of the big iron gate. Golzar nodded to Hafez who ran back to the front door of the station house and reached inside hitting the button to open the gates. The Land Rover peeled out on the dirt surface and sped away.

The other three Greenstone operatives pulled the clips out of both the jailer's and Golzar's pistols, disassembled the slides, and dropped the guns and the parts in the dirt.

"And now, Colonel, we will leave you to get on with your day. If I were you, I would instruct my staff to keep silent about today's events, lest you find out who really has the power in Fars Province!"

With that, they released Golzar and left the two jailers where they lay in the dirt, still cuffed.

Jalal had remained in the cockpit of the Huey, preferring to witness the event from afar. The governor climbed up into the pilot's seat, and Mr. White and his team members got in the back with Evan and Amar.

Khani turned to the Greenstone team leader, "Mr. White, I will fly you directly to Shiraz International Airport. We will land on the ramp, and you won't have to go through security. I will put you all on a plane myself. Where would you like to go?"

Mr. White deferred to Dr. Chatterjee.

"London, I think, Governor, will suit us quite well," said Evan. "By the way, Governor, I suggest you visit the dig at Persepolis as soon as you can. I suspect you will find the discovery to be very intriguing."

Khani was distracted with his switches and controls and simply acknowledged Evan's request. "I will be sure to do that Mr. Chatterjee; I assure you. Jalal, call Turkish Airlines and explain that they will be transporting five passengers going to London under diplomatic passports approved by me. Tell them the governor wishes to personally escort his friends onto the plane."

Jalal grinned. "Yes, sir. Governor, it will be my pleasure."

Mahmoud Khani quickly went through his checklist and fired up both turbines. In another cloud of dust, he established a hover, turned the chopper, and departed over the courtyard wall.

Hafez was busy cutting the flexicuffs off the two jailers when yet another blast of wind and dust swept over them. All four of the religious policemen covered their eyes as the chopper took off. The two jailers each took one of Colonel Golzar's arms and helped him across the yard and into the headquarters building. His legs were still shaking like a newborn fawn's from the Taser. They sat him down in the reception area and gave him a glass of water.

No one spoke. They were all waiting to hear what he was going to say first. Hadi came down from his lair and sat next to the colonel, who looked wretched and defeated.

"My Colonel," he whispered into Golzar's ear. "I'm sorry the infidels got away. I tried to bug the prisoner's phone, but it cannot be hacked in any way. For the first time since he'd been shot with the Taser, any hope Golzar harbored for revenge, vanished into the morning light.

CHAPTER TWENTY-FOUR

Seattle

While Tom Parish sat on the sofa in his office trying to comfort Rachael, Jan Meyer was monitoring the satellite display of the drama unfolding in Shiraz. They'd been at it all day and into the night. After the last contact with Mr. White, Jan had zoomed the image back far enough to observe five blinking cursors approaching the target area. At that image altitude, the police compound was no longer discernible from the surrounding landscape.

Off to the left side of the display was a medical data window which listed the medical stats of all six people. The cursors were labeled G1 through G5, EC for Evan Chatterjee, and ECP for his phone. Amar, being completely separated from the technology, had no cursor.

She had seen the five cursors of the Greenstone team stop and pause for a few minutes and then tear away to the south at a much higher rate of speed. Renfro confirmed that Governor Khani had picked up the team, and they were approaching the police compound in the Governor's helicopter.

Evan's watch was still transmitting medical data and so far, his stats were well within limits. Evan still had two cursors, one for his phone, and one for his watch showing on the display. Neither had moved in hours, indicating that he and Amar were probably in some sort of detention cell. They could only hope Amar was still healthy, as well.

The display issued a beep, which indicated a status change. Jan stood up and approached the screen. The indicator came from Evan's watch, which started moving. His phone cursor remained in place. His pulse was quickening. Jan zoomed the image back down to show the courtyard and the roofs of the buildings.

"Sir, Evan is moving, and his pulse has quickened."

They could clearly see a group of people emerging from the building and moving out into the courtyard, though they couldn't tell who was who.

Tom and Rachael jumped up and ran over to Tom's desk to peer into the picture. When Jan zoomed in to show just the compound, the cursors for the Greenstone team had dropped off the display. Then the display beeped loudly, and they could see that Evan's pulse had risen to 120 beats per minute.

Rachael put her hand over her mouth in concern. All of a sudden, a large helicopter entered the frame from the left side. Five men jumped out and approached the group on the ground at a dead run. A window came up off to the right side of the display. Renfro's face appeared.

"Okay, everybody, the rescue is about to go down."

He could see Tom, Rachael, and Jan from his monitor.

"How're you guys holding up?"

Rachael's voice broke, "I'm terrified, Gary. Will they be alright?"

"We'll know very shortly, Rachael. Not to worry, this team is among the best in the world."

The team from the helicopter surrounded the policemen and their prisoners. Tom and Rachael could identify Amar and Evan as the two men on their knees. Two of the policemen were subdued immediately. One of the policemen fell to the ground in a heap. Renfro didn't try to speak to Mr. White, who obviously had his hands full. Then things settled down. Three men were on the ground. Amar and Evan were being helped to their feet. After a few minutes, Renfro's team escorted Amar and Evan to the helicopter. Two of Renfro's men got in a vehicle and drove away. The chopper took off and flew away from the compound at high speed.

Renfro addressed White through his earpiece. "Mr. White, report," he commanded.

Mr. White responded in code speak so as not to give anything away about the events that had just transpired, just in case anyone had the capability to listen in.

"All safe, sir, the threat has been neutralized non-lethally. We are inbound to the airport with the package, in company of highest authority. He will accompany to means of egress. Will report back destination, once principals are aboard."

"Well done, Mr. White. Renfro out."

Gary Renfro was sporting a huge grin on the monitor. Rachael threw her arms around Tom's neck and wept into his shirt.

Tom said, "Thanks, Gary, no man ever had greater friends than you and your team."

"Thank you, sir. All's well that ends well. I'll report back when their departure is confirmed and let you know their destination. I'm sorry for the scare. We'll need to have a conversation with Mr. Chatterjee about future activities when he returns."

"Yes, I believe we will. Thanks again, Gary."

Renfro, ever the military man said, "Renfro out." His picture faded from the screen.

Jan Meyer was wiping her eyes. She looked exhausted. They all looked exhausted. Tom held Rachael at arm's length.

"He's alright, my dear. Let's all settle down. Why don't we go up to the Tower Club, and I'll buy you both dinner?"

Rachael's eyes were all red from crying. She nodded, "I think I want to have that talk with Evan myself."

Tom agreed, "And so you shall, so you shall."

The two ladies wiped their eyes again. Tom, Rachael, and Jan Meyer left the office and crossed the hallway to the bank of elevators that would carry them up to the restaurant on the 75th floor for a sumptuous and much-needed meal.

CHAPTER TWENTY-FIVE

London to New York

Evan and Amar arrived at Heathrow at 5:00 p.m. and bought first class tickets to La Guardia on the American Airlines flight at 7:45 p.m. Mr. White and his crew faded away into the London cityscape. Evan and Amar had just taken their seats when the flight attendant put a hand on Amar's shoulder. He looked up to see who was being so familiar. Kelly's deep green eyes twinkled back at him.

"Kelly, it's good to see you. I didn't know you were on the London run."

"I just changed from the New York to Seattle run last week. How are you, Amar?"

"I'm doing very well. Kelly Bates, I'd like to introduce my friend and colleague, Dr. Evan Chatterjee."

Evan looked up and beheld a lovely green-eyed redhead. She was wearing a dark blue American Airlines blazer over a white blouse that did little to conceal an ample bosom. Just a sprinkling of freckles crossed the bridge of her nose.

Evan was familiar with Amar's reputation as a ladies' man. He would have expected nothing less.

He extended his hand, "Kelly, it's nice to meet you."

Kelly replied in kind and then focused on Amar. "It's been at least a month since I've seen you Amar."

"I've been out and about," he said. "Evan and I are just returning from a dig in Iran."

"Still playing in the dirt, I see. Iran, no less. That's pretty risky for an American these days. Is there anything I can get for you?"

Evan cut in, "Two glasses of champagne, I think, Kelly."

"Are we celebrating?" she asked.

"Just celebrating being alive," Amar sighed contentedly.

"I'll be back with your drinks in a minute," she said and headed for the galley.

Evan nudged his colleague in the ribs, "What a lovely young woman, and those eyes are quite striking."

"She does have green eyes, but she wears colored contacts to enhance them a little. I agree, the effect is striking. That's the only thing about her that isn't her own. Her other attributes are, shall we say, completely natural."

Evan took his meaning. "I take it you know each other well?"

"I met her on the New York to Seattle run. We've seen each other a few times. There's no commitment, but we're good friends." He grinned lasciviously.

Kelly returned with the champagne. She served the two men and bent over to whisper in Amar's ear.

"When can I see you again?" she asked.

"What are you doing tonight?"

"I'm off for the next two days."

"I'll meet you at baggage claim, and we'll go to my place?" Amar offered.

"I thought you'd never ask," she said and went to attend to her duties.

Amar leaned toward Evan, "The photos you took in Persepolis, where are they stored?"

"They were downloaded directly from my phone to the server at my office."

"I know I'm going to have to answer to Tom for the cost of our rescue. He might be mollified a little when he sees what we've discovered. Can you send them to me somehow?"

"Sure, I'll download them to your Dropbox in the morning. You'll be able to retrieve them whenever you want. Then I'll get busy with the translation. I take it you'll be heading back to Seattle soon?"

"I'm expecting a phone call from my dad at any moment. Will you need a ride anywhere when we land?"

Evan replied, "No thank you, I can see you'll have your hands full tonight, literally. I'll have Terrance from the office pick me up."

It had been a spectacular evening. Amar and Kelly took a car service from the airport to his apartment in Turtle Bay. They'd enjoyed some cocktails, spent themselves more than once, and had only been asleep for three hours. Kelly lay cuddled against him. His arm held her close, his right hand cupping a breast. Her luxurious red hair spilled across the pillow. Amar's phone rang.

Kelly moaned, "Turn it off, turn it off!"

Amar rolled over and picked up the phone from the side table. It was 10:00 a.m. in New York and 7:00 a.m. in Seattle. He knew it was the chairman.

"Morning, dad."

Tom was a man of few words, "Amar, I need you here at the office tomorrow. Ted will be at LaGuardia on his way back from Boston to pick you up. He'll be there at 1:00 this afternoon. See you at the house tonight for dinner. Got to go." He hung up.

Amar's father had been extremely generous with him, giving him a ten percent stake in both PCI and GES on his 21st birthday. Amar had been able to use the resulting dividends from the company to fund his expeditions. When Tom Parish said, "You come now," then he went. Amar rolled over and got out of bed. He showered and wrapped a towel around his waist. He began repacking a bag for the trip.

Kelly woke and sat up. The sheets fell away, but she wasn't the least bit modest. She noticed what he was doing. "Oh, are you leaving so soon?"

"I've been summoned by the great man. I have to go. You can stay as long as you like. I'll call you when I'm coming back to town."

Kelly knew about Amar's father and his company. She pouted facetiously. "Just take what you want and leave. I know who you are, Mr. Playboy Parish."

Amar jumped onto the bed and pushed her back down. With an ample breast in each hand, he smothered her face with kisses. "It's true," he said. "If you don't give me what I want, I'll have to take it."

Kelly comically placed a wrist over her forehead. "Oh no, you cad, how dare you!" She felt his enthusiasm through the towel. "Then take me if you must!"

So he did.

CHAPTER TWENTY-SIX

Ashgabat, Turkmenistan

Harrison Warburg took in the view of the capital city of Ashgabat, Turkmenistan from his window in the presidential suite of the Yyldyz Hotel. The city and its architecture were surprisingly cosmopolitan in a country where sheepherders and oil wells co-mingled across the countryside. Sixty-nine years old, perpetually tanned, five foot ten inches tall with coifed white hair, Warburg still counted himself amongst the wealthiest of the beautiful people. As is the habit amongst the super wealthy, his clothing had to bear the names of the best designers: shirts by Brioni, suits by Desmond Merrion, shoes by Zegna, watch by Patek Phillipe. Just the clothes on his back would have supported an entire family of Turkmen sheepherders for about a decade.

Warburg had been born in West Germany in 1950. His father made his mark in the construction business feeding off of Marshall Plan funds provided by the Allies for the reconstruction of West Germany after World War II. The older Warburg passed away in 1975, leaving his twenty-five-year-old son in charge of the family fortune. Harrison showed an aptitude for making money. His only sister Alma did not, opting to marry into a wealthy family from Romania by the name of Dragan.

Mr. Dragan was well-connected as a minor minister within the Ceausescu government. He watched in horror as the dictator mismanaged Romanian oil field investments, plunging the country into skyrocketing foreign debt. In 1980, Ceausescu implemented his Austerity Policy distributing the losses to the general population. It was all downhill from there. The population was growing restless.

Dragan was a patriot and insisted that his and Alma's identical twin sons, Viktor and Marko, join the armed forces and be ready to participate in quelling the coming unrest. Dragan was no fool and knew from experience that opportunities come when there is blood in the streets. Predictably, the people began to revolt, and they convinced the military to side with them.

Dragan knew it was now or never. If the Dragans and the War-burgs joined forces economically, they would have the financial clout to convince Ceausescu to sell Romanpetrol, the national oil company, for a song. It would be Ceausescu's last-ditch effort to raise money to prop up his government and soothe the masses. The sale took place in mid-1989, but it was too little too late for the General Secretary.

On Christmas day in 1989, the revolt reached its zenith. Nicolae Ceausescu and his wife Elena were arrested and stood before a firing squad. Two of the shooters that day were the newly enlisted, seven-teen-year-olds, Viktor and Marko Dragan. The revolt backfired on the twin's parents who, due to their relationship with the former dictator, were both killed during the bloody revolution. The boys knew nothing about their father's business, so Uncle Harry Warburg quietly ab-sorbed the parent's shares and became the sole owner of Romanpetrol.

Viktor deserted from a post-revolutionary military unit which was in disarray and didn't care to look for him. Marko followed in short order. The twins went to Uncle Harry seeking refuge. Warburg felt some family obligation. After all, Viktor's parents had provided half of the capital with which to acquire the oil company.

While they were identical in appearance, Viktor was prone to vio-lence, and Marko, on the other hand, was interested in mechanical things. Warburg hired Viktor as his new head of security. Marko would do odd jobs for the oligarch, eventually taking charge of main-taining all of the weaponry used by his growing security force to protect him.

Warburg saw a unique opportunity in the twins. In the chaos fol-lowing the revolution, Warburg placed some strategic bribes and had all records of the boys destroyed. He made sure they were never seen in public together. If Warburg needed to have someone removed, Viktor would take care of it. During the hit, Marko would go to a pub-lic bar or nightclub posing as Viktor, thus establishing an airtight alibi protecting his brother.

In 2002, Warburg sold Romanpetrol to Kazakhstan's state-owned oil company for 2.7 billion dollars. It was just the beginning of a for-tune that would soon span the globe.

Warburg pulled his Greenstone satellite telephone from his inside jacket pocket and checked his text messages. The news wasn't good. He had come to Ashgabat to meet with officials of the Turkmenistan Central Bank. He was attempting to privatize the country's national bank, as he had done in smaller countries on several continents. In return for a controlling interest in the new central bank, he would make substantial investments in local oil field infrastructure that would directly benefit several high-level ministers.

The door to the presidential suite swung open, and Viktor Dragan walked in. Dressed in a dark suit, he was a couple of inches taller than his uncle. At forty-four, he was well-muscled and in very good physical condition.

"Harry, the situation is deteriorating. The secret police have just arrested thirty-two people who were conspiring in a plot to kill the president of this stinking country. Some of the officials at the central bank are among them. The police think that somehow you may be involved."

Harry turned from the window. "The hell you say? It's true I've been trying to acquire the central bank, but I don't know anything about an assassination plot. What else have they told you?"

"They've impounded your Gulfstream at the airport. We aren't allowed to leave while the investigation is ongoing. We could be trapped here for weeks, or worse if they think you're in on it."

Dragan took off his jacket and went into his bedroom. When he returned, he was wearing a shoulder holster and screwing a silencer onto the barrel of an FN Five-Seven pistol. He slipped the pistol into his holster.

"What's our next move?" he asked.

Warburg always made a point to spread the wealth to key local figures before mounting a takeover bid. "I have a friend in the secret police. Let me make some calls."

He dialed his phone. "Arslan, this is Harry; I need your help."

Arslan replied, "Harry, you know what's going on, right?"

"Yes, I understand. Are they going to charge me?"

"It hasn't gone that far yet. They're still investigating. Look, it's tense around here. They're looking for an excuse to implicate anyone who seems the least bit suspicious. I can't be caught talking to you."

"Arslan, I have taken care of your family's needs; you owe me. You don't want to cross our friendship, believe me."

The Turkmen Secret Service agent didn't need to envision what might happen to him or his family if he didn't cooperate. He had met Viktor Dragan.

"Okay Harry, I'll try to keep you up-to-date. Please don't call me, though; I'll call you." Arslan hung up.

Harry stared thoughtfully at his nephew. "I think it's time to call the cavalry." Holding his phone with both hands, he pressed the two little orange buttons on the bottom corners marked EXT.

CHAPTER TWENTY-SEVEN

Seattle

Ted Lockhart had just dropped off one of Tom's business partners in Boston. Sitting in the queue to be cleared for takeoff took almost as long as the thirty-minute flight to La Guardia. Amar was waiting at the Sheltair FBO when the Citation taxied up at 1:15. The airstair door came down just long enough for him to scramble on board. The door went back up, and Ted called La Guardia ground for taxi instructions. After a four-hour flight, they touched down at Boeing Field at 2:30 local time. Amar had parked the now restored and heavily upgraded Land Rover Defender 110 in the hanger on his way to Persepolis. He drove to the family home on Mercer Island. Rachael was in the kitchen, putting a roast in the oven for the evening meal.

"There you are!" she said. "How was your flight?"

"The usual Parish Airways standard of excellence," he quipped. "How've you been, Mom?"

"Much better now that you've come back from that horrible country. Whatever possessed you and Evan to go there in the first place?"

"I'll tell you exactly what it was." He reached into his duffle bag and extracted his Apple laptop. Placing it on the kitchen counter, he pulled up the photos from Persepolis and scrolled through them for her.

"Oh, what a beautiful room!" she exclaimed. "How did you even know it was there?"

"We didn't. Evan was summoned by the old guy who runs the place because he couldn't read the inscriptions on the stairway outside. We excavated to the bottom of the stairs and found the doorway. This find has the potential to change our version of human history. Evan is still working on translating the text, but we think this room was built more than ten thousand years ago. That was a time period when humans were supposed to be wearing animal skins and hunting mastodons, not showing a very high level of skill in creating mosaic tile murals!"

Amar was thirty-three years old, but what child doesn't still want the approval of his parents, particularly when the recent accomplishment came with a substantial price tag? Rachael's response was less than he had hoped for.

"Well, that would be a significant discovery, wouldn't it? Have you shown these photos to your father?"

"No, not yet. I take it he'll be home for dinner tonight?"

"He said he'd be here around 6:00. You can show him then," she noted, taking a taste from one of the bubbling pots on the stove.

Tom Parish was home at precisely 6:00 p.m. After a lukewarm greeting, he fixed himself a scotch on the rocks. Amar launched into the discovery at Persepolis. Tom sat still as they reviewed the photos. Amar described the Vimana and showed the workman moving big stones about.

"Well, I do admit, it's a fascinating picture, but how can you be sure of its age, and what makes you think the depictions are of real events and not someone's imagination?"

"Evan thinks he can date the work by the arrangement of stars on the ceiling. He's still working on translating the text, as well, and that may help pin down the age of the find. If it is as old as we think, the architecture alone wouldn't have even been conceived of, much less a flying machine."

"I see. Evan is the best there is when it comes to translations. That is why I've kept him on board all of these years. His language skills have been instrumental in helping us to work with foreign governments around the world. I hope it'll be worth the expense."

Amar knew this was coming. He gulped and asked, "How much did it cost to pull us out of there?"

Tom paused, then delivered the quote, "Without the GES markup, it cost more than half a million dollars to mobilize the troops and equipment, son."

Amar whistled. "I was afraid of something like that."

Rachael cut in, "We're not going to talk business at the dinner table. So, you two can save it for tomorrow at the office."

It was almost impossible for the Parish men to have a conversation without lapsing into their various projects, all of which qualified as business in Rachael's mind. They spent most of the evening talking about current events and listening to her tell what had been accomplished recently on behalf of the environment.

Tom Parish went into the office at 7:00 a.m. Amar arrived around 10:00 in the morning. Jan Meyer produced coffee and pastries. At

Tom's request, she also produced a printout of the cost of the Persepolis extraction. Amar felt as if he was on his way to the woodshed, which in a manner of speaking he was. Tom gave a copy to Amar, and they went down the line items.

A prorated cost for the use of the C-130 at $10,000.00 per hour. Combat pay for the pilots, Mr. White, and his crew. Combat pay for the two advance men already in country. The cost of usage of the Greenstone Satellite System. The cost of staff time in the office. The cost of weapons and munitions that had to be disposed of once in country, and on and on. The total came to $598,625.50. Amar was no pauper, but this was a fairly big chunk even for him.

Tom softened the blow, "I had no idea this project would turn out the way it did. But, since I helped arrange passage into the country for both of you and since I should have paid more attention to what you were walking into—you, Evan and I will each take a third of the expense. That will be approximately $200,000.00 each."

Amar slumped in his chair, "Thanks, Dad, that makes it a little easier to swallow."

Tom shoved a small box across the table toward his son.

"There's one condition, Amar."

"What's that?"

"The condition is that you will carry a Greenstone phone from now on so I can protect you better on these foreign digs you love so much."

Reluctantly, Amar accepted the box. "If you say so."

Tom summed up, "Let's hope Evan comes up with evidence that this is actually a significant find. That will help soothe our wounds. Now, I want to talk to you about the company."

Tom droned on for another hour about how he wanted Amar to begin to take an active role in the future of the company. He sighed, listened politely, and was relieved when Jan came back in.

"Mr. Parish, there are further developments in the Warburg extraction."

"Put it on my screen please, Jan."

Tom pressed a button on a remote on his desk, and a wall panel behind him slid up into the ceiling, revealing a large flat screen monitor.

He turned to Amar, "Now you can see what it takes to do an extraction. Gary, are you there?"

The picture on the screen was from a miniature camera embedded in a lapel pin in Gary's suit coat jacket. The extraction had begun the previous day.

"Here boss," Gary said. The main picture showed the flame-like outline of the Yyldyz Hotel. There was a small frame in the upper left showing a live satellite photo of a Gulfstream 650 parked at Ashgabat International Airport. An armed sentry from the Turkmen secret police was standing guard.

Tom slipped into his persona as a long distance commander, "We have your body cam on screen and also a live overhead at the airport. The client's medical data is within normal limits. How did you travel there and how many crew did you bring with you?"

"We came in the white C-130, which has been fitted with logos of a less than legitimate international aid company. Mr. White is monitoring Warburg's plane while looking after our own at the same time. Our pilots have remained on board."

"Okay, Gary, what's the sit-rep, please?"

"We arrived in country yesterday at 14:30 local time. I was able to talk directly with Mr. Warburg while in flight. He wasn't entirely forthcoming about his reasons for being in country. I also started back-channel communications while inbound on the plane. I was able to connect with a mid-level functionary by the name of Andrei Dumitru. That connection came through a mutual friend we have in Germany. Our German contact verified my creds, and Dimitru agreed to meet me at Ashgabat airport, subject to an appropriate amount of compensation.

"Dimitru revealed that Warburg was in country engaged in an attempt to privatize the Turkmen Central Bank. In return, he offered to make investments in oil field infrastructure that would directly benefit several high-level cabinet officials by lining their pockets.

"Unbeknownst to Warburg, he walked into the middle of a coup being staged by said cabinet officials that included an assassination attempt against the president. Apparently, the ministers needed Warburg's contribution to help fund their post-takeover plans. The plot was foiled, and the secret police arrested thirty-two people accused of playing a role in the attempt. They cast a pretty wide net, and Warburg fell into it, but only upon suspicion.

"I don't trust Warburg's impressions of the situation and am not relying on him to tell me what contacts he has within the government who might be sympathetic to our goal of extraction. I decided instead to rely on Dimitru's knowledge of the local situation and his recommendations as to which palms to grease to accomplish our objective."

Tom broke in, "Did you bring adequate funds for that purpose?"

Renfro continued, "I pulled a million in cash from the safe at GES. I believe that will be plenty since $100,000.00 US is considered to be a fortune to most of these people. Warburg's credit limit with us is far above this level, and reimbursement will not be a problem. The secret police have Warburg and his stooge, Dragan under house arrest. They've impounded his Gulfstream 650, and his pilots are in jail undergoing interrogation. I'm in the process of beginning to influence some key local officials, and I should have an update later this afternoon.

Tom asked, "Anything else we should discuss?"

"No, I don't think so, boss. This is just a normal pay to play scenario. I suspect we will have him out of here by tonight or tomorrow morning at the latest."

"Thanks, Gary, talk to you soon."

"Renfro out," he said, as the picture went dark.

Amar was glued to his seat. "Who is this guy, Warburg?"

"Harrison Warburg is our wealthiest GES client. His main investments are in oil and banking. His fortune makes ours look like food stamps," Tom said. "He was one of the original subscribers to the GES program. He likes to push the limits of the law wherever he goes. This will be the second extraction we've performed in as many years. Frankly, I don't really like or trust the guy. He's what you might call a master manipulator. You never know if he's giving you the straight story or trying to set you up somehow."

CHAPTER TWENTY-EIGHT

Ashgabat, Turkmenistan

At 3:00 in the morning, Renfro walked out of the elevator on the 19th floor of the Yyldyz Hotel. Two armed secret policemen stood guard outside the door of the Presidential Suite. They had been informed that Renfro would be coming. He slipped a 500 Euro note into each man's outstretched hand, whereupon the two men left their posts and headed toward the elevator.

Renfro knocked. Dragan swung the door open. His hair was wild, his shirt wrinkled from a sleepless night sitting on the sofa waiting, an empty shoulder holster under his left arm. Renfro was familiar with this guy from the last extraction and frankly considered him to be a hack. Dragan stood there with a pistol pointing at Gary's chest.

"Put that away, Viktor before I shove it up your ass and pull the trigger."

Dragan seethed. He would like nothing more than to pull the trigger right here and now. But it wouldn't do to kill the guy who was going to get his boss out of this jam.

Warburg's voice came from the living room behind Dragan. "Stand down, Viktor."

Glaring at Renfro, Dragan holstered his pistol and stood back to allow the man from GES to enter. He slammed the door behind Renfro to emphasize his opinion.

"Nice digs, Harry," he said.

"Never mind that," Warburg snapped. "Are we getting out of here soon?"

Renfro mused, *Warburg could slather on the charm, making you feel as if he was your best friend when he wanted to.* In truth, neither one of these guys was capable of civil behavior when the chips were down. He suspected that they were both sociopaths. Renfro sat next to Warburg and outlined what he had accomplished and what would happen next.

Amar had spent the day at the conference table in Tom's office face-timing with Evan in New York regarding his progress on the Persepolis translation.

At 4:30 in the afternoon, Renfro called back on the landline, "Okay, boss, we're on our way to the airport. Warburg's plane has been released. I only had to use about 750K to get it done. The secret police have agreed that Warburg had nothing to do with the coup, but that he should leave at once and not return for a couple of years. He is coming back to Seattle and get this; he wants to take us all to dinner tomorrow night by way of thanks."

Tom didn't really want to spend an evening with this man, but Warburg was his wealthiest client, and he would be sending the man a serious bill.

"Ok, tell him I'm swamped, so we'll do it here at the Columbia Tower Club at 6:00. Will you be back by then?"

"I should be, just. I'll see you then."

Tom hung up and looked over to where Amar was sitting. "You might as well come, too," he said. "You might find it interesting."

Warburg strolled into the Tower Club, with Viktor Dragan in tow, at 6:00 p.m. the following evening. Tom, Rachael, Gary, and Amar were seated around a table with a fabulous view of the lights of Seattle before them. Renfro looked up from his menu long enough to determine that there was a lump under Viktor's jacket. Renfro expected as much and unbuttoned his jacket to expose the grip of his own weapon.

Dragan was not invited to sit at the table and settled himself at the bar. Warburg was introduced to Rachael and Amar who were both cordial toward him, having no reason to disdain the man other than Tom's opinion. Warburg and Renfro ordered the beef tenderloin, Tom and Rachael the King Salmon, and Amar ordered the lamb.

Rachael, looking to participate in the conversation, asked, "Where are you staying, Mr. Warburg?"

"My yacht is here in Seattle. I'll be staying aboard her while I travel back and forth to various business destinations for the next few weeks."

Rachael noted innocently, "It must be nice to have your home with you wherever you go."

Warburg's tone was slightly condescending, "It's very comfortable, thank you."

When the table was cleared and coffee served, Warburg got down to business.

He addressed Tom, "I wanted to take you all to dinner to thank you for helping me out of an awkward situation. I was attempting to do some business in Ashgabat and just happened to walk into the middle of a coup being staged against the president. Of course, I had nothing to do with those events, and things were getting a little tense until Mr. Renfro arrived."

Warburg raised his wineglass toward Gary. "Many thanks for a job well done, Mr. Renfro."

Gary nodded in his direction.

"In fact, I am so impressed with Greenstone Executive Security, that as I have indicated to you before, I would like to buy the company."

Tom's face grew perceptibly red. "As I have indicated before, Harry, GES is not for sale."

"I would make it worth your while, Tom. I am prepared to pay an above market price."

Tom Parish had fought off takeover bids for GES before. Tom and his son were the sole owners of both GES and PCI. There was little anyone could do to force them to the table. Tom made it clear he was not going to discuss the matter further which vexed Warburg, though he didn't allow it to show on his face. Warburg elected to change tactics. Maybe he could ingratiate himself with the son.

Somewhat formally, he asked, "Young Mr. Parish, where do your travels take you these days?"

Amar was guarded in his father's presence and replied vaguely, "I've just returned from an archaeological dig in Iran. I'll be heading back to New York tomorrow to work on translating some of the hieroglyphics we found there."

Rachael protested, "Oh, Amar you are going again, so soon?"

"I have to, Mom; Evan needs my help."

Warburg picked up the thread, "How very interesting; I take it that you are passionate about the subject of ancient history?"

Amar told some stories about his travels to different archaeological sites around the world. Dinner was served and eaten. The small talk was a little strained and contrived. Finally, Tom folded his napkin and placed it on the table to indicate that the dinner had come to a close.

Warburg cast a fly in Amar's direction. "As it happens, I'll be taking my Gulfstream to New York tomorrow. I would be happy to give you a lift."

Amar knew that his father wasn't in the mood to spend thousands more having Ted Lockhart ferry him back to the Big Apple. He had planned to fly commercial, enduring the hassle of waiting in line and being scrutinized by the TSA.

"That's very kind of you, Mr. Warburg."

"It's the least I can do under the circumstances."

Warburg took a small leather notebook from his inside jacket pocket. He wrote the address of the hangar at SeaTac and his personal phone number on it, tore out the page, and handed it over to Amar.

"Shall we say 11:00 in the morning?"

Amar agreed. Tom stood up, his disapproval evident. He shook hands with Warburg.

"I'll be sending you an invoice, Harry. If memory serves, it will be $1,950,000 dollars. Try to stay out of trouble, will you?"

Warburg didn't even flinch at the amount. "It will be paid promptly," he said.

Once Tom, Rachael, and Amar were in the Lexus on the way home, Tom turned to Amar, "You be very careful around that man Amar; he's a snake."

Amar dismissed the remark, "It's just a plane ride dad, no more."

"All the same, son; be very careful. You never know what Warburg is planning."

Warburg and Dragan walked the two blocks over to Safeco Plaza and rode the elevator up to the Fourth Avenue Heliport on the roof. Warburg was silent while he digested the snub from Parish. Dragan knew when not to interrupt the boss's thought processes. The Airbus H160 was on the pad with its engines warm. As they walked out to the chopper, Warburg revealed his intentions.

"Viktor, there's no need for you to accompany me to New York tomorrow. Once I drop the kid off, I'll be heading back here. I want Tom Parish out of my way. The son will be much easier to deal with than the father. I want you to study the situation and, when I return, you will tell me what the best method will be to accomplish that."

CHAPTER TWENTY-NINE

Seattle to New York

The following morning, Amar took an Uber from Mercer Island to Warburg's rented hangar at SeaTac. The navy blue jet had just been washed and sat gleaming in the morning sun. The tail of the Gulfstream 650 bore a logo saying Zoltan Holdings. As Amar pulled his bag from the car, a tall, striking blonde descended the airstairs and walked over to greet him.

"Good morning, Mr. Parish, my name is Julie Barton. I am Mr. Warburg's personal assistant. If you will follow me, please, Mr. Warburg is already on board."

The Gulfstream 650 would have dwarfed his father's Citation had it been parked alongside. They entered the cabin. The two pilots were in the cockpit running through their pre-takeoff checklist. The interior of the jet did not disappoint. It was everything Amar had come to expect from a highly successful businessman: white leather seating, exotic tropical woods, gold fittings. Warburg was seated at a small desk in front of a bulkhead that separated a bedroom suite from the main cabin. He was on the phone and motioned to Amar to take a seat on the leather sofa facing his airborne office.

Warburg ended the call. "Good morning, Amar. Do you mind if we proceed on a first name basis? You may call me Harry."

"All right, Harry, good morning to you," he replied.

"Coffee?"

"That would be great, thanks."

"How do you take it?"

"I prefer black."

Warburg motioned to Julie, who was seated in the front of the cockpit. "Julie, two black coffees, please."

Julie nodded and set about her task in silence.

Warburg inquired, "Where would you like to be dropped?"

"Oh, ah, the Sheltair FBO at La Guardia would be great."

Warburg pressed a button on his desk phone, allowing him to talk to the pilots. "Thomas, file your flight plan for La Guardia, please."

Amar buckled in, and the two men made small talk over coffee until the plane was airborne. Warburg had done his homework overnight and read everything he could find about the young man. Once they leveled off at 41,500 feet, Warburg began to weave his web.

"I'm very interested in your work, Amar. Will you tell me more about your recent discovery?"

Maybe it was because of the less-than-stellar reception he had received from his parents for the discovery at Persepolis. Maybe it was because he hadn't been roughed up much in his young and privileged life and he tended to take people at face value. Maybe there was just a tinge of rebellion against his father's advice. Harry Warburg had shown himself to be polite and sincerely caring so far.

Amar proceeded cautiously. "Harry, we're still working on translating the text we found at this site, and we aren't ready to make our discovery public yet. In order to tell you more, I'll need your word not to talk about it until I say it's okay."

Warburg chuckled, "I'm usually the one who demands a non-disclosure agreement! Certainly, you have my word. I will not discuss what you tell me with third parties."

Amar rummaged around in his duffle and extracted his Mac Book laptop. He pulled up the photos from Persepolis and narrated as they scrolled through them. He reiterated his theory regarding the extinction of civilizations due to overspecialization. Finally, Amar summarized his personal quest.

"My colleague, Evan Chatterjee, tells me that this chamber is at least 10,000 years old, maybe older. I truly believe that we are not the most advanced civilization to ever inhabit the earth. If the images from Persepolis are an accurate depiction of one of those civilizations, who knows what kind of technology might be waiting to be discovered? It could be something so advanced as to literally change to course of humanity's future!"

On the surface, Warburg pretended to have a common interest in the welfare of the human race. Underneath, he was calculating. If what the kid was saying ended up being true, the profit potential could be incalculable. The image of one man levitating large blocks of stone was of particular interest. That technology alone could revolutionize the construction industry.

"What do you plan to do next?" he asked innocently.

"I plan to scour the planet looking for the ruins of this city. There must be remnants of it somewhere."

"How will you go about the search? I don't recall ever hearing or seeing anything like what you have shown me. Where will you begin?"

Amar paused, considering what he was about to say. He elected to reveal his latest idea. "Once we've completed the translations, I intend to create a digital file of everything we know so far. As you are aware, the Greenstone Satellite System has a built in surveillance capability. I haven't talked to my dad about this yet, but I'm wondering if we can program the satellites to scan the entire planet looking for certain architectural or geological features that we see in the images. The satellite cameras also have an infrared capability that can show us what can't be seen with the naked eye. Maybe then, we'll be able to home in on the location of the ruins and go take a closer look."

Warburg's mind was racing. He almost blurted out that he would certainly favor such an effort were he to be able to buy the company but thought better of pushing too far too fast. This young man had to be cultivated.

"Well, Amar, I'm very impressed with what you have accomplished. Will you keep me posted on your progress?"

Amar hesitated, a subtle voice in the back of his mind was hinting that he may have gone too far already. "Uh, yeah, sure I will," he said, somewhat insincerely.

Just then, the pilot came over the intercom, "Gentlemen, we are on final approach to La Guardia. Please buckle up and prepare for arrival."

Part 4: The Imbrium Codex

CHAPTER THIRTY

Seattle August 2018

Tom Parish had grown weary of being the busiest man on the planet. A stellar career in technological innovation was coming to a close. He'd hardly paused in the pursuit of his fortune since the day he left NASA almost forty-six years ago. With Rachael's assistance, he'd taken good care of himself. Finally, it was time to smell the roses and take time to play. Six months ago, he pulled back from the day-to-day management of PCI. Bob Alford, PCI's president and chief financial officer, was a capable executive, and Tom really had no qualms about letting him run the show. After Barsukov succumbed to cancer, Tom had let Lunokhod 1's control room equipment sit idle in a back corner of the museum's workshop for nearly a decade.

He wasn't a golfer or a fisherman, and he was tired of traveling. Frankly, he was tired of business in general. Tom liked to relax by playing with what his wife referred to as "his space junk." Some people might have said he was trying to relive the glory days of his past, as older people sometimes do. There was more to the story than that, though. Very quietly, after he had turned operations over to Bob Alford, he enlisted the help of Gary Renfro, Robby Harris, and Trevor Guilford for his next project. They gathered in Trevor's office at the museum.

"Guys, we're going to complete the control room display for Lunokhod 1. Whatever equipment is missing we will replace with modern components. We are going to make the control room display operational."

All of the men agreed without being aware of the chairman's real intent.

"Here's the twist," he said. "I'm ridiculously wealthy, and I can afford to blow a few hundred thousand on anything I want. What I want, is to attempt to revive Lunokhod 1, just for the fun of it. According to Barsukov, there's a chance that the mission extender module, or the MEM as it was referred to in the drawings, might actually work after all of these years. We have all of the specifications and frequencies for this device. We just need to complete the control setup, and we'll give it a try."

Robby sat up straight. He locked eyes with Trevor, who was also nodding his approval.

Gary said, "Boss, you've been so good to all of us over the years, we don't care if you want to fly a balloon over Antarctica; we're in."

"I thought you might say that. I hate to deceive anyone, but this effort has to remain secret. Our intentions are not to leave this room. This could be a complete fool's errand, and I don't want to see headlines that say, *"Telecommunications magnate wastes millions trying to resurrect defunct spacecraft!"*

The gears were grinding away in Robby's head. "No worries, boss. When you developed the S-band system for NASA you had the benefit of a worldwide communications system, right?"

"We had ground stations at Goldstone, Canberra, and Madrid. We also had ship-borne and aircraft-mounted systems, as well. But you must remember that while the earth spun on its axis, we were also communicating with a ship hurtling through space. This project is much simpler," Tom said.

This was out of Trevor's area of expertise, so he sat quietly while PCI's computer whiz went on, "we can't use the Greenstone satellite system for this project because it speaks a different language than a fifty-year-old rover. How do you plan to make the radio connection?"

"Good question, Robby. Lunokhod 1 also operates on the Russian version of the S-band signal. We have the frequencies. I was wondering if we can link the control room equipment at the museum to the Greenstone backup dish mounted on the roof over at SatCom. It should be relatively easy to reconfigure that dish for S-band."

Robby paused for a few seconds, "We'll need to replace the attenuator since the moon is much farther away than our satellites, but yeah, that should work."

The four men talked into the night making lists of the equipment that would be needed and tasks to perform.

Six Months Later

Tom made some coffee and sat in front of his control console. Trevor was in his office. Tom told Rachael and Jan that he would be at the museum working on the Russian display late into the night. They were both used to his ways and thought nothing of it. Gary called and mentioned that he had something important to take care of but would be there later in the evening. The control console looked like it was right out of the sixties, which, except for half a dozen high tech up-grades, it pretty much was. The original Russian computer was the size of a small chest freezer. Above that, Tom had mounted one large flat screen monitor which was flanked by three smaller antique screens on either side. A bank of instruments sat to the right with voltmeters, oscilloscopes, an S-band transceiver, an inclinometer, and a whole collection of minor dials and readouts.

It was probably unlikely the rover could be brought back to life af-ter suffering through forty-seven years of 300-plus degrees of temp-erature swings from lunar night to lunar day. Then, there was the fact nobody really knew exactly how the rover had ended its operational life. Maybe it had fallen into a crater and was upside down. No one knew.

The last known coordinates were in the package Barsukov had supplied. Barsukov was positive about the viability of the mission ex-tender module. He described in detail how it was built, and the quality of the materials used. The files supported his opinion. The Russians had installed a pressurized lubrication system for all the rover's bear-ings utilizing a special fluoride-based lubricant that wouldn't freeze or boil with extreme temperature fluctuations. Would it work after all of these years?

This was completely uncharted territory. Nobody had ever tried to resurrect a piece of space junk after a mission that was completed one year earlier much less five decades ago! But what the hell, Tom knew he'd give it a try; he'd known it since Barsukov came forward and changed his whole relationship to owning the rover.

If the attempt was successful, he'd become the only private citizen in history to have owned and operated a spacecraft on another planet. What a museum display that would make!

He plugged in his headset, giving him a direct line to Robby at his office in the SatCom building in Everett. "Robby, are you there?"

"Here, boss, all ready to go. Are Gary and Trevor there with you?"

"Trevor is here; Gary will be late. We have a lot to do, though. Let's proceed without him."

The Russian display was in the northwest corner of the museum near the double doors to the workshop. The rest of the museum sat quietly in semi-darkness with only the nightlights on. The mock-up of Lunokhod 1 rotated, gleaming on its turntable, under the high-intensity spotlights. A large high-definition monitor was mounted to the wall above the old analog instruments. Below that to the left and right, mounted in cabinets that could be closed, were banks of digital video recorders and the most up-to-date digital radio signal equipment. The keyboard and joystick were the latest high-tech video gaming models.

It had taken six months of spare time to assemble everything. It would take a couple hours more for him and Robby to configure the equipment. He consulted his moonrise tables. Today the moon would rise around 3:00 in the afternoon.

They no longer enjoyed the luxury of a networked system of transmitters located around the world like Tom had at his disposal with the Apollo program. That meant they could only communicate with the rover by direct line of sight. The moon had to be in the sky over Seattle in order for any transmission to be received by the spacecraft. As a result, the amount of time they could work with the rover would be greatly reduced. Today being Sunday, the museum was closed, and they would have from 3:00 in the afternoon until midnight or so. Once Robby dialed in the coordinates Barsukov had supplied, he engaged the dish's clock drive so it would track the movement of the moon across the sky.

At about 3:30, Tom turned the master switch to the "On" position. He turned the broadcast selector switch to "Encrypt-Interrogate". He knew this part of the procedure would take a while. He switched on the digital recorders that would record all signals coming and going. The first broadcast would prod the rover's mission extender module and look for a weak return signal to localize upon. According to Barsukov's files, the last known location of Lunokhod 1 was in the Mare Imbrium, which when translated meant, "The Sea of Rains." That region would be visible at the upper left of the moon's surface after it got dark in Seattle.

Once the rover's approximate location could be determined, Robby could fine-tune the antenna and begin to transmit commands that, according to Barsukov's drawings, would cause the rover to deploy a small solar array that would charge the auxiliary battery bank in the MEM. Then, maybe they would get a live picture from the moon. Maybe they would even go for a drive.

Viktor Dragan had researched Tom's home and office and rejected both for being too difficult to approach. He had tailed Tom Parish for the last week and decided that the best possible location for delivering Warburg's final message to him would be at the Parish Museum of Communications. Every time Parish was there, Renfro was too. Renfro's presence would increase the degree of difficulty, but oh how he'd like to put the former SEAL down at the same time as his master.

However, Parish was the primary target, and he would make doubly sure not to let his personal desires compromise the mission. This task had to be executed perfectly. Warburg wouldn't stand for any mistakes.

Dragan had previously visited the museum during regular business hours. He noted that there was a security camera in the parking lot but none inside the building. Perfect. He'd even had a conversation with the curator, a Mr. Guilford. He'd gone into the museum pretending to be a fan of the famous entrepreneur. He was advised that Mr. Parish was a very private person and would not be available to talk. But, as they were looking at the Russian display, Guildford let it slip that Mr. Parish was actually working on the display himself from time to time, mostly on the weekends when the museum was closed.

Dragan tailed Parish to the museum the following Sunday at 3:00 in the afternoon. For the benefit of the parking lot security camera, he was wearing a navy blue hoody over a black ball cap that obscured his face. The driver's window of the 1983 Oldsmobile sedan he'd stolen the previous day from a Seattle gang member was open. He'd stalked the gang banger the previous week photographing him from a distance with a telephoto lens while he hatched his plan. Then he had kidnapped the man and his car at the same time.

At this moment, the gangster was sedated with a dose of Ketamine and resting comfortably under a tarp in the passenger seat. Before stuffing the limp, but still breathing body in the car, Dragan photographed his forearm tattoos. Dragan's left sleeve was rolled up and one arm perched on the sill of the driver's window revealing fake MS-13 tattoos that matched the ones on the forearms of the car's owner. Dragan planned to leave the body, overdosed on Ketamine, in the car when he was done with it.

He passed through the lot and parked behind the warehouse on the south side of the museum. Despite the show he'd just put on for the cameras, Dragan preferred to look as ordinary as possible on the off chance that something might go wrong, and he would have to walk away from this confrontation. It was a chilly 45 degrees with low cloud cover. Exiting the low rider, he slipped on a tan-colored Miguel Caballero jacket against the cold. Under the coat, he wore the navy blue hoody, dark green whipcord pants, and soft-soled brown leather tactical boots.

The roof of the warehouse would give him a perch from which to monitor the comings and goings from the museum parking lot. A service ladder with a safety cage was mounted to the west side of the building, out of sight from the museum. It was locked with a cheap

Master padlock. Dragan slipped on a pair of nitrile rubber gloves—best not to leave any prints behind. He easily defeated the lock with a bolt cutter. Shouldering his Maxpedition Gearslinger backpack, he climbed up to the roof and selected the perfect spot in the shelter of a large air handler. He pulled a pair of Zeiss binoculars from the pack and settled down to look, wait, and listen.

CHAPTER THIRTY-ONE

Mare Imbrium, The Lunar Surface

The silence was complete. The inviting blue and white form of Earth hovered just over the horizon, the only color in a deep black sky. The tracks leading up to the rover were the sole disturbance in the magnificent desolation of the thick gray lunar dust. Lunokhod 1 sat slightly nose down on the collapsed edge of a lunar crater created by the impact of a meteorite long before men walked the Earth.

The rover sat undamaged, just where the Soviets left it decades before, when the primary battery banks finally ran down. Due to its position on the incline, the main solar array on the lid covering the instrument bay couldn't be oriented toward the sun.

If there were any atmosphere with which to transmit sound waves when Tom pressed the button, someone standing near the rover would've heard a soft whirring sound. A small rectangular door on the front side of the mission extender module opened, a miniscule auxiliary solar array slid out, unfolded and oriented itself to the Sun. Tom Parish got a green indicator light.

He stood, "Well, I'll be a sonofabitch!" he said to Robby Harris.

"So will I!" Robby agreed.

According to the specs, the auxiliary solar array would trickle charge the module's battery bank. Theoretically, when the MEM's batteries came up to a full charge level, he could then move the rover and have a live TV signal. He doubted that any of the instruments in the main payload bay would be operational, but he didn't really care about that. He wasn't here to repeat the experiments the Soviets had done; he just wanted to go for a drive on the moon. The first step in the rover's revival had been accomplished!

Trevor came into the control room at 5:00, "Tom, I have some pepperoni pizza here when you get hungry."

"Perfect timing, Trevor, I'm famished, and we're charging the batteries, which will take a little while."

Trevor asked, "You've made contact?"

"Well, I have a green light from the MEM's battery charger. Time will tell. Let's have a bite shall we."

After eating more than he should have, the pizza wasn't agreeing with Trevor's stomach. "Tom, I'm not feeling well, I think I'm going to go home."

"I'm sorry to hear it, Trevor," Tom said in between bites. "By all means, go take care of yourself. Leave the door open for Gary, will you?"

Trevor took his leave.

An hour later, Tom returned to his seat at the control panel. Robby was sitting at his desk at SatCom sipping from a Big Gulp. Tom cycled a switch labeled "Camera 1 Cover" and got a green light indicating that the front camera cover was open. The battery needle dipped slightly lower.

He turned on the inclinometer, and it showed that the rover sat nose down on a ten percent grade. He switched on the main CRT and the high-definition screens and recorders. After all of these years, he couldn't contain himself. He thought, *what the hell, I can always recharge.* With his eyes on the charge needle, he pressed the button labeled "Camera 1 On/Off." The charge needle dipped dangerously low, and after a few seconds, he quickly switched it back off.

Best to let the batteries come all the way up to a full charge. He looked up and saw that the forward camera's digital recorder read 3.26 seconds. He scrolled the display back to 0.00 and hit the play button. The high-definition screen above the console showed a crystal clear picture of the dusty gray lunar surface. The hair on the back of his neck tingled.

"Robby, are you seeing this? We had live video, for a few seconds anyway! Looks like the rover is upright!"

Robby's monitor was linked to Tom's, and he was seeing the same picture.

"I see it, boss; I hope we get to see some little green men!"

Tom and Robby busied themselves with various tasks for two more hours until the charge needle was further into the green. At 8:00 p.m., Tom turned on the aft camera. He could just make out the rover's tracks behind it in the lunar dust, black sky above. A strange feature of the lunar landscape was its immutability. With no atmosphere or wind to erode the surface, even the footprints of the Apollo astronauts still remained as they were the day they left the surface.

Without benefit of peripheral vision, it was impossible to tell from either camera exactly where the rover was. If the rover would move, he could safely back it up in its own tracks and get to level ground where they might be able to get a better picture of the local lunar terrain. Around 9:30, green lights shone all around.

"Okay Robby, all indicators in the green. Here we go."

Tom threw a switch labeled "Drive Train On/Off" and waited a few seconds. There was a five-second lag in control times owing to the time it took for the radio signal to reach the moon. He supposed the lag might have been what caused the original operator to drive the rover onto an incline where it finally ran out of power and wouldn't move any more.

Tom gently nudged the joystick back and held it for five seconds. Nothing happened. The forward camera was still off, but now that the sunlight had improved, the aft camera showed a slightly better picture than before. After a few seconds, the picture showed the tracks out behind the rover jiggling slightly in the frame.

In a miracle of Russian engineering, the rover's bearing lubrication system came up to pressure. Each of the eight wheels on the machine had its own sealed electric motor and brake. The special antifreeze lubricant, still in its reservoir, flooded into the rover's wheel bearings aided by a surface temperature of 150 degrees Fahrenheit. As Tom pulled back and held the stick a second time, each motor wound up slightly, causing the rover to buck a little.

After a tense few seconds, the bearings broke free and both the analog and the high-definition screens showed that the rover was backing up. Tom continued to make five-second control inputs until the picture showed that the rover had crested the slope and the inclinometer read one degree nose down. Behind the rover, both Tom and Robby could see the horizon of the lunar surface against the deep black backdrop of outer space.

Tom jumped up from his console, let out a whoop and did a little dance high fiving the air. The goddamned Russians were fucking geniuses!

Robby came over the intercom, "Way to go, boss; this is so cool!"

Tom settled down and took his seat. He switched to camera 1 and verified that the recorders were on. The MEM's cameras were not gimbaled, so in order to take in a panorama, it would be necessary to pivot the rover. Tom held the control stick to the left for two seconds. Five seconds later, the picture on his monitor began to pivot to the left, as well. When it came to rest, the left side of the screen was partially blocked by a vertical black surface with a straight edge.

"Robby, do you see that? What do you think it is?"

"Yeah, I see it. Maybe a piece of the spacecraft is obscuring the camera?"

"Huh, okay, I'm going to pivot left a little more, and we'll see if it moves with the camera."

Tom tilted the control stick to the left for three more seconds. They waited. Finally, the picture began to move. Tom jumped up, knocking his chair over. Robby shot back in his chair as if he needed more room to see what Tom was seeing.

Both he and Tom hollered at the same time, "What the hell is that?"

The rover's camera had come to rest perfectly framing a large rectangular black object in the foreground. It sat a little below the rover's line of sight, in the middle of a shallow lunar crater. The rover's tracks were clearly visible in the foreground. Tom could see where it had gone over the edge. The monolith looked as if it was made out of black granite. It was much larger than Lunokhod 1. Drawn on its surface in gold lines was the image of a large book which lay open as if it were poised on a music stand. Both exposed pages had some sort of language written upon them. It was clearly manmade—or maybe not. Maybe it was of extra-terrestrial origin. Tom couldn't read the script. He took in a sharp breath. There, on the top of the left page, he recognized the same double oval symbol that Amar had shown him in the photos from the underground chamber at Persepolis.

"Are you recording this?" Robby yelled. "What is that?"

"Yep, the recorders are running." Tom stared for all he was worth. "I don't know what that is. But whatever it is, it is likely one of the greatest discoveries in human history. There are no straight lines on the moon. Anything up there that has straight lines was put there by us. Or maybe by a visitor from somewhere else!"

Tom reached into his pocket and pulled out his Greenstone phone. He shot off a text to Ted Lockhart, "Call Amar now. Then take the jet to New York tonight, and bring him back here immediately. He'll know why; this is of the highest priority—no questions please."

Then he took a screenshot of the monolith and texted that to Amar, "You may have been right all along. Come at once! Ted is on his way. Dad."

CHAPTER THIRTY-TWO

Seattle

The sun went down around 5:00 p.m. Two cars were parked in front of the museum. The high-intensity LED parking lot lighting cast eerie shadows across the lot. Dragan watched through his binoculars as a pizza man came and went. The curator opened the door to receive the pizza and clearly had not locked it afterward. It wouldn't have made any difference; Dragan was fully equipped to defeat any commercial deadbolt. After a while, the curator came out, got into his car, and left. That was good; the curator was not a target.

Renfro, Parish's bodyguard, was nowhere to be seen. Dragan decided to wait; he really wanted to add Renfro to the confrontation as retribution for the disrespect Renfro had shown him during the Turkmenistan extraction. Renfro was almost always somewhere near his boss. Dragan would wait for him to make an appearance. He lay in silence on the roof of the warehouse waiting hour after hour. No activity took place in the parking lot.

It was now 9:40 p.m. Tom Parish was still alone. Perhaps Renfro wasn't coming. He couldn't wait any longer. He'd deal with Parish's man at another time. Slipping on his pack, he silently descended the ladder. He made his way around the edges of the parking lot, keeping to the shadows. Quietly, he slipped in the front door of the museum. The interior was dark except for some lights in the back left corner of the display floor. From his earlier visit, Dragan knew that was where the Russian display was located.

He went to the right passing the displays on Graham-Bell, Marconi, Edison, and Tesla. Slowly, rolling the soles of his boots so as not to make a sound, he came into the section of the museum that was dedicated to its founder. On his left was a mock-up of an Apollo landing craft sitting on a faux lunar surface. The curator had used dark drapes behind the display to simulate the blackness of outer space. Dragan crept behind the capsule and peered through a seam in the drapes. He was directly behind the chairman of PCI.

Tom Parish wore a headset. He was sitting in front of some sort of control room diorama. Another spaceship of some kind was lit by spotlights to his left. A flat-screen above Parish's position showed what looked like photographs of the moon Dragan had seen in National Geographic. In the upper right-hand corner of the monitor another man, also wearing a headset, looked back at Parish. The two men were talking.

Dragan was fascinated. He paused. *What the hell were these two doing?* Less than a minute had elapsed before Dragan realized that whatever was taking these photos of the moon was doing so in real time. *These guys were actually live on the moon! But why? What were they up to?* Then, a large black object came into view on the screen. Parish jumped up knocking over his office chair. He yelled, "What the hell is that?"

Dragan recognized the Greenstone phone Parish pulled out of his pocket. Warburg had one just like it. Standing there, Parish took some screenshots and texted for a minute. Then he slid his phone back into his shirt pocket. Dragan pulled back into the shadows as Parish turned, picked up his chair, set it back on its feet, and sat down. As Dragan watched for a few minutes more, Parish pulled a thumb drive from what looked like a modern version of an old video recorder and put it in his pants pocket.

Dragan thought, *I don't know what's going on here, but I'll snatch that thumb drive on my way out. Maybe it will be of interest to Warburg.* The Maxpedition Gearslinger pack he wore had one unusual feature. It could be pivoted around to the front of its wearer for easy access, without wiggling out of the shoulder strap. Dragan twisted the pack around and took out a small black leather briefcase and the silenced FN Five-Seven pistol. In one easy motion, he slung the pack back into the carry position. Leading with the pistol, he stepped through the drapes. Dragan made one minor mistake. He failed to realize that the man in the monitor could see him.

Robby Harris screamed, "Tom, behind you!"

Gary Renfro was attending his ten-year-old daughter's birthday party at the Chuck E. Cheese in Kent, Washington. The kids loved this place. If you had enough rolls of quarters, they would stay busy for hours, giving him time to sit and chat with his wife. They gathered the kids up and left only after the manager told them the arcade would be closing at 9:00 p.m. Gary's wife piled all of the kids in her Denali to take them home. She understood Gary would be pulling late night duty at the museum and probably wouldn't be home until long after she had gone to bed. Renfro pulled into the museum's parking lot at 9:55 and got out of his car.

Dragan stepped through the drapes. The guy on the monitor yelled something as he raised his pistol. Tom Parish stood up and turned around, pulling his headset off, a questioning look on his face. Dragan looked him in the eye. Without uttering a word, he pulled the trigger, twice. The first 5.7 x 28mm, 40 grain jacketed bullet plowed through the Greenstone phone in the chairman's pocket and then through his heart at 2,000 feet per second. The second bullet severed his spine. Both bullets went clean through his body. One crashed into the original Russian control computer and one into the modern PC. All of the monitors went blank.

Tom Parish looked confused for one second as if he hadn't comprehended what just happened. His dying thought was, *What's Dragan doing here?* Then he fell, blood streaming from his lips. The assassin stepped forward, took the dead man's hand and wrapped it around the handle of the briefcase. He placed the briefcase under the console in one of the lower cabinets, as if Parish had left it there. Standing over the dead man, Dragan snatched the thumb drive from his pants pocket and stashed in it his own.

Renfro approached the front doors of the museum. Contrary to what is commonly portrayed on television, silenced handguns are not really silent. Renfro saw two flashes through the glass and heard two distinct pops. He drew the Wilson Combat .45 and shoved his way through the doors. Leading with the gun, he ran up the stairs and to the left around the displays, directly to where he knew Tom Parish would be sitting.

As Renfro came around the last display in the darkness, he saw a man standing over Tom Parish, who was lying on the floor in a pool of blood. The man's face was shadowed by a black ball cap and hoody. Renfro flipped off his safety and fired two shots at the man's center mass. The man raised his gun and fired back. His shot was a little late; the impact of Renfro's 45 caliber slugs had pushed him back and thrown his aim off. Renfro paused in confusion for a tenth of a second. He was sure he had hit the man directly in the chest.

The man turned and ran. Renfro shot him twice in the torso, but he kept running toward the double doors to the museum's workshop. In frustration, Renfro squeezed off one more shot at the man's legs as he disappeared through the workshop doors. The man stumbled but kept going. Dragan was gloating that the Miguel Caballero bulletproof jacket he was wearing had done its job as advertised. Then a searing pain erupted in his leg as Renfro's last shot plowed a deep groove through his left calf. Dragan ran on through the workshop, burst through the man door next to the loading dock, and disappeared into the night, blood squishing in his left boot.

Renfro pursued the man as far as the double doors to the workshop and saw him exit through the exterior door. He dropped the magazine from the butt of his pistol and inserted a fresh one. Tom Parish might still be alive! Renfro turned and ran back to where his best friend lay on the floor of the museum in a widening pool of blood. He reached down and felt for a pulse. There was none. As if someone had drained all of the energy out of his own body, Renfro dropped to his knees and wept. Robby Harris heard and saw the shots just before his monitor went black. He called 911.

Sitting on his knees in a pool of blood, with gun in hand, Gary Renfro wept for the loss of his dear friend, for the loss of his mentor and for the loss of one of the great men of our time. In the distance, he could hear the sound of approaching sirens.

Dragan peeled out of the south side of the warehouse's parking lot and headed north on Marginal Way. He merged onto Highway 99 north, and a few minutes later, exited at Elliot Avenue. At this time of night, no one was around to notice as an old Oldsmobile pulled into the parking lot of the Elliot Bay Marina. Dragan parked the car. The driver's floor mat was covered in his blood. His left calf was throbbing with pain. He removed his boots and socks and tossed them into the passenger seat footwell. It wouldn't do to leave bloody footprints on the dock. He had already checked to make sure there were no security cameras in that area of the marina parking lot, so he wouldn't be seen exiting the car.

Dragan pulled the Gearslinger pack onto his lap and extracted a water bottle, a pair of scissors, and some QuikClot bandages. Cutting away the lower part of his left pant leg, he cleaned both the wound and his bloody foot. He dressed the gash with the QuikClot bandage. Since Renfro's first four rounds seemed to have no effect, his last shot had been taken in frustration. The .45 caliber bullet plowed a furrow across the back of Dragan's left calf. The wound would hurt like a bitch for a week or two but ultimately wouldn't slow him down much. He reached back in the pack and took out a small round black plastic device, which he put in one of the bulletproof coat's cargo pockets.

Dragan scanned the area for witnesses. Seeing none, he exited the vehicle, slung the pack on his back, and opened the passenger door.

He removed a tarp that had been draped over the gang banger and dragged the unconscious hoodlum across the bench seat, leaving him upright in the driver's seat. He took a syringe loaded with Ketamine from his pack and jabbed it into the gangster's arm, delivering enough of a dose to kill the gangster. He removed a two-gallon can of kerosene and sloshed the contents over the interior of the car and unfortunate criminal, dropping the empty plastic can in the footwell on top of his boots. Dragan pulled the plastic incendiary device from his pocket and twisted the cap until the readout indicated six hours. He placed it on the passenger seat and locked the car door.

Still limping from the pain, Dragan entered an access code into the locked gate that prevented the general public from walking onto the docks and made his way down to slip A-7. The 2008 Linetti 20.5 speedboat was idling quietly in the slip. Two former mercenaries, now in Warburg's employ, were waiting, one at the wheel and one standing guard. Both men were armed with 9mm submachine guns. The guard noted that Dragan was limping and helped him aboard. The guard cast off the lines, stepped onto the swim step, and sat down on the engine cover, looking over the transom, to face any pursuit that might come.

The driver motored out of the marina slowly so as not to attract attention. The three men then faded away into the dark and calm waters of Puget Sound. They would maintain a 20 mph speed for the next two hours so as not to attract the attention of the coast guard.

At long last, they left Puget Sound and turned into the Juan De Fuca Strait. The driver opened her up to 50 mph.

Three hours later, the sun was rising in the east as the Linetti bumped against the swim platform of Warburg's 106 meter mega yacht, the Zoltan, which had been cruising in international waters, just outside the 12-mile limit.

Just as the early morning fishermen began to arrive at Elliot Bay Marina, the interior of an old Oldsmobile in the parking lot suddenly and quietly began to burn. A marina employee, who had arrived at work early, grabbed a fire extinguisher and ran toward the car. He could see there was a body in the driver's seat, the clothes on fire. The door was locked. He smashed the window with the extinguisher and put the fire out. The man was badly burned. The employee checked for a pulse. The man was dead. He called 911.

Marko Dragan had returned to the yacht by helicopter only an hour before, having established an alibi for his brother by partying at a popular Seattle night club, an establishment with security cameras. He made sure to locate several of the cameras and look in their general direction so his presence would be recorded at the time of the hit.

Marko picked up the bowline as the Linetti bumped into the swim platform of Warburg's mega-yacht. Viktor Dragan was stiff from so many hours in the left seat. His calf was screaming as he climbed up onto the platform. Marko was used to obeying direct orders from his brother, no matter how strange they might seem.

"Did you establish my presence in Seattle?" Viktor asked.

"Yes, I was there for a five-hour period," Marko replied.

"Good, sink this boat," Viktor said. "Then ask Mr. Warburg to meet me in the infirmary." He limped off into the bowels of the ship.

Marko complied by opening the boat's seacock and watching it slowly slip beneath the waves. When Warburg came into the ship's medical center, Viktor was sitting on a gurney, a doctor stitching up and re-bandaging his wound. At the same time, he was scrubbing the fake tattoos off of his left forearm. Warburg looked at Dragan's leg but didn't bother to inquire about the wound.

"Was your mission a success?" he asked.

Dragan recounted the evening's events, noting Parish was dead but that Renfro still lived.

"That's too bad; there will be other opportunities. But you got away clean? There won't be any blowback?"

Dragan had enjoyed a conditional family bond with Warburg for years. He wasn't dumb enough to test the older man's loyalties and so did not mention that he had left some blood behind. It wouldn't matter since Dragan had been very careful over the years to make sure his DNA wasn't on file anywhere.

"No sir, Marko established my alibi; there will be no blowback. I was able to conceal my identity during the hit. They will think a certain gang member committed the murder." Holding up the thumb drive, he said, "This might interest you; though I'm not sure how to explain it."

Warburg accepted the thumb drive, moved over to a computer monitor used primarily by the medical staff, and plugged the thumb drive into a USB hub. He played the 3.6 second video and recognized the lunar setting at once. He played it again and paused on the monolith. Clearly visible was the same double oval symbol he'd seen in the photos from Persepolis that Amar Parish had shown him on their shared flight to New York.

"The object appears to be part of the lunar landscape?" he asked incredulously.

Dragan explained what he had observed at the museum while waiting to complete his mission.

"Amar Parish is up to something. I'm not sure what it is. He indicated to me that he was on the trail of an ancient technology that could change the world as we know it. I want to know what that technology is Viktor. You find someone in their organization who can be bought. Dangle some cash; threaten his family if need be. I want someone on the inside. I want to know what they're after."

CHAPTER THIRTY-THREE

New York

It was 1:00 a.m. in New York. Amar spent most of the evening working on photos while Evan attempted to translate the text from Persepolis. Amar didn't have a lot to contribute to the translation process and contented himself with organizing digital files for the photos. On the off chance that Tom Parish would allow the satellite system to be used to scan the planet for ruins, he created a file of the most notable archaeological aspects of the city that might be visible from space. That file included prominent elements of the architecture, the shape of the valley, the configuration of the lake, the location of the waterfall, and even the strange zigzag pattern in the foreground.

Evan was still working when Amar gave up for the evening and walked the four blocks home to his apartment in Turtle Bay. He'd gone to bed around midnight and was sound asleep alone in his apartment. His phone buzzed and rattled on the side table. He opened one eye long enough to see that it was a text message. He sat up with his back to the headboard and picked up the phone. Through sleepy eyes, he squinted at the phone's screen. As usual, it was from Tom.

The message said, "You may have been right all along; come at once! Ted is on his way." That got his attention, but the attached photo made him bound right out of bed.

"Holy shit!" He exclaimed, recognizing the double oval symbol from Persepolis on the face of what looked like a large granite monument. He plugged his phone into his laptop, downloaded the photo, and enlarged it. His jaw dropped as he stared at it. Amar had seen enough photos of the moon at Tom's museum to recognize the background. How could this be? Gray dust all around, the vast blackness of outer space behind it. Whatever this was, it appeared to be located on the moon! He dialed Tom's number. It rang and rang—no answer. He sat on the edge of the bed staring at the laptop when his phone chirped.

It was Ted Lockhart. "Amar, this is Ted. Sorry to call this late at night. Your dad insisted I come get you immediately. Jason and I will

be landing at La Guardia at 5:00 a.m. your time. We can have breakfast while the plane is being refueled and then we'll return to Seattle
immediately."

"What's going on, Ted? Have you seen the photo Tom sent me?"

"No sir, I didn't actually talk to him, but his message to me said to
come get you and don't ask questions."

Amar didn't know what to make of the secrecy. "Okay, I'll be at the
FBO at 5:00 a.m. See you then."

Amar texted the photo to Evan. Evan was still at the office working
on the translation. He called, and Evan picked up.

"Did you get my text?" Amar asked.

"No, sorry, I was engrossed in the Persepolis translation. Since you
left, I used one of my graphic analysis programs to compare the difference between the depiction of the night sky in the chamber at
Persepolis and the night sky that we see today. Amar, the chamber is
at least 12,000 years old, and you aren't going to believe what the text
says!"

"We can talk about it on the plane."

"Plane, what plane?" Evan asked.

"Never mind that right now; look at the picture I just texted to
you."

"Hold on. I'll put you on speaker while I look." Evan looked, spied
the double oval symbol on the monolith, and gasped audibly. "Well,
I'll be damned. When it rains, it pours! Who sent this to you?"

"Tom sent it. What do you think?"

"The two finds are definitely related. This cannot be a coincidence.
You do recognize the location?"

"Yep, I've seen enough pictures of the moon to know it when I see
it. This has something to do with my dad's rover."

"I daresay it does," Evan replied.

"Tom wants me to come right away. Ted is on the way and will be
at the FBO at 5:00 this morning. I want you to come, too. Maybe we
should get some sleep first."

"Hah, I'm not going to sleep a wink between now and then. This is
the most unbelievable set of circumstances I've ever been a party to. In
the next few days we're going to rewrite the history of the world, Amar. Do you understand how huge this is?"

"Yeah, I do Evan. We're going to be deluged by the media, probably sooner than later."

Evan considered that. "Let's not say anything to anyone until after
we have talked to Tom and gone over all we know about both finds."

"Good plan for now. You're going to take a cab to the airport, right? So, stop here and pick me up at say 4:30?"

Evan agreed. He began organizing all of his materials from Persepolis for the trip to Seattle.

Ted Lockhart was nothing, if not precise when it came to the operation of the jet. He taxied up to the FBO at 5:00 a.m. on the dot. He parked the jet and called for the fuel truck which came alongside a few minutes later. Ted and Jason Hall, his co-pilot, entered the passenger lounge.

Ted greeted Amar and Evan, "It'll take at least thirty minutes or so to refuel the jet. As you know, we'll pick up three hours on our way back to Seattle. We don't need to get there that quickly since no one will be available at 7:00 a.m. I'm famished; can I buy you two breakfast over at La Guardia Cafe?"

They went to breakfast, were back at the plane at 6:00 a.m., and took off for Seattle shortly thereafter. Once airborne, Evan began to share his notes from the translated text at Persepolis.

Amar listened carefully, then exclaimed, "Oh my god, Evan, this is exactly what I had hoped it would be!"

Gary Renfro had been up all night with the Seattle Police crime scene unit and the coroner at the museum. Robby Harris was on the phone from his office at SatCom to tell them what he had seen. A Detective Manning was running the show. Finally, Tom's body was removed by the coroner. After hearing Renfro's story three different times, Manning bagged his pistol and asked him if he could come to the downtown station later in the day.

He could and would, but first, he had to break the news to both Amar and Rachael. Renfro would see Rachael in person. He knew Amar was out of town and called his cell phone. Amar mentioned he was in the air and on his way to Seattle. Renfro broke the news to him. Amar felt a searing pain just behind his eyes. He was so upset he couldn't speak and handed the phone to Evan. Once Evan understood what had happened, he was visibly shaken. Renfro promised to call them back later; he had to go tell Rachael and needed to do so in person.

CHAPTER THIRTY-FOUR

Seattle

Ted Lockhart made his final approach to Boeing Field from the north. He set the Citation down gently on Runway 14R and taxied over to the PCI hangar. The whine of the Rolls Royce jet engines subsided as he parked the aircraft. Evan opened the airstair door and helped a shaky Amar Parish down the stairs to find Jan Meyer waiting beside the hangar door. Renfro called her early that morning with the disastrous news before heading over to Tom's house to tell Rachael.

Jan had worked for Tom Parish for over twenty years. She'd watched Amar grow up from boyhood. Amar could see the strain in her face as he approached. She clung to him rather than simply embracing him. The tears came freely as he wept onto her shoulder. She was clearly grief-stricken and doubly so the moment she saw him and Evan. After a moment in Amar's arms, she pulled away and gave Evan a hug.

"Oh, Amar, what a mess this is. I'm so sorry." It was difficult for her to speak.

"I know, Jan. I guess everything's going to change now."

Jan slowly gathered herself, wiped her eyes, and returned to a semblance of the trooper that she was. "I have your dad's car out front. I suspect you'll want to go to the house and see Rachael first?"

"Yeah, that would be best. Evan, you're welcome to stay at the house with us if you like."

Evan said, "Amar, you and Rachael are going to need some privacy. I've booked a room at the Fairmont Olympic; you can just drop me there, and I'll see you tomorrow."

"Here, can you drive?" Jan said, handing the keys to Amar. "I'm so upset, I might get us killed."

"Sure, I'll drive; no doubt there are things we need to talk about on the way."

Jan nodded in the affirmative. "That's putting it mildly," she said. "but all business matters can wait for a day or two."

They walked out into the parking lot, threw their bags in the back, and got into Tom's Lexus. They pulled out onto Marginal Way heading north. After dropping Evan at the Fairmont, they turned onto Interstate 90 East, took the first Mercer Island exit, and made their way down the west side of the island to Forest Avenue. The 7,000 square foot, six-bedroom house sat on two acres that fronted on the waters of Lake Washington with a view of downtown Seattle. Tom purchased the home eight years earlier after Amar had started trekking all over the globe, chasing his dream. Amar had a suite consisting of a bedroom, bathroom and sitting room, but he had only spent a few holidays there, and it had never really been his home.

They parked the Lexus in front of the garage and went in through the front door. The home was a split level, with one flight of stairs leading down into the great room below, which looked out upon Lake Washington through a wall of glass. The kitchen, dining, and utility areas were on the lower level. One flight to either side of the main staircase led up to two separate bedroom wings.

Rachael was sitting on a love seat in the living room, a handkerchief in one hand, Renfro holding her other hand. They were both staring into space across the water at the view of downtown Seattle with the Olympic Mountains in the background when Amar and Jan came in. Rachael stood. She wore pleated black gabardine slacks and a cream-colored silk blouse. At sixty-eight, she was still a handsome woman. Her skin was pale, the only signs of aging in her face were little crow's feet at the corners of her eyes and just a smidge of loosening skin under her chin. She had remained fit over the years, primarily due to a regimen of exercise and healthy foods.

The shoulder-length black hair still radiated glowing highlights, just a hint of silver here and there. She came around the sofa and embraced her son. With tears in her eyes, she held him tight. Then she motioned back toward the couch. "Come sit down and tell me everything."

Jan broke in, "Rachael, I'll be in Tom's office. You two need some time alone. I'll answer the phones and keep things quiet for you. Just call me for whatever you need."

Renfro's phone buzzed; he stood and looked at the screen. "I have to go to the police department for a while, but I'll be back later in the day. In the meantime, I have ordered one of our security people to stand guard. He's sitting in his car in front of the house. Jan has his name and phone number if you need it."

Rachael smiled at them; one could always count on Tom's loyal staff to be at the ready in a pinch. "Thank you, Gary and thank you Jan, so much."

Renfro left by the front door. Jan turned and went into the north wing where Tom kept an office at home. There was also a small guest suite, which she stayed in occasionally to be available if he needed her.

Rachael and Amar sat, and he recounted all the events of the past two days, starting with Tom's text to him in New York, telling him that he'd made a significant discovery, and he needed to see Amar right away. Amar showed Rachael the photo Tom had texted him, but at the moment, it paled in significance against the death of his father.

"I'm worried about you, Mom. How will you cope with all of this?"

Both Amar and Rachael were aware that grief comes in waves. She squeezed his hand, and the tears flowed. "This is all so senseless, Amar. Why would anyone want to kill your father? He was such a good man."

"I don't know, Mom, but we're going to find out."

"There's a lot I need to tell you, Amar." She couldn't bring herself to refer to her husband in the past tense just yet.

"You know how your dad is. He's always been married to his work. Over the last ten years, we've grown somewhat apart. He's been traveling a lot on business, and when he's home, he spends most of his time at the office or the museum. We still love each other very much, but I've had a lot of practice living on my own since you've been away."

"God, I had no idea."

"Well, no, you wouldn't have. Whenever you came home, we all spent time together. I'm not saying that I won't miss him—I will. I already miss him terribly." She gave a little sob.

She finally let the past tense slip in. "He was a self-made man, a force of nature. All I'm saying, I guess, is that I'm somewhat used to living on my own, and I think I'm going to be alright." Having said that, she fell into deep sobbing.

Amar teared up as he held her. "I'm sorry, Mom. I never knew all that was going on. I mean, I guess I never took the time to see it."

She wiped her eyes. "You've been away for a long time. I think you always favored my side of the family. But whatever else you may be, you're still your father's son. Just like your Dad, when you're concentrating on a project, everything else fades into the background. It's not a bad trait. Your ability to concentrate and to focus is what has made the Parish men who they are.

Amar, you've never had to worry about money. Your father saw to that. I doubt that you ever will have to worry about it. I know your interests have always been more along the lines of academia than business. But the company is the engine that has funded our financial security. I don't think it was your father's intent to place a burden upon you that you couldn't carry. That's why he built such a strong company. You have Bob Alford to look after the day-to-day stuff. But, since the company is completely owned by our family, your dad wanted it to remain under the direct control of a family member. I don't have a head for business. He knew that. That's why he wanted you to succeed him as chairman of the board."

"He's been after me to take a more active role for years. As you know, I've resisted his desires. Never in my wildest dreams did I imagine it would all happen at once. So, I guess I'll be taking care of both of us now."

"Well, I'll expect you to look in more often. Tom set up an investment fund in my name a long time ago. I have fifty million or so in liquid assets and investment capital that returns a healthy income to me. I also have this house. Anyway, I'm quite well set up for the rest of my life. I have enough to indulge my charity work, too."

Amar gave a low whistle in appreciation of the amount. "I feel like such a dope, Mom. I never paid any attention to the family fortune; I just always assumed there was enough to do whatever we were doing."

"You had no need to, Amar. You've been pursuing your course of study like the man that you are. Your father respected what you're doing."

"You think he did?"

"It was all he could do to refrain from making demands on you. He was very positive about your working relationship with Evan. He liked him a lot. Evan, you know, was instrumental in helping your father to break into international business because he could speak to nearly anyone on the planet in their own language."

"Evan and I had some time to talk when we were in jail in Iran. I knew he and Evan were close friends, but I didn't know Evan had played such a key role in establishing the family fortune."

"That was your father's way, Amar. He wasn't one to casually reveal details about his business activities to anyone who didn't need to know, or in your case, someone who wasn't really interested."

Amar rubbed his face with both hands. "This is giving me a headache. You know Mom, I don't even know what we're worth."

"Jan will set up meetings with the accountants for you. The net worth of our holdings fluctuates all the time with changes in the market. But I think the current net worth of PCI and GES, along with your father's other investments, hovers somewhere around 8.5 billion dollars. I don't know for sure, but I think the annual income the business provides is something around five percent. It's more than you could possibly spend."

Amar sat back. His eyes wide, his jaw dropped. He was stunned, nearly beyond words.

Rachael was sympathetic to his reaction. "I know that's a lot to take in, honey. Your father was a well-established billionaire, but because the company was privately held, he had no obligation to reveal that information to anyone."

Amar looked stricken. The number was so large; he feared...he didn't know what he feared. Maybe, that his life had just involuntarily changed from anthropologist to businessman? That wasn't what he'd been planning for himself.

"You need to understand, Amar. Once the will is settled, both PCI and GES are yours to do with as you wish. Yes, it will be something of a burden for a while and no, your lifestyle won't change all that much. The Citation will be at your service. You can have nice homes wherever you would like. You can fly to your digs anywhere on earth.

We've never been the kind of people to flaunt our wealth. Your father was always content to drive a Lexus instead of a Bentley or a Maybach or some such thing. He dearly loved having the jet, though, so he could move around at will."

Amar and Rachael talked for hours in a way they never had before. They laughed and cried and when they were done, they had completely renewed the bonds of their relationship. Jan had kept everyone away so that Amar and Rachael could talk themselves out.

They hadn't noticed the afternoon turning to evening as the lights of downtown Seattle came on, and reflections of the city danced off the ever-changing surface of Lake Washington.

CHAPTER THIRTY-FIVE

Seattle

Jan stayed busy all day Thursday setting up appointments for Amar on Friday. The next morning Amar, Rachael, and Jan drove to the office in Tom's Lexus.

Jan returned to her duty as executive assistant. "Amar, there are a lot of people who want to meet with you, most, of whom you've met in the past but don't know well."

"Who would that be?"

She went down her list. "First up, I need to schedule a meeting for you with PCI's President, Bob Alford. Then, Tom's in-house accountant, Al Hemmings. Then we need to meet with the estate lawyers, and all the partners are calling. The lease on the offices is up for renewal. You need to review the documents. The South Korean acquisition is in a critical stage, and there are some new executive-level employee hires that will need your approval."

"Why does all this stuff fall to me to decide? Why can't Bob handle it?" he asked.

"You don't know?"

He shook his head to indicate that he didn't.

"Oh dear," she said. "Bob Alford gave his notice last week, just before your father's death. He'll be leaving in a month to pursue his own interests!"

The Lexus drifted onto the shoulder before Amar caught it and pulled back onto the road. "Jesus Christ, Almighty! Please tell me you aren't serious!"

Jan had reached out for the grab handle as Amar swerved. "Okay, okay, let's calm down and at try to stay on the road; maybe he'll reconsider under the circumstances," she said.

Bob was already in Tom's outer office with Beth Landis, his secretary, and some hot coffee. They went through greetings and condolences all around. Jan sat at her desk with Rachael nearby on the sofa. Beth stood nearby for any directive that might come from Bob Alford. Bob and Amar retired to the chairman's office.

Bob motioned for Amar to take his father's seat behind the big burlwood and black glass desk. Amar looked out at the view of downtown Seattle and gave a heavy sigh. Bob sat down across from him.

"Amar, Jan told me that you only found out yesterday about Tom's wishes that you succeed him as chairman of the board. I imagine that has been something of a shock to you."

"That's putting it mildly. I understand you're leaving us?"

"I don't want to put any pressure on you at a time like this. I can postpone my plans for a while until you feel more settled. For the moment, there's a long list of items to consider. I'm sure you realize that you'll be having some contact with the press in the days to come. The funeral will receive a lot of coverage."

"I know. It's not something I'm looking forward to. The press coverage, I mean."

"Amar, I know you haven't had time to adjust to what's happened, but there are hundreds of people that depend directly on PCI and its affiliates for their livings. We have quite a few partners in some of our regional telecom systems, as well. They all want to know if big changes are going to be made. A press release is probably in order before the funeral."

"Bob, my dad had a great deal of faith in you. He told me so on more than one occasion. I have no reason to doubt your abilities or your intent. I know Dad pulled back a lot in the last couple of years. He was excited about his activities outside the office and confident in your management of the company. In fact, you provided him with a level of freedom that he never had when I was younger.

"Even after he pulled back, he still managed to fill his time with other projects like the museum and his space junk. That's just who he was. I'm happy with the way he left things for now. If you're looking for my first directive as the new chairman, you can tell whoever needs to know, including the press, that no changes are going to be made in the short term, it will be business as usual."

"Thank you, Amar. I'll continue to serve your interests the same way I served your father's for as long as I remain on board."

Amar nodded. As if she had been summoned psychically, Jan Meyer walked in from the outer office and came to a stop next to Bob's chair, steno pad in hand. Bob had asked her to broach this subject, but she still hesitated a little.

"Amar, we need to establish some ground rules regarding our communications with each other. I've known you since you were a little boy. Though I was very fond of your father, I always addressed him as Mr. Parish or sir, around the office.

We never really discussed that sort of thing in detail; it just happened that way. We've been in the habit of being a little formal around here mostly because of all the VIPs that your father did business with. The question is, how would you like Bob and me to address you?"

Amar sat lost in thought for a moment. "I guess it's going to be a steady stream of decision making?"

Bob replied, "More like a conveyor belt, I think."

"How about this?" Amar queried, "I've known you both nearly forever, so I don't want to be formal with you. When we're alone around here and when you call me on the phone, I want to stay on a first name basis. Whenever you think it's appropriate to refer to me in the third person, as Mr. Parish, feel free to do so. When I have to meet with the bigwigs you can be as formal as you think is appropriate."

Both Jan and Bob nodded. Bob continued, "Okay, good start. I have Al Hemmings lined up, and some of the folks from our accounting department have come in to meet with you. Can you take the time?"

Reluctantly Amar agreed, "Okay, let's do it. Jan, would you get hold of Evan and find out what time he can come by? After these meetings, I want to go to the museum. I want to see where it happened. I understand Trevor is still in charge there?"

Jan came back, "Yes, he is. He offered to come into the museum today if you need him."

"Let's get Trevor to meet us at the museum this afternoon. Ask Rachael if she'd like to go with us, too. Then I imagine we should go to the funeral home and check on everything."

Jan left the room as Al Hemmings and the accountants arrived. They set up an easel with a chart of the corporate structure and passed out spreadsheets to everyone showing all the divisions and their related values. They presented Amar with the up-to-date financial data on all his holdings. The total net worth was nearer to nine billion. Al had all the information compiled in a briefing binder and also on a thumb drive that Amar could take with him to study. Al presented a list of the contract negotiations that were ongoing and outlined the major issues that Amar might want to weigh in on. They signed some paperwork relating to him taking over the position of chairman of the board.

Jan buzzed, "Amar, Evan has arrived, and Gary Renfro is here with a detective from the police department."

"Okay Jan, thanks. Guys, if we're done for now, I need to meet with Gary and the detective for a while."

Al Hemmings and the accounting crew stood up and thanked the new chairman for his time. Al gave Amar his card and asked him to call with any questions he might have about the spreadsheets he'd been given or anything else. Without a doubt, for the foreseeable future, Amar knew his life wasn't his own anymore.

Al Hemmings and the accountants filed out of the office. Evan was sitting on the sofa outside of Tom's office with an arm around Rachael, sharing her sorrow. Amar left them alone. Gary introduced Perry Manning, a Seattle homicide detective and an old friend of Tom's. The three men entered the chairman's office and closed the doors behind them. "Gary, you were there at the museum when my dad was shot?"

Gary teared up, "I was late because I was at my daughter's birthday party. I got there just as the gunman was making his escape. I managed to wing the guy, and he left some blood behind. We'll probably get some DNA from that. I couldn't take the time to pursue the shooter; your father was down, and I needed to attend to him. By the time I got back to Tom, he was already gone. I'm convinced the shooter was a pro. I know how these people move, and this guy was definitely a professional."

Manning cut in. "Mr. Parish, I'm sorry to bother you at a time like this, but I've been talking with Mr. Renfro, and he tells me that you may have satellite coverage of the Seattle area on the night in question?"

"Is that true, Gary? Did we have a bird over Seattle? Can we trace this guy's movements?"

"We always have a bird over Seattle. Tom demanded it. I've been so busy with everything else I haven't had time to look. I put Robby Harris on it; he's over at SatCom. Let's get him on screen and see if he has anything for us."

Gary pressed a button on a remote on Tom's desk. The cherrywood panel behind the desk slid up, revealing the large flat screen. The screen came alive with a camera view of Robby's office at SatCom, showing him hard at work punching keys on his computer keyboard.

"Robby, I'm here with Amar and Detective Manning from the Seattle Police Department. Were you able to find our shooter?"

Robby jumped in his seat and looked up, "Jeez Gary, you snuck up on me!"

Robby could see the chairman's office on his screen. He spotted Amar and expressed his condolences. He then greeted the detective. "Yep, I found the guy. Mostly."

"Show us what you have," Gary said.

Robby narrated as the edited footage played on screen. "This first bit is from the outside security camera. There are no security cameras inside the museum. From the clock counter in the lower left of the screen, you can see that it's 3:03 p.m. The scene you are looking at is the parking lot at the museum. The sun is still up, so the image is of fair quality. Here comes the shooter driving an old Oldsmobile sedan; he drives through the parking lot. You can see the bottom half of his face in the driver's window. He's wearing a ball cap and hoody, so we probably won't be able to identify him by facial recognition. However, the dumb bunny has his arm out the window showing his tattoos for all to see.

Detective Manning interrupted, "Robby, can you zoom in on those tattoos?"

"Yes, sir, I can."

The screen showed a grainy close up. It was enough to identify the man should they ever find him.

Manning was about to ask if he could have a printout when a printer in one corner of the chairman's office began clacking away.

"I've sent the image to Tom's printer," Robby said, and continued with his narration. "The car disappears around the corner of the warehouse next door, and that's the last we see of him until about 9:45. Here he comes sneaking around the edge of the parking lot, trying to stay out of the lights. The doors to the museum aren't locked, so he goes right in. If they had been locked, I doubt that would have slowed this guy down much."

Gary spoke up, "The reason the doors were open is because Tom was expecting me. He was going to try to revive the Russian rover, and he wanted me to be there."

"Revive the Russian rover?" Manning asked.

Gary gave a brief explanation regarding the rover. He emphasized the need for discretion.

Manning said, "No word will pass my lips about this. Tom Parish was one of the most amazing men I've ever known."

Amar pulled out his phone and looked up his father's text. He showed the image to Renfro and Manning. "He sent me this text at 9:50, about five minutes before you got there, Gary. Apparently, he was successful."

"What the hell is that?" Gary asked. "It looks like some sort of black granite monument in the desert."

"I don't know exactly," Amar said wistfully. "But you see that symbol in the upper left corner of the slab? That's the same symbol that Evan and I saw in the underground chamber at Persepolis."

Gary read the text aloud, "Amar, come at once; maybe you've been right all of these years, I'm sending the jet. Dad. Well, he was never one to waste words was he."

Amar buzzed, "Jan, will you send Evan and Rachael in here? You come too, please."

The doors opened, and Evan, Rachael, and Jan came in. Chairs were drawn up, so they were all sitting around Tom's desk in a semi-circle.

Amar asked Evan, "Did you bring the images from Persepolis with you?"

Evan felt around in his pocket and pulled out a thumb drive. He handed it over. Amar plugged it into a USB port on Tom's desk. The images from the underground chamber popped up on screen. Everyone present was impressed by the beauty of the discovery.

Amar pointed to the screen. "We see the same symbol at the doorway to the underground chamber here and again on the floor inside the chamber here. Evan hasn't had time to completely finish translating the language in the room yet, but the two discoveries are clearly related. Anyway, I just wanted to point that out before we continue. Robby, you can pick up where we left off."

"Okay, we had two camera feeds that were recording from the moon, but we weren't recording the camera feeds that were on me or Tom. So all I can tell you about the shooter is what I saw before my screen went dark." Robby continued the narration. "So here comes Gary in his truck. He gets out; there you can see two flashes in the windows. Gary hears the gunshots. He draws his weapon and rushes into the building."

With tears in his eyes, Gary looked at Rachael, "I was just a few minutes too late, Rachael. I'm so sorry."

Rachael grabbed his hand and held it. "It's not your fault Gary. How could you have known?"

Robby went on, "You can see a few more flashes here as Gary returns fire. Now, here comes the gunman. He exits the warehouse door and runs across the parking lot. You can tell he's been hit because he's limping as he runs. He runs around the corner to his car. Here, he peels rubber out of the parking lot.

"Now we'll switch to our Greenstone satellite feed. We zoom back up a little, and we can follow the car north on Marginal. It's an easy car to track. He gets on 99 North, jumps off at Elliott Avenue, and pulls into Elliott Bay Marina. He parks the car, fiddles around in the interior for five minutes, and then makes his way to a slip. He piles into a very fast looking speedboat, and a few minutes later, he pulls out into Puget Sound. We follow him north for forty-five minutes until he gets to Juan de Fuca Strait where we lose him under cloud cover. The only other thing I can tell you is that I saw the shooter step out from between the drapes behind Tom. It was dark. I couldn't see his face. He didn't say anything. He just raised his gun and fired. Then my screen went blank. I haven't been to the museum yet, but I'm pretty sure his bullets damaged the main computer. That's all I have."

Manning asked, "Were you able to get a plate number off the car?"

"Yeah, right, I almost forgot." Robby punched a button and an enlarged photo of the back of the car traveling north on 99 came on the screen. The printer clacked again.

Manning pulled the sheets from the printer and said, "I'll run this plate, and I'll send a cruiser over to the marina. The car will probably still be there, and we might be able to pull some prints off of it. This is clearly the work of a gang member, but it's not a random killing. This guy spent some time planning the hit. Mr. Harris, please send the security camera footage to my office for further review. Mr. Parish, I need to get moving before the trail gets cold. I'll get back to you when there is any new information." Manning got up, shook hands all around, and left the office.

"Okay, I want to go to the museum and see where it happened. Mom, do you want to come?"

"No, I don't want to see it, Amar. Perhaps Jan could drive me home?"

"Of course," Jan said. "I spoke with Trevor earlier, and he'll be there to meet you, Amar."

CHAPTER THIRTY-SIX

Seattle

The police had closed the museum as a crime scene. The techs had finished bagging evidence two hours earlier. Manning left instructions for Amar, Evan, and Renfro to be admitted. Trevor met them at the door and accompanied them to the Russian display. They strolled quietly through sections devoted to the Mercury, Gemini, and Apollo programs. Mock-ups of the space capsules and the spacesuits worn by the astronauts for each program were on display.

The four men rounded a corner and came upon a section dedicated to Tom Parish and unified S-Band communications. The display was set against a backdrop of oversized photos of the five transmitting stations located around the world, which Tom had been in charge of during the Apollo program.

The last area contained all the equipment from the Soviet Space program. They walked around the S-Band display and came face-to-face with the full size mock-up of Lunokhod 1. The rover's gold and polished aluminum surfaces sparkled under the spotlights. A Plexiglas information board was bolted to the floor nearby. It told all about the rover and included a copy of the ownership papers Tom had obtained from the Russians. On the main wall behind the rover was a giant photo of the Proton K launch vehicle emphasizing its size. A few examples of the moonscape photos sent back by the rover in 1970 adorned the side walls.

Evan hadn't been to the museum in many years. "So, this is the copy of the rover that Tom bought?" He asked.

"Yep, this is it," said Amar.

"And the original is still on the moon?"

"It's still up there, and it seems to be working. Or at least it was working," Amar sighed.

"I never thought it would be this big!" Evan exclaimed.

"Tom liked what the Russians did," said Renfro. "He always remarked how well he thought they had built things."

The three men moved over to the control panel. The floor had been cleaned and the only remaining evidence of the shooting were two bullet holes through the center of the huge Russian computer processor that controlled the rover. All of the screens were blank. Trevor bent over and opened one of the cabinet doors under the control panel. He extracted a black leather briefcase and handed it to Amar.

"I think this belonged to Tom. I didn't see it until I was on my knees cleaning the floor."

Amar opened the flap and looked inside. The briefcase contained a one-inch-thick bound booklet that said, "Transaction Summary" on the cover. Amar closed the flap. It was probably something to do with one of Tom's many deals. He'd give it to Bob Alford the next time he was in the office.

Amar asked Trevor, "Will we be able to make repairs and get the rover running again?"

Trevor looked a little gloomy and shrugged his shoulders. "I have some serious doubts about that. I was mainly responsible for how the display looks. Tom and Robby handled all of the technical issues. I did hear them say that this computer used some sort of Russian computer language, and the whole project wouldn't have been possible without it. You can ask Robby. I would have no idea how to go about finding a replacement."

Amar turned to Renfro, "Anything to add, Gary?"

Renfro considered before responding. "I guess you could say that I was only the gofer on this project. All I did was hire some of the contractors to help Trevor build the display. I arranged for shipping some of the equipment purchases. Basically, I did whatever Tom asked me to do, but I wasn't involved in the technical side."

Trevor's face brightened, "There is a file box of information on the rover; it's in my office. I'll get it for you." Trevor disappeared into this office and returned shortly carrying a banker's box.

"These are the files that Tom bought from a Russian by the name of Barsukov, who actually worked on the rover for the Soviets. All of the information that allowed Tom to revive the rover is in here. Unfortunately, Barsukov passed away about ten years ago, but maybe you can find something in here that will help." He passed the box to Gary. Amar took out his phone and photographed the damage to the control panel and the rest of the Lunokhod 1 display.

He shook Guilford's hand, "Trevor, I want you to reopen the museum as soon as the cops will let you. Tom would want it to be reopened. You can close this display until we can make repairs. For now, I need to get over to the funeral home."

Tom Parish's funeral was held the following Saturday at St. James Cathedral in downtown Seattle. Four hundred twenty people attended along with several news team satellite vans. Amar and Rachael were besieged by well-wishers. The police investigation was nowhere near completion. CNN led, and all of the rest of the news hounds followed, reporting that the United States had lost one of its great industrial innovators to a senseless gangland killing.

Amar was sitting on the floor of Tom's office, the contents of the file box from the museum and printed copies of all of the photos from Persepolis spread around him. In between teary eyed waves of grief, he was flipping back and forth through the various images when he came across a photo of the full moon showing the last known location of the Russian rover. Something about the picture was prodding his memory. He searched through the photos from Persepolis until he came to a close-up image of the moon rising over the stone city. He looked closer and for the first time noticed a small black dot in the upper left quadrant of the image of the moon. He'd never noticed it before.

He compared the two photos. The black dot was in the same exact location on the lunar surface as the last known location of the Russian rover.

He jumped up with a photo in each hand. "Holy shit!" he exclaimed.

Just then, Evan entered the office, laptop case in one hand and a cup of coffee in the other.

Amar didn't bother with a greeting. "Evan, look at this, will you?"

Evan laid his things on the conference table and compared the two images. He knew right away what he was looking at. "This just keeps getting better and better. Now, in addition to the presence of the double oval symbol, we have yet more concrete evidence that the two finds are inextricably related. What joy it brings me! This photo of the moon is from the files Trevor gave you?"

"Yep, the last known coordinates of Lunokhod 1 were in a region on the moon known as the Mare Imbrium." Amar looked like a bereaved cat who had eaten the canary. "Decoding this mystery is the most satisfying thing I've ever done. How are you doing with both the translation from Persepolis and from the artifact on the moon?"

"That's why I'm here. I've managed to crack the code. I was right; the text is a very early version of Indo-Iranian Sanskrit. It is clearly the precursor language from which the ancient language of Sanskrit has evolved into its present form."

"Don't torture me, my friend, what does it say?"

Let's start with the band of text from the chamber at Persepolis. It consists of three sentences. In the center above the image of the village it says, "Vandalay, Planetary Capital City of Ularia."

"The city is named Vandalay? I like it! But what does Ularia mean?"

"You are to consider Amar, that over 12,000 years ago, the inhabitants of the Earth would have had a different name for our planet. They also would have a different system for marking the passage of time. As you can imagine, they wouldn't have had a calendar based upon the birth of Christ. It is also interesting to note that there was a capital city for the whole planet!"

"Right, of course. What else does it say?"

"The sentence on the left says, "Look to the heavens for your salvation.""

"What do you think that means?" Amar asked.

"I don't think it refers to the Christian concept of divine salvation. As you know from my writings, I believe the concept of divine judgment and salvation from above was created by the church as a means to control the population during medieval times. I think the intent of this sentence is much more literal, and you may have just uncovered part of what it means yourself. The explanation is twofold. I believe it means that the keys to the destiny of the human race may be contained within the artifact that was placed on the moon and that we should look there for the information.

"I also think it indicates that we should look to the pattern of stars depicted on the ceiling to determine how old the room and the message from Persepolis actually is."

"Have you been able to decipher the constellations?"

"I have, though it's hard to be precise. I estimate that the room in Persepolis was built in approximately 10,000 BCE, which would make it right at 12,000 years old. That date would place the construction of the room at the tail end of the last ice age. As you know, the sophistication of the tile work alone forces us to rethink the technological history of humanity. It supports your thesis that highly advanced civilizations may have existed on the Earth at that time."

"Okay, we're really making some progress here. What does the third sentence say?"

"The third sentence is quite short. It says, "We are among you.""

Amar was triggered in a way he had never experienced before. Some kind of déjà vu. As he stared at the photo image of Vandalay in his hand, he was overwhelmed with the feeling that he was staring into a past that somehow, he knew. He plopped down into one of the conference table chairs. The sensation passed. He took a few deep breaths.

"Are you quite all right?" Evan inquired.

"Huh? Uh, yeah, I'm fine. I just felt dizzy for a minute. That sentence implies that there are people here on Earth, right now, that remember their ancient heritage. A heritage that goes back over 12,000 years?"

"I suppose you could interpret it that way. We probably shouldn't jump to conclusions. They might have intended the chamber as a message for cultures only 1,000 years in their future, not knowing it would remain hidden for this long."

"Valid point. What about the artifact my dad videoed with the rover? Have you been able to translate that?"

"Yes, I was able to read it. Having a few weeks to work on Persepolis made this translation fairly easy. The language is very similar. First I would like to establish that you and I believe that both of the artifacts we have discovered are describing the Earth and not some other far away planet."

"You know Evan, I've been assuming that all along, but at this point, we don't have any actual proof. You know what can happen when you assume. I suppose we should keep an open mind about it until we know more."

"I think that's wise Amar. Before I get into that translation, I believe I have enough information to name Tom's discovery. It looks like a book etched into the surface of a large chunk of granite. An ancient manuscript in book form is referred to as a codex. So, we have a codex located in the Mare Imbrium. Logically, it follows that the name of this discovery is the Imbrium Codex. Do you like it?"

"I like it just fine. Let's go with that. Now, if you will quit teasing me, maybe we can get on with the translation?"

Evan chuckled, "Okay, already! Try not to get your knickers in a knot!" Evan pulled up Tom's video on his laptop. "You can see that the engraving shows the image of a book laying open with two pages visible. Unfortunately, there is not a lot of information on those two pages. Look at the symbol we now know so well. In a way, it is both a symbol and a map. The text says that the Ularian sun takes another star as its partner and revolves around it in approximately 24,000 of our solar years. The double oval symbol is actually a map showing what is known in astronomy as a binary orbit. It's also a clock.

"In order to understand what that means, let's have a little astronomy lesson. In 1543, Copernicus established that the planets in our solar system revolve around the sun. The heliocentric model, as it is called, has been proven over the intervening years to be correct."

"Everybody knows that now, except maybe the flat earth guys," Amar quipped.

Evan smiled knowingly, "It wasn't until the late 1800's that we were able to view the first pictures of another galaxy. That was a spiral galaxy named Andromeda. It wasn't until the launch of the Hubble Space Telescope in 1990 that we began to understand how many types of galaxies there are in the universe. Subsequent measurements have determined that our galaxy, the Milky Way, is also a spiral galaxy very much like Andromeda. You realize that our galaxy is so large we haven't been able to send a camera far enough away to look back at it?"

Amar noted, "That's right, I know from my dad's work that the farthest manmade object from Earth is Voyager 1 which is only now leaving our solar system. There's some information about that in the museum."

"That's true. So our conclusions about our own galaxy are not based upon a visual image from afar but upon astronomical measurements. What we do know about our galaxy is that it has approximately 200 billion stars in it that seem to rotate around a luminous galactic core in about 240 million years.

For a long time, we thought that the stars were all rotating around galactic center in unison, and that's why they seem to stay in the same place relative to each other in the night sky. But then there's this pesky thing called the precession of the equinoxes where the equinoctial points move backward around the Zodiac at the rate of 1 degree every seventy-two years. This phenomenon is not well known because it moves so slowly. You can't see it with the naked eye. One system of thought concludes that the precession of the equinoxes is caused by a wobble in the Earth's axis.

The translation of the codex refutes that idea. It specifically says that the precession of the equinoxes is caused by the Ularian sun, together with its planets, orbiting around another sun, with its planets, in about 24,000 years. That's what is known as a binary orbit and is what the double oval symbol represents. In addition, the text claims that the symbol is also a clock. The little dots on each oval represent the relative positions of each solar system."

"I've never heard of a binary orbit before, and how does it work as a clock? How can an engraving on granite change like a clock with the passage of time?" Amar asked.

"Here's where it gets really interesting. Apparently, the long axis of our elliptical orbit faces toward galactic center. For half of the orbit, or 12,000 years, our solar system approaches the center of the galaxy. Then for 12,000 years, we speed away from the center of the galaxy. The translation says that the luminous galactic center is inhabited by conscious beings who radiate the intelligence that manifests the natural world kind of like a radio broadcast.

Our movement toward galactic center causes human intelligence to evolve and its subsequent technology to accelerate. Our movement away from galactic center causes human intelligence and its technology to be forgotten. These are referred to as the ascending and descending cycles."

Amar sat up straight in his chair. "You're telling me that the luminous center of our galaxy is inhabited by conscious beings?"

"That's what the translation says. It's not such a big stretch when you consider that conscious beings are present in the region of the galaxy we live in. Our galaxy is a container for life. Why shouldn't we find life everywhere we look within it? I have no direct proof for that supposition, but it's fun to think about."

Amar pondered, "The codex says that the ebb and flow of consciousness, due to this binary orbit, is the cause of the rise and fall of civilizations, correct? The descending cycle would explain why we have evidence of previous advanced civilizations, but no knowledge of what happened to them. We just forgot our own history?"

"So it would seem" Evan replied.

"What else does it say?"

"I don't have an answer for how the binary orbit symbol engraved on granite could change over time. I'm not sure how the clock works. Unfortunately, that's all the two pages of the codex says."

Amar was beginning to pace around the room. "There has to be more, Evan. There just has to be. Maybe it's on the backside of the monolith. I know in my bones that the Earth and Ularia are one and the same. This is our story. I want to know the whole story. We've got to get this rover fixed!"

Amar pressed the intercom button on what was now his desk. "Jan, can you get Robby Harris for me?"

A few minutes later, Robby's gaunt face came on screen.

"Robby, you look tired," Amar said.

"So do you boss. I guess we're all working overtime. What can I do for you?"

"Robby, I'd like to have your assessment of the damage that was done to the rover control system at the museum. We need to get Lunokhod 1 up and running. It's critical."

"I was down there yesterday, boss. Both the original Russian computer, and our modern processor were damaged beyond our capability to repair. Our processor will be easy to replace. The Russian computer is another matter. We'll have to see if we can find one over there. I have no idea how to go about that."

Amar's gaze swept across all of the file box contents spread around on the office floor. "I might have an idea about how to do that. I'll let you know. While I have you, there is another task I need you to focus on. Our satellites have a surveillance capability, don't they?"

"Yep, that's how Tom was able to see what was going on during an extraction. That's how he knew where you and Evan were in Iran."

"Robby, can the satellites be programmed to look for something specific, like architectural or geologic features?"

"Yes, boss, no problem, we can do that."

"Okay, great. I'm going to send you a file containing a batch of photos from Persepolis, and I want you to search for them from space."

"What part of the planet are we looking at?"

"The whole planet, Robby. All of it." Amar declared.

CHAPTER THIRTY-SEVEN

Seattle

Evan and Amar spent the rest of the afternoon poring through every piece of paper that had come in Barsukov's file box. Amar kept returning to the working drawings for the MEM. Then he realized what he was looking at. Every drawing bore the name and signature of the MEM's designer, a Russian by the name of Nikolai Chubukin.

Amar didn't bother with the intercom. He just hollered, "Jan, I need Gary Renfro here as soon as possible."

Jan came into the office, so she didn't have to yell back. "That's a coincidence; he just pulled into the garage and is on his way up to his office."

"Please have him come here, first," Amar instructed.

Two minutes later, Renfro entered the room. "What's up boss? Jan said you wanted to see me?"

"Gary, I need you to find someone for me. In Russia."

Amar explained what he was after. "This guy might be the only person on the planet who can get the rover up and working again."

"No worries, boss, I have contacts in Moscow. Shouldn't be a problem. It's the middle of the night over there, so it will be a few more hours before I can make the calls. I'll stay late tonight and get them up at dawn. If this guy can be found, I'll have some information for you in the morning."

"Okay great. In the meantime, let's bring you up-to-date on the translations."

Renfro was waiting in the outer office, drinking coffee and chatting with Jan Meyer, when Amar arrived the following morning. He seemed a little more cheerful, having gotten his first decent night's sleep since his father's passing. Jan Meyer was her normally flawless self. Gary looked quite disheveled.

"Good morning, you two. Gary, did you sleep in your clothes?"

Renfro made a face. "I haven't gone to bed yet, boss."

"That must mean you have information. Were you able to locate Chubukin?"

Renfro pulled a small notebook from his shirt pocket and flipped it open. "Yes, I was. Here's the lowdown on him. Nikolai Chubukin is seventy-three years old. He lives with his daughter Katya, in a small town about a half hour to the southwest of Moscow called Peredelkino. Nikolai was employed by the Russian version of NASA in the 1970s. He is a machinist by trade but is also known as a mechanical genius. He was the man in charge of the design and fabrication of both Lunokhod 1 and Lunokhod 2. As you know, he also designed, and I believe, fabricated the mission extender module that Tom used to fire up the rover.

After the robotic missions to the moon, Chubukin had a brilliant career in front of him. But, when his wife, Jumaana, died in 1983, he lost his way and became a functioning alcoholic. It was mostly downhill from there. He was reassigned as an aircraft mechanic, finally retiring in 2010.

The daughter, Katya, is thirty-nine years old. She was raised by the grandparents until her 16th birthday. It seems that she was quite exotic looking, being a combination of white Russian and dark-skinned Kazakhi. She had trained as a gymnast in her youth. Her beauty on the mat was noted by the hierarchy, and she was recruited for the FSB's sparrow program in 1995. You know what the sparrow program was?"

Amar did not. "Never heard of it, Gary."

"The sparrows were good-looking women who were trained to use their femininity as a weapon. They would use sex to compromise a foreign dignitary or spy and then blackmail him into becoming an intelligence asset for mother Russia."

"Oh, right," Amar said. "I think there was a movie about that recently."

Renfro continued, "Katya served with distinction until 2010 when one of her missions went bad, and she took a bullet to her right leg. The scar was not repairable, and she ended up walking with a slight limp. She could no longer play the part, and her career ended with distinction. Both she and Nicolai were put out to pasture at about the same time. They now live together in a modest dacha in Peredelkino, which is southwest of Moscow. Nicolai does not speak English; Katya does, having learned it at the sparrow school. Here is her phone number."

"Gary, how the hell can you know all of that?" Amar asked.

"Never underestimate the value of business contacts, boss. Also, we just happen to be the ones who built the cell phone system that Katya uses. We have people in the area."

With both Jan Meyer and Gary Renfro in the room, Amar made the call.

Peredelkino, Russia

It was eight o'clock in the evening when Katya's phone rang. Noting that the phone number of the calling party was from the United States, Katya answered in English.

"This is Katya; who is calling, please?"

"Katya, my name is Amar Parish. My father was Tom Parish, chairman of the board of Parish Communications International. I am very interested in talking to your father. I believe his name is Nikolai—is that correct?"

"That is correct, Mr. Parish. His English is not very good. Why do you want to talk with him?"

"My father was instrumental in placing men on the moon during the American Apollo missions. He also purchased the rights to Lunokhod 1 and has the original mock-up on display in his museum in Seattle. I understand that your father was the man who actually built the rover?"

Katya had heard the stories about the Lunokhod rovers since she was a toddler. She was used to dealing with high-level businessmen, but slightly puzzled as to who this man could be.

"Yes, that is correct. Papa was in charge of both the design and fabrication of the two spacecraft. Why do you want to talk to him?"

"My father was recently killed in the museum..."

Katya remembered, "Oh yes, we saw that on the news recently. His death was noticed here in Russia due to his relationship with our lunar rover. I'm sorry for your loss. I apologize for interrupting you; please continue."

"As I was saying, my father was killed at the museum. Just before he died, he was actually able to revive the rover using something called a mission extender module. He was able to use the module's cameras to take some live pictures from the moon. Unfortunately, the antique Russian computer that controls the rover was damaged by gunfire. I was hoping I might be able to hire your father to come to the United States and help put the system back together."

"You have live pictures taken from my father's spacecraft after almost fifty years?"

"I do. Can your phone accept a text message?"

"Of course, it's an iPhone X," she said, being well aware that most Americans thought Russia was technologically backward.

"Ok, hold for a second, and I'll send you some photos."

Amar fiddled with his phone and sent images of the Lunokhod 1 display and the damaged control room in the museum. Then he sent the 3.6-second video the rover had taken.

Katya received the photos. "I recognize the spacecraft, but what is the object in the video?"

"That is what I need Nikolai's help to find out."

"Just a minute," Katya said. She turned to her father who was sitting on a sofa in the living room. Amar could hear her speaking in rapid-fire Russian. Niki jumped to his feet and grabbed the phone from Katya. He looked over the images. His reply was equally frenetic.

"Mr. Parish, he says that he always knew the mission extender module would work. He just didn't think the test would happen after so many years. He also says that the strange object on the moon is what he saw in the control room, for only one second, on the last day that Lunokhod 1 remained in operation. That was in 1971! He is very eager to know what he can do for you!"

"Please tell him that the rover appears to be drivable. But I need a replacement computer to control it. I need to know if he can find that replacement computer. Also, I would like to bring you both to America to help us revive the spacecraft and find out exactly what the object is. This could be one of the greatest discoveries in the history of mankind."

"We are not wealthy people, Mr. Parish. What do you propose?"

"I will fly to Moscow in my private plane. I will take care of the visas and all of the paperwork. I will pay both you and your father a generous fee for helping me along with all of your expenses. I will return you to your home when we are done. What do you say, will you come?"

"One moment," Katya said. Amar heard more rapid Russian in the background before Katya returned to the phone. "We would be pleased to come to America, Mr. Parish."

"Okay, Katya, I will make the arrangements and call you back. In the meantime, perhaps Nikolai can see if he can locate a replacement for the computer."

"He says he will do his best."

"Thank you, Katya; I look forward to meeting you."

"So do I Mr. Parish." She hung up.

Amar laid down his phone. Jan Meyer was flipping through her Rolodex. Before he could speak, she beat him to the punch. "Let's see, flight plan to Moscow, and visas for all parties both coming and going. Anything else, Mr. Chairman?"

"Nope, not for you, Jan. But Gary, will the Russian computer fit into the cargo hold in the Citation? Maybe we should take the old one with us. If we can't find another one, maybe they can fix it."

"I'm on it, boss," Gary said.

CHAPTER THIRTY-EIGHT

Peredelkino, Russia

The first leg of the flight from New York to Reykjavik was uneventful. The sky over the Atlantic had been clear at 45,000 feet. Ted Lockhart refueled the plane while everybody else took a breakfast break. The second leg took them into Moscow. The Citation touched down at Vnukovo International Airport on the southwest side of Moscow at 10:30 a.m. local time. Amar Parish, Dr. Evan Chatterjee, and Gary Renfro cleared customs by 11:00 a.m. Jan had done a masterful job acquiring the visas quickly. The original Russian computer from the Parish Museum wouldn't fit through the cargo hatch door. One of the forward seats was removed and the computer, the size of a small chest freezer, was strapped in its place inside the passenger cabin. The computer and the pilots remained on board waiting to hear what the boss wanted to do. The sky was gray, a drizzle wetting the pavement.

Evan, the only one who spoke Russian and the only one who could read the road signs, drove the rental car to the modest dacha on Derevnya Street in the small town of Peredelkino. Amar took the lead as the three men entered through a garden gate and filed up the flagstone walk to #26. Amar knocked on the door. It swung open, and he came face to face with Katya Chubukin.

Amar stared into dark almond-shaped eyes. For the second time in as many weeks, he felt a dizzying sense of familiarity. He shook it off. Katya was not surprised by his reaction. Many men had been struck speechless upon seeing her for the first time. That was, in fact, why she had been recruited for the Sparrow Program. She cocked her head to one side and paused, as if to say, "Come on, mister, find your tongue!"

She was five foot eight and about 125 pounds. Tight black denim jeans and a clingy velour top revealed an athlete's body with all of the proper attributes required of a sparrow agent. Renfro's intelligence was right on, as usual. She had shoulder-length black hair, slightly oriental eyes, and cafe au lait skin. She wasn't just beautiful; she had a kind of presence he had never experienced in a woman before. The kind of presence that made you want to look and keep on looking.

Amar regained his composure and offered his hand. "Katya, I'm Amar Parish, and these are my colleagues, Dr. Evan Chatterjee and Gary Renfro. It's very nice to meet you."

She was thoroughly gracious. "It is very nice to meet all of you, as well. Won't you please come in? You are all getting wet."

Nikolai Chubukin raised himself from his recliner and came forward to shake hands all around. The four men sat down.

Nikolai spoke, and Katya translated. "He says, you can call me Niki; everyone does." Katya offered, "Some tea, perhaps?"

Everyone nodded approval. Both Amar and Renfro noticed a slight limp as she walked into the kitchen. Evan began conversing with Niki in Russian. Amar got up and followed Katya into the kitchen.

"Can I help?" he inquired.

She turned away from the counter and locked eyes with him. At once, the dizzy feeling came back.

"Have we met before?" she asked. "Somehow, you seem familiar to me."

Amar liked what he saw but was not tempted to exhibit his usual ladies' man routine. He could tell that this woman was not the kind you trifled with. It was difficult to maintain eye contact with her. He felt that those deep dark eyes were looking right through him. He had a sense that no matter what he said, she would be able to extract his most hidden motivations. Authenticity was the only option.

Amar delivered an offhanded compliment. "Uh, no, I don't think we have met before. I would have remembered, for sure."

She smiled, "I think you are right. I would have remembered, as well. You can take the tray."

Once everyone was seated and sipping their tea, Amar nodded to Evan to begin. Evan removed a thick sheaf of eight-by-ten glossy photographs from his shoulder bag and began narrating in Russian for Niki's benefit. He outlined how Tom had bought the rover at Sotheby's. He showed photos of the restored mock-up and the damaged control panel at the museum. He showed Niki photographs of the working drawings for the MEM.

Niki asked, "Those are my drawings; where did you get this information?"

"A man named Barsukov came forward, and Mr. Parish bought these files from him," Evan replied.

Niki recounted the story of Koslov doing work outside of channels and how he had been sent away. "Anatoly told me that he destroyed all evidence of the MEM. That's why there has never been any official mention of the module. We covered it up to save our skins. How is he? He was my roommate for many years."

"He died in the United States from prostate cancer in 2009."

Niki paused for a moment to take that in.

Evan laid down an enlarged still photo of the Imbrium Codex taken by Lunokhod 1 and continued, "Just before he died, Mr. Parish was able to photograph this artifact on the moon."

Niki scooped up the photo and stared at it for a long minute. His eyes bore the glassy look of someone receding into the past. "I've been looking at the smaller image from Katya's phone. I remember this. The main camera swept across it as that idiot, Evginy, drove the rover over the side of a crater. He and I were the only ones to see it. But then the rover's batteries died, and that was it, until now. Tell me, what is that thing?"

Evan summarized the finding, "We believe the monolith is approximately 12,000 years old and that it was put there by an ancient civilization that flourished on the Earth at the time. It's a message for mankind. We also believe there may be more information, perhaps on the back side of it. We want to revive the rover again, if possible, to investigate. We want you to help us do that."

Niki placed a hand over his heart, "You must excuse me; this is more excitement than I've had in quite a while."

Amar and Renfro sat quietly while Evan, Niki, and Katya rattled away in Russian.

Amar shifted in his seat, finally interrupting, "Evan, can he help us with the computer?"

Evan smiled at Katya, who also understood both parts of the conversation. "Be patient, Amar. I was just about to ask him that."

Niki said, "I have looked for another computer, and as far as I can tell there is nothing available. However, I may have found something better."

"Oh? What would that be?" Evan asked.

"I found the man who built the original computer. His name is Boris Yakov. He is a little older than I am, and he still lives here in Moscow. Katya texted the photos of the control panel to him. He says he has boxes of old analog vacuum tubes and computer parts. He may be able to repair it."

Evan grinned and nodded at Amar. He told Niki, "We wondered if repairs were an option, so we brought the original computer with us. It's on the plane. Can he come look at it? The plane is over at Vnukovo Airport."

Niki asked Katya to call Yakov and see if he could come. She dialed and spoke to Yakov. She addressed the three Americans, "He can come this afternoon if you like. He wants to know if you will pay him?"

That was Amar's department. "Tell him five hundred dollars U.S. to come and see and five thousand U.S. if he can fix it. I have Euros if he prefers them."

Katya told him and nodded his approval.

Renfro cut in, "Tell him we may not be able to take the computer off of the airplane without getting all tied up in customs. Can he bring what he needs with him?"

Katya told Yakov, who indicated that no guarantees could be made, but he would bring what he thought might be needed and would be there at 2:30 this afternoon.

Renfro indicated that the jet was at the Jet Aviation FBO at Vnukovo and gave Katya the tail number. Amar called Ted Lockhart to let him know what was happening. Ted and Jason had been napping in preparation for the return flight. Lockhart noted that he would make arrangements with the FBO to allow Yakov access to the ramp. In the meantime, Amar offered to take everyone to lunch at the Grenki Pub over at the airport.

Yakov arrived at the Citation in a UAZ 452 utility van at 2:45 p.m. He was a short man, slightly overweight with a wild gray beard. After all of the introductions, everyone filed into the cabin and took a seat. Both Niki and Katya expressed their admiration for the opulence of the jet's interior. Yakov entered the cabin carrying a briefcase tool kit. One bullet had penetrated the Russian computer, exiting out the back side. The second one had blasted a hole in the modern PC, which Robby Harris was in the process of replacing.

Yakov smiled, stroking the top of the computer, as if he was greeting a very old friend. He removed the case and probed around in the innards of the device. He narrated his findings to Katya and Niki over his shoulder. "The bullet entered the case here and plowed a furrow through all of these vacuum tubes and circuit boards exiting through the back over here." The diagnosis was positive. "The computer's chassis has been spared. The mechanical hard drive is intact. I believe I have all of the components that will be needed in the van. I can't fix the bullet holes in the case, though."

Katya relayed the information. Nobody cared about the bullet holes.

Yakov turned and faced Katya directly, "Ask the pilots if they can have an extension cord run out here from the FBO. I wouldn't want to take a chance plugging this thing into the airplane's electrical system when it comes time to test it."

He set about vacuuming out the broken shards of glass and disconnecting the antique circuit boards to be replaced. Two hours later, he was finished. Yakov plugged the computer into the extension cord and pushed the start button. The computer whirred to life as a green indicator light came on. He probed some more with an ohm meter and was satisfied. He reinstalled the case.

While packing up his tools, he spoke to Katya and Niki, "I think all will be well."

Evan looked at Amar and Renfro. "It's fixed!" he said. Renfro held up the high five, and Amar slapped back.

Amar pulled a silver Vanguard briefcase from an overhead compartment next to the galley. "Katya, will you ask him if he wants dollars or Euros?"

He says, "Euros would be preferable."

Amar counted out eleven 500 Euro notes, not caring about the exchange rate. Yakov grinned and shook his hand. 5,500 Euros was about six months' salary for him. That was the most money he'd ever made in an afternoon in his whole life. Amar stood in the jet's doorway while Yakov climbed into his van, smiling and waving as he departed. He turned and walked back to the group immediately noticing that Niki's countenance had turned gloomy.

"Is Niki alright?"

Katya hadn't noticed her father's change in demeanor until she faced him. "Papa, are you okay?"

Niki replied wistfully, "Now that the computer is fixed, what do they need me for?"

Both Katya and Evan relayed Niki's concern to Amar at the same time.

Amar shook his head, "Tell him not to worry. I need him to teach me how to drive the damn thing! Tell him we are all going to America, and then we're going for a drive on the moon!"

CHAPTER THIRTY-NINE

Moscow

Amar Parish was getting used to being in charge. "Here's what I'd like to do. Evan and I will take Katya and Niki back home so they can pack their bags. We'll all return here to the airport hotel and stay the night so the pilots can rest. Let's be wheels up first thing in the morning. When we get to New York, I can put Katya and Niki up at my place. Evan can stay at his apartment, and I will have Jan book hotel rooms for Gary and the pilots. The following morning, we'll head for Seattle.

He called Jan Meyer on his Greenstone phone. "Jan, I need hotel rooms for seven people at Vnukovo airport just for tonight. I'll need three hotel rooms in New York for tomorrow night for Renfro and the pilots. Evan can stay at his place, and I have two guest rooms at my apartment for Katya and Niki. We'll be back in the office the day after tomorrow. What's going on around the office that needs my attention?"

Jan replied, "Nothing that can't wait until you return, except Mr. Warburg has been trying to reach you."

"Tell him I'm in Russia; he can wait along with everyone else. I'll talk to you tomorrow."

They all checked into the Vnukovo DoubleTree Hotel at the refreshing price of $80.00 per room. Everyone gathered for dinner at the Legends restaurant. With Katya translating, Niki took up most of the dinner with tales of the Soviet Space Program. Amar, Evan, and Gary agreed beforehand not to question Katya about her job in the FSB. They were unsure how she would react to the fact that they knew her history as well as her father's. Everyone was back in their rooms by 10:00 p.m., preparing for an early departure. Katya couldn't sleep. At 1:15 a.m. she was sitting at the bar in the Sky Lounge. She had already turned two different men away.

"You couldn't sleep either?"

She looked up from her drink. Amar was standing next to her, appreciating the highlights in her dark hair.

She motioned for him to take a seat. "I guess it is all of the excitement," she said. "What keeps you from your sleep?"

"Same thing. I'm so glad you and Niki are available to come to Seattle and help us out. I can't wait to see if the computer will work." Amar ordered a scotch and soda for himself and sat there with his forearms on the bar, both hands wrapped around the glass.

"Me too. I've never been to America. Niki has always wanted to go, but we've never had a reason or enough money for that matter. Russian pensions are not exactly luxurious."

She placed a hand on his arm. He hoped she hadn't noticed the goosebumps that were forming there. He'd been with lots of beautiful women in his life, but he had never experienced the kind of energy that seemed to radiate from her. He couldn't even come up with a word to describe it. The feeling was completely new to him. He didn't want to describe it. He just wanted to feel what it was.

"So, tell me about yourself, Mr. Amar Parish. Have you traveled much?"

"I was fortunate to be the son of a self-made man. My childhood wasn't that much different from what any only child, born into a wealthy American family, would have experienced. I never really thought about being wealthy. I've always known there would be enough for whatever I wanted to do and so I just focused on my interests. I'm not sure why, but for as long as I can remember I've been obsessed with human history. As a child, it was the Revolutionary War period of American history. It was a fascinating time during which the founding fathers really strained themselves, trying to come up with a plan for the new country based upon individual freedom.

"I couldn't get enough of it. I read all of the books. Fortunately, my father's wealth allowed me to tour our country and see as many of the historical sites as I wanted. I studied the philosophies of the founding fathers and their fight for freedom. I thought they were brilliant.

"In my teens, I expanded my inquiry to include world history. I'm still obsessed with it. I've been to archaeological sites on every continent. For the last ten years or so, I've been working on the theory that modern civilization is not the most advanced culture ever to inhabit our planet. It seems that we have uncovered irrefutable evidence that my theory is true."

"That must be very exciting for you. Will you publish your findings?"

Amar had often wondered why the subject of previous advanced cultures didn't immediately inspire and excite his listeners the way it inspired him.

"Truthfully, I haven't thought that far ahead. We'll figure it out as we go. Will you tell me about yourself?"

"There is not much to tell. I was raised, mostly by my grandparents, in Tyuratam, Kazakhstan. That is where Russia launches its spacecraft. Both my grandfather and Niki worked in a machine shop for the space program. Niki was well-known as a child prodigy in the workshop. Before I was born, he was assigned to go to Moscow to work in the lunar robotics division of NPO Lavochkin, kind of like your NASA, I think."

Katya frowned a little as if she was telling a painful tale.

"Niki and my mother had a long distance relationship. He was only able to see her when he had leave. The government promised Niki that he could have housing for us in Moscow, but they never delivered on their promise. My mother died in Tyuratam when I was four years old, so I never really knew her well. My grandparents took over from there. I was a normal schoolgirl with schoolgirl interests.

"When I was sixteen, I was recruited to work for the government. I was good at my job and stayed in that post for twenty-one years. I was injured on the job three years ago and am now retired. You may have noticed I walk with a bit of a limp."

"I did notice that. Does it hurt?"

"No, I'm not in pain. The wound healed some time ago. I have regained a full range of motion, but the muscles are still a little stiff."

"Where did you learn to speak English so well?" Amar asked.

"It was a requirement at the government school."

"And what keeps you busy these days?"

"Mostly, I just take care of my father, who needs me. Like a lot of Russian men, he is a functioning alcoholic."

"I'm sorry, Katya, I didn't know that."

"Don't mistake what I say, Amar. Niki is a good man, a great man, some say. He accomplished a lot for mother Russia and deserves to be taken care of."

Amar tried to sound casual, "I understand. Is there any other man in your life?"

Katya smiled, "No, not at the moment. But that is a very long story; maybe I will tell you someday."

The bartender leaned over and mentioned that it was 2:00 a.m., and the bar would be closing. Amar paid the bill and left a generous tip. All of their rooms were on the same floor. He walked Katya back to hers. She swiped her key card and opening the door a little. She turned and faced him in the doorway.

She grinned, "Good night, Mr. American Big Shot. I will see you in the morning."

Amar grinned back, "Good night, Katya, I will definitely see you in the morning."

CHAPTER FORTY

Moscow and New York

After having breakfast at the Legends restaurant, the entire group went through customs and gathered at the plane. Katya had flown in private jets before as a part of her job. Niki had not. Ted Lockhart filed a flight plan for Reykjavik. The plane was fueled, and the pre-flight inspection completed. Jason Hall loaded their baggage and made sure everyone was buckled in. The Citation left the runway at 7:30 a.m. local time.

At 44,000 feet, the air was clear and smooth. They were well above the weather. The first leg to Reykjavik took only three hours. Everyone stayed on board while Ted had the plane refueled.

They arrived at La Guardia at 4:00 in the afternoon. Everyone went their separate ways promising to be back at the FBO first thing in the morning for the flight to Seattle.

Amar unlocked the door to his three-bedroom, two-bath, second-floor apartment on East 43rd Street and held it open for Katya and Niki.

"It's not all that fancy, but it's home," he said. "Niki, you will be in this room and Katya over here."

Niki pulled his suitcase into the bedroom and then disappeared into the hall bathroom.

Amar took the opportunity to question Katya, "Can I offer him a drink? Is that appropriate?"

"Oh, sure. He is very disciplined. He will have two or three drinks, and then he will go to bed early. I can see that he is fatigued. What would you like to do for dinner?"

"I'm tired of restaurant food. I thought we could eat here. I asked my housekeeper, Marta, to stock the refrigerator for one night. Let's see what she left."

Amar opened the refrigerator and pulled out a freshly made spinach, cheese, and sausage casserole. "Looks like Marta left us enough vegetables for a salad, as well." Amar put the casserole in the oven to heat.

"That looks delicious," Katya said. "If you give me the tools, I will make the salad."

Niki reappeared and seated himself at the breakfast bar.

"Something to drink, Niki?" Amar asked. Katya translated.

"Da, vodka on rocks, please," Niki replied in limited English.

Amar rooted around in his liquor cabinet and came out with a bottle of Grey Goose and an everyday Chateau Vieux Poirer Bordeaux for himself and Katya. Niki approved. So did Katya.

She stood at the kitchen island chopping vegetables on a wooden cutting board. Every time Amar walked behind her, he felt as if he was passing through some sort of force field that caused involuntary ripples in his skin, a very pleasant feeling.

They sat down to dinner. The casserole was delicious. Marta acted like a mother hen in the building, looking after the needs of several tenants who traveled on business.

"Niki, do you anticipate any problems reinstalling the computer?"

Katya replied, "He says he is not much of a computer expert, but if you had it hooked up before, reconnecting it shouldn't be a problem. He wants to know if you have a computer person at your museum?"

"I do. He works at SatCom in Everett. SatCom is where we control the Greenstone satellite system. He will be available to us if we need him."

They talked about the rover. How amazing that it should still function after all of these years. What was this thing they were calling the Imbrium Codex? What did it say? Amar explained what he knew so far. After consuming his third vodka, Niki excused himself and retired for the night. Amar and Katya finished the dishes and sat on the living room sofa in front of the gas fireplace. He poured the last of the wine. Sirens wailed in the distance. Traffic could be heard in the street below.

"It is very noisy here," Katya noted, kicking off her shoes. She leaned back on the armrest.

"Yes, I suppose that's just New York. It's a very busy place."

She tucked both feet under his thigh. "Do you mind? My feet get cold sometimes."

"No, I do not mind." He turned toward her until their eyes met. He struggled to maintain eye contact.

What an extraordinary woman. She was very attractive, but there was so much more to her than that. Was she being forward, or was she just comfortable around strangers? He didn't have a clue. Looking into her eyes was unlike anything he had ever experienced in the company of a woman. Even though they had just met, he felt as if she knew everything there was to know about him. It was unsettling to say the least.

He looked away, lest his most lascivious thoughts be exposed without saying a word. There were aspects of her presence that were wholly new to him. He was possessed by a deep level of respect that was unfamiliar. It was as if they had been through lifetimes of trials and challenges together, and each of them had proved their undying loyalty to the other.

It wasn't that he lacked respect for Kelly Bates or the other women he'd been involved with, but this was something very different. This was the kind of bond two people who had survived a war together would share. He was deeply attracted to her. If a move were to be made, she would have to make it. He would do nothing to screw this up.

They sat in silence for a while, staring into the flames. Finally, she reached out, took his hand, and held it.

"It's alright," she said.

"Yes, it is alright," he replied, without being completely sure of what she meant. He was sure of what he meant.

Attractive little creases formed on either side of her mouth as she grinned at him. "So, Mr. American Big Shot, we will rise at the crack of dawn and get into your fancy airplane one more time!"

He laughed, "Yes, we will. Well, maybe not the crack of dawn. You know, I never wanted to be a big shot; it just happened."

"Sometimes the world demands that we play a role we never anticipated. When that comes into our lives unbidden, it should be looked at as divine intervention. The key is to accept it with dignity and to do the best we can. If you can do that, your destiny will be revealed. Now, I am tired and must go to bed."

She untucked her feet, leaving a warm spot under his thigh. She rose from the sofa, put on her shoes, and leaned over kissing him on the cheek.

"Good night, Mr. Amar Parish." She closed the bedroom door gently behind her.

Amar remained on the sofa puzzling over what she'd said about destiny.

CHAPTER FORTY-ONE

Seattle

They touched down at Boeing Field late the following morning. Amar's Land Rover and Renfro's pickup were still in the hangar. Amar and Gary loaded the computer into the back of Gary's truck. It was a short hop across the street to the museum. There were several cars in the parking lot, and the museum was open for business. Renfro backed his truck up to the loading dock. Guilford's two assistants helped him unload the machine into the museum's warehouse. Amar, Evan, Niki, and Katya went in through the front door. Trevor Guilford was waiting for them inside. Introductions were made.

Trevor took the lead, "I suspect you will want to install the computer right away, so I took the liberty of asking Robby Harris to come down from SatCom. He should be here within the hour. In the meantime, would your guests like to tour the museum?"

Yes, they would. Trevor followed the same path through the history of communications that was dictated for the public. Niki and Katya kept up a dialogue in Russian through the displays on Morse, Marconi, Bell, Edison, and Tesla. When they walked into the room displaying the capsules and space suits from the Apollo missions, Niki was silent for a moment as if he were standing in front of the holy grail of the space race.

Finally, he spoke. Evan picked up the translation. "He says he didn't know the Apollo capsule would be so small."

Evan replied in Russian, "When I saw Lunokhod 1, I had the opposite reaction. I didn't know it would be so big!"

Niki laughed, "It is here? Can we see it?"

Evan pointed to the next doorway. "It's right through there, Nikolai."

Trevor had installed a drape over the damaged control panel, but the mock-up of Lunokhod 1 sat on its turntable under the spotlights. Niki approached slowly, with tears in his eyes. The rover had been cleaned and polished to a state that rivaled the condition of the original before it left the clean room to be mounted on the Proton K launch vehicle.

Niki asked Evan, "Can I touch it?"

Evan relayed the request to Trevor who reached behind a drape and threw the switch that stopped the turntable.

Evan said, "Under the circumstances, that would be entirely appropriate." Amar pulled out his phone and snapped a bunch of pictures as Niki mounted the turntable. The tears coursed down his cheeks as he gently passed his hands over the machine.

In a low and hesitant voice, he said, "I built this you know, almost fifty years ago." He motioned to Amar and Katya to come up. They each took a position on either side of the great craftsman while Evan snapped more pictures of the event.

Niki leaned down and whispered in Katya's ear, "I wish your mother was here to see this."

She squeezed his hand. "So do I, papa. So do I."

Robby Harris arrived at the museum moments later. He was carrying a new PC, which wasn't anything special. The original Russian computer was used to control the rover's drive train and cameras. The test equipment on board the original rover had been controlled by another computer that Tom had never been able to acquire. It didn't matter, since no testing was on the agenda. In truth, a modern cell phone had vastly more calculating power than the original consoles that controlled Lunokhod 1. The purpose of the new PC was to interface between the MEM's cameras and the modern video recording equipment.

Once again, introductions were made. It was closing time, and Trevor made sure the last visitors were out of the building before locking the doors. The two assistants brought the Russian computer in on a four-wheeled dolly. It still had a bullet hole in it and didn't look any different to Robby. He asked about what had been done, and Amar relayed the story about the repairs Boris Yakov made in Moscow.

Robby was a little skeptical. "Well, let's get all of this hooked up and see what we have."

Robby and Niki went to work assembling the equipment. Pizza at the museum was beginning to be a tradition. Trevor called for it, but Renfro answered the door, the Wilson Combat .45 at the ready under his jacket. It was just the pizza guy, no more. Everybody sat around one of the tables in the museum's workshop eating, while Niki and Robby worked on the control room equipment.

An hour later, everything was in place, and Niki and Robby came in for some pizza, reheated in the workshop's microwave.

"I guess I forgot to tell you something critical, Amar," Robby said. "Our communication with the rover is by line of sight. That means that the moon must be visible over Seattle for radio communication to be possible. Since the rover's cameras have no lighting system, the moon will need to be nearly full, so we have sunlight on the Codex. If we turn it on now, all we will see is black."

Not being up-to-date on the phases of the moon, Amar asked, "and when will that be Robby?"

It's been twenty-six days since Tom and I fired the rover up for the first time. The next opportunity will be the day after tomorrow around 10:00 p.m."

Amar was disappointed. He was ready to drive on the moon right now. Robby made a show out of removing his laptop from its case. He turned it on.

"In the meantime," he said. "I have something else that will interest you. We have a hit on the location of Vandalay."

"You do? When? How?"

"I programmed the search criteria you gave me from Persepolis into the satellite system. We don't have full coverage of the earth at all times, so it took a while to retask some of the birds to cover the globe. This video image came in this morning. Robby hit enter and what was obviously a satellite image zoomed in over the North Sea. The zoom stopped, and the image began to resolve. Robby hit another key, and a smaller photo appeared in the upper right corner of the screen. This is one of the photographs that Evan took at Persepolis. Remember the white zigzag pattern that was on the floor? You can see Evan's feet in the photo, too."

The larger image finished resolving. It showed what appeared to be a glacier, which was clearly melting. A huge lake of ice melt had formed on top of the glacier. Water was streaming out from its base. Sticking out from under the leading edge of the mammoth wall of ice was the same white zigzag pattern.

Amar pounded the table with his fist. "I knew it. Where the hell is this?"

Robby's answer consisted of one word. "Greenland," he said. "It's in Greenland, boss."

Robby zoomed back out a little. Everyone could see the east coast of Greenland as well as Iceland to the south. "It's here at the east end of a waterway called Nordvest Fjord, which is off of Scoresby Sound."

Amar was incredulous. "Damn, we practically flew right over that area yesterday afternoon!"

Katya was puzzled, "What is this Vandalay, did you say? What does it have to do with Greenland?"

With everything else going on, Amar and Evan had neglected to even mention the find at Persepolis to Niki and Katya. Evan brought out his shoulder bag and slid the photos onto the table.

Amar narrated, "Recently, Evan and I were summoned to the ancient ruins of the city of Persepolis in Iran. We were called there so Evan could help to translate some text that they found on the sides of a very old staircase. We excavated the stairway until we came to a doorway, which collapsed, revealing this underground chamber."

Amar nodded to Evan, who produced the photos from his shoulder bag.

Katya gasped at the beauty of the room. She pointed, "There is that same double oval symbol you found on the moon! What does it mean?"

"These images are from a very old city that was once the capital of our planet. It was called Vandalay. They referred to themselves as Ularians. My personal opinion is that their civilization was more technologically advanced that ours. Evan and I believe that the inhabitants of that city knew their civilization was going to be destroyed during the last ice age. We believe they placed the codex on the moon as a message to mankind." Amar had never put it quite like that before. Evan nodded his approval.

Amar went on, "We intend to find out who these people might have been and what their message to us is. Now, it seems, we may have found the location of the ruins of Vandalay. Gary, we need to go there. What's the best way to do that?"

"My first guess is by ship, boss. From these photos, there doesn't appear to be any kind of town within five hundred miles of this location."

"Actually, there's a small town of 450 people called Ittoqqortoormiit at the mouth of Scoresby Sound, but it's not like we can just stop in there and pick up whatever we need at the local big box store," said Robby. "I also think a ship is the right way to go, but if we don't go soon, that ship will need to be an ice breaker."

"Robby, can you zoom in?" Evan asked.

Robby played with the touch pad on his laptop. "The Greenstone Satellite cameras produce very high resolution images, so we can zoom in pretty close."

Amar commented, "The mountains are dramatic, but they look worn down, and there aren't any trees like we see in the chamber at Persepolis. How would you account for that, doctor?"

"Quite easily," Evan explained. "The one thing that could change a landscape that much would be a glacier. Perhaps a much deeper glacier than we see here, one that might have been formed during the last ice age. For all intents and purposes, Greenland is still in the middle of that ice age, though the people who measure such things are telling us that the ice cap is melting at an accelerated rate. That's probably why the white zigzag pattern hasn't been noticed before now. I suspect it has only recently become visible."

Amar stepped back into his role as chairman. "Gary, can you pull together the logistics for such an expedition in the next two days?"

Renfro looked up and to the left as if accessing a mental database. "I won't have all of the details, but I'm sure I'll be able to give you an overview of what's involved and when it can happen by then."

"Okay, great. Gary, if the three-bedroom apartment at the PCI warehouse is vacant, can we put Katya and Niki up there?"

Gary extracted his Greenstone phone from a vest pocket. "Yes, it is; I'll call ahead and make sure it's clean."

"Evan, will you be staying at the Fairmont?"

"I have reserved my usual suite, Amar. I'm quite well taken care of."

"If you like, I can drop you there on my way home," Trevor offered.

Amar turned to Katya. "We have a nice little apartment at the PCI warehouse, which is just across the street at Boeing Field. Gary and I will get you and Niki set up over there. I'll have my secretary, Jan Meyer, arrange to show you and Niki the sights around Seattle tomorrow."

"You are very kind, Amar. I would like to go there now, if possible, and freshen up before dinner," Katya said.

CHAPTER FORTY-TWO

Seattle

Amar drove Katya and Niki across the street to the warehouse located in an unremarkable cinder block building at the south end of Boeing Field. Renfro followed in his truck. Gary punched a code into a security keypad, and they entered the building to be greeted by Alice Turnbull, the sixty-five-year-old, somewhat wizened PCI den mother. Introductions were made. Alice maintained a presence in the building and looked after PCI's technicians and Greenstone Security's operators when they were in town.

Gary conducted a tour of the facility. The first floor of the building consisted of a large warehouse stuffed with cell phone tower equipment, switch gear, and other land-based cell phone equipment used in PCI's contract work around the world. The building also housed a locker room, kitchen, mission planning room, office, armory with a large gun vault, a gym, and an underground pistol range. The second floor had a three-bedroom, two-bath apartment for crew layovers, and a studio apartment where Alice lived. Katya took particular interest in the gym, which had the full complement of exercise machines as well as a boxing ring.

They went upstairs; Niki and Katya selected their rooms and dropped off their bags.

Katya translated for her father, "Niki would like to take a nap, but I would love to work out before dinner. Is that possible, Amar? Do you like to work out?"

"Sure, I'd like to work out as well," Amar said. "How about you, Gary?"

"It would be good to blow out some cobwebs. I'm in."

Alice announced, "Dinner will be ready in about an hour and a half; you have time to exercise if you want."

"Katya, change into your workout clothes, and we'll meet you in the gym," Renfro said.

Gary and Amar both had lockers downstairs. They changed and were warming up on two side-by-side elliptical machines when Katya came down. She wore a form-fitting black spandex pullover top, black yoga pants, and canvas gymnast slippers, her dark hair worn in a ponytail. The rpms of Amar's machine began to drop off immediately as he stared at her. She was very well-toned and really quite beautiful.

Katya slipped between the ropes of the boxing ring and did some stretching on the mat. After a ten-minute routine, she laid on her back and raised her legs over her head into a handstand. She walked across the mat on her hands and did a walk over onto her feet. She turned and took two bounds followed by a backflip. Amar and Renfro stood motionless on their machines. More than just beautiful, she moved with grace and expertise.

"Mister Gary, do you do the martial arts?" she asked.

"Huh, ah, yes, I do," Gary stumbled.

Katya picked up a rubber knife from a bench containing various training weapons and tossed it to him. "Then come to attack me, please."

Renfro was 190 pounds of solid muscle. He dismounted from his machine, turned to Amar and said under his breath, "I'll take it easy on her."

He climbed into the ring and squared up on his opponent. He approached her with the knife raised above his head and ready to strike. So quickly, the movement barely registered, Katya seized the wrist of his knife hand from underneath, pivoted inside his grasp, and did something Renfro had never seen before. It was a sort of a combination hip and arm throw with a certain kind of twist at the same time. His body went up and over her head, was turned upside down at the same time, and slammed into the mat with incredible force, the confiscated knife already at his throat. He lay there stunned, the air knocked out of his lungs.

She reached down and helped him to his feet. "Are you all right?" she asked.

Somewhat sheepishly he grunted, "What was that, and where did you learn it?"

"It is a Russian technique known as SAMBO. It stands for Samozashchita Bez Orvzhiya. You would say, self-defense without weapons. I was taught this during my time with the FSB. Do you wish to go again?"

"I think I'll take a break." With a malicious grin he said, "I'm sure Amar would like to try his luck."

Katya looked at Amar where he was standing like a stone statue. "Mr. American Big Shot, would you like to try to kill me?"

"I can't think of anything I'd rather not attempt to do more than that." He said. His only foray into martial arts was a short stint on the wrestling team in high school. Not wishing to be shown up so quickly, he offered, "Do you like to wrestle?"

She waived him into the ring, "I can wrestle; you can bring it on now, before I get too hungry." There was a glint of mischief in her eyes.

Amar squared off and made his move. He grabbed her right bicep with one hand and wrapped the other around the back of her neck. She gave a little hop, wrapped both of her legs around his thighs and squeezed hard. Both of his feet came together in a one-pointed stance and he toppled to his left landing on his hip. Somehow, she slipped behind him as he bounced and ended up underneath him. Her legs were wrapped around his torso, and she applied intense force, preventing his diaphragm from moving. She clamped a choke hold around this neck. Amar tapped the mat before he blacked out, and her grip was released.

His back was to her; she smelled like rose water. He lay there just a little longer than was quite appropriate. There wasn't an ounce of fat on her body. She didn't move but kept still. All of Amar's senses were screaming at him. Finally, she tousled his hair, "Are you going to get off of me, Amar?"

Reluctantly, he rolled off of her. "Sorry, you caught me off guard there."

Renfro could see that a dance was in progress. It made him want to fill the silence. "I suppose you can shoot as well? he asked.

"I love to shoot, Gary. Do you have a range here?"

He motioned toward a doorway in the side wall of the gym. "Right this way, ma'am." Renfro opened the side door, revealing a stairway that went down into a long skinny underground room. The walls, floor, and ceiling were solid concrete. Renfro flicked on a light switch.

In the foreground, were some steel lockers. Renfro punched a few numbers into a keypad, and one of the lockers popped open. He removed three Glock 19's, three sets of earmuffs, two boxes of 9mm cartridges and an UpLula speed loader and set them on the shooting position countertop. He mounted a man profile target on the cable slide and ran the target down in front of a steel bullet trap about forty feet away. He handed one of the guns to Katya and one to Amar.

"Katya, you go first," Amar said.

Katya counted fifteen cartridges onto the countertop and began methodically clicking them into the magazine using the loader. Renfro had observed beginners fumbling with the loading device which was awkward to use if you weren't familiar with how it worked. Katya clicked fifteen cartridges into place in about thirty seconds. She donned a pair of earmuffs, picked up the pistol, shoved the magazine home, racked the slide, took aim, and began firing. When the pistol slide locked open, Renfro reversed the target and brought it back in. Ten shots center mass, three shots in the head, and one in each hand.

"Why am I not surprised?" Renfro said. He mounted a new target, loaded his weapon, and reproduced Katya's pattern. He might be a little off of his game with respect to martial arts, but he made a point of keeping his shooting skills current.

Renfro looked at Katya."Do you want a job?"

She smiled, "What do you have in mind, Mr. Renfro?"

Renfro put a hand on Amar's shoulder. "I'm busy doing other things, and I need a bodyguard for the boss. From what I've seen here today, you are eminently qualified."

Katya grinned at Amar. "An interesting proposition. I will think upon it. Now you, Amar?"

Amar was way out of his depth in this company. He placed one hand behind his ear. "It's getting late—isn't that the dinner bell? We should go, we don't want to irritate Alice!"

Renfro laughed while stuffing the equipment back into the locker. "If there is one thing that is universally true around here, it's that you do not want to irritate Alice!"

Renfro begged off, preferring to have dinner at home with his family. Alice made a mouthwatering chicken pot pie for the four of them. Nikolai, somewhat revived from his nap, had managed to find the liquor cabinet and was already into his first vodka and tonic.

Katya instructed him in Russian, "Papa, you must pace yourself. It has been a long trip, and I can see you are still tired. No more than three drinks tonight."

Niki replied in broken English, "Da, okay, three only."

The four of them engaged in light conversation until 8:00 p.m. Alice retired to her apartment to watch her favorite TV show, and Niki retired at the same time, having fully medicated himself with vodka. Katya and Amar seated themselves on the sofa in the living room facing each other. They both started to speak at the same time.

"Please, you go ahead," Amar said.

"I just wanted to tell you how much I appreciate what you are doing for my father. I haven't seen him this inspired in a very long time."

"He 's a remarkable man. So was my father. The things they both did during the space race are incredible, given the technology they had to work with."

"It's true, I have heard that my cell phone has more computing power than Lunkohod 1 or even the Apollo spacecraft, for that matter. To have men travel all that way to the moon and come home safely with such primitive equipment is really a miracle. Then to find the Imbrium Codex using papa's rover is an even bigger miracle. Do you think we will be able to drive on the moon again?"

Amar's face lit up. "Yes, I do. We'll know in two days' time. I can hardly wait!"

His passion for the quest he had undertaken was reflected in his boyish good looks.

Amar put his hand on her forearm. "There's something I've been meaning to ask you. I don't mean to be forward, but from the day we first met, I've felt like I have known you forever. Am I delusional, or do you feel it, too?"

She moved closer to him. "I was going to ask you the same thing. I don't know what this is between us." She smiled, "I was minding my own business at home, and all of a sudden, here comes Mr. American Big Shot, and then everything changed. Now here I am, halfway around the world. The strange thing is, I like being here, and I like being with you."

Sex hadn't been motivating for her in a very long time. That was one reason she was living with her father. That, and an inner need to take care of him. It wasn't that she abhorred sex, but once you've used sex professionally, it loses some of its luster. In order for her to enjoy it, there had to be something more involved, something much deeper than she had experienced in the past. She hadn't met the man who could fulfill that requirement, or perhaps now she had.

Amar couldn't stand it any longer. He placed both hands on either side of her face and kissed her long and tenderly. The kiss was returned with an open mouth. She rose and took him by the hand lapsing into Russian, "idite za mnoy dorogoy." (Come with me, darling.)

Leading him into the bedroom, she closed the door. She backed him up to the bed and pushed him down into a sitting position. Reaching behind him, she pulled his shirt up and over his head. He held her by both hips as she stood between his legs stroking his well-tanned shoulders. He peeled off her spandex top. She was wearing an athletic bra. He unhooked it and let it drop to the floor, releasing very nicely shaped full breasts. He buried his face between them, kissing and nibbling while he slipped the yoga pants off of her hips. She pushed him back onto the bed and removed his gym shorts.

Amar ached with desire; he'd never felt so hard. She straddled his hips and took him into her. Slowly and rhythmically she did things with the muscles surrounding him, that he had never experienced before. Katya's history of sexual contact was one of domination and deceit, but this was something very different. She didn't quite know what. It took some effort to quiet her mind, let her training go, and just allow herself to feel.

They closed their eyes and together were transported to a realm of lights, colors, and sensations. It was strange and yet familiar. Together, they lost all sense of being separate from each other. It was as if they were the gods of old conceiving the entire human race right now. Thousands of years scrolled by in that moment. This was more than a physical experience. This was some sort of spiritual communion of the ages. Their climax came all at once. She wrapped her arms around him and his around her, clinging to each other for dear life. It went on and on until they were both completely spent. Amar could feel her tears dripping softly onto his own cheeks.

He whispered in her ear, "It's okay, you know."

She nuzzled his neck, "It is okay...finally. I didn't know it could be like this."

"Neither did I," he said.

She lay on top of him, he still inside her. Together they fell, down, down, down, into soft white clouds of unconsciousness.

CHAPTER FORTY-THREE

Seattle

Amar woke at first light. They had lain like spoons, scarcely moving the whole night. He slipped out of bed and put his gym clothes on.

Katya stirred, "Must we get up now?"

"You don't need to, but I have to go to the office. Why don't you and Niki sleep late. I'll have Alice make a brunch for you. Then, I'll have Jan come by and take you on a tour of Seattle this afternoon. Would you like that?"

She rolled onto her belly, face in the pillow, "Yes, that will be good, I will like to meet her. Send Jan to me." She sighed, closed her eyes and went right back to sleep.

Amar shut the door gently on his way out noting, with some relief, that Nikolai was still sleeping, as well. He didn't want to cross the *I'm in love with your daughter bridge,* just yet. He went downstairs and showered in the locker room where he kept a change of clothes. Alice was in the kitchen and handed him a cup of coffee when he came in. Amar explained his desires for Katya and Nikolai.

"That's no problem; I just have some light cleaning to do and Gary asked me to load a thousand rounds of .45 ACP P-Plus for him. You know how he likes that special custom load."

"I didn't know your duties extended to loading ammunition." Amar declared.

"It's easy," she said. "We have two Dillon 650 loading machines in the armory. One is set up for rifle cartridges and one for pistol cartridges. All you have to do is put a bullet on each casing and pull the handle. It's a little more complicated than that, but I load ammo for all of the boys."

"Well, you are a woman of many talents, Alice. I'm happy to get to know you better."

Amar arrived at the office at 8:00 a.m. Jan Meyer's day was already in full swing when he walked into the office. "What's on the schedule for today?" he asked.

"Your 10:00 meeting has been canceled, and Mr. Warburg has been trying to reach you."

"Okay, I'll return his call. Would you mind taking the afternoon off and showing Katya and Nikolai around Seattle? They're staying at the apartment at the warehouse."

"I'd be happy to. I'll call Rachael and see if she wants to go. She needs to get out of the house. We can go do the Space Needle restaurant for lunch, and I'll dig up several ideas so Katya and Nikolai can choose what they would like to do."

"Great idea, thanks, Jan. Mom said she wanted to meet them."

The phone buzzed. "Speaking of the devil, Mr. Warburg is on line one."

"Thank you, Jan." Reluctantly, Amar went into his office and picked up the phone. "Harry, what can I do for you?"

"Amar, I'm calling to express my deepest sympathies over the loss of your father."

"Well, thank you, sir, I appreciate the sentiment. It's been a little difficult around here of late; he left big shoes to fill."

"I have no doubt that you must have your hands full. Perhaps I can help. I would like to have a face-to-face meeting if you would be so kind."

The hairs on the back of Amar's neck were tingling. "What about?" he asked.

"I have a business proposition for you that I think will both simplify your life and end any monetary issues you may be having, forever."

"Oh, and what might that proposition entail?"

"I would prefer not to discuss it on the phone."

Amar looked at his appointment book. "I have an opening this morning at 10:00. Would you like to come here?"

"If you wouldn't mind, I would like to have you come to my office," he said.

Amar thought, Jesus, one more thing to do, but said, "Harry, I was not aware you had an office in Seattle."

"I have offices all over the world, Amar. Do you know where the 4th Avenue heliport is?"

"Yeah, sure, I can see it from my office window."

"My helicopter will be at the pad at 10:00 and will bring you to me. Can you allocate say, three hours, for the meeting?"

Amar thought to himself, *this is Greenstone Security's wealthiest client, I have to accommodate him.* "Alright Harry, I'll meet your pilot at the helipad at 10:00 a.m.

"Thank you, Amar, you will not be disappointed." The line went dead.

Amar buzzed, "Jan, will you call Gary and ask him if he can attend a meeting with me this morning? I'll need him here at about 9:30. Tell him it's important."

Gary arrived at the office at 9:30 and strolled into the chairman's office. "So, we've been summoned by the great Warburg?" he said, respect not evident in his tone of voice.

"Yep," Amar replied, "he wants to make some sort of a business proposition."

"He wants to buy the Greenstone Satellite System, Amar. He's been after your dad to sell it to him for a couple of years now. You're not going to sell, are you?"

"Gary, with everything I've had to deal with lately, that subject hasn't even crossed my mind. That being said, he is our wealthiest client, and I suppose we should hear him out. By the way, are you packing?"

Gary pulled back his blazer to reveal the Wilson Combat 45. "Never leave home without it," he said.

"Good, I've been thinking about your bodyguard idea."

"Better to be safe than sorry, boss."

"Do you really think Katya would make a good bodyguard?"

"Yes, I certainly do. We'll have to get her a green card and a concealed carry permit. I can handle all of that."

"Well, if she really wants to do it while she's here, then let's put her on the payroll."

"Will do, boss."

At 9:55, both men were standing behind the glass door to the helipad on top of Safeco Plaza. Amar was wearing his trademark cargo pants, hiking boots, and a light nylon jacket. The sun was out, and the windsock on a pole at the railing wafted in a light west wind. Gary, being much more of an expert on aircraft than Amar, gave a whistle as the chopper approached. "That's an Airbus H160," he said. "About 22 million coming our way."

The highly stylized silver and navy blue chopper flared and set down gracefully on the pad. The left side door opened, and Julie Barton stepped down and approached them. She was built like an athlete and wore low healed black leather boots, black pants with a razor sharp crease, and a light cream colored jacket.

As she approached, Gary nudged Amar in the ribs while gesturing with his eyes toward the lump under the woman's left arm. "I'll bet she can run the hundred in under ten seconds. She's packing, too. Not to

worry, it's common for men of Warburg's status to have armed security. At least it's not that clod Dragan."

Amar nodded as the young lady addressed him while treating Renfro as the hired help, "Good morning, Mr. Parish, nice to see you
again. If you will come with me, please."

"Good morning, Julie, lead on."

Renfro was intimately familiar with Amar's reputation as a ladies'
man. When Barton turned toward the chopper, Renfro held his arms
out as if to indicate, "What, her too?"

In a low voice so Barton couldn't hear him over the din of the helicopter, Gary followed up with, "You know her, too? Of course, you
do! What was I thinking?" Amar just grinned back at him.

The H160 was configured with two pilot seats up front and five
passenger seats in the rear compartment. Barton installed them in the
back and gave each man a headset to wear. She buckled in facing
them.

"You can speak to me through the intercom if you wish, the flight
will take about twenty minutes," she said.

The chopper lifted off, turned due west, crossed Bainbridge Island,
then the southern edge of Olympic National Park, and sped directly
out to sea at 200 miles per hour.

Gary leaned forward in his seat, addressing the woman, "Uh,
where exactly is Warburg's office?"

"She replied with just a hint of emphasis on the word mister, "Mr.
Warburg's office is on his yacht, which is currently at sea; we are
about ten minutes out."

The tumblers in Renfro's mind were clicking at a high speed as
they crossed over the coastline. When they accessed the satellite surveillance footage immediately after Tom Parish had been shot, they
lost the shooter under cloud cover as he piloted a speed boat due west
in the Juan De Fuca straight. He could have been headed to any point
on shore in the ninety-six-mile long strait, or he could have been going out to sea. Gary was on high alert. Ten minutes later, the yacht
came into view.

She had been built by Lurssen in Bremen, Germany and launched
in 2008. She was 106 meters in length and could host a gathering of
fifty guests. With a crew of fifty-five, she was 15,000 tons of gleaming silver, blue, and white mega-yacht. She could cruise the world's
oceans at twenty-two knots. The pilot circled the ship, as if to display
her attributes, and lined up for his approach to the helipad on the aft
deck. The yacht's name was displayed on both sides amidships: *The*

Zoltan. The chopper set down gently on the pad, and the engines were throttled down.

Aboard the Zoltan at Sea

Barton opened the door. "Gentlemen, if you will follow me, please." They left the chopper, crossed the helipad, and made their way past a large swimming pool and outdoor bar. Renfro, an experienced para-military man, nudged Amar in the ribs and gestured toward an odd looking tubular device protruding from the deck. It was about five feet in diameter with a domed top and two strange looking brackets on either side. Renfro recognized it from his time as a Navy Seal. In a low voice, so Barton couldn't hear, he said, "Boss, that's a British Sea Skua missile launcher. I'll bet this tub is armed to the teeth."

Amar nodded his understanding. As they passed the swimming pool, they observed two very good looking young women lounging in a hot tub at the end of the pool. Amar figured the hot tub probably cost more than his Land Rover. Barton ignored them, but one of the women rose slightly from the water, giving Amar a little wave and demonstrating clearly that the two pretty ladies were sans clothing. Amar smiled back at them. Renfro rolled his eyes.

Two double glass doors to an opulently furnished salon slid open automatically as they approached. The interior of the salon brought the decor of the finest Manhattan penthouse into question: sumptuous carpet, exotic tropical woods, gold plated window trim and fittings, a hand carved bar and back bar, a fabulously expensive grand piano, and multiple seating groups of the finest leather. It was everything a master of the universe would want or need. Barton escorted them across the room to a door on the far wall.

She motioned for Amar to enter, "Mr. Parish, Mr. Warburg will see you in his office."

She turned and put a hand on Gary's chest, and though he had not given his name, she said, "Mr. Renfro, you and I will wait out here. Would you care for a coffee or perhaps something stronger?"

Gary didn't protest. Maybe he could extract some relevant information from their conversation. Amar entered the equally opulent office. A large hand carved desk, with a seating group and coffee table in front, dominated the room. A conference table with eight chairs took up the right side of the space. A leather recliner was positioned in front of a panoramic window with a view of the ocean, stretching to the horizon. Warburg was not in evidence. Amar looked around and spotted a small 8" x 10" painting on one wall. He strolled over for a closer look. An engraved gold plaque under it said, "Girl with a Pearl Earring".

"Do you like the artist, Amar?" came a voice behind him. Warburg appeared as if by magic; Amar hadn't heard him come in.

"I'm more of an expert on ancient stone carvings, but I do recognize a Vermeer when I see it, Harry. The original is hanging in the Hague, isn't it?"

Warburg chuckled, "As difficult as it may be to believe, this is the original. The painting in the Hague is a copy, but don't tell anyone. Vermeer produced only thirty-four paintings—I own six of them."

Amar turned around. Warburg's white hair was neatly barbered. He was dressed casually in dark slacks and a tailored white shirt in a subtle houndstooth pattern with French cuffs, and heavy gold cufflinks at each wrist—the perpetual suntan. The two men shook hands. Warburg motioned toward two wing-backed chairs in front of his desk. Amar noted a hint of disapproval as Warburg took in his cargo pants and hiking boots. *At least they were clean,* he thought.

"Please, have a seat."

As if on cue, a steward entered through the same door, hidden in the paneling, that Warburg must have used. "Can I get you anything?" Warburg asked.

"A cup of coffee would be great, thanks. Nice boat, by the way," Amar said.

Warburg nodded to the steward who disappeared through a sliding door in the back wall without a word. *Nice boat, my ass,* he thought. *This is 550 million dollars of nice boat; this kid will be a pushover compared to his father.*

Smiling at Amar, he began, "You're probably wondering why I asked you to come here."

If Renfro had been present, he would have noted the slight gleam of malevolence in the older man's eyes. Amar wasn't naturally cynical. He tended to take people at face value, which left him vulnerable to a master manipulator like Warburg. The coffee came in. Amar sipped and nodded his approval.

"Yeah, I've been wondering. Why did you want to see me?"

"Amar, in short, before your father's death, I entered into an agreement with him to buy the Greenstone Satellite System. I have invited you here to bring you up-to-date on what has been agreed to. It is my hope that we can complete the transaction in the short term."

Amar's brows furrowed. "I'm not aware of any such transaction. As far as I know, my father didn't want anything to do with the idea of selling the Greenstone system."

Warburg picked up a remote from the side table. "He changed his mind while you were in New York recently. Here is a video of the transaction." Warburg pressed a button on a remote and a TV screen rose out of the credenza behind his desk. A video played showing Tom Parish entering the yacht in the same way that Amar and Renfro had. He was alone. Warburg greeted him on camera, and they entered the office. Two other people were present. They all sat at the conference table, which was covered by several documents. Then followed a fifteen-minute sequence during which documents were read, signed, and notarized by Julie Barton. Copies were placed in a black leather briefcase and given to Chairman Parish. Then he exited the office, boarded the chopper, and took off toward the coast.

Amar couldn't put his finger on it, but something didn't pass the smell test. As far as he knew, Tom had been adamantly against this sale. Why would he have changed his mind so suddenly? Why hadn't he revealed that fact to either him or Rachael? If the deal was already signed and sealed, what did Warburg want or need from him?

Warburg lied, "Your father was given a copy of the video."

"What was the purchase price?" Amar asked.

With a straight face Warburg said, "Nine billion dollars for GES alone. The deal includes the satellite system, the SatCom facility, and the robotic satellite factory. You retain ownership of PCI. The value of its land-based infrastructure will fade away in a couple of years anyway."

Amar gave a low whistle. "If this is all done, then what do you want from me?"

Warburg smiled, "There is still the matter of the ten percent of the company personally owned by you."

Amar studied the man's face. "Judging by this yacht, your Gulfstream jet, and whatever else I presume you own, why does a man that has more than everything want the Greenstone Satellite System badly enough to pay that kind of money for it?"

CHAPTER FORTY-FOUR

Aboard the Zoltan at Sea

Warburg knew the kid wouldn't be able to hold his own during these negotiations. He just didn't have the business acumen needed to compete at this level. Ordinarily, Warburg wouldn't bother to explain his motivations to an opponent. But in this case, his massive ego got the better of him. He really wanted to see the look on the kid's face when he told him what this was all about. He wanted to revel in his victory as he took down the offspring of his victim.

The purchase of the Greenstone Satellite System was, in fact, a highly sophisticated fraud. The deepfake video had been digitally re-created, from an earlier visit to the yacht by Tom Parish. The documents were brilliantly forged and notarized. In a gross display self aggrandizement, Warburg allowed his ego to take over. He wanted to gloat out loud.

He leaned in a little. "As you know Amar, GES is the most highly developed privately owned satellite network on the planet. It's perfect for my purposes. You were very forthcoming about your work and your passion for what you've discovered. Since you have something I want, I'm going to tell you about my work and my passion for it. I'm going to explain to you how the world really works. It can be summed up in one sentence. *Those who control the currency, control the world.* Let me explain it to you this way. When you borrow money, you borrow it from the people who have it, right?"

Amar was no genius at business, but he could read people, and he was feeling the oppressive energy coming off of this man. He decided to play along and see where this was going.

"I've never had to borrow money before, but yes, I suppose that's true."

Warburg continued, "Are you aware that in 1971, the total amount of outstanding U.S. private debt, was just under one trillion dollars?"

Amar came back, "I've never studied such things, but I have no doubt you have, so I'll take your word for it."

Warburg asked, "And are you aware that in 2019, there is now twenty-eight trillion dollars in U.S. private debt outstanding? That is to say that in the last forty-eight years, we have created twenty-seven trillion additional dollars in the form of debt?"

"No, I was not aware of that fact."

"Are you aware, that independent of household debt, every town, city, and state in the nation is staggering under record levels of debt?"

"Yeah, I do know about that. You hear it every day on the news. The interest on all forms of debt is consuming a higher and higher percentage of nearly every nation's budget, both private and public. So, there's not enough left to pay the bills, and everyone has to borrow to make up the difference."

"The question you and everyone else should be asking, my young friend, is—where did all of that borrowed money come from? Do you think that people like me had kept boatloads full of gold coins for decades just waiting for 1971 to roll around so we could begin lending them out to cities, states, and nations as well as the general public?"

Amar's face took on a genuinely chagrined look. "I guess I never thought about it."

"No, my friend. You haven't thought about it because you never took the time to understand what's really going on in the world. Don't feel alone; most economists, and indeed, most politicians, don't understand it either. Those who do understand this system, are so dependent upon its favors that they do not choose to protest. Why would they? It has made them rich."

"So, what you're telling me, Harry, is that twenty-seven trillion dollars has been created from nothing in the form of debt since 1971. How is that possible? Who has the power to do something like that?"

"This is a very old game, Amar. We've been playing it in countries around the world since the invention of paper money nearly four hundred years ago. It is so simply sophisticated that it hides in plain sight. The average person lacks the intelligence to understand what we've created. I'll put it in simple terms, so it will make sense to you. When you put 1,000 dollars in your bank, by law the bank is allowed to lend 900 dollars of that money out to third parties. Are you with me so far?"

"Yeah, I've heard about that; it's called fractional reserve banking, right?"

"Very good, Amar. Even though the bank has lent 900 dollars of your money to a third party, they are still allowed, by law, to say they have your 1,000 dollars on deposit. How can your money be in two places at once? So, what has just happened?

"I'm sure you're going to tell me," Amar said.

"What has just happened, is that the bank has created 900 dollars out of nothing in the form of debt. Warburg paused. "You don't borrow money to save it. You borrow money to spend it, right? Once that 900 dollars has been spent, re-deposited and relent again and again, eventually it will result in the creation of 9,000 dollars in new debt." That's 9,000 dollars of new debt created for every 1,000 dollars the system holds in deposits.

"So that's how 27 trillion dollars in new debt came into being since 1971? Who do we owe that money to?"

"You all owe it to us," Warburg noted casually.

"And who is us?" Amar asked.

"We are the people who control the creation of currency."

"And what gives you the right to control the creation of currency for your own benefit?"

The smirk on Warburg's face was obvious. "Why the law, of course."

Amar grabbed the bridge of his nose with thumb and forefinger as if to ward off an ice cream headache. He was starting to feel like a youngster asking, "'Cause why, Daddy?" He already knew the answer, but asked the question anyway, "Who writes the laws that allow you to do that?"

"We do, of course," came the reply.

"So you have written the laws that allow you to gain an unfair advantage over any competitor in any market place that you choose? Why you? Why not somebody else?"

"That should be obvious, Amar." Warburg held out both arms as if to contain the yacht. "Do you recognize all of this for what it is? This is evidence of our power and superiority. We have the right because we have the power to take it. You might say it's our destiny to rule over mankind."

"And you accomplish all of this through the retail banking system?"

Warburg laughed, "No, retail banking is only one part of our business. One of our closely held secrets is that we also own most of the central banks in the world. Our power to create money has made us lords over the stock market, the munitions industry, big pharma, agribusiness, and the oil business, just to name a few."

Warburg's attitude was beginning to be extremely offensive.

"So, tell me what all of this debt has to do with satellite telephones?"

"You'll need a little more background for that understanding. We began to consolidate our control of the U. S. currency system when we created the Federal Reserve in 1913. At that time, the dollar was backed by gold. Since there was only a limited amount of gold in existence, it restricted our ability to inflate the currency by issuing more and more debt. In 1971, President Nixon, at our behest, took us off the gold standard, removing that restriction. That move, and the advent of the computer gave us all the power we needed to gradually take what we wanted."

"And what did you want?" Amar asked.

"We wanted to continuously harvest a little value out of every dollar in existence for our own use. I probably should mention that we don't limit our activities to the United States or to the dollar. The amazing thing is, that as long as inflation hovers at the two-to-four percent level, the population thinks the resulting price increases for nearly everything are normal. But nobody seems to realize that two-to-four percent inflation, compounded year after year, is a staggering amount of money.

"The little people even joke about how the car that cost 1,500 dollars in 1971 now sells for 35,000 dollars as if to say, 'wasn't it quaint in the old days?' You may not know it, but the value of the dollar has been reduced by ninety-nine percent since 1913."

Showing some irritation, Amar retorted, "You're saying that you are the ones who benefit from the process of inflation in which prices are continually going up?"

"Historically that is true. The mass creation of currency in the form of debt is actually the cause of inflation. But things are changing. We are on the cusp of bringing the process of inflating currencies to an end."

"Let's see if I have this right. You continuously reduce the purchasing power of the dollar by confiscating its value for your own use. The common people, and all forms of government, having to pay higher and higher prices all of the time, must borrow from you to make up the loss of purchasing power. Then, whether public or private, they spend their lives in subservience to the phony debt they owe to you. Isn't that fraud?"

Warburg laughed at the young man's naiveté, "I assure you Amar, all of our activities are quite legal. That's not hard to do if you also own the government. The governments of the world are just brands that we own."

"Well, if it can't be classified as fraud, then it's definitely a form of slavery!"

"You could look at it like that. However, in the United States, it's slavery with a house and a car, nice clothes, and entertainment. When you compare the lifestyle, this system has produced to what was common in the 1800's or even the early part of the 1900's, how can you say the people are worse off?"

"You think that living a life mired in debt is an improvement?"

"Yes, when compared to the lack of creature comforts most people used to live with, I do think that."

Amar considered that statement for a while. "So, again, what does this have to do with satellite telephones?"

Warburg sighed, having to explain all of this to an under-informed kid was beginning to be a little tedious.

"When we loan money to you under the old system, we have created the money that we lend out. However, we have not created the money that will be needed to pay the interest on your debt. That money must come from the existing money supply. The problem arises when debt increases exponentially as it has in recent years. Then, the amount of money needed to pay the interest also increases exponentially. That means the money needed to pay the interest on money created as debt, consumes a larger and larger percentage of everyone's budget. Eventually, the only alternative is more borrowing. That system has been good for us in the past.

You should be able to visualize how it all works. Unfortunately, the process isn't mathematically sustainable, and at some point, the amount of interest due will completely overshadow the amount of money that remains with which to pay the bills. At that point, recession sets in again, and the economy, which was based upon debt, contracts suddenly.

If the contraction is too violent, the population suffers. Eventually, they will grow restless. At that point, to avoid civil unrest, we will crash the old currency system and replace it with a new one. We have drained so much value from the dollar, the entire U.S. monetary system is now at risk. The same thing has been done in countries around the world where we are in control of the central banks. It's a global condition. That's where we are now.

It's to everyone's benefit that we create a new system before the old one self-destructs. We've come to realize that it's time to design a completely new monetary system that does away with the problems inherent in the old paradigm. We're creating a new system, which reduces debt and keeps wages on a par with the cost of living. We want prices to be stable.

We want to eliminate the ravages of inflation and deflation that plague the old system. We're about to unveil a new, one world, digital currency to that end. The reason I convinced your father to sell me the Greenstone Satellite System is that we're going to use it as the new medium of exchange."

Now Amar really looked puzzled, "I don't understand."

"First we'll outlaw cash. Paper money will be a thing of the past. Checks will no longer be written. Then we'll close out the credit card system. Everyone will receive an appropriate amount of digital money in return for the liquid assets they own. Everyone will purchase a Greenstone phone, without the extraction feature of course. The phones will be used both for communications and as the new payment system. When you go to the store, you will wave your phone in front of the card reader to complete your transaction. No more button pushing or entering of pin numbers. The amount of your purchase will be deducted from your account. We will centralize and manage all of your financial data. Identity theft will be a thing of the past, since the system cannot be hacked. Your father saw to that.

"There won't be tax returns any more. We'll institute a flat tax system. Taxes will come out of your earnings on a daily basis. You'll hardly notice. We'll create a new foundation for the prosperity of the masses. As you know, the Greenstone phones have a worldwide signal. You'll be able to do business in any location, anywhere on the planet. It may take a few years, but prices and labor rates around the world will stabilize as a result. Consistently higher prices will be a thing of the past."

"Excuse me if I'm a little skeptical. If you are going to homogenize the worldwide labor pool, that means American labor rates will go down and the population will suffer, right?"

"That will be true in the short term, but the population will adjust," Warburg offered.

"You're not telling me that you are voluntarily giving up the income you've amassed by printing currencies as a humanitarian gesture, are you?"

Warburg grinned wolfishly, "No, I'm not telling you that. I am saying that we'll no longer need the mechanism of interest-bearing debt to fund our activities. We'll be instituting a transaction fee. It will be very small, maybe one percent, but it will be one percent of every transaction that takes place globally—about two trillion dollars a year to start, tax free, of course. That's more than enough to pay for the lifestyles of those of us who own the system of exchange.

"But the Greenstone phones are super expensive to buy. How will everyone be able to afford one?"

Warburg could see that the kid was smart, but he really didn't get the whole picture. "Amar, we're going to make so much money rolling out this new system, we could afford to give the phones away for free. But we'll be charging a reasonable fee for each phone. With no money down, that cost will be added to each person's account as a debt when they sign up. Believe me when I tell you, the people will line up to buy them for convenience, fashion, and safety."

"With the capabilities of the Greenstone system, you're talking about a total surveillance state. Anonymity will be a thing of the past. You'll be in total control of all systems of exchange and of society!"

"What you've failed to grasp, young man, is that we're already in control and have been for a long long time. This is just the next technological development on that path."

"You'll need many more satellites than we have in orbit now, won't you?"

"Very perceptive, Amar. We are well aware of the capacity of the robotic satellite factory that your father built. It is more than capable of keeping up with demand. You may not realize it, but satellite production isn't the bottleneck that prevents the expansion of the system. Launch capability is."

"I suppose you have that issue handled as well?"

"Yes, we do."

"You realize that the phones are manufactured in Taiwan? Will they be able to keep up with your demands?"

"Of course, I have TaiwanCom under contract. In about a month, I'll be its new owner. We'll be expanding their assembly line to meet demand."

"You're going to data-mine the entire planet! How will you manage all of that data?"

Warburg chuckled again, "Our data farm in Utah already has the capacity to deal with it."

"What if the people don't want your system?"

"Well Amar, if the absorption rate doesn't match our projections, there might be some sort of terrorist incident that shuts down regional power grids. Maybe no one will have electricity for a while and access to the Internet will be lost. The only Internet access available will be through the new phone system. We'll come forth and save the day on behalf of the people."

"I don't believe this!" Amar exclaimed.

"You would be wise to believe it, Amar. You have no idea how far our power extends throughout the world."

Amar put his elbows on his knees and held his head with both hands. Amar hadn't met very many people he would classify as being truly evil. Along with Colonel Golzar of the Iranian Religious Police, now he had.

"You're giving me a massive headache. I need some time to talk to my people."

"I understand, I've just dropped a lot on you. However, time is short. I want your ten percent of GES. You have thirty days to complete the transaction. After that, I might have to be a bit more persuasive. You will find documents to sign in the black leather briefcase your father took with him. I believe you will also find a copy of the video I just showed you. Look it over and call me with your decision."

Suddenly Amar remembered the black briefcase Trevor had given him. He'd tossed it in the back of Tom's Lexus. The document in it had been titled, "Transaction Summary." He'd forgotten to give it to Bob Alford. It was probably still there.

With a tone of defeat in his voice, he said, "Okay, I'll look it over."

Warburg stood and brought the meeting to a close. Even though he was physically shorter than Amar, he felt himself towering over the young man. A frightening expression crossed his face like a black cloud in an afternoon thunderstorm.

"Just to be clear, Amar, I don't like to take no for an answer."

It was a veiled threat, but Amar received the message loud and clear. They rose. Amar didn't bother to shake hands with Harry Warburg. He simply turned and left the office the way he came in. Warburg didn't follow. Barton and Renfro were waiting at the bar when he came out.

Renfro observed the dazed look on Amar's face, "Everything okay, boss?"

He mumbled, "I don't know, Gary. I need to collect my thoughts for a while. I need to digest what I've just heard."

Barton accompanied the two men to the helicopter but didn't go with them.

Once they were airborne, Renfro asked, "What went on in there, Amar?"

Amar nodded toward the two pilots up front indicating he didn't want to risk them overhearing.

"We'll discuss it back at the office."

The rest of the ride back to Seattle was uneventful and dead quiet. No one spoke a word.

CHAPTER FORTY-FIVE

Seattle

The two men deplaned at the 4th Avenue Heliport. In the elevator on the way down to ground level, Renfro asked again, "So what happened in there, boss?"

"He showed me a video of Tom signing the papers to complete the sale of GES to him. Now he wants my ten percent, as well."

"What? I don't believe it Amar. I know how Tom felt about selling the company. I also know what he thought about Warburg. He'd never sell the company to that pompous ass."

"Do you remember that black briefcase that Trevor gave to me at the museum?"

Renfro nodded.

"I completely forgot about it. It's in the back seat of my dad's car. According to Warburg, our signed copies of the transaction are in there. Let's go down to the garage and get it. I'll tell you the rest in the office."

Amar strode purposefully into the inner office carrying the black briefcase, Renfro right behind him.

"Jan, I need Al Hemmings and Bob Alford up here now, please. This is urgent. Bring them in as soon as they get here."

Amar slapped the briefcase onto the conference table, and he pulled out the bound Transaction Summary notebook. Renfro pushed the button that revealed the monitor behind Tom's desk. Amar fished around in the side pocket of the briefcase and came out with a thumb drive, which he passed to Gary. Renfro plugged the thumb drive in just as Hemmings and Alford entered the office with Jan in hot pursuit.

Alford asked, "What's going on, Amar? What has happened?"

"Gary and I have just returned from a meeting with Harry Warburg." Holding up the notebook, he declared, "He presented us with these documents and a video showing Tom signing over GES to him. I, that is we, all need to know if this is real,"

Renfro pushed another button on the remote showing a date-stamped video of the transaction. Jan and the men seated themselves and watched the short film showing Tom signing the documents. Afterward, Alford paged through the papers with Hemmings looking over his shoulder.

"I don't believe this," Alford said. "Tom would have told me if he was going to sell the company. I'm sure our lawyers have never seen any of this material. That's his signature, and the documents do appear to be genuine. So does the video." Alford's gaze swept across the faces of everyone in the room. "Did any of you know about this?"

All present shook their heads. Alford looked at the last section of the document and gave a low whistle. "Apparently the purchase price is nine billion dollars for the company. That money is in escrow waiting to be released. There are documents here for your ten percent position in the company as well Amar. He is offering an additional one billion for that. I'll admit that is substantially above our current estimates of the system's value."

Jan Meyer's eyebrows shot up as she reached for her appointment book.

"I have Tom attending a meeting with Mr. Warburg on the same date that the video was taken. I understood the purpose of that meeting was to collect a check for the Turkmenistan extraction and to renew Warburg's subscription to the Greenstone Executive Security program. I didn't know he was going out to Warburg's yacht."

Renfro said, "He never said anything to me about going out to Warburg's yacht."

Jan reminded him, "Gary, I have you in Los Angeles on that day."

Gary remembered, "Oh, right, I remember now. I had a telecom meeting at the Bonaventure."

Hemmings cut in, "I produced the invoice for him, and he dropped the check off when he returned. He never said anything to me about selling the company."

Knowing for the first time that it was up to him to decide the direction of this and all future meetings, Amar took charge.

"Bob, I need to have the lawyers look all of this over and tell me if it's real. Check that, I'm beginning to understand that it's not real, I need to know if he can make it stick. I don't care how much it costs in legal fees; I need an assessment by tomorrow morning. Please have Robby look at the video and tell me if it's real or not.

"Al, I need to understand all of the financial issues that will fall out of this deal. Give me two versions: one without selling my ten percent and one if I do sell it. If this goes through, we will be carving out GES as a wholly owned subsidiary of PCI. Are there common assets, that when gone, will leave PCI in a wounded state? If so, what will that look like? Tell me about the tax issues. What personnel will be affected? I presume this deal includes SatCom—does Robby go with the deal? Does it also include the satellite factory? I need to know anything else that's relevant.

"Gary, I need a threat assessment. Did Warburg have anything to do with my father's death? Are any of us in physical danger? Do we need to put more bodyguards in place? Do you still have a guy at the house? Get me an update on the police investigation, too.

"Jan, please check in with my mom and see if she's okay. Then call Evan; I'd like to meet with him and Rachael later this afternoon at her house. Let Katya know I'll be busy tonight but would like to have her here in the morning to begin her duties as my bodyguard. Let's reconvene tomorrow morning at 10:00 to see where we are. There's a lot of work to do people—so let's get to it."

Amar arrived at home to find one of Renfro's men parked in the driveway keeping watch. They spoke briefly about the security schedule, who was coming on duty and when. Jan Meyer, while acting as a chauffeur for Rachael, Niki, and Katya had informed Rachael that she would be having two more people for dinner. Amar found her in the kitchen, busily preparing pasta and scallops with a Caesar salad for the three of them. Evan arrived shortly after Amar. Red wine was poured, and the two men sat at the breakfast bar watching her cook.

"So Mom, you met Katya and Nikolai. What did you think?"

"I think that they are lovely people," she said. "That Katya is quite the beauty." She raised one eyebrow in Amar's direction. "I'm sure you noticed."

Amar smiled a little sheepishly, "Uh, yeah, I did notice that."

Rachael recounted her recent activities and charitable contributions. She teared up several times and talked about how her grief came in waves. Her sorrow was infectious, and all three expressed how much Tom was missed in their lives. They talked about the ongoing police investigation into his murder.

After dinner, both Amar and Evan brought her up-to-date on everything else that had happened since Tom's death, some of which she knew and some of which she was hearing for the first time.

Amar told her about their trip to Russia to meet Niki and Katya. He explained Katya's skills and Renfro's idea that she could serve as his bodyguard. "She's really extraordinary, Mom."

"I liked her a lot," she said. "Nikolai had some interesting stories to tell about the Soviet space race. Your father would have enjoyed meeting him."

Amar outlined how the computer had been repaired and how, if possible, Niki would help them drive the rover the following night.

Evan brought her up-to-date on what they knew so far about the Ularian civilization, the state of the translations, and what they hoped to find next. He mentioned Robby's hit on a potential site for Vandalay in Greenland.

"You are going to Greenland? When is that going to happen?"

"I'll know more tomorrow. Gary is looking into a ship to rent. We'll need to approach the site from the water. I'll let you know as soon as I know."

Like any mother would, she said, "You will be careful, won't you?"

Amar assured her that all relevant precautions would be taken. Finally, the conversation turned to Harrison Warburg.

"I never liked that man; neither did your father."

Amar explained everything that had happened that morning, the suspicious buy/sell agreement, the video, the perceived threat. He explained in detail how Warburg wanted to use GES for the next monetary system. Evan hadn't been in the earlier meeting and was hearing some of this for the first time as well.

"That's the main thing I wanted to talk to you both about. The lawyers are going to tell us tomorrow whether he can make this hostile takeover stick. I suspect they'll tell me that he can. He's one of the richest men on the planet, and I doubt he would go to so much trouble if he didn't think he could pull it off. He doesn't own my ten percent yet, but he wants it badly. The conundrum is this: if I keep my ten percent, I'll have a minority interest in a high tech bid for the establishment of a planetary surveillance state. I won't have a say in what that entity does or does not do. I will certainly incur his wrath, and that could be potentially dangerous for all of us. Also, I don't want our family name to be associated with that kind of a scheme.

Once people discover what his system is really about, I could become a target by being associated with him. I'd like to stop what he's doing, but I doubt I can accomplish that from the inside. If I sell, he'll have complete control of the satellite system, which in effect he already has. Funds from the sale in the amount of nine billion dollars are already in escrow. If I sell my ten percent, we'll have an additional one billion dollars to work with, some of which we could use to engineer a way to oppose his plans. I'd like to know what you both think."

Evan deferred to Rachael.

"Amar, your father wasn't all that keen to be in the executive protection industry. He had no interest in currying favor with the ultra rich. He was only interested in the technology. He saw GES as an opportunity to bring very expensive satellite phone technology into the mass market. He hoped that once it was introduced to a prosperous clientele, the cost of the technology would gradually decrease, making the convenience of it available to ordinary people.

You're not passionate about satellite phones. I can tell from what you've told me tonight that discovering the remains of your lost city is what gets your juices flowing, not doing battle with a sociopath. From what you've said, Warburg already has control of the system. I know you don't want him to have any kind of control over you. If you stay in, it will be a constant battle for supremacy. He is a devious man, and you are not. I can't see you choosing to do battle directly with that kind of a man. I recommend that you sell and put all of this behind you. Perhaps you can find some other way to get the word out about who he is and what a terrible thing his system will be for the world. In the meantime, you can pursue your archaeological dreams, which will be so much more rewarding!"

Amar turned to Evan with a question mark in his eyes.

Evan concurred, "I couldn't have analyzed it any better myself. I'd like to add one more thing to what Rachael said. I believe that the system Warburg is proposing represents the essence of your theory about overspecialization. It's entirely possible that he won't be successful, and he'll cause his own extinction."

"Wouldn't that be nice. Thank you both. Depending on what the lawyers tell me in the morning, I think I'll put this behind me. Maybe we can find a way to hasten Warburg's self-inflicted extinction."

CHAPTER FORTY-SIX

Seattle

Jan had coffee and pastries delivered to Amar's office the next morning. At 10:00 a.m., Gary Renfro, Katya, Al Hemmings, Robby Harris, Evan, and Amar all crowded around the conference table. Niki elected to remain at the apartment resting up for a drive on the moon that evening. Bob Alford came in and introduced the corporate lawyers, Lewis King and Bill Wright.

Amar presided over the meeting. "Gentlemen, thank you for coming. I apologize for imposing upon you yesterday. I hope you were able to review all of the documents and reach a conclusion."

Bill Wright was the senior lawyer. "Not a problem, Mr. Parish; the overtime will be reflected on our bill. We spent the evening looking over the documents and the video. We brought in our handwriting expert, who has verified that the signature on the documents is indisputably your father's. We also engaged a graphics expert to determine if the film is an original and has not been edited in any way. He believes it is genuine. The form and substance of the documents are legal. If this is a forgery, it is one of the best deepfake video forgeries ever created. I doubt that any effort to overturn this transaction in court would be successful."

"PCI and GES are very closely related. Will there be any kind of lasting damage to PCI from the separation?" Amar asked.

Lewis King provided the answer, "In terms of the volume of annual transactions, PCI is the larger of the two companies. GES was created as a vehicle for introducing your father's satellite technology. The break between the two companies should be relatively clean. You retain all of the land-based cellular networks, infrastructure, and contracts that are currently owned by PCI. GES owns the satellite system that is in place, your father's small robotic satellite factory, and what you commonly refer to as SatCom in Everett, all of which go with the sale.

The warehouse at Boeing Field belongs to PCI. That facility, as well as the three C-130 airplanes, are one hundred percent owned by

PCI, and are not part of the deal. There is a simple usage agreement between the two companies for the airplanes and the cooperative use of the building, which can be dissolved. None of the contracts that GES has with its employees and subcontractors require them to remain with the company. They are free to resign if they wish."

"That's right," said Robby. "I'm not working for that crooked bastard."

"Me either," Renfro agreed.

"Not to worry, gentlemen," Amar assured them, "You will both have positions within PCI's corporate framework. I have decided to sell my holdings in GES since I don't want to have a relationship with Harrison Warburg either. What do I need to do to make that happen?"

"You can sign and notarize the documents that have been provided. We have reviewed them and find them to be in order. I need to caution you; there is a fiduciary clause regarding the hand over," said Bill Wright. "Robby Harris is the most knowledgeable person when it comes to the satellite system. The agreement calls for a thirty-day transition period during which you will need to provide an executive-level employee to help Zoltan Holdings become familiar with the workings of the satellite system."

Amar agreed, "I'd like you to take care of that in good faith, Robby. It's to our benefit to have a clean break with no blowback. Then you can thumb your nose at them when you leave."

Robby relented, "If you say so, boss, I'll do it for you."

Amar signed, and Jan Meyer notarized the paperwork.

"One more question, Bill: What is the status of the museum?"

"The museum is a foundation and a completely separate entity. It'll remain unaffected by the sale of Greenstone Executive Security."

"Thank you, Bill and Lewis, for handling this so quickly. Please make sure the funds are processed through escrow properly. One more thing, I want you to hold these documents until the very last minute before telling Warburg we have agreed to his terms. Let him stew."

The lawyers indicated that they would, with pleasure, and they withdrew.

Amar addressed the group, "What's next?"

Jan reported, "Detective Manning is here from the police department to give us an update on his investigation.

Jan brought the detective into the room. Amar said, "Detective, will you tell us what you know so far?"

Manning greeted everyone.

"We discovered the partially burned body of one Jose Luis Perez in an Oldsmobile in the parking lot of the Elliot Bay Marina the morning after the shooting. Quick action by one of the marina's employees using a fire extinguisher, prevented the car and the body from being fully engulfed by the flames. We have determined that the car was actually owned by Mr. Perez, who was a small-time drug dealer and MS-13 gang member. The results of the autopsy tell us that the cause of death was an overdose of Ketamine. There was no evidence of smoke in Mr. Perez's lungs, indicating that he was already dead when the fire was started by someone else. This was clearly a murder.

"I'm convinced that this was a rather clumsy attempt by third parties to blame your father's death on a disposable gang member. In truth, no one in law enforcement will be mourning Mr. Perez's passing. As you recall, from the parking lot camera at the museum, the driver of the car made a point of showing off the tattoos on his left arm as he arrived at the scene. Those camera shots match the tattoos on the dead man's left arm. That could have been a decoy, or Mr. Perez could have been the get-away driver who ended up being framed for the shooting.

"That being said, we also found some blood on the driver's side floor mats that does not match the blood type of the deceased and which could indicate that he was not the driver. It does match the blood sample found inside the museum. We were able to get a DNA sample from that blood but got no hits from the national database. We found the remains of an incendiary device in the car that was used to delay ignition of the accelerant until the real perpetrators had time to escape.

"We believe the parking spot at the marina was selected for its lack of camera coverage. What the perpetrators didn't know was that you had satellite footage of the area. In that footage, we saw someone park the car and then manipulate something inside the car. We suspect he was pulling Mr. Perez's body across the bench seat and positioning it on the driver's side to give us the impression that Perez was both the driver and the shooter. The murder weapon was also found in the car with Perez's fingerprints on it.

"However, in your satellite footage, we then saw a man with a slight limp, consistent with Mr. Renfro's claim to have wounded the shooter in the leg, get on a boat with two other men and motor away into the night. We have been unable to trace that boat or its destination, once it was lost under cloud cover. We know the approximate age and make of the boat and are continuing to look for witnesses who might have seen it. Whoever this guy is, he has a leg wound that might help to identify him. He also had at least two helpers. That's the state of our investigation to date. We have no further leads at this time."

Manning looked around the table. "Do you have anything to add that might be helpful?"

Renfro pitched in, "Yeah, we might. There's a hostile takeover of the Greenstone satellite system in progress that could be a motive for Tom Parish's murder."

Renfro explained the circumstances of Warburg's takeover in some detail. "One of the problems preventing further discovery is that Mr. Warburg's headquarters are on his yacht, which conveniently cruises in international waters. Am I right to assume we have no probable cause to stop him and search his ship?"

"I agree; we don't have enough evidence for probable cause yet. We are aware of the Zoltan because Mr. Warburg frequently travels back and forth in his helicopter. The ship flies a Romanian flag. We would need some solid evidence that our shooter is on board in order to search that vessel. For now, I'll do some research on this guy, Warburg, and I'll keep you informed."

Renfro said, "Warburg would never do his own dirty work. You'll want to focus on his bodyguard, Viktor Dragan."

Manning wrote the name in his notebook. "I will do that," he said.

Amar gestured in Katya's direction, "Detective Manning, I'd like to introduce Katya Chubukin. I have a favor to ask. Katya is going to be acting as my personal bodyguard. This is a position for which she's very qualified. She is an expert marksman. In order for her to carry concealed, she'll need a permit. Can you help with that?"

"Amar, your father was one of the leading donors to police charities in this state. I will be happy to reciprocate and will walk the paperwork through myself. All you need to do is fill out the forms. I'll send them over this afternoon."

Amar thanked the detective, and he departed. "Okay, what's next?" he asked.

Bob Alford took the invitation, "As you know, I'm going to be leaving PCI to pursue other personal interests. I've agreed to remain on board until the sale of GES is completed and things have settled down. I know there's a lot of activity going on regarding the museum and the discoveries made by both you and Tom. I'd like to have an overview of what you are planning so I can anticipate how to allocate the cost of these activities within the corporate structure. If intellectual property is created, I want to make sure it doesn't get buried in the museum's foundation as public property and that you have full access to it."

"I have similar concerns from an accounting perspective," added Al Hemmings. "I would also like to know what is going on."

Evan took the initiative. "I've been collecting images as things unfold. I have a short slideshow of what we know so far." He pressed a button on this laptop, and the images came up on the monitor over Amar's desk.

Amar cautioned the group, "What Evan is about to tell you must remain confidential. You are not to discuss any of this information with third parties, including wives or lovers."

Everyone nodded their assent, and Evan began with their trip to Iran. When he came to the photographs of the chamber at Persepolis, Amar took up the narrative.

"There are two things about these photos that excite me. One is a clear depiction of a flying machine, there in the upper left corner. The second is the image of a workman moving a large piece of stone by himself with some sort of levitation device. We have dated this room to be more than 12,000 years old. The sophistication of the tile work itself indicates a civilization much more advanced than anything we've ever seen from that time period.

Indeed, these pictures imply the presence of a civilization that may have been more advanced than our own. The images of a flying machine and a levitation device tell me these people had technology that could move human evolution forward by leaps and bounds if we can find any remaining trace of it left on Earth. You'll note the double oval symbol in the foreground. That's the same symbol we found on the artifact in the Mare Imbrium. I believe that's proof that the two finds are from the same civilization."

Evan selected images of the Imbrium Codex and put them on the screen.

Bob Alford cut in, "The profit potential for that kind of technology is off the chart! I can see why we need to keep our efforts under wraps."

Amar frowned, "Bob, I understand that you'd want to approach what we've found from a traditional profit making point of view. However, I'm not interested in making a profit from these discoveries; I have more than enough money. My interest in pursuing this inquiry is for the benefit of all mankind."

Alford's face took on the gray cast of someone who had just been reprimanded. "I see, so you're willing to give away technology potentially worth hundreds of billions as a humanitarian gesture? That's madness."

"We're putting the cart before the horse here. Let's table this discussion until we actually find something of value," Amar replied. "Evan, go back to the pictures from the chamber at Persepolis, please.

I asked Robby to configure the satellite system to do a worldwide search for the valley and anything else from these images that could be seen from space. He did so and got a hit. Robby, would you explain?"

"Sure, boss. From the position of the moon in these pictures, I was able to determine the direction of the hydrological axis; I mean the direction of water flow in the valley. That data filtered out thousands of possible sites for the city of Vandalay. Once that subset was filtered out, I entered other data from the images into our search criteria and got a hit on the white zigzag pattern that you see in the foreground of the chamber. Evan, can you pull up the satellite photos?

Here you see the identical pattern sticking out from under the leading edge of a glacier on the east coast of Greenland. The ice cap in this area is melting at an accelerated rate, which only recently revealed this pattern. We believe it's possibly some kind of irrigation system that may be a remnant of the city. Amar asked us to analyze the logistics involved to go there. Gary has been leading that effort. Gary, would you like to tell us what you've found?"

"Be happy to," Gary said. "The area in question is approximately 500 miles to the north and slightly west of Reykjavik, Iceland. It is on the inland side of a fjord that empties into Scoresby Sound. There is a small village of 450 people at the mouth of the sound, which won't be much help in mounting an expedition. There isn't a lot there, so we'll need to bring our own equipment. The site Robby found is another 150 miles west on the inland waterway, or fjord as they call it.

The best way to access the site is by ship. I've found a research ship called the Aurora Star, which is owned by a consortium of German companies. She is an icebreaker used to sailing in the Norwegian Sea, which is good, because we may encounter various kinds of ice floes. Normally she's only available by reservation years in advance. However, her most recent mission was cut short and there is a thirty-day window during which she could be available to us.

The mission profile will be as follows: We'll determine what kind of equipment we'll need to take and stockpile it at the PCI warehouse at Boeing Field. One of our C-130's is currently tied down on the ramp there. We'll load and fly that plane from here to New York for layover. The second leg will take us into Reykjavik, Iceland. Each flight will take eight-to-ten hours, depending on headwinds. At Reykjavik, we'll offload the equipment and meet the ship. From there, it's a three-day sail into the target location. Let's figure three days onsite and a three-day return trip. Then two more days to fly the C-130 back to Seattle. The total mission from beginning to end will take about two weeks with no complications."

Al Hemmings interjected, "What's the proposed cost of this expedition?"

Renfro continued, "The ship is $150,000.00 per day. With the C-130's, crew and equipment expenses we are looking at approximately 1.85 million."

Hemmings looked across the table, "Amar, are you willing to invest that kind of money without knowing what you'll get in return?"

"Absolutely," Amar said. "That's a small fraction of the nine billion currently residing in escrow from the sale of GES."

Both Alford and Hemmings sat shaking their heads as if the inexperienced heir to Tom Parish's fortune had no idea what he was doing. The dissention did not go unnoticed.

"Robby, can you zoom in close enough to give Gary a sense of the conditions we'll encounter onsite so he can plan what equipment we will need?"

"I can do that, boss."

"Gary, I'd like you to proceed with the mission planning. You may commit to renting the ship. How soon can we go?"

"Let's be prepared to take off ten days from now," Gary said.

"Okay people, last but certainly not least, tonight we'll be attempting to drive on the moon. What time should we be at the museum, Robby?"

"I will be at SatCom in Everett running the dish from there. If you all get to the museum by seven o'clock, we should be ready within an hour. Katya, will Niki be ready to go for tonight?"

Katya replied, "Da, I mean yes. He hasn't been feeling all that well, but he is resting now, and I think he will be able to work tonight."

Amar brought the meeting to an end. "You are all invited to come to the museum tonight. It could be a historic event. If there is nothing else to discuss, this meeting is adjourned. Gary and Katya, if you don't mind, please stay, I'd like to have a word."

Everyone else filed out. On his way past Jan's desk, Alford declared, "Jan, I have a meeting; I'll be back midafternoon."

CHAPTER FORTY-SEVEN

Seattle

Alford took a cab to a restaurant on Nickerson Street. He loved his wife and children, but he'd made the all too common mistake so many top executives fall prey to. He'd had an affair. He not only had an affair but had become so smitten with the leggy blond that he set her up in a nice apartment of her own and now had money problems as well. He was petrified that his wife would find out and ask for a divorce. Should that happen, the resulting financial split would devastate what was left of his meager fortune.

A solution was at hand. He arrived at the restaurant at 2:00 p.m. and ordered lunch, while he waited for his party to arrive. A half hour later he was startled by a not so gentle hand on his shoulder.

"Good afternoon Mr. Alford," Viktor Dragan said as he took a seat opposite PCI's president and CEO.

Alford had never been given the man's name. He had never revealed who he worked for, though Alford could guess. The man took a heavy envelope out of his jacket pocket and laid it on the table. "One hundred thousand dollars deposit as agreed upon."

Alford reached for the bundle, but the man put his hand on it. "First, the information please."

"I don't feel good about this," Alford said.

"That's fine," the man said. "You can refuse to comply, and your wife will receive these pictures this afternoon."

He slid a folder across the table. Alford opened the folder and found photos of himself and his mistress in several compromising positions.

"How the hell did you get these?" he demanded.

"You have no idea what I can do," the man said. "If you don't comply there will be no money, your wife will be informed, and I might even send your children home in pieces."

Alford hadn't known much in the way of fear in his life, but his hands began to shake under the table. This man was evil personified.

"Now, tell me what you know."

Alford recounted all of the information from the morning's meeting, including the police report and what Parish hoped to find in Greenland.

When he was done the man said, "See, that wasn't so difficult was it? I want you to keep me informed. You go to the museum tonight and report back to me here as soon as they have completed the translations. We want to know what this Codex thing says."

Amar and Evan were chatting with Trevor Guilford in his office when Nikolai and Katya arrived at the museum. Amar gave Katya a hug and shook hands with Niki. "Nikolai, I've heard you aren't feeling well. Are you up to this tonight?" Amar asked.

Katya translated, "He says he has rested and is anxious to go for a drive."

Renfro and Alford arrived at the same time. Al Hemmings had begged off, having family duties to attend to. Jan Meyer and Rachael were having dinner together at the house on Mercer Island. Renfro locked the doors, checked the chamber of the Wilson Combat .45, and re-holstered the pistol. They all moved to the control room display. Trevor turned on the large flat screen monitor, and Robby's face appeared. Through the windows behind him they could see a full moon hovering over Everett. There was no way to see the moon from the museum without going outside.

"Hi everybody!" Robby greeted them. "Looks like all conditions are in the green. I have oriented the dish, the clock drive is functioning, and I have already verified our location signal with the rover."

Trevor had helped Tom Parish set up the control room and was the most familiar with all of the knobs and switches.

"Trevor, shall we begin to turn things on?"

"Ready when you are, Robby."

Robby went down the list, and Trevor affirmed, "Master switch on."

"Check."

"Recorders on."

"Both recorders are on."

"Turn on the PC."

"PC is on."

"Switch on the Russian computer."

"Russian computer is initializing."

"Let's wait until the Russian unit is up and running."

After less than a minute, Trevor reported, "Okay, it's up and running."

"Drive train master switch on."

"Drive train is on."

Robby could monitor the radio signal from his location, "S-band signal strength in the green," he said.

Robby didn't have access to the battery indicator; only Trevor did.

"How's the battery level? Robby asked.

"Just below full charge," Trevor answered.

Robby continued, "Camera covers open."

"Check, camera covers are open. I have a green light."

"Now the moment of truth," Robby said. "Camera one on."

"Turning camera one on," Trevor said.

Robby punched a button, and the picture of his face shrank to a thumbnail at the top right of the monitor.

The tension was palpable as they waited for five seconds. Slowly the image began to resolve and there directly in front of Lunokhod 1, which hadn't moved since Tom Parish was murdered, sat the Imbrium Codex. The gold script, unintelligible to anyone except Evan Chatterjee, glistened in the sunlight. Everybody applauded.

Amar asked for verification, "Are we recording this?"

"Yes, sir, we have two recorders running," Trevor indicated.

Trevor got up from the chair, and Amar motioned for Niki to take over. Niki sat down and asked Katya, "What do they want me to do?"

Amar instructed, "There is a natural slope on the right-hand edge of the crater. Ask him if he thinks we can drive down it. I would like to go around behind the Codex to see what's back there if possible."

"Niki narrated through Katya, "Control inputs should be from three-to-five seconds. Due to the time it takes our signal to reach the moon, there's a five-second control input delay. So, we'll make a control input and wait to see the camera move. Look there; you can see where Evginy, that idiot, drove the rover over the edge of the crater to our left almost fifty years ago. The natural slope on the right is nowhere near as steep, and I think we can drive down it."

Niki made a series of control inputs waiting for the camera to move each time. The codex went out of view as he slowly drove down the slope. When the rover got to the bottom and leveled out, they could see the gray lunar surface, extending behind the codex to the horizon, with a black sky above. Niki moved the rover forward to clear the monolith, and then began to turn left to position the camera directly behind the monument. As the rover pivoted again, the back of the monument came into view. It was blank and had no writing on it.

"Battery level at seventy-five percent." Trevor said.

Amar was incredulous. "There has to be more! They wouldn't have gone to all of this trouble and then leave us so little information. Can we drive around the right side to view it up close from the front?"

Niki replied that he could, and then he began to cough. He coughed so violently; he couldn't go on. Trevor brought out another chair, and Niki slid over. "Now you, Amar," he gasped in heavily accented English.

Amar took the control stick and pivoted the rover to the right ninety degrees. He made two additional control inputs to move it past the end of the monolith. Then he pivoted ninety degrees to the left again and drove past the edge of the monument. After clearing the side of the granite, he began to pivot back 180 degrees to face the codex head on. He misjudged the distance and held the stick in place for too long. Lunokhod 1 pivoted 180 degrees but was very close to the face of the monument.

The picture showed the camera closing in on the surface with the gold script upon it. Closer and closer, there was nothing Amar could do to recall his input. The picture rocked slightly as the rover bumped into the front of the monument.

"Battery level at fifty percent," Trevor advised.

The camera was close, so only a portion of the writing could be seen. Then, to everyone's surprise, the writing changed.

"Did you all see that?" Amar practically screamed. "The writing has changed. Niki, can I back it up?"

With a handkerchief over his mouth, Niki nodded. Amar entered the control input. There was enough room between the edge of the crater and the codex for the rover to back up and still see the entire surface. The recorders were running. The position of the dots that symbolized the relative position of the two solar systems had also changed.

"Trevor, is there any way to check that we got the footage of this panel?"

"Sure, boss, I can route the feed to one of the smaller monitors."

"Please do that and tell me we have the image; I want to bump it again."

Trevor's eyebrows rose in surprise. He pressed some buttons and reported that the image had been captured.

Amar glanced at the video, "Look, the binary orbit symbol has changed. That's how it acts as a clock. When you touch the codex, everything changes. How can writing that appears to have been engraved in granite over 12,000 years ago suddenly change like that?"

Evan commented, "As you've said many times Amar, their technology was more advanced than our own. The presence of the codex alone is direct evidence of that fact."

"I'm going to try it again. There may be more information."

Amar made a series of one-second control inputs and watched very carefully as the rover closed in once more. Finally, it bumped into the monolith, and the writing changed again. He backed up while that panel was recorded.

"Battery level at 25 percent." Trevor reported again.

Amar bumped the front of the monument again. The writing changed again. He backed up while the recorders documented the new writing on each panel. On the third try, the writing didn't change.

Amar backed up to verify that the panel had remained the same. It had.

Trevor reported one final time, "Battery level at one percent."

Then the picture went black. Through the heroic efforts of everyone involved, Lunokhod 1 had been raised from the dead, a feat unparalleled in the history of the space program. A thorough check of all systems revealed that the Russian rover had finally and irrevocably died for the last time.

Amar turned to Evan, "Okay, Doctor, there are six pages in total; now it's up to you to tell us what it all means. Can you complete the translation overnight?"

"I might as well; I'm certainly not going to be able to sleep until it's done."

"Then let's meet at the office tomorrow morning at 10:00," Amar said.

CHAPTER FORTY-EIGHT

Seattle

Amar and Katya put Niki to bed. After he was settled, they spent the night together again in Katya's room. Any doubts they may have had about the nature of their relationship were completely dispelled. The lovemaking had been long and tender, and they had fallen asleep in each other's arms once again, completely exhausted.

Amar woke at 7:15 and found that Katya was already up. He pulled on his cargo pants and padded out into the living room to find her on the sofa with a laptop computer.

"What are you looking up?" he asked.

"You," she said. "If I'm going to act as your bodyguard, then I'm entitled to know everything about you." She turned the screen in his direction. "I have Googled you and found your website."

"It's just a blog really," he confessed. "I use it as a place to park the papers I've written."

"I'm interested in your theory of overspecialization. Will you tell me about it?"

"I've been all over the world investigating the remains of civilizations that no longer exist. When I stand in the presence of the great ruins of history, I'm haunted by questions:"What happened here? Why are the people who built these magnificent structures gone? Where did they go?" The theory of overspecialization basically says that the larger and more embedded any artificially created social structure is, the more likely it will precipitate an extinction event when it fails. It could explain why some ancient civilizations have disappeared.

Social structures are comprised of the rules a society might put in place to manage the behavior of its citizens. An artificially created social structure can be a government, a religion, a belief system, a system of commerce, or as we are now discovering, a monetary system.

Let's consider the food production system here in America. The family farm was once the backbone of commerce in the United States. The typical family farm produced vegetables, poultry, dairy products, red meat, and more. The family farmer understood the need to keep all of his agricultural systems in balance to feed each other. The manure from the animals fertilized the plant material. The plant material supported both the animals and the people. Nothing was wasted. No chemicals or fertilizer had to be imported. If one farmer went under, his demise would not necessarily endanger all farmers.

Then, we decided that the objective of agriculture was to make money. Food in this country is no longer grown so much as it is manufactured. They say the average meal comes from 1,500 miles away and is shipped to your local market. They say every city only has a three-day supply of food on its shelves, which is replenished on a daily basis. What would happen if the transportation system broke down for some reason? That would be an example of the effect of overspecialization.

In our pursuit of profits, we instituted a monoculture. Now we have these vast agri-business farms that grow only one kind of crop. They deplete the soil and rely heavily on the application of chemical fertilizers and pesticides. We're just starting to be aware how much of these substances remain in the food we eat. The question is, will we see the point of no return before some sort of autoimmune disease born of the ingestion of pesticides descends upon the population at large?

The stock market is another good example. When their obscenely profitable mortgage revenue bond scheme failed in 2008, it caused a global financial crisis. The day before the crisis became visible, the CEO's of the major companies that went bankrupt were touting that the fundamentals were sound. Most of us didn't see that one coming.

The problem with large social structures of all kinds is that they are unresponsive to changing conditions at the local level. There are local differences, regional differences, and national differences in how people customarily organize themselves. One size doesn't fit all. Centralized management of large portions of the planetary population must take those differences into account, or they will most certainly fail and do great damage to society at large when they do fail.

Larger and larger social structures place both economic and political power in fewer and fewer hands. We're watching global trends toward the consolidation of power occur in most every area of endeavor. Amazon.com is an example of a massive social structure that's changing the way that we shop. Amazon is causing brick and mortar stores to go out of business. They have single-handedly changed the book-selling business. Don't get me wrong, I shop at Amazon. They have great prices and deliver the goods right to my door. Amazon's success has put enormous power in the hands of very few people. The question is—can we trust their ability to foresee the unintended consequences of their actions?

I envision a world where the means of production are returned to the local level. We should be able to go visit the butcher, the baker, and the candlestick maker in our local area to see how the goods and services we use are produced. Our young people should understand how the built environment around them was created. I envision a world where national governments take a backseat to local governments, where the people who legislate have a face to face relationship with their constituents and are held accountable by them.

What Warburg and men like him want to do is a form of overspecialization. They want to put all of their faith and all of our wealth into a single monetary system controlled by them. Their monetary system is not based upon the most good for the most people. It's based upon control of all by a small class of ruling elite. The truth is that the bigger any imposed social system is, the less responsive it is to the needs of the people. That was proved in your country Katya. If Warburg and his people are temporarily successful in setting up their one-world electronic slavery society, the damage will be on an unheard of scale when it collapses, and I am certain it will collapse.

The theory of overspecialization calls for decentralization, smaller government, and locally-held ruling power. Goods and services would be produced locally instead of being hauled all over the globe and hopefully reduce the global ruling class.

Katya sighed, "You're talking about a revolution, Amar. It's always the same. The elite want too big a piece of the pie. The common people rise up to take their power back. They are met with the fury of resistance from the people whom the current system has served. In order to overcome that resistance, they overpower the old guard and eventually become what they despised in the first place. How can we prevent that from happening again?"

"I don't know yet, Katya. I'm hoping Evan's translation will supply the next clues we need."

Everyone gathered around the conference table in Amar's office at 10:00 that morning. Evan walked in a few minutes late, looking slightly haggard.

Amar inquired, "Doctor, were you able to get any sleep at all?"

"I managed to grab a couple of hours between six and eight this morning. Is there any coffee for all love?"

Jan jumped up and returned with a cup made just the way he liked it.

Amar continued, "Were you able to complete the translations?"

"What a slave driver you are, Amar Parish!" he said in between sips. "Wait one moment while I attempt to put the photos on screen."

Evan punched a few keys on his laptop. A still photo of the first two pages of the codex popped up on the monitor over Amar's desk. Evan downed the rest of his cup in two swallows and held it up for Jan to refill.

Feeling slightly more human, he began, "You recall that I was able to translate the first two pages that Tom sent you just before he died, God rest his soul."

They all bowed their heads in respect. Evan realized that not everyone in the room had heard the translation of the first two pages yet. "I'll go back over that part so that we're all have the same information. We now know that the people who inhabited our planet over 12,000 years ago called themselves Ularians. At first, we thought that the double oval symbol we see both at Persepolis and on the Codex was simply some sort of logo that represented their civilization. Subsequently, we found that it is actually a diagram of what is called a binary orbit. This photo was taken before Amar accidently discovered more pages by blundering into the monolith."

"Hey, Doctor, I did not blunder! No blundering took place!" Amar grinned. "Well, maybe a little bit."

"As I was saying," Evan smiled, "the two dots represent two different solar systems. The two ovals represent the orbital paths that the solar systems take through space relative to each other. One dot represents our own solar system, which was known by the ancients as Ularia 2. We haven't had a chance to identify which star in the night sky represents the other solar system, but we now know it was referred to by the Ularians as Ularia Prime.

Note that the two dots are at the closest point they can be to each other on the first page. I have interpreted this to be the position they were in when the codex was placed on the moon. I'm going to switch to the next page, so you can see how that has changed. We'll return to the text in a minute."

Evan punched some more keys. "Once pages 3 and 4 became visible, we see that the position of the dots has changed. I believe that the new positions of the two dots indicate the relative positions of the two solar systems today. In that way, the diagram is not only a map but also a clock."

Evan returned to pages 1 and 2. "The text explains the binary orbit in detail. The codex says that it takes approximately 24,000 years for the two solar systems to complete one revolution around the binary orbital path.

Evan changed the slide. "This is a picture of the Andromeda galaxy which is very similar to our own. We do not have pictures of our galaxy since no camera has ever been far enough away to take one. Let's pretend that Andromeda is our galaxy. You can see that it's made up of spiral arms of stars emanating out from a luminous center."

Evan overlaid the orbital diagram over the picture of the galaxy and continued. "Our two solar systems are locked in a dance and are floating together in one of those spiral arms. Apparently, the long axis of the two ovals points directly toward galactic center. That's an important distinction, which I will elaborate on in a minute. The long axis divides the orbit into two parts. For half the orbit, or 12,000 years, we approach the center of the galaxy. For the other half of the orbit, or the remaining 12,000 years, we move away from the center of the galaxy."

Bob Alford interrupted, "But why is that significant?"

"According to the text, the archetypical energy that animates the intelligence of human beings, is broadcast from the luminous center of the galaxy. The idea is referred to in modern Gnostic texts as Emanationism. You might think of it like a radio broadcast that gets stronger as you approach a radio station from a great distance. As we approach galactic center for 12,000 years, both human intelligence and the technologies that flow from it increase. You are all familiar with the acceleration of modern technology over the last two hundred years. I believe that is an example of how the binary orbit works upon us. As we travel away from galactic center for 12,000 years, both the higher state of human intelligence and the technologies that once flowed from it, are gradually forgotten."

Amar jumped in, "And that's the answer to why we have physical evidence of higher civilizations being on the planet, but we can't remember who they were or what they knew!"

"I believe this discovery proves that your theorems are correct, Amar. In both the Imbrium Codex and the chamber at Persepolis, we have direct evidence of civilizations that were more advanced than our own, and of whom we have very little knowledge." Evan said, "The half of our elliptical orbit during which we approach galactic center is referred to as the ascending cycle, and the half of the orbit during which we move away from galactic center is called the descending cycle."

Katya could not restrain herself. "I have to know; where are we now?"

"I spent a couple of hours calculating our position last night," Evan testified. "When Amar caused the display to change, the diagram changed with it. You can see the relative positions of the solar systems here. From my calculations, I estimate that the codex was placed on the moon in approximately 11,500 BCE and that now 13,520 years have elapsed. We passed that point in our orbit that was farthest away from galactic center around 499 CE.

That period roughly correlates to the fall of Rome, a time when the entire planet was suffering from ignorance, pestilence, and an overall lack of intelligence. We are all familiar with the vast leaps technology has taken since then. According to our current position, we are now approximately 1,520 years into a 12,000 year acceleration toward the light of galactic center."

"So, the news is good?" Renfro asked.

"Yes and no," Evan replied. "In order to qualify that statement, we'll need to move to pages 3 and 4 of the text. Before we move on, I should mention that the codex is signed, and we know the name of its author."

Everyone sat up and started talking all at once.

"Calm down people," Amar demanded. "Tell us, Doctor, who put it there?"

Evan announced, "The Imbrium Codex is signed by a man named Sanjay, who was the Royal Historian to the Court of Vandalay."

Robby Harris cut in, "How cool is that, people? But what did you mean by answering yes and no to Renfro's question? Is the news good or not?"

"On pages 3 and 4, Sanjay tells us that the release of this information has come at a particular time in human evolution. He says that the codex was placed upon the moon so it would survive a great period of global cleansing. I have interpreted that to mean the end of the most recent ice age. The resulting melting of the ice caps, and the biblical deluge created by the release of so much water, have transformed the planet. Sanjay mentions that the earth has gone through this cycle many, many times.

Anyway, he says that every subsequent class of humans comes to a point in the development of their technology, where for the first time, they are capable of destroying themselves. He says the codex was placed in a location where the level of technology required to destroy ourselves is the same level of technology that would be required for us to go find the codex and benefit from the wisdom contained in it.

We created the atomic bomb in 1945. That was the first appearance of the technology required to completely destroy ourselves. We walked on the moon in 1969, only twenty-four years later. That's pretty close in the context of a 24,000 year cycle. You will all agree that we still live in a society that is haunted by the specter of nuclear annihilation. That being said, Sanjay takes it even further."

"What more is there to say? Are we doomed?" Trevor asked.

"Actually, as it turns out, Sanjay has quite a lot more to say. As to whether we are doomed or not, that appears to be the question that humanity is being collectively called upon to answer. Sanjay refers to something he calls the Planetary Free Will Experiment. He says that the design for humans on our planet is for us all to be free to act creatively in our own evolutionary interest. He makes the point that free will is a gift that comes with a responsibility to recognize everyone's God-given right to create the life they want.

"He seems to have been aware of what our approximate position on the binary orbital path would be when we made this discovery. We've been through the dark ages and are now accelerating toward the light. According to the Royal Historian, we have come to that point in human evolution where we must realize that we can no longer enslave one another for material gain. He says that our collective failure to have that realization may endanger our species.

"Sanjay tells us that the power behind creation is increasing as we approach the light of galactic center. He says that a great quickening is at hand, and that the affairs of humanity will begin to move very fast. He also says that the power behind creation can be used to manifest our dreams or our nightmares. He makes it clear that we will either stop the practice of enslaving each other as a species, or we may face a terminal extinction event brought upon ourselves by ourselves. The question being asked is—will we see the point of no return before we cross it? The experimental part is that we are free to fail."

Amar connected the dots, "We are faced with just such a dilemma right now. Warburg wants to set up a global monetary system and a total surveillance state wherein every human is monitored and manipulated from the cradle to the grave for the personal gain of his group of elites. I can't think of a better example of overspecialization, not to mention moral decay. If you've read any of my papers, you know that overspecialization can lead to extinction. The battle is becoming clear. Warburg, and all of those like him, must be stopped."

"I agree," Evan said. "However, we must take great care in how that's done lest we become what we're opposed to. The story of past revolutions in which the rebels eventually became the oppressors is all too common. Let's move on to pages 5 and 6. Sanjay says that two forces are acting upon the inhabitants of our galaxy.

He describes beings known as the Aeons and the Archons. Historical references to such beings are present in the very early Gnostic writings found in the Nag Hammadi Library, a collection of thirteen ancient books that were discovered in Egypt in 1945. According to his description, the Aeons inhabit the luminous region of galactic center. He says their role is to create the three-dimensional world by dreaming it into existence. He refers to what he calls the Aeonic influence, which is based upon freedom, creativity, and happiness.

He also describes beings known as the Archons. According to his description, the Archons are scattered throughout the galaxy. He says they are parasitic in nature, and they project materialism, subservience, and misery into the three-dimensional world. They feed upon discontent. Sanjay makes the point that the Archontic influence is adopted by those who make it their life's purpose to defraud the common people.

He says that the Archons are aware the planet is accelerating toward the light. At this point in our trajectory, they will make a final play to consolidate their dominance over humanity. You will know this is taking place when honor is lost, and the truth becomes lies. A very apt description of the world today, don't you think?

So far, I don't recognize these two forces as a collection of conscious beings, but I certainly recognize them as cultural influences. In my words, these two forces are like radio channels. You can tune them in or out. That attunement is the essence of the Planetary Free Will Experiment. The question is; will we collectively attune ourselves to freedom, creativity and happiness in time to save humanity, or will we go the other way into mass hypnosis, subservience and possibly extinction?"

Katya had something to say, "My country has been taken over by the oligarchs. They dismantled the Soviet Union in 1991 and divided up all of the assets for themselves, leaving almost nothing for the common people. Creativity is frowned upon. Their system is neither creative nor productive. You are told not to smile because the people, who have been oppressed for centuries, will think you are crazy. Here in America, you can't find anything that says it was made in Russia. My country is in serious decline at the hands of a dishonest ruling class.

It is interesting to note that the Russian revolution in 1917 took place to stop the very same kind of abuse by the ruling class of that time. Then the communists created an elite class of privileged bureaucrats to administer their system, and the cycle of abuse started all over again. When that system failed, the communist elite were replaced by the oligarchs.

Sharing a border with China causes Russians to be interested in what they are doing. The Chinese are well on their way to creating the total surveillance state that you fear. They have installed 200 million cameras, with facial recognition, to keep watch over their population. They reward their citizens for reporting any action that doesn't match the state's version of proper behavior. They inform on each other and keep score by electronically punishing those who do not comply. They have created a society based upon fear and conformity, which they think is a good thing."

"I think the battle lines are becoming clear," Amar said. "Is there any more from Sanjay, Doctor?"

"Yes, there is, and this may be the most exciting part. Sanjay says that at the time the codex was created, even he was not allowed to know what the exact condition the planet would be in after the great cleansing. He says if the archive still exists, we will find technology there that will weaken the control of the Archons and help all humans to move forward. He also says it would be quite useless to try to describe where the remains of Vandalay might be located, since the world will most certainly not look the way it did prior to the great cleansing. He signs the codex saying—'Blessings Be Upon You, Sanjay, Royal Historian to the Court of Vandalay.'"

"Thank you, Evan, from the bottom of my heart, for your expertise and commitment to this cause," Amar said. "I just want to add a couple of thoughts. I believe that the codex was intended to be viewed in person on the moon. It might have taken another fifty-to-one-hundred years for us to have enough of a physical presence there to stumble upon it.

"I'm not sure that Sanjay anticipated we would discover it using a robot. I'm also not sure that Sanjay anticipated that we would have satellites to help us zero in on the probable location of the ruins of the ancient city of Vandalay. I'm saying that because I believe we may be slightly ahead of schedule in discovering who the Ularians were. That gives me hope that we may be in time to stop the technological takeover of the human race."

CHAPTER FORTY-NINE

Seattle

Alford was summoned to the restaurant on Nickerson St.

"What have you got to tell me?" asked Dragan.

Alford considered all that there was to tell and decided to leave out parts of the translation that seemed to him to be philosophical.

"They have completed the translation of the codex. All of the information they have gathered so far points to the possible existence of an ancient city unlike anything discovered up to this point in human history. The part that will interest you is that contained within that city is an archive. Supposedly, in that archive, they should find technology that will completely change the world as we know it."

"What kind of technology?"

"The codex does not say what kind of technology."

"And do they still think this city is located in Greenland?"

"They don't know exactly, but they have some satellite surveillance that shows where it might be. Here are the coordinates."

Dragan opened his laptop and pulled up Google Earth. He entered the coordinates and zoomed in. "There's nothing in this part of Greenland but dirt and ice!"

"That could be the reason the damn thing hasn't been found yet," Alford commented dryly.

"When are they planning to go there?"

"According to Renfro, they will be ready next week."

Dragan slipped another envelope across the table. Alford put it in his jacket pocket.

"I want to know exactly when they plan to leave, what they are taking with them, and how they plan to go there," Dragan commanded.

Alford sighed. He wasn't a traitor by nature, and he didn't like the way this was coming down. But he was in too deep and had no choice now.

"Okay, I'll get all of that information to you as soon as I have it."

"See that you do, Mr. Alford. You know the penalty for failure in this matter."

Alford rose from the table and made his way out of the restaurant on shaky legs. This man, whoever he was, scared him to the deepest part of his soul.

Part 5: Hostile Takeover

CHAPTER FIFTY

Seattle

The expedition team, consisting of Amar, Katya, Robby, Evan, and Gary, gathered in the mission planning room at the PCI warehouse at Boeing Field. Nikolai was judged to be too frail to go along on this adventure and would stay in the apartment with Alice. Bob Alford and Al Hemmings were instructed to remain behind to keep PCI running smoothly. Robby Harris and Gary Renfro spent hours studying the high-resolution satellite photos of the edge of the glacier on the east coast of Greenland.

Robby was able to zoom in close enough to see the white zigzag pattern that had recently been revealed by the retreating ice. He also noted two distinct points of interest that would affect the coming expedition. First and foremost, a large lake of ice melt had formed on top of the glacier, less than a kilometer inland from its edge. The second point of interest was a small opening under the base of the leading edge of the glacier, out of which an icy river was flowing.

Robby put the satellite feed up on the monitor. He zoomed in to show the edge of the glacier and summarized their findings. "It looks like there might be an ice cave under the base of the glacier. That's not uncommon in this area. Glaciers don't necessarily melt from the top down. We may be able to walk in under the ice. I've seen photos of ice caves in Greenland; they can be really beautiful."

He zoomed back out for an overview of the lake. "The lake on top of the glacier could be a real problem. We have no way of knowing how stable it is. I've heard stories of this kind of lake water melting its way down to the underside of the glacier and then completely draining in less than an hour. That would be a lot of water moving at high speed. If we're in the ice cave when that happens, it could be potentially life-threatening. Based upon these conditions, Gary has assembled a travel plan and acquired the equipment we will need to journey under the ice."

Renfro stood up and pointed toward a photo of a ship, now on the monitor. "As you know, the Aurora Star will meet us in Reykjavik.

We've signed an agreement with them that anything we might find onsite will remain the property of the expedition. It will be a three-day sail into the site of what we hope will be a significant archaeological discovery. We'll each have our own staterooms, and the ship will provide all of the food and beverages we could want, so we should be very comfortable. The ship can't sail right up to the end of the fjord, so we'll need to use their shore boat to ferry us to the gravel beach." Renfro clicked and a picture of a smaller boat appeared on the screen. "This is a Norsafe Munin 1200 fast rescue boat. It is designed for use in the North Sea. It's powered by jet drive and is highly maneuverable. It's designed to withstand extreme weather and if it rolls over in heavy seas, it will right itself automatically. We can run this boat right up on the gravel if we need to. It has sufficient cargo capacity for us and any artifacts we might be able to salvage."

Renfro went over to two tables piled high with equipment.

Katya quipped, "Looks like Christmas in August!"

Renfro grinned and pulled down a large black Pelican case. He opened it.

"This is a DJI M-600 industrial drone. It has six propellers, a flight duration of about a half hour and a range of five kilometers. Robby will pilot the drone from on board the ship which will be anchored less than one kilometer away. He'll fly ahead of the shore party to get a bird's eye view of whatever conditions we are likely to encounter before we get there. He'll also use the drone to monitor the lake and warn us if any conditions are changing up there. Robby will also be in charge of communications not only with us but also with the ship's crew.

The shore party will consist of Amar, Katya, Evan, and myself. Because we're going into unknown and potentially dangerous conditions, I've assembled the following equipment."

Renfro held up each item as he described it. "Each member of the shore party will be wearing a red and black Hollis BTR-500 dry suit with matching rock boots and insulated gloves. We will each have an open-faced helmet with a built-in waterproof radio, a helmet camera, and a retractable visor."

"Why do we need radios, Gary?" asked Katya. 'I should think an ice cave would be relatively quiet."

"I've consulted with some experts on the subject and they tell me that it can be quite noisy inside one of these caves. There will be the sound of fast-moving water and sometimes the ice actually "sings" making all sorts of creaking and groaning noises. So, the radios are a good idea. Each of you will also have a Mantus mini scuba tank carried in a small backpack. They are very compact and don't weigh much at all. Each tank has a 2.7 liter capacity and will provide air for up to twenty minutes. I don't anticipate being under water, but these tanks will give us a margin of safety if we have to swim for any reason."

"Doctor, I have a little something else for you here."

Renfro pulled out a small black Pelican case and opened it. "This is an Olympus TG-5 waterproof camera with a transmitter. We'll have lots of coverage from the helmet cams, but we would like you to keep this handy for close-up shots of any artifacts or text you might want to look at later. Every time you take a picture, it will automatically transmit the image back to Robby's computer on the ship. That way we won't lose any images if the camera is destroyed during the mission."

Seeing the worried look on Evan's face, Amar stepped in, "Doctor, we've been in tighter spots before and have made it through. If we determine that an area is too dangerous to enter, we will not go in."

Evan pretended he was reassured, but the worried look remained.

"Finally," Renfro said, "there are the usual assortment of crampons, ice axes, shovels, and instruments of destruction. We've already loaded a Yamaha Grizzly ATV into the airplane. I'll be using the quad to pull a sled with all of the tools. We'll also use the quad to haul back any artifacts we might find. Robby will handle communications. Evan will be responsible for photography, and Amar and Katya will lead the way. Amar is the boss, and what he says goes. We'll still have three days aboard ship to iron out the details. Any questions?"

"Yes," Amar asked, "when do you want to leave?"

Renfro answered, "We'll load the plane this afternoon and depart tomorrow at 7:00 a.m."

CHAPTER FIFTY-ONE

Seattle to Nordvest Fjord, Greenland

A steel gray overcast day was dawning as Ted Lockhart and Jason Hall completed the pre-flight inspection of the C-130 Hercules at 6:00 a.m. Gary Renfro was supervising the loading of the remaining equipment when Amar, Katya, Robby, and Evan arrived. Everyone had been advised to bring warm clothing since daytime temperatures in both Iceland and Greenland were not expected to top 45 degrees Fahrenheit during the day and somewhat colder at night.

This particular C-130 cargo plane was used by PCI primarily to transport cell phone tower equipment and switch gear along with construction crews to foreign countries. Two rows of heavily padded reclining seats had been installed just aft of the cockpit bulkhead for the comfort of crew members. A large flat screen TV was mounted on the back wall of the cockpit to allow the crew to watch movies on long international flights.

The airplane was fitted with long range fuel tanks allowing one-hop flights from Seattle to New York and from New York to Reykjavik. A part-time flight engineer named Jerry Hanson was also on board for this mission. Everyone strapped in, and the C-130 was wheels up at 7:00 a.m. sharp. The turbo-prop was substantially slower than Amar's Citation X. At 350 miles per hour, the flight into La Guardia took 8-1/2 hours. Amar and Katya talked quietly in their seats, holding hands in between movies, naps, and snacks. They were on the ground at La Guardia and taxiing to the tie-down area at 6:30 p.m. local time. They would lay over that night in New York and be wheels up again the next day at 7:00 a.m.

The flight from New York to Iceland took just a little longer, and they arrived at Keflavik International Airport at 11:00 p.m. the following evening, having crossed five time zones. The sun had set around 9:00 p.m., but it was still light enough to see. Jan Meyer arranged for a box van and a passenger van to haul both people and gear over to Skarfabakki Pier where the Aurora Star waited for them. The three pilots would go on holiday until the members of the expedition returned. They were looking forward to visiting the Blue Lagoon geo-thermal spa and seeing the sights around southern Iceland.

Jan also greased the skids with the customs agents, and processing at the airport took only a few minutes. They made a cursory inspection of all of the equipment and did not even look through personal luggage. Since they were not really entering the country, a customs officer accompanied them to the departure pier to verify that all equipment would be transferred on board the ship. That was a good thing because both Renfro and Katya had weapons stowed in their gear. Seagulls were squawking overhead as the vans pulled up next to the ship. The sky was clear, and the stars looked close enough to touch. The late evening air was a brisk 40 degrees.

Katya was the first out on the pier wearing a black one-piece Bogner jump suit and matching ball cap, her hair in a ponytail under the cap. Amar loved that go-anywhere look. As tired as they were, she still looked spectacular. The team gathered at the base of the gangway to be greeted by the ship's captain, who had done his homework and recognized Amar Parish on sight.

"Mr. Parish, welcome aboard the Aurora Star. My name is Stefan Fischer." He waved toward the ship. "I am your captain. Allow me to present my first officer, Harvey Kline."

Amar shook hands with both men. "Captain and Mr. Kline, it is very nice to meet you. Allow me to introduce my crew." Amar proceeded with the introductions and then gestured toward the box van. "We have a truckload of equipment that needs to go with us."

"I'll have my people load your gear aboard. If you will follow me, I will direct you to your cabins."

The Aurora Star was ninety-four meters of stout, steel ship. Her ice breaker's hull was painted navy blue with a white superstructure above. There wasn't a flake of rust on her. Two cranes towered above them, one on the foredeck and one on the aft deck. The cranes and all the deck equipment were painted bright red. The aft crane creaked and groaned as it pivoted over the pier to pick up Renfro's quad and place it on the deck.

The ship carried a crew of twenty-one and had space for twenty-three scientists or researchers. She would be vastly underused on this expedition, but the crew wouldn't mind at all. This would be an easy cruise for them compared to a normal scientific expedition.

Amar and Katya were sharing one of the larger staterooms. Evan, Renfro, and Robby each had their own cabins. The crew was used to operating at odd hours during late summer evenings near the arctic circle. No one was surprised when midnight came, and Captain Fischer ordered them to unmoor ship and proceed into the Norwegian Sea on their way toward Scoresby Sound. Once the helmsman set the course, the captain retired to his cabin for the night.

Amar and Katya stood by the rail outside of their cabin admiring the bright green northern lights shimmering in a crystal clear night sky. The display was so mesmerizing, they remained at the rail, finally giving up and retiring after 3:00 a.m.

Over the next two days, the crew busied themselves preparing their equipment, studying real time satellite images of their destination and whale watching as they crossed the arctic circle. Renfro instructed Evan and Katya on the use of the scuba tanks. Both Renfro and Amar were certified divers and needed no refresher. The weather was cooperating as the Aurora Star steamed north through gentle eight-foot swells spaced one-tenth of a mile apart. The ship entered Scoresby Sound after an uneventful cruise through relatively calm Norwegian Sea waters. As a matter of back country courtesy, Captain Fischer stopped at the little town of Ittoqqortoormiit to deliver supplies and fuel which were off-loaded onto the port's ship tender.

The Aurora Star departed Ittoqqortoormiit at dawn on the third day of the voyage. They still had 125 miles to sail through Scoresby Sound just to get to the mouth of Nordvest Fjord. The expedition crew spent many hours on deck admiring the giant ice mountains that were floating by. Finally, they entered the mouth of Nordvest Fjord. At eighty-seven miles in length, Nordvest Fjord is one of the longest fjords in the world. The winter pack ice was just beginning to form in the four-mile-wide passage, and the ship easily plowed a path up the middle of the waterway. Bleak looking snowcapped mountains rose up to 5,000 feet above them on either side. The ship shunted the smaller bergs out of her path as she made her way up the fjord. Two men were required on the bridge at all times to keep an eye out for larger icebergs, particularly those that might be submerged.

At 9:00 p.m. on the third day, the ship arrived at the end of the north fork of the fjord. They were surrounded by giant floating mountains of ice, with colors varying from aquamarine blue to bright white. Captain Fischer turned the ship around, pointing back in the direction from which they had come. The fjord was over 500 feet deep, too deep to make anchoring practical. The captain would rely on the vessel's GPS dynamic positioning system to keep the ship in one spot for the duration of the expedition. There was a narrow channel into the gravel beach kept clear by the slightly warmer river water running out from under the glacier.

It wouldn't be long before that river and everything else froze solid for the winter. Timing was critical. They had to complete their mission and sail out of the fjord before the pack ice became too thick to break through. The sun had already slipped from view behind the mountains on shore and Amar decided to wait until morning before sending the drone aloft to recon the area.

In anticipation of the next day's adventure, nobody slept well that night. Just before dawn, the expedition team gathered in the chart room to review the plan and safety considerations for the day's exploration. Everyone was grateful for the coffee and pastries offered up by the galley crew. Amar noted that the quad and all of the team's equipment was being loaded onto the shore boat, which sat in a cradle on the aft deck. When that was done, the overhead crane lifted the entire boat, with all of its gear, and placed it gently on the water next to the boarding stairs on the starboard side of the ship. Amar smiled; that was so much easier than ferrying all of the gear down the boarding stairs, one bag at a time. These sailors knew what they were doing.

Amar addressed the group, "The galley is preparing a full breakfast and some sack lunches for us. I know it's early, but I suggest you all take advantage of the opportunity. We're going to get some exercise today, and we don't really know if and when we might be able to break for lunch. Harvey, the first officer, will pilot the shore boat and land us on the beach.

"We're bringing some loading ramps so we can offload the quad onto the gravel. He'll wait there for us in case we need to evacuate in a hurry. I want everyone to kit up before we get in the boat, including helmets, radios, all safety equipment, and the air bottles, too. Both Gary and Katya will be armed. Polar bears are not uncommon in this part of the world.

"Gary will drive the quad and pull the sled with all of our tools. Evan, I'd like you to document our progress with your camera as we approach the glacier. Robby will be receiving all the feeds from each helmet cam on this large flat screen monitor as well as Evan's handheld and the drone. We'll be in audible and visual contact at all times."

Robby cut in, "I have also taken the liberty to set up a satellite link with the office so Jan and Rachael and key members of the staff can watch the expedition directly from your helmet cams, live as it unfolds. It's the middle of the night there, but I let Jan know when the feed would be available. They'll be able to see what you see in real time."

"That's a great idea, Robby; thanks for taking care of it. I know my mom will be delighted to have a front row seat. Robby, do we have enough light to launch the drone?"

"All set boss. If you gather around my monitor, I'll put this baby into the air."

Robby manipulated the controls. The drone took off from the aft deck and flew out over the ice-strewn water on its way to the glacier.

Robby narrated, "It's still early enough in the autumn for heat from the sun to melt portions of the glacial ice, creating the big lake we have seen on top of the glacier from our satellite feed. Obviously, that lake water is warmer than the ice that supports it. Some of that water is draining through the glacier and forming the river that flows out from its leading edge and which has created an open channel through the ice."

The drone flew up the channel toward the glacier at fifty feet above the water.

"The shoreline is coming up. We follow the river on up the gravel area and look there to the right! There's your zigzag pattern, Doctor!"

Evan was wide awake now, "Can you get closer Robby?"

"Sure can; let's take her down and hover right over it."

Evan squinted at the close-up picture, "It looks like clay pipe! Most of it is crushed into shards, but you can see a small section here and there that is still intact. We're looking at manmade technology that could be more than 12,000 years old. It's amazing to me that it has never been seen before now, but apparently, this is the first year the glacier has retreated far enough to reveal it!"

"Robby," Amar said, "let's proceed to get the overview, and we can investigate all of the details when we get there."

Robby pulled back on one of the control levers, and the drone rose back into the air. He adjusted the camera angle, and the edge of the glacier loomed 500 feet into the air before them. The drone sped up-river toward what they all hoped would be a monumental discovery. Robby slowed the drone's speed as it approached the vertical face of the glacier, bringing it to a hover directly above the opening out of which the river flowed. Gently, the drone descended to a human eye level.

"It's hard to tell the scale, but it looks like the opening is only ten feet or so high. Can you fly inside Robby?" Amar asked.

"It's too risky, boss. I'm not an expert with this drone, and if I hit something, we'll lose our ability to monitor the lake above."

"Right," Amar said. "we'll be there in a little while anyway. Can we have a look at the lake?"

"Sure thing. Going up now."

The drone rose 600 feet straight up and the lake came into view atop the glacier, less than one kilometer away. Robby tweaked the controls, and the drone sped on toward the tenuous body of water. The drone flew over a small round crevasse about 150 feet in front of the lake.

Robby hovered the drone over the hole. "It's hard to tell how deep that is since it's in shadow. We should be able to see better when the sun rises higher in the sky.

"Let's move on to the lake," Amar said.

"How big do you think that is?" Katya asked.

"Looks like twenty-to-thirty acres," Amar answered.

"That's a shitload of water," Renfro commented.

Robby was flying the drone with one hand and punching numbers into a keypad with the other. "Looks like a couple of hundred million gallons if it's fifteen feet deep," he said.

Evan chimed in, "It looks stable for the moment."

A red light began to flash on Robby's controller. "I have to bring her back and change batteries. I'll wait until you leave, and then I'll put the drone back in the air and keep an eye on the lake for you. Every half hour, I'll have to come back for fresh batteries, though," Robby said.

Amar was grinning from ear to ear. "Okay folks, let's have breakfast and get ready to go discover the ancient city of Vandalay."

CHAPTER FIFTY-TWO

Iceland

The Augusta Westland AW609 tiltrotor aircraft took off from the west helicopter pad of the newest of Zoltan Holding's thirty-two oil platforms. This one was located off of the north coast of Iceland. The AW609 is a tiltrotor aircraft capable of vertical takeoff and landing as well as cruising at 300 mph. The aircraft was configured with seven seats and a small cargo area. It was primarily used to ferry crews back and forth from the mainland to various oil platforms owned by a hierarchy of shell companies that were ultimately traceable directly to Harry Warburg, but only if you knew how to navigate the corporate layers.

Viktor Dragan sat in the co-pilot's seat as they sped across the Norwegian Sea on a beeline for Ittoqqortoormiit, Greenland, some 500 miles to the west. Five of the passenger seats were filled by Dragan's crew of eastern European mercenaries. He referred to this group of men as Alpha team. Dragan's call sign was Alpha one; the other five mercenaries were known as Alpha two through six. Alpha seven was the pilot.

These men worked for pay and had no qualms about what they might be asked to do, so long as the money was good. They were professional warriors for hire. The flight across open water took less than two hours. Dragan had made previous arrangements with the FBO at Nerlerit Inaat Airport to refuel with Jet A, which in an ironic twist of fate, had been delivered the previous day by the Aurora Star. The refueling took place in less than an hour. As the chopper rose into the air on its way into Nordvest Fjord, Dragan reached up and shut off both the transponder and the GPS beacon. Best not to have a record of where they were going or what they were going there to do.

Dragan and his Alpha team were all kitted in black fatigues with helmets and full combat vests. This mission would be like taking candy from a baby. They would be in and out very quickly. Resistance, they knew, would be minimal. No provision was made for prolonged exposure to cold temperatures, they wouldn't be there long enough for it to matter.

Each one of the soldiers of fortune carried his own choice of semi-auto pistol. The cargo area contained ice climbing and rappelling gear along with a Sig Sauer MPX 9mm machine pistol for each man. Dragan checked his wrist display. He should be getting a satellite feed from Amar Parish's helmet cam and communication radio any minute now, courtesy of Bob Alford, his man on the inside. Dragan made a mental note to eliminate that sniveling moron as soon as he returned from this mission.

Vandalay

After a hearty breakfast, Amar and his crew donned their dry suits, helmets and communications gear. They strapped on the backpacks containing their mini scuba tanks and some food and water. Both Renfro and Katya loaded a Wilson Combat .45 caliber 1911 semi-auto pistol with spare clips into their packs, just in case. The rest of their gear was already aboard the shore boat.

Amar turned to Katya knowing that his mother and Jan could see him through Katya's helmet cam. He waived. "Hi Mom! Well, this is it. We're either going to make history today or go home empty-handed. Either way, I'm glad to be here with you all."

He gave Katya a peck on the cheek.

Katya looked up into his eyes and grinned, "I have been on some intense missions, but so far this is the most fun I've ever had on a first date! I am happy to be with you too, Mr. American Big Shot. Let's go and make some history."

Evan, also grinning, chimed in using a fake Russian accent, "You guys can get to a room after we make this history!"

They all laughed. One by one the team descended the gangway steps in single file and took their places in the boat.

"Com check," Amar said into his microphone.

Renfro said, " I have you five by five."

Katya replied, "I can hear you."

Evan repeated, "I can hear you, too."

Robby was up on the aft deck of the bridge, preparing to launch the drone. "Everybody is coming in loud and clear. I have four helmet cam pictures."

Amar took command, "Okay Harvey, let's go to the beach,"

"Aye, sir," said the first officer. One of the deck hands let go of the mooring lines, and the fast rescue boat began to move slowly away from the ship.

Renfro asked, "Harvey, can we beach this craft stern first so we can unload the quad?"

"Yes, sir, that won't be a problem."

They motored down the deep blue channel, the sun glaring off of large chunks of floating ice. Renfro pointed out that each of their helmets had a retractable tinted visor they could use if it became too bright. It was only about a half mile to the gravel beach. Harvey pivoted the boat and used reverse thrust to ground her on the gravel bar just to the north of the river's mouth.

Evan jumped out, and Amar helped him to place the ramps over the stern. Renfro climbed onto the quad, started the motor, and very carefully drove it up over the stern and down the ramps onto the gravel. Evan and Amar shoved the ramps back onto the rear deck of the boat. Harvey handed out the sled and the rest of their tools and equipment.

"Harvey, can you stay here until we size up the situation? If we're going to be in there for a while, I'll radio out to you, and you can go back to the ship. We'll call when we want to be picked up. Before I make that call, I'd like to assess the situation, and have you wait here just in case we need to make a hasty retreat."

Harvey held up his thermos and lunch box. "No worries, boss. I have my coffee and my lunch. Just let me know what you want to do, and I will make it happen."

Renfro put the quad in gear and began to motor along the gravel bar on the north side of the river. The river was flowing gently along, and it looked like they would have no trouble crossing to the other side if need be. Katya, Amar, and the Doctor hiked along behind him.

After ten minutes, they came upon the white zigzag pattern that had drawn them there.

Evan was the first to comment. "Look here—the white streaks are actually pulverized clay pipe. There are a couple of shards that are still intact. This has to be some sort of ancient irrigation system."

Amar pulled out some large plastic Ziploc bags. "Let's take some samples, Doctor. We may want to analyze them later."

Samples were taken, placed in a plastic container, and stowed in the sled. The pattern of what used to be piping led directly to a gaping semicircular maw at the foot of the glacier. As they approached, the vertical wall of blue and white ice loomed 500 feet above them, shining in the sun.

Renfro stopped the quad one hundred yards away from the leading edge and addressed the group, "I'm no expert, but the face of the glacier looks pretty solid. If it were out over the water, I wouldn't be so sure, but since it's resting on solid ground, I don't see any evidence that it's about to calve. It's only fair to warn you that we're all putting our lives at risk here. If you want to turn back, now's the time. Do you all want to continue?"

Each member of the team indicated that they were prepared to keep going. When they had studied the satellite photos and observed the area earlier that morning with the drone, there was nothing present to indicate the scale of the opening. As they approached the sheer wall of ice, it became apparent that the arched hole was about fifteen feet high and thirty feet across. The small river ran out of the center, leaving enough of a gravel path on both sides so they could walk directly into the heart of the glacier. Amar grabbed Katya's hand, and they entered the cavern with Evan and Renfro behind them.

Amar decided to test coms with Robby. "Robby, are you getting all of this?"

Robby came back, "Yes, boss, I have four helmet cam feeds, and I'm recording everything you say and see. It's beautiful!"

"Roger that, we're going in."

It was midnight in Seattle. Jan Meyer, Rachael, and Bob Alford sat mesmerized in Amar's office as they watched the mission begin to unfold.

The arched tunnel curved away to the right. The slick icy surface of the walls and ceiling above them glistened as if they were wet. An eerie blue light seemed to emanate from somewhere in front of them, illuminating the whole tunnel. Remnants of the white clay piping disappeared under a wall of ice on the opposite side of the river. They walked slowly around the bend, and everyone came to a sudden stop. Renfro shut off the quad's engine.

The tunnel opened up into a gigantic ice cavern that strained each of their abilities to perceive how big it actually was. A smoky ray of sunlight shone down through a hole in the top of the ice cave causing the very walls and ceiling of wavy blue ice to emanate a deep aquamarine glow. The small river snaked its way across what appeared to be a dry lakebed. A waterfall cascaded down the rocks on the north side of the cavern where the ice met the mountains. Tumbled down carved stone edifices littered the shores of what was once the ancient capital city of Vandalay.

The four friends stood together in silence for several minutes. Chitchat somehow seemed sacrilegious. Something about this place commanded respect. A deja vu of epic proportions coursed through both Amar and Katya's minds and hearts at the same time. Amar stumbled; he and Katya held onto each other for support. Together, they sank to their knees, awestruck by what they were seeing and feeling. Neither of them could utter a sound. Time stood still for a moment as the essence of 14,000 years of human history washed over them. Amar knew somehow that he had been here before.

Evan unzipped his dry suit and pulled a photo of the chamber at Persepolis from an inside pocket. He held the photo up in front of the landscape.

"Well, my dear friends, at long last, behold the lost city of Vandalay," he said quietly. "We are finally here."

The sounds of running water echoed off of the walls and ceiling. The creaking and groaning of the glacial ice were loud enough to make hearing each other difficult without the radios.

"It's a good thing we elected to bring the coms gear," Renfro said. "It is kind of noisy in here."

"I never thought it would be so big," Evan said respectfully.

He pulled out his camera and began taking pictures. Amar staggered to his feet and pulled Katya up alongside him.

He looked at his friends with tears in his eyes. "Let's go see our city," he said.

Slowly they made their way around the eastern edge of the dry lakebed. The glacier had ground the exposed homes and structures on the east bank into great piles of loose and eroded stones. Shards of slate roof tile were scattered about. They entered what they supposed had been a residence at one time. None of the walls were still standing. The floor plan of the simple four-room residence was still discernible. Floors, walls, and roof surfaces had been made of stone. Any timbers used in the roof structures had long since become petrified and lay scattered around the ruins. No human remains were in evidence. Stone door sills could be seen in between the rooms. They stepped over knocked down dividing walls indicating that some residential units had been connected.

"This must have been some sort of row house," Amar concluded.

Evan was clicking away with his camera. Renfro had to navigate around the piles of stone with the quad.

From some distance away he called out, "There's a stone road over here. Looks like it goes into the heart of the city."

Evan, Amar, and Katya climbed up and over a pile of loose stones to see what Renfro saw. A wide stone street meandered in pleasing curves around the edge of the lakebed and on up to an area where one giant stone column still stood in the distance.

"I want to go see that building," Katya said into her helmet-mounted microphone.

The four explorers slowly wandered their way toward what was once the main plaza and gathering place of the Ularian people. With some difficulty, they ascended the very tall stone steps up to the carved facade of what might be a temple or meeting place.

"Evan noted, "If these steps are any indication, I venture to guess that the Ularians were much taller than we are."

Seven ornately carved columns lay scattered about in front of a building that had been carved out of the living rock many thousands of years ago. Only one still stood in place. Two huge sculpted bronze doors had been torn from their hinges and lay at odd angles against the stone entryway.

Katya gasped as she recognized the double oval symbol that graced the upper third of each door. "Look, when these doors were closed, the binary orbit diagram would have been prominently displayed for all to see. These doors look like they weigh many tons! Can we go in?"

"It looks safe enough to me; let's go in," Amar said.

Renfro left the quad outside and the four explorers entered the council chamber. The high-ceilinged space was in very good condition. Some beautifully made tiles remained on the floor. The carved stone walls were intact. At the back of the room, a raised dais with thirteen stone thrones rose above them.

"It stands to reason that spaces carved out of the mountain would be in better condition than the rest of the city," Evan noted. "It looks like this area may have been submerged at one time, but the mountain has protected this space from being ground up by the glacier like the rest of the city."

Renfro jumped up on the dais and sat in one of the seats which made him look like a child sitting his father's chair. "I think you're right; Evan, looks like they were a couple of feet taller than we are."

Just then, a loud thunderclap echoed through the chamber. Amar pressed a push-to-talk button connecting him with Robby.

"Robby, do you copy?" he asked.

"Here, boss," Robby came back.

"We just heard a noise like thunder. Where is the drone?"

"I've got it circling over the lake, boss."

"Can you see anything unusual?"

"Yep, there's a wave running down the length of the lake, north to south. Things might be shifting up here. Maybe you should come out!"

Amar grabbed both sides of his head as if he was in pain. Ancient memories were trying to surface in his mind, but they weren't quite making it to his inner eye. The memories were expressing themselves as feelings rather than pictures, but he remembered the feelings.

"Okay, copy that. Everyone, I can't explain it but I am remembering why we're here. I think our time in the city may be short; we need to get moving."

Katya nodded as if she understood. Renfro held up his hands toward Evan and shrugged as if to say, "Remember? What is there to remember?"

A second thunderclap got them all moving. They ran back down the tiled floor and out onto the plaza. Amar stopped and looked around. "Over here; follow me!" He ran across the stone plaza toward an opening in the face of the mountain on the north side of the lakebed. Everybody was straining to keep up.

Amar glanced over his shoulder as he ran, "In here, I remember this building."

The facade of the building had long since crumbled, leaving a large hole in the side of the mountain.

They ran into the room, which had been carved out of the rock long ago. "This used to be the archive!" Amar hollered.

They ran after him into the back of the room. Mounds of unidentifiable material that might have been what was once stored here were piled up against the back wall. Amar began digging frantically.

Renfro didn't hesitate to pitch in, "What is it, boss? What's behind this stuff?"

"There's a door here, Gary. I know there is."

Katya and Evan helped move the debris revealing a much smaller but also very heavy bronze door with a small round glass porthole, still on its hinges. Next to the door, a series of nine tiles with Ularian symbols that were unfamiliar to any of them seemed to glow from within. Without knowing why or how, he knew what to do. Amar pressed each tile in a particular sequence, and the door, which was animated by some internal power source, opened toward them. Amar ran through the door into a tunnel that disappeared into the mountain. A ten foot patch of bright white walls and ceiling began to glow as they entered the tunnel, and the light followed them as they went in.

Amar ran on for fifty feet and halted in front of a handprint on the side wall. The rest of his crew skidded to a stop behind him. Amar placed his hand on top of the print, and a hidden door in the side wall slid open revealing a small storage space. Inside was a white cube with rounded edges, about two feet on each side. Renfro pulled the box out into the hallway. Amar reached down and undid two latches. The lid of the container popped open with a hiss. Inside the container was a small cube shaped ornate metal device that looked very old, which indeed it was. They could all see some sort of crystal under a small glass dome. There was an image of a handprint on the front of the device. Amar reached down and placed his hand over it. The crystal began to glow bright violet white. It lit up the hallway.

"What is it?" Evan asked.

"Don't ask me how I know," Amar said, "but this is what, in our time, we would call a free energy machine. It extracts an unlimited amount of power from the space in between the atoms. This is what Sanjay wanted us to find. This is the technology that he said would change the world. It'll make fossil fuels obsolete!"

The creaking and groaning coming from the glacier started to get louder.

Amar took charge, "We don't have much time. Gary, we'll haul the machine out into the archive while you run for the quad. We need to get the hell out of here. Robby, do you copy?"

"Yes, boss, I'm here. There was another wave on the lake, I suggest you come out as quickly as you can."

"We're on our way. Ask Harvey to stay on station."

"Will do, boss." Robby said.

CHAPTER FIFTY-THREE

Vandalay

Viktor Dragan and his crew had refueled at Ittoqqortoormiit two hours earlier and were speeding toward the site of the ancient city. A half hour into the flight, Dragan had picked up the satellite link provided by Bob Alford. He and his crew had been watching Parish's helmet cam feed on Warburg's Greenstone phone and were listening to his crew as they talked. Dragan's people were beginning to understand what the stakes were.

His team would have to act fast. There was some danger that the lake on top of the glacier was unstable. If Parish was right about this artifact, he needed to go in and take it away from them. If it was what Parish thought it was, it had the potential to destroy Warburg's vast oil empire. On the other hand, a free source of unlimited energy would ensure that Warburg would continue to be in control of the world's supply of wealth into the distant future. Dragan could only imagine what his reward would be for pulling this off. Maybe an apartment in Monaco. If Parish and his entourage died during the effort, so much the better.

"Com check," Dragan hollered over the noise of the rotors.

All members of the Alpha team indicated a positive connection. The tiltrotor aircraft roared over the Aurora Star on its way toward the glacier.

Robby Harris and Captain Fischer both looked up and said in unison, "What the hell?"

Alpha seven was moving the rotors back into the vertical position in preparation for landing on the glacier.

"Alpha seven, I want you to circle the lake and come to a hover over that hole so I can see how deep it is."

"Roger that one," the pilot said.

The sun was high in the sky, and Dragan could see a small river flowing across a mud flat 500 feet below the hole.

"Alpha seven, I want you to set down fifty feet to the south of this crevasse. We can get in there quicker if we rappel down from the top of the glacier. We'll attach our fast ropes to the landing gear. In an emergency, you can pull us up using the ropes. Otherwise, if we can, we'll go out the way Parish and his people went in. Alpha seven, once we land on the ice, I want you to set a dozen C-4 charges between the hole and the lake. When we get clear, I will radio you to blow the lake. That should destroy everything that remains down there and make sure we are the only ones who possess the technology."

Renfro was running back to the council chamber to grab the Quad so they could load up Amar's device. Amar had heard the roar of the Augusta's rotors through Robby's mic as it thundered overhead.

Robby transmitted, "Boss, do you copy? We've got company. Some sort of helicopter with a logo on it that says, Zoltan Holdings."

Amar came back, "Shit, Warburg is here? How the fuck does he know about this?"

Amar had this sinking feeling—he was the reason Warburg was here. He remembered how he couldn't keep his mouth shut on that plane ride to New York. He resolved, if he ever got out of this alive, he would never again tell anyone anything they didn't need to know.

"Gary, you copy? Warburg is here!"

"I doubt that, Amar," Gary said breathlessly into his mic. "It's not Warburg; he would never come this far. It's got to be Dragan!"

Renfro reached the quad and jumped on. Just prior to hitting the starter button, he looked up and saw six fast ropes plummeting down from the roof of the cavern. The ropes were followed by six men in black fatigues, with submachine guns strapped to their backs, sliding into the cavern at a high rate of speed. Renfro recognized Dragan even from some distance away. He pulled his pack around and drew the Wilson Combat .45; then he hit the starter and raced toward the archive building.

Dragan was first on the ground in the middle of the dry lakebed. He clearly saw and recognized the squat form of the man he hated most—Gary Renfro, speeding along the edge of the lakebed on a quad cycle. Dragan shouldered his sub machine gun and let off an entire thirty round magazine in Renfro's direction. He changed his magazine, but Renfro was traveling too fast.

Renfro zigged and zagged the quad, managing not to get hit. He emptied a full clip in Dragan's direction as he drove, unsure if he hit anything. He sped right into the archive building, screeching to a halt next to Amar, Katya, and Evan. Katya, having heard the exchange of gunfire, had her weapon out. Renfro inserted a fresh clip into his pistol.

"Six is hit!" One of Dragan's crew screamed.

Dragan looked at the man writhing on the ground. One of Renfro's bullets had entered his abdomen just under his vest. Without giving it a thought, Dragan fired a two-round burst into the man's face.

"You all knew the risks!" he shouted and took off running toward the archive with Alphas two through five hot on his heels.

Renfro screeched to a stop in front of the door to the tunnel. "It's Dragan, boss," Renfro said over the radio. We're totally outgunned. What do you want to do?"

Before Amar could answer, Dragan and his team came running through the opening into the archive, spraying a barrage of nine millimeter bullets in their direction. Bullets were pinging and ricocheting all over the place.

"Get back in the tunnel! Katya, covering fire!" Renfro shouted.

Amar pushed Evan through the door. Renfro and Katya laid down a curtain of fire as they backed in behind them. Dragan's men took cover behind fallen stones.

"What about the device?" Renfro shouted.

"No time, if you want to live!" Amar shouted over his shoulder.

Amar hit the same code on an identical set of tiles inside the tunnel and the door closed automatically. Dragan's team poured bullets into the door, but it was far too heavy to be breached by nine millimeter rounds.

Dragan screamed into his mic, "Stop firing, you idiots. You'll damage the machine!"

They all ceased firing. Alphas two through six took up defensive positions, training their weapons on the door, in case Parish tried to come out again. Amar and Renfro observed them through the small window, which was thick enough not to be damaged. Dragan stooped over and undid the latches on the white container. He looked over the machine.

"This is what all of the fuss is about? Doesn't look like much to me!"

He closed the container; his men loaded it onto the sled and strapped it down. Dragan moved over to the door and looked at Parish and Renfro through the window from inches away.

"Well, here we are, Mr. Renfro. You put a bullet in my leg the night I killed old man Parish. Turnabout is fair play, now you're all going to die here today." With that, he mounted the quad and prepared to move out.

A rage from deep down engulfed Amar Parish. Renfro watched his face turn red. Amar reached for the keypad to open the door. Renfro grabbed his wrist, preventing him from exposing the crew to more gunfire.

Amar screamed, "I'll kill that bastard."

"Not now, Amar, this isn't the right time. He'll get his in the end." Renfro gave Dragan the middle finger salute through the window.

Dragan looked over his shoulder and laughed, knowing they would all drown in a few minutes. He motioned for his men to leave the archive.

"Alpha seven, we have the package and will exfil out the south tunnel. Blow the charges on my mark and pick us up on the gravel bar below."

"Copy that Alpha one; I just need a few more minutes to finish setting the C-4," Alpha seven said.

After a hasty battery change, Robby had the drone back overhead. "Boss, red alert! They're mining the lake—they're going to blow the damn thing!"

Amar came back, "Robby we're stuck in this tunnel; is there anything you can do?"

"Stand by, boss. I have an idea."

Alpha seven had worked up a sweat setting the charges and ran back to the Augusta. He was dripping sweat and opened the cockpit window to cool down while he went through the engine start sequence. He gently placed the detonator on the co-pilot's seat and began flipping switches. The Pratt and Whitney PT6A turboshaft engines huffed and began to whine as the rotors started to turn.

Robby thought, *this is it, I can't screw this up.* He cut the feed to Seattle. Jan and Rachael didn't need to see this. From one hundred feet overhead, he dove the drone at the helicopter, and dodging the pilot's side propeller, flew it right in the pilot's window. Alpha seven saw something move out of the corner of his eye and looked up just as the twenty-five-pound drone, with all six propellers whirling at high speed, smashed into his face at thirty miles per hour.

The impact dislodged both of his eyeballs, severely lacerated his face, and threw him onto the co-pilot's seat—right on top of the detonator. Robby's drone camera feed went black. The twelve C-4 charges Alpha seven had just set on the ice, went off in rapid succession, boom, boom, boom, boom...followed by one thunder clap after another as the glacier that had lain over top of the ancient city of Vandalay for thousands of years, began to break apart.

From their vantage point on board the Aurora Star, both Robby and Captain Fischer could see a giant fireball rising into the sky from the top of the glacier.

"Oh, shit!" Robby exclaimed, not knowing if his actions had caused the conflagration. The Captain grabbed his handheld radio, "Harvey, get out of there now!" He screamed.

The ice under Dragan's chopper started to collapse. The aircraft tilted; the spinning rotors struck the surrounding glacier sending propeller shards over a wide area with some of the shrapnel penetrating the chopper's fuel tanks. The spilling fuel ignited from the surrounding C-4 fireball.

Dragan and his team had just come out of the archive and were moving out onto the stone plaza when the charges went off. They looked up and saw huge chunks of ice falling from the roof of the cavern, followed by the mangled and flaming remains of the chopper. A great roar filled the cavern.

Dragan was paralyzed where he sat on the quad. There was no point in running. He had time to scream only one word, "Fuuuck!"

His epithet was followed by huge chunks of the glacier and 250 million gallons of ice cold water pouring into the cavern with tremendous force.

He had less than one second to review his life. A massive wall of water, traveling at high speed, with a wave front full of stones, chunks of ice, pieces of slate and debris from the city enveloped him and his evil crew grinding them into pulp. Their body parts were washed across the lakebed and through the ice tunnel, pouring out into the deep waters of the fjord. What was left of them sank 500 feet to the bottom. There would be nothing left to find but fish food.

Amar still had Dragan and his crew in sight through the porthole in the bronze door. He was seething with anger when a gigantic wave of roiling water engulfed Dragan and his five accomplices and washed them away in a fraction of a second. Amar was astounded at the instant finality of it all. Five men, gone in less than a heartbeat.

When the massive wave hit the relative restriction of the ice tunnel, the water backed up and very quickly rose, covering the city and the window Amar was looking through. In a flash, he knew what was coming. He grabbed Katya by the hand, and he also had only one word to say. "Run!" he yelled.

They raced down the tunnel deeper and deeper into the mountain, the eerie light source following their progress. The water was rapidly rising in the tunnel. Robby lost both coms and helmet cam feeds as they ran further into the mountain. They came to a set of double doors which opened automatically as they approached and ran into a room that Amar knew at once.

He hit a button on what appeared to be a somewhat weathered control console, and a single door opened into a second room. They all ran inside. The white walls and ceiling glowed with an eerie light of their own. Amar closed the door.

"What the hell is this?" Renfro wanted to know.

"No time, Gary; just follow my lead."

The room was filled with what looked like six beds made of the same luminous white material as the walls. Each bed had a curved glass cover. Katya knew what to do immediately. She took off her pack, jumped up onto one of the pods and laid down, holding her pack against her chest.

Amar said, "Save your air bottle for last. I love you."

Katya sat up and kissed him hard, "I love you, too." She lay back down.

Amar hit a button on the side of the bed closing the lid. Evan and Renfro understood right away, and both removed their packs holding them against their chests as they each jumped into a pod. Amar hit their buttons, and the lids closed. Ice cold water flooded in under the door and through cracks in the ancient walls, rapidly filling the room.

After making sure everyone else was safe, Amar got into his own pod, reached out, and hit the button. The lid came down just as the water rose up over the edge of the glass. In a few minutes, all of the pods were under water. Each of them contained a small bubble of air that wouldn't last long. Their waterproof radios were still working.

"Okay everybody, if I'm right, the water level won't stay up very long. Get out your scuba bottles and get ready to use them but wait until the last minute. We want our air to last as long as possible."

Fourteen thousand years is a long time for any piece of equipment to function. As the water rose to the ceiling, the stasis pods began to leak. Amar could see through the water that Evan was terror-stricken.

Renfro tried to talk him down, "Doctor, what would you like to do once we get out of here?"

Evan replied, "I'd like to go to a sunny white sand Caribbean beach somewhere and have a few drinks."

Katya picked up the thread and said, "Me too, I'd like to put on a skimpy bikini and slather myself with suntan oil while lounging next to a crystal clear lagoon, drinking a Mai Tai." Katya went on about the wind and the waves, the palm trees moving in the breeze, how luxurious it felt, how nice the sun was...

The images distracted Evan at least for a moment. Despite his present circumstance, the prospect of seeing Katya in a bikini was pleasant, if only just for a moment. The water began to seep into each pod. The coms gear was waterproof, but the helmet cams were not. As the water rose, any future video feed was lost for good.

"Okay folks, time to go scuba diving," Amar said. "Not to worry, this won't last long. It's been a pleasure so far."

Amar had been keeping track of their air supply using his dive watch. With only five minutes of air left, the water began to recede from the ceiling. The water level seemed to take forever to drain out of the room. With only one minute of air left, the water drained below the edge of the stasis pods. Amar hit a button in his pod and all of the lids rose together. Katya jumped out and sloshed through the water to him. They held each other. Slowly, Renfro and Evan swung their legs over the side and stood up.

Renfro looked at his boss and wondered, "How did you know about this?"

"I can't tell you exactly, Gary," Amar said. "It was kind of like an instinct—I just knew."

Harvey Kline, the first officer, was sitting on the back deck of the shore boat, eating his lunch, when the chopper flew over. He looked up quizzically, wondering what it was all about. A few minutes later, he heard the booms from the detonation of the C-4 charges.

His radio crackled, "Harvey, this is the Captain; get out of there now!"

Harvey had known the Captain for years. When he said to do something, it was for a good reason. The first officer jumped up and ran into the cabin tossing the remains of his lunch onto the chart table. He slammed and locked the cabin door behind him. He flipped on the blower switches to ventilate the engine compartment. The specs said to wait two minutes before starting the engines to avoid an engine compartment fire caused by diesel fumes.

He looked at the clock mounted on the dashboard. "Come on, come on," he said impatiently to no one. The hell with it, at one minute and thirty seconds, he pressed the starter, and the engines roared to life. He engaged the jet drives, but it was too late.

A twenty-foot-high wall of ice-cold dirty water ripped through the tunnel, pulling part of the icy ceiling with it. The hole in the front of the glacier blew out to twice its original size as the wave bore down on the shore boat. Harvey hit the throttles and managed to get far enough from the gravel beach that all of the heavier debris sank to the bottom of the fjord behind him. The massive wall of water engulfed the small craft. The shore boat rolled inside of the wave—once, twice, three times it rolled over. Harvey was bounced around inside the cabin like a ping pong ball trapped in a jug, rolling down a hill.

Robby and the Captain watched in horror from the aft deck of the Aurora Star as the giant wave ripped its way through the ice tunnel. The mangled remains of the chopper's fuselage appeared in the face of the wave, and then it was gone. The wave continued on its destructive path until Harvey and the shore boat were lost under the frothing water. Robby ripped off his headset in disgust and threw it down on the deck.

But, then the Munin 1200 did what it had been designed to do; it righted itself and popped back up to the surface unharmed, engines still running. Harvey was bruised and battered. The salami from his sandwich was stuck to the ceiling by a generous dollop of mustard, and his coffee was splattered everywhere. He picked himself up, engaged the jet drive, and followed the leading wave out toward the ship. Halfway there, something bumped into the side of the boat. At first, he thought it was a chunk of ice, then he looked closer.

The wave had diminished in size by the time it got to the Aurora Star and only caused the ship to bob up and down a little. The thrusters of the ship's dynamic positioning system kept the icebreaker on station. Harvey tied up to the boarding stairs. Captain Fischer was on the radio again, "Harvey, are you okay?"

"I think I broke a finger and I'm gonna be sore in the morning, but I'm fine boss. Send down a cargo net, will you?"

The captain gave the order, and a deck hand swung the crane around, lowering a cargo net over the side and into the water next to the shore boat. Harvey pulled a floating object into the cargo net and gave the signal to haul away. He stood on the net and rode it up onto the aft deck where both the Captain and Robby Harris were there to meet him. He stepped off the net, and the three men walked to the aft rail.

"I'm sorry, Mr. Harris," Harvey said. "I don't know how anyone could have survived that."

The Captain stood there with his binoculars trained on the now much bigger hole in the base of the glacier. No survivors were evident. Tears began to flow down Robby's cheeks. This was the worst thing that could have ever happened. He was sure he had caused the detonation. Then again, they were going to blow the charges, maybe he had just made it happen one minute sooner. He hoped in his heart it had been quick and no one had suffered. Mercifully, he'd cut the feed to Seattle. Jan and Rachael were spared having to watch everybody die.

The water receded, leaving only a few inches on the floor of the chamber. Amar hit the exit button, and mercifully, the door opened. The four survivors sloshed their way down the tunnel to the bronze door. Amar pressed the tiles in the correct order, and the heavy bronze door, which had some debris piled against it, opened only about four inches.

Amar said, "Gary, give me a hand."

Together, they placed their shoulders against the door and pushed with all their might. It gave a little.

"Again," Amar sputtered.

They heaved and heaved against the door, and finally it moved enough so they could each squeeze through the opening. The archive was filled with large chunks of ice, but they could see a small opening at the ceiling line where the front wall once stood. Daylight was shining through. They climbed up and over the ice, shimmying through the small opening. Standing on top of the gigantic pile of ice chunks, they surveyed the damage.

The sounds of dripping water echoed through what was left of the cavern. What was once a fifty foot hole at the top of the ice cavern, was now a hundred yards wide. Blue sky with broken cloud cover was visible overhead. The village of Vandalay was once again buried under mountains of ice. Holding hands in a line, they descended the ice slope carefully to keep from dislodging the large chunks.

At the bottom, Katya hollered, "The river of water carved a path through the ice floe! We can walk out of here!"

Robby's mind was chattering away in despair, when he heard a familiar voice in the distance. He was much too far from the glacier to hear anyone calling for help. For a moment, he thought his mind was playing tricks on him. Then he realized, his headset—the sound was coming from his headset! He scooped it up from the deck and put it on.

"Aurora Star, come in. Robby, are you there?"

The Captain focused his binoculars on the hole under the glacier, immediately recognizing the black and red dry suits as the four survivors walked out into the dappled midday sun.

"Oh my god!" he screamed. "They made it!"

Katya came through his headset, "Hey Robby, what does a girl have to do to get a lift around here?"

CHAPTER FIFTY-FOUR

Vandalay

Captain Fischer said, "Harvey, you go to sick bay and have that hand looked at. I'll take the Munin back and pick them up.

"I'm going with you!" Robby exclaimed.

The flash flood caused by the draining of the lake was over. The Captain was able to back the boat into the beach where Amar and his crew were waiting. "Do you have anything to load?" he asked.

"Just us," Amar said. "Nothing else made it through."

All four friends climbed on board.

Robby hugged each of them in turn. "Oh my god, I thought you all bought the farm on that one. I'm so glad you made it through. What the hell happened?"

Amar told the story. When he got to the artifact, Robby remembered the white box that came up in the cargo net with Harvey. At the time he thought it was some piece of equipment from the shore boat.

"We may have a surprise for you," he said.

Amar finished describing how Dragan had confessed to killing his father and then how his men had been washed away.

"Who were those men in the helicopter?" Fischer asked.

"They were enemies of my father. They wanted to make sure our expedition wasn't a success. It's a long story. Talk about instant Karma," Amar said. "I've never seen anything like it. One moment, five men were there; the next moment, they were—just gone. Did you see any human remains come out in the flood?"

Both Robby and Captain Fischer indicated that they had seen part of the helicopter sink out of sight under the advancing wave, but no bodies were visible. All they had seen was a big wave of dirty water that rolled the shore boat over, which then popped up unharmed. Fischer looked thoughtful as he put the boat in gear and pulled away from the beach.

"I guess we should report their deaths."

"Who would we report them to?" Amar asked. "We only know the name of one of them."

Evan took charge, "Greenland is a part of Denmark. I speak the language. I'll take charge of reporting their demise through diplomatic channels in Copenhagen when we return to Seattle."

Evan had no intention of doing anything of the sort but felt the need to take the issue off of the Captain's plate.

"Fair enough, thank you," said Fischer. "Technically it didn't happen on board my ship, so I have no firsthand knowledge of the event. All I saw was a fireball." Fischer gazed at the sky with the knowledge of a master mariner, "Looks like there's some weather coming in. We should get back to the ship."

They tied up at the boarding stairs and slowly, one by one, made their way in single file up to the aft deck. Harvey and members of the ship's crew were waiting at the rail. A round of applause erupted as they stepped onto the deck. Harvey's right hand was bandaged, but he shook all of their hands with his left.

"What's the surprise, Robby?" Amar asked.

Robby parted the crowd and there on the deck, under a cargo net, was the white box containing the machine that would change the world.

Amar "whooped" and ran over, pulling the net away. The surface of the box was badly scarred, but not broken.

"I don't know what this material is, but it's tougher than nails!"

He opened the box, and they all peered in. "Looks like it's no worse for the wear," Renfro said.

Stefan Fischer peered into the box over their shoulders. "What is it?"

Amar, realizing at once that security must begin now, answered the question evasively, "We don't really know. It's a historical artifact of some kind. We'll have to study it and try to figure out what it was used for. Captain, will you have it taken to my cabin?"

"Harvey, make it so, please," the captain ordered.

Harvey directed a couple of the deck hands who took the box away.

Evan, seeing the need to change the subject, turned to Katya, "I'm going to hold you to that trip to the Caribbean. Thank you for what you did back there, Katya."

She laughed, "It'll be my pleasure to keep that promise, Doctor."

Amar thought a Caribbean beach was a great idea. He put an arm around Katya's shoulders.

"When we get back, we'll all take the jet and fly to one of my favorite beaches for a nice vacation where Doctor, you may look but you may not touch!"

Evan bowed toward Katya, "I never had any intentions of touching, but there's nothing wrong with appreciating great beauty where one finds it!"

Katya smiled; she wasn't the least bit offended.

Renfro rubbed his stomach. "Okay people, my sack lunch was ruined, and now I'm famished. Can we please go to the galley and eat?"

Fischer looked at his watch, "You're in luck; the cook should be putting lunch out right about now. Once you've peeled off your gear, please join me at my table."

Grabbing Katya by the hand, Amar announced over his shoulder, "I'm going to need a half hour to get out of this dry suit and take a shower."

Renfro addressed the captain, "It won't take me a half hour; I'll meet you in the galley in a few minutes."

Evan concurred, "Me too. I could eat a whale!"

Amar closed the door to their cabin and locked it. The white box was sitting on the carpet in the middle of the room. He turned to Katya and put both hands on her shoulders. Their eyes met.

"Tell me, Katya; what did you feel in the ruins of Vandalay?"

"The same thing you felt, Amar. Though I've never set foot in that place, I know it. I felt like I had come home."

"That's exactly what I felt," Amar said. "I have no visual memory of ever having been in the city, yet, in a flash, I knew why we're here and what we came here to do. How do you explain that?"

"It's just one of the great mysteries of Vandalay. I suspect there are many more to unravel over time. I know one thing, though."

"What's that?" Amar started to unzip her dry suit and help her step out of it.

"I know I'm supposed to be here with you now, doing what we're doing. I know there's a greater purpose here."

She unzipped his dry suit but didn't stop there. They took turns peeling off each other's long underwear. Amar pulled her to him, gazing down at her naked body.

Appreciating her form, he said, "If you're lucky, and I happen to be a very lucky man, you might come to that point in life where all the seemingly unrelated events you've experienced line up to point out your destiny. That's what I'm feeling right now."

She reached down and wrapped her fingers around him. That wicked Katya look, that he was beginning to know, stole into her eyes. After less than a minute of foreplay, she said, "It feels to me like Mr. Lucky is inspired; that's what I'm feeling right now."

Then she did what only an experienced gymnast could do. She gave a little hop, wrapped her legs around his waist and gently slid down onto him in one smooth motion. He carried her into the shower.

Twenty minutes later, pink and freshly scrubbed, Amar and Katya entered the galley. They served themselves from the buffet and sat down at the Captain's table where Evan, Renfro, and Robby Harris were well into their meal. The Captain was curious about what had happened under the ice, and the story was recounted again from different points of view. Stern looks from Amar conveyed the message to avoid discussing the artifact.

Finally, the Captain asked, "Do you wish to go back in tomorrow? Is it safe now that the lake has drained?"

"Where's a glaciologist when you need one?" Amar quipped. "I need to have a meeting with my people, and then we'll let you know what we want to do." He addressed his team, "Let's meet in my cabin in ten minutes." As they filed out, Amar took Robby aside. "Robby, bring your electronic instrument kit and be discreet about it, please."

"Sure thing, boss; see you in a few."

A few minutes later, they all gathered around the white container. Amar undid the latches, and the lid popped open with its characteristic hiss. He took out the device and set it on the coffee table. It was a cube approximately one square foot on each side. The surface was made of some sort of bronze-colored metal. It was highly decorated and bore the double oval symbol of Vandalay. They all sat staring at it for a moment.

Renfro began with a question, "One thing I want to know, Amar: before the big flood, you said you remembered why we're here and where we should go. Then you knew the code to open the door. How did you know all of that?"

"I can't explain it, Gary. It was kind of like intuition. I just knew."

"You are to consider, Gary, that there are a great number of mysteries yet to be solved regarding the lost city," Evan said. "It's going to take some time to unpack it all. Like this device, some of those mysteries may challenge our sense of what's real or even what's possible. How good is the video coverage, Robby?"

"I recorded everything up to when you disappeared into the tunnel," Robby said. "The helmet cam footage is a little shaky as you might expect, but the stills you took with your handheld camera are outstanding. We have enough footage for a nice documentary." Robby gestured toward the machine on the coffee table, "Boss, just before I lost the video feed, you said this was a free energy machine. You said that it extracts an unlimited amount of power from the space between the atoms?"

"That's what popped into my head at the moment we opened the container," Amar admitted.

He placed his hand on the handprint on the outside of the case, which was somewhat larger than his own hand. A crystal under the glass dome began to glow. The florescent light on the ceiling of Amar and Katya's cabin, which had not been turned on when they entered the room, cast a bright light upon them. They all looked up in amazement.

"Robby, can you tell us if it's true? Is that what we have here?"

Robby's jaw dropped, "I think it might be boss. Doctor, you told us that the city and this device are over 14,000 years old?"

"It would seem so, Robby," Evan confirmed.

"This is amazing. It still works after fourteen millenniums!" Robby took an instrument from his tool kit and held it close to the machine. The tester chirped and glowed red. "It's definitely putting out some power. I'm going to need some time to analyze this."

Renfro asked, "That brings us to the next question boss. This is your mission; do you want to go back into the city, or do you want to leave now?"

Amar knew that he and Katya were of one mind.

She didn't hesitate, "The city is buried under ice again. It would be difficult and dangerous to go back in. We don't know if Warburg is going to send another crew or not. What's left of the city will still be there next spring and in fact, may be much easier to get to as the ice melts and the glacier recedes. If this machine is what it appears to be, it's priceless. In my opinion, we need to get this device to safety where we can analyze what it does and discover whether or not we can duplicate its technology."

"Katya's right," Amar said. "While I'd dearly love to poke around in the ruins, Sanjay's message was clear. This device will change the fate of humanity. That's the main mission."

Amar pointed out the cabin window. Large flakes of snow were falling into the waters of Nordvest Fjord. Two inches of snow had already accumulated on the ship's main deck. "I say we head for home. We can come back in the spring."

Renfro said, "Once we get back to Seattle, we can store the device in the gun vault at the PCI warehouse. It'll be secure there while we figure out our next move."

"There's one thing I want to understand," Amar said. "How did Warburg know what we were up to?"

Speaking from years of spy work, Katya pronounced, "It's quite simple, Amar; you have a leak inside your company. The conclusion is inescapable, Warburg has bought one of your employees."

CHAPTER FIFTY-FIVE

Aboard the Zoltan at Sea

Harry Warburg sat in the leather recliner in his office on the top deck of the Zoltan which was cruising just outside the twelve-mile limit to the west of Seattle. The head of one of his stable of exotic female play toys bobbed up and down on his lap. He thought her name was Brittany but couldn't remember. She finished her work and managed to zip him up without letting a drop of bodily fluids fall onto his obscenely expensive slacks. She knew such a violation of his protocol could cause her to be dropped onshore, penniless, in some strange town, or worse.

There was no mistaking her job as being anything but a harem girl, but she loved the opulent surroundings and was willing to trade her dignity for nice clothes, good food, and life aboard the yacht. Occasionally, Warburg would reward the more compliant girls with expensive trinkets which they could save for the future. Besides, there were enough of the girls to spread around the more distasteful chores.

Harry Warburg had willingly adopted a philosophy that inflicted elite sociopaths around the world. He was convinced that he occupied his position at the top of the monetary heap by right. To the victor go the spoils. He was certain that he deserved the obscene wealth he had confiscated, without discrimination, from less fortunate peoples around the world.

He shared what he felt was a natural attribute of the ruling class— everything that came in contact with him must be costly and perfect. Nothing but the finest wine, the best food, the most expensive clothing or the most coveted artwork would do. He went to great lengths to isolate himself from experiencing anything that was undesirable. He viewed the Zoltan as a symbol of his superiority. He lived in a rich man's bubble, traveling from one posh environment to another in fabulous luxury at all times.

Julie Barton came over the intercom, "Mr. Warburg, Bjorn Admunsen, the drilling boss from Iceland Platform 14, is on the line."

Warburg moved to his desk and picked up, "Admunsen, have you heard from Dragan? What do you have to report?"

"Good morning, sir," Admunsen said. "I wanted to get back to you as soon as possible."

"Get on with it, please," Warburg demanded testily.

"Dragan took off from the platform yesterday in the AW 609 tiltrotor aircraft. He hasn't been seen or heard from since. About three hours after he departed, both the GPS beacon and the transponder ceased to operate. I fear they were lost at sea."

"That was a twenty million dollar aircraft. Who is responsible for maintaining it?"

"Why, I am, sir. But I assure you all of its maintenance records are up-to-date."

"Admunsen, you better hope they are. You borrow a chopper from one of the other platforms and go find either Dragan or his crash site!"

"Dragan didn't tell me where he was going. All I know is that they were headed northwest toward Greenland."

"Then go there and find him!" Warburg hollered as he slammed the phone down. He buzzed his secretary, "Julie, come in here."

A moment later, Julie Barton entered his office, "Yes, sir, what do you need?"

"Check Dragan's company credit card; find out if he bought fuel anywhere. Call Lloyds of London and tell them we may have lost one of our tiltrotor aircraft at sea. They'll send an investigator to look for it."

Barton researched Dragan's account. She found a fuel charge at the FBO at Nerlerit Inaat Airport in some little town by the name of It-toqqortoormiit, Greenland, that was truly in the middle of nowhere. Barton knocked on Warburg's office door.

"Come," he said.

"Mr. Warburg, Dragan refueled at a little town located on Scoresby Sound in Greenland. I called the FBO at the airport. The man I talked to said they don't see many tiltrotor aircraft, and he definitely remembers him. Dragan never indicated where he was going, but when the aircraft took off, it headed due west. The man at the FBO, I can't pronounce his name, took the time to look up the range of the aircraft. In his opinion, they could have crossed the continent to Aasiaat or Ilulissat but only if they flew directly there with no stops in between. I called all of the airports on the west coast, and no one has seen Dragan or the aircraft. I fear they have either crashed or are stranded on the ice somewhere. That's all I could find out."

"Damn, what a pain in the ass," Warburg cursed, showing no concern for Dragan's life. "Get my M&A attorney on the line in New York."

"Yes, sir, right away, sir." Barton disappeared back into her office. A few minutes later, she buzzed him, "Mr. Denescu on line one."

Warburg never wasted words, "Alex, where are we on the acquisition of TaiwanCom?"

"Hi Harry, we are scheduled to close the purchase tomorrow."

"Have you verified that they'll be able to manufacture the Greenstone phones in the quantities I require?"

"We've been through this, Harry. Julie has the projections on the expansion of the assembly line. It will take a couple of months to achieve the production numbers you want, but there is nothing, short of a violent takeover by mainland China, that would prevent them from achieving those numbers."

"Good, where are we on the close of Greenstone Executive Security?"

"I just got off the phone with Bill Wright, Parish's attorney. He assured me that Mr. Parish has signed off on his ten percent ownership and that the final executed documents will be in escrow in a few days. I just need you to deposit the last billion dollars into escrow, and we are good to go."

"I'll have Julie take care of that today," Warburg said. "Any fires to put out anywhere?"

"No, sir. I believe we have done our homework and you should own both companies within a week."

"Keep me informed," Warburg demanded.

"I will sir," Alex said, but Warburg had already hung up.

CHAPTER FIFTY-SIX

Seattle, Five days later.

The C-130 Hercules landed at Boeing field and taxied up to the PCI warehouse. Alice had been notified of their arrival and was waiting next to the open warehouse door; an AR-15 hung from a sling over her right shoulder. Two of Renfro's telecom operatives had come in to provide additional security and to help unload the plane. They would be departing the next day on PCI contract work.

"Glad to see you all got back in one piece," she said.

Katya was standing by with her pistol drawn. Renfro grabbed a dolly from inside the warehouse, and he and Amar wheeled the white container through the warehouse and into the armory where the gun vault was located. After placing the item in the vault, Renfro closed the door, shot home the bolts, and spun the dial, locking it up tight.

Everyone except Robby climbed the stairs to the apartment. Robby remained in the plane hunched over his laptop. Nikolai had not been feeling well and was in bed under Alice's care. Katya disappeared into his room to check on him. Alice had put out a nice buffet, and they all dug in.

Amar took a call from his attorney. "Amar this is Bill Wright; glad you're back. I'm calling to remind you that in two days we'll enter the documents into escrow, conveying your ten percent ownership of GES to Zoltan Holdings. Escrow will then close, and the sale will be complete. Do I have your permission to proceed?"

"Yes, Bill, you can proceed. I have a question, though."

"What would that be?"

"The contract states that I must provide an executive-level employee who is intimately familiar with the Greenstone system to Zoltan Holdings for a thirty-day turnover period. Does it specify specifically who that employee must be?"

Amar could hear the sound of paper shuffling in Wright's office.

Wright came back, "No, the contract does not specify that person by name. Just that he or she must be intimately familiar with the work-

330 · W.O. JOSEPH

ings of the system. We always assumed it would be Robby Harris. Do you want to name somebody else?"

"I might, but I'll need some time to think it over. Thanks, Bill, I'll get back to you."

Just then, Robby entered the room with his laptop under his arm.

"I saw you all lost in thought on the flight back," Amar said. "Were you working on the mole?"

"I was boss. I know who did it."

"Who was it, and how do you know?"

"First, I ran a diagnostic on the GPS coordinates of Warburg's Greenstone phone. It showed the phone located in Greenland while we were there. Dragan had it in his possession. It went offline less than a minute after the fireball erupted over the glacier. Next, I ran the phone records of every PCI and GES employee who has one of our satellite phones. I was looking for any phone that had contact with Warburg's phone during the time we were in Vandalay. I got a hit on a continuous transmission that covered most of that day."

Amar's features grew grim. "Who was it, Robby?"

"I'm sorry to tell you, boss. It was Bob Alford."

"I see," Amar said. "He was one of Tom's most trusted employees. What a shame that is."

Renfro added his two cents, "That skunk—I'd like to break a few of his bones!"

"I have something else in mind, Gary. We'll get into that in a minute."

"There's something I've been meaning to talk to you about, boss," Robby said.

"What's that?" Amar asked.

"After everything we've all been through, I can't go to work for Warburg, not even for thirty days. If you have to fire me, I'll understand. I just can't do it."

"Robby, you won't have to work for him. Besides, I need you to get going on the free energy machine and tell me as soon as possible if we can duplicate the technology."

"Yes sir! You have no idea what a relief that is to me."

"Yeah, actually I do. Escrow is going to close on the sale of GES in two days. You need to get up to SatCom today and clean out your desk. You need to make sure nothing is left behind that can come back and bite us later. Pack up any technology that does not relate to the sale of GES. You can set up an office here at the warehouse. Alice will make a spot for you. This is where the device is anyway. Did you ever talk to the two guys who run the satellite factory about their jobs?"

"Yeah, I talked to them before we left. Their jobs are highly specialized. They both want to stay at the factory and will go along with the sale. All they know is that GES has been sold. They don't know to whom or why. They're big boys; they can figure it out."

"Alright Robby, feel free to purchase any equipment you will need to analyze the machine." Amar gestured toward the buffet, "Have some lunch and then scoot up to SatCom. Hopefully, we can meet again tomorrow."

"Gary, can one of your guys go with Robby to SatCom and provide security while he cleans out his office? There's no telling what that villain Warburg will spring on us next."

Renfro put a hand over his mouth while he finished chewing a bite of scalloped potatoes, "Sure thing, Amar. I'll take care of it."

"Thanks, Gary." Amar dialed Jan Meyer.

She answered, "Hello Mr. Chairman, glad to have you back. How was the expedition?"

"Hi Jan, nice to be back. I'll tell you all about it soon. I'm coming into the office this afternoon. I'd like to meet with Bob Alford at three o'clock."

"I'll set that up for you. Anything else you need?"

"No, thanks Jan, not at the moment. See you soon."

Katya came into the kitchen.

"How is Nikolai?" Amar asked.

"I'm afraid he's doing poorly. If he doesn't improve soon, he'll need to go to hospital."

"I'm sorry to hear that. I'll stop in to see him before I go. I suspect you'll want to stay here?"

"I wish to stay by his side. You will come back tonight?"

"Absolutely, I'll probably be back around six this evening."

Amar put a hand on Gary's arm, "Since my bodyguard will be staying here, I'd like you to go with me to meet with Alford."

"I wouldn't miss it for the world, boss. By the way, Katya, I almost forgot. Alice has something for you."

Alice took her cue and came forward with a small box. She opened it and began to hand items to Katya. "Here's your green card; you are now an official employee of PCI. Here's your first paycheck; your starting salary will be 100,000 dollars. Here's your concealed carry permit along with a pamphlet explaining the rules for carrying a firearm in Washington State. Last but not least, here is a beautifully crafted leather shoulder rig we had custom-made for you along with a new Sig Sauer P-229 Legion in 9mm."

Katya teared up a little and embraced Amar. "You sure know how to make a girl feel welcome." She kissed him passionately on the lips. Everyone applauded. Amar blushed bright red. Katya reached behind her, pulled out the Wilson Combat .45 that Renfro had loaned to her, and placed it on the table in front of him.

"How did you know that I love the Sig? It's lighter than Gary's Wilson. Also, I really do like the de-cocking lever. It's so much more comfortable carrying the pistol loaded with one in the chamber when the hammer is de-cocked!"

Amar grinned at Alice, "I had good advice from the experts. You are so welcome, Katya."

Katya's eyes grew bright. "Now, I get paid for watching my boy-friend, to keep him from cheating on me! I love America!"

Amar blushed again, and they all howled with laughter.

Evan asked, "Katya, would it be alright if I went in to see Niki?"

"Of course, Doctor, he is sitting up taking some soup. I'm sure he would be delighted to see you."

Katya rose from her seat. "Mr. American Big Shot, you can come too."

The three of them entered Niki's room. He looked as if he had aged ten years while they'd been away. Evan sat down next to the bed and began rattling away in Russian. Niki was pleased to have his own language spoken to him. Amar stood next to Katya but couldn't follow the conversation. She put an arm around his waist. Niki motioned them forward. They came to opposite sides of the bed and Niki held out both hands. They each took one of his hands in theirs.

Niki was beaming at them as well as he could. He placed their hands together as if to give his blessing to their union. He spoke in Russian while Evan translated. "He says this is right. You two are made for each other."

Niki began to cough.

Amar put his hand on Niki's shoulder. "Thank you, Niki, I guess we should get going," Amar said. "I'll see you here later on." He kissed Katya on the cheek. "I'll be back later this evening. Gary, are you ready to go?"

He turned to Evan, "Can I drop you at your hotel, Doctor?"

"Yes please," Evan said. "I'm looking forward to some hot tub time and a date with a cocktail."

After they dropped Evan at his hotel, Renfro brought up Bob Al-ford. Amar explained his plan.

"That's fitting, boss," he said. "I'd like to do physical harm to the slug, but your idea is more elegant."

Amar dialed Bill Wright and explained what he wanted.

Amar and Renfro entered the office at 2:55. Amar hugged Jan, and both men poured themselves a cup of coffee. "Let me know when Alford gets here. Also, I'm expecting a document by email from Bill Wright; will you bring that in as soon as it comes through?"

The two men went into his office. Jan could tell by his tone of voice that something was up, but her years of experience with the Parish men told her it was not the right time to inquire. At 3:00 on the dot she buzzed, "Amar, Mr. Alford is here to see you."

"Send him in, Jan, and hold any phone calls."

Bob Alford looked upbeat when he entered the office. He offered his hand, but Amar didn't shake it. To add a little drama to the event, Renfro took off his jacket revealing his shoulder holster and pistol. The blood drained from Alford's face like the air leaving a party balloon. He knew he'd been found out.

"I know what you did, Bob. What I can't figure out is why. You almost got all of us killed."

Alford stammered, "I never intended for anyone to be harmed, Amar. That guy who works for Warburg threatened my wife and my children. He said if I didn't do what he wanted, he would send my children home in pieces. I believed him."

"How much did your loyalty cost, Bob?"

"I didn't do it for the money," Alford lied.

"How much, Bob?"

Alford hung his head, "Two hundred thousand. What are you going to do to me?"

"Gary here wants to break your legs. I told him no."

Alford seemed to shrink in his chair. Jan knocked on the office door.

"Come," Amar said.

The door opened, "Here's your email from the attorneys."

"Thank you, Jan."

Amar looked over the document. "I thought about taking you to court for industrial espionage and reckless endangerment. But truthfully Bob, you aren't worth the expense. My mercy has a condition."

He pulled a pen out of his pocket and signed two copies of the document. "First of all, as president of PCI, you're fired, effective right now. Your paycheck will be prorated through today. You can pick up your check from Al Hemmings on the way out."

334 · W.O. JOSEPH

Amar handed him a copy of the document. "I'm appointing you President of GES without pay. You're only there to act in an advisory capacity. Your signing privileges have been revoked."

Amar pushed the document across the table to him. "By signing this document, you agree to remain at GES for a period of thirty days and do whatever the new owner wants."

Alford signed the document.

"You wanted to work for Warburg; now you'll have your chance. Escrow will close in two days, and you can negotiate a salary with him if he is inclined to keep a traitor in his employ. Good luck; I hope you enjoy your new boss. Gary, get him out of my sight."

Renfro rose and grabbed the man by his arm, steering him out of the office. Alford clutched the document, and shuffled out the door, a beaten man.

Having seen Renfro escorting the president out of the office, Jan came in immediately. "What just happened, Amar?"

Amar told her the whole story from the time they boarded ship in Reykjavik until the present moment.

"Rachael and I were able to see you enter the cave and wander through the city. It was so exciting. Robby was smart to cut the video feed before all of the mayhem started. It wouldn't have been good for Rachael to see that. Were you scared?"

"There were more than a few moments when none of us knew if we'd survive, but it turned out well, for us anyway. Gary made sure we had just the right equipment. Dragan and his punks got what they deserved. The odd thing was, they basically died by their own hand with only a little help from Robby, which no one regrets. I guess there's justice in the universe, at least some of the time."

"What's next, Amar?"

Jan Meyer had known him since he was a kid. She wasn't just a trusted ally; she was a member of the family. He confided in her now.

"Well, for one thing Jan, for the first time in my life, I'm in love. It's the best, most complete feeling I've ever had."

CHAPTER FIFTY-SEVEN

Seattle

Amar had just pulled out of the underground parking lot on his way back to Boeing Field when Jan called him in the Land Rover. "Amar, Katya and Alice have just taken Nikolai to Virginia Mason Hospital in an ambulance. He's having trouble breathing. They'll be taking him directly to the emergency room."

"Oh my god! I knew he wasn't feeling well, but he seemed to be in reasonable health earlier today. I'm on my way. Thanks, Jan."

Amar parked the car in the hospital parking lot and ran into the emergency room. He found Alice and Katya in the waiting area. He sat next to Katya and took both of her hands in his.

"Tell me," he said.

"After you left, Papa started to have trouble breathing. I looked around and found a bottle in his nightstand. He'd been drinking in the afternoon. He promised he wouldn't ever do that again. He passed out, and we called the ambulance right away. They stabilized him and took him in for testing. That's all we know so far."

Amar hugged her and kissed her on the forehead. Just then, the doctor appeared. All three of them stood.

"Miss Chubukin," he began, "your father is suffering from advanced cirrhosis of the liver. His liver has already failed, his kidneys are shutting down, and his heart is failing. I'm afraid he has only hours left."

Katya placed a hand over her mouth. She knew this day would come, but she hadn't allowed herself to think it would come so soon.

"Is there anything you can do, doctor? Amar inquired. "Money is no object."

"I'm sorry, preventative care is no longer an option. All we can do is make him as comfortable as possible. He's partially sedated at the moment, but you can go sit with him if you like. I'm so sorry."

Tears were coursing down Katya's cheeks. She'd been her father's caregiver for many years. Reluctantly, since her retirement, he'd become her reason for being. Now everything would change.

Alice approached Amar and said in a low voice, "I'll leave you to it, boss. I'm going to head back to Boeing Field. Let me know if you need anything."

"Thank you, Alice, if you wouldn't mind, let everybody know what's going on. The doctor might want to come by and visit."

"Will do," she said and left through the emergency room entrance.

Amar escorted Katya to Nikolai's room. His bed was elevated slightly at the head. He lay motionless, a breathing tube causing his chest to rise and fall gently. They went to opposite sides of the bed and each took a hand. Niki's eyes fluttered open. He couldn't move his head but looked to his right, his gaze fixing upon his daughter. Katya stared into his eyes. She saw no fear there. Even with the breathing tube taped to his face, she could just make out a little crinkle at the corners of his mouth. She knew under the stress of the moment, he was smiling. She kissed his hand, and his eyes closed again.

They sat by the bed for hours. Just before midnight, Evan arrived. He went to Katya and embraced her, quietly speaking Russian into her ear. She smiled and hugged him back. Amar had no idea what was said, but it seemed to please her. The three of them sat quietly with a man who had been one of the most gifted machinists ever to grace the planet.

Close to five a.m., the heart monitor flat-lined. The staff arrived with a crash cart, but Katya waived them off. Nikolai Chubukin had been a genius in his field. He'd lived a brilliant but troubled life, as geniuses often do.

They sat in respect for another hour before Amar stood behind Katya's chair, his hands on her shoulders and asked, "What would you like us to do, for the funeral, I mean? Did you two ever discuss it? I'll help with any kind of arrangements you want."

She placed a hand over his. "Papa wanted to be cremated and buried alongside of his parents at the cemetery in Baikonur. That's in Kazakhstan, you know?"

"Would you like to have a service here before we take him home?"

"I don't think so. My father was a very quiet and somewhat lonely man. He never wanted people to gather around him. Can we have the cremation done here and then fly him back home?"

"Of course, I'll make all of the arrangements," he said.

"Thank you so much *dusha moya* (my soul).

"Is there anything I can do?" Evan asked.

Katya smiled at him; she had become fond of the diminutive doctor, "He really enjoyed talking to you in his own language, Evan. He said so many times. Would you be willing to write an obituary in Russian? We can send that on ahead before we get there."

"I'd be honored to do that for you," Evan said. "What would you like to say?"

For half an hour Katya told the story of her father's life while Evan took notes. Jan arrived at the office at 7:00 a.m. and called Amar for an update. Upon hearing of Nikolai's death, she went into action and called the funeral home they had used for Tom Parish's passing.

An hour later, the funeral home hearse arrived at the hospital and prepared to take the body away. After all of the tubes had been removed, Katya bent over her father, kissed his forehead, and said her goodbye in Russian.

Amar reflected; Nikolai Chubukin had built a magnificent machine that could be revived after sitting in the harsh lunar environment for almost fifty years. Without his help, they would never have been able to photograph the Imbrium Codex. It remained to be seen what impact all of their efforts would have on the world, but Amar had high hopes for what would come next. Both Tom Parish and Nikolai Chubukin's passing marked the end of an era. Amar wondered if the world would see such great innovators ever again.

CHAPTER FIFTY-EIGHT

Seattle to Baikonur, Kazakhstan

Amar was at his desk on the 65th floor of Columbia Tower, "Jan, send out a memo to Gary and Evan; I promised them a vacation on the beach, but we're going to have to postpone that. Katya and I will be flying Nikolai home to Kazakhstan. Also, see if you can locate Bob Caffrey, he's one of my high school buddies. I'm pretty sure he's in real estate in northwest Montana. I'd like to speak with him."

"Right away, Amar, do you need me to book accommodations in Moscow?" Jan replied.

"That won't be necessary; we'll stay at Katya's *dacha*."

Katya was sitting at his conference table making arrangements for Nikolai's funeral. She wore a nicely tailored short brown leather jacket over a white cotton blouse and form-fitting black slacks. The jacket had been specially made to conceal the Sig Sauer P229, which rested in the very comfortable leather shoulder holster, a gift from Amar. Her hair was pulled back in a ponytail. Amar gazed at her across the room. God, he loved the way her ponytail swished from side to side when she turned her head. She felt his gaze upon her, looked up, and smiled at him.

"Katya, would you mind if we made a stop for a couple of days on our way to Moscow?"

"Whatever you want to do is fine with me, Amar," she replied.

"I have Bob Caffrey on the line," Jan said over the intercom.

Amar picked up, "Bob, it's been a long time. How've you been?"

"Amar, it's been a very long time. I'm doing well, and you?"

"I can't complain. Life has been good to me."

"I heard about your father's passing. You have my sympathy."

"Thank you, are you still in real estate?"

"I am. I have an office in Bigfork, Montana. Are you considering joining us here in God's country?"

"That's why I'm calling. I'm looking for something very private. I've been researching properties in a place called the Swan Valley. Is it common for rural properties to have both a house and a large work-shop?"

"It's very common around here. The north end of the Swan Valley is just a few minutes from my office. What exactly are you looking for?"

"I'd like to have a minimum of 200 acres, a five-bedroom home with a garage, a guest house, and a 5,000 square foot workshop. It has to be very private, with no neighbors anywhere near the buildings. I want to stress that privacy is the most important attribute I'm seeking."

"I understand, Amar. I've noticed when you've popped up in the news over the years. Amar Parish, the celebrity playboy! I can see why privacy is a concern. No offense intended."

"None taken, Bob. I'm well aware of my media presence. But things have changed, a lot. I'm looking for a place I can go relax where nobody knows who I am."

"I understand, Amar. You'd be surprised how often this sort of thing comes up here. There are more than a few wealthy people seek-ing refuge in Montana. One of the nice things about our culture is that people mind their own business. For some reason, a lot of the trophy properties have come on the market recently. There are a couple I can think of that might be what you're looking for. One even has its own grass airstrip. I'll put together a package for you. Are you planning to come any time soon?"

"I have to fly to Moscow in two days and thought we'd stop in on our way."

"I'd be happy to pick you up at Glacier Park Airport and show you around. What price point are you looking for?"

"Oh, let's try to keep it under five million. Thanks Bob, I'll give you a call as soon as I know when we'll arrive. You'll be able to find us at the Glacier Jet Center. Talk to you soon."

Two days later, Amar's Citation X taxied up to a tie-down spot at Glacier Jet Center. Ted Lockhart and Jason Hall were in the cockpit. Amar and Katya were seated comfortably in the cabin. Jan had given Bob Caffrey the jet's tail number but had neglected to mention what kind of an aircraft it was. Caffrey pulled up next to the jet in a Chevy Suburban. Jason let down the airstair door, and Caffrey entered the cabin carrying a leather briefcase.

Amar rose, shook his hand, and introduced Katya. "Bob, it's great to see you after all of this time. This is Katya Chubukin. Katya, meet Bob Caffrey, one of my high school buddies."

Caffrey looked around and gave a low whistle, "Very nice to meet you Katya. I knew you were doing well, Amar, but I had no idea it was this well!"

"The credit goes to my father, Bob. I'm merely the recipient of his genius. I've just had a thought; why don't we fly over the properties you want to show me? Then we'll return here and drive down to take a look."

Grinning, Bob said, "That works for me. We can take as much time as you want."

Caffrey opened his briefcase and pulled out some maps. Amar hollered, "Ted, can you come back here and look over these maps? We'd like to take an aerial tour of the Swan Valley."

Ted looked over the maps and indicated, "I'll need a few minutes to file a VFR flight plan; then we can be on our way."

"While we're waiting to take off Bob, can I offer you a drink?"

"Scotch on the rocks if you have it."

"No problem. Katya, how about you?"

"I'll have a soda, thank you."

Fifteen minutes later, they were cruising over Swan Lake at 6,000 feet. The first snow fall of the year had gently dusted the Swan Mountains to the east and the Mission Mountains to the west.

A few minutes later, Bob pointed out the window, "The first property is coming up on our left. It's 100 acres and has a nice 4,000 square foot house with a large barn. There is a one-bedroom guest unit inside the barn.

Amar looked it over, "It's too close to the highway, Bob. I want something more private than that."

"Okay then, maybe the second property will be more what you want. It will be coming up on your right in a few minutes."

Bob handed over some photos of the property.

"It's on the west side of Lindbergh Lake. This is a legacy property of 250 acres. It's totally surrounded by state forest; there are no neighbors. It has views of both mountain ranges and the lake. The main house is 7,000 square feet and has five bedrooms, six baths, and a three-car garage. All bedrooms are en suite master bedrooms. The guest house is equally beautiful and has three bedrooms, three bathrooms, and a two-car detached garage. There's a grass airstrip and a 4,000 square foot hangar. It doesn't have a workshop, but you could build one or use the hangar for that purpose. It also has two 1,000 gallon underground propane tanks and an emergency generator capable of powering the entire compound. I'm afraid it's somewhat more than you wanted to spend."

"What's the price?" Amar asked.

"It's on the market for 7.5 million furnished, Amar."

"Is it occupied?"

"I believe the owners are traveling in Europe, so we can go in this afternoon if you like."

Let's go see it," he replied.

They toured the property late that afternoon. It was exactly what Amar wanted. Bob Caffrey was delighted. They drove back to his office to pencil out the offer. Amar offered full price, a cash sale with no contingencies, a thirty-day close, and the right to enter the property for surveying and planning prior to the close of escrow.

"How would you like to take title, Amar?"

Amar gave him the name of a recently formed anonymous New Mexico LLC. "I want you to know, Bob; I'd prefer that my name isn't used anywhere. You can tell the sellers that this property will be used as a corporate retreat. I need you to agree never to use my name in any form, written or verbal until I'm ready to release the information.

"I understand, Amar, you have my word," Bob pledged.

Two days later, they landed at Vnukovo Airport in Moscow. Jan had a rental car waiting for them, and Amar asked Katya to drive since all of the road signs were in Russian. They pulled into #26 Derevnya St. at 5:00 p.m. Katya's *dacha* was a seventy-five-year-old, two-story clapboard home with a corrugated steel roof. It was surrounded by pine trees. The last time he'd been here, he didn't really get a good look at any part of it but the kitchen and living room. Though it was only 47 degrees outside, Katya began opening windows to air the place out. Nikolai's bedroom was on the first floor. She led the way up the stairs to her suite, which was once two bedrooms and a bath. Many years ago, she had a door cut in between the two bedrooms so she could use the second bedroom as a sitting room.

"Please bring your bag; we will sleep here in my room."

Amar placed his bag in the closet. What would you like to do for dinner, Amar?"

"Since we're in your country, I'd like you to decide, Katya."

"We left no food in the house six weeks ago, so I will take you to someplace special."

Arm in arm, they strolled down the street to what appeared to be just another small home but was in fact, a small family-run restaurant with only twelve seats.

"*Dobri vecher*, Marissa," Katya greeted the proprietor.

"Good evening, Katya. We haven't seen you in quite a while," Marissa said in Russian.

Katya told of her travels to America and recounted her father's recent passing. She introduced Amar as her boyfriend. Marissa seated them in a small private booth with a window facing the garden. After the appropriate condolences, Katya ordered the beef Stroganoff for both of them along with a bottle of Stolichnaya. "Now that you're back home, Katya, what are your thoughts on the future?" Amar asked. "I guess, I mean, maybe things seem different to you since we've returned."

She reached across the table and took him by the hands. "I asked that myself as we went through the house. I don't think this is my home anymore." She smiled at him. "Besides, I have this job protecting Mr. American Big Shot. It pays well and there are, how do you say? Fringe benefits!"

Amar grinned; he was getting used to her sense of humor. Being ignorant of Russian law, he asked, "What about your house. What will happen to it?"

"When I was in the FSB, I managed to make what you would call, "side income." The house is in my name, and I don't owe any money on it. I make enough money at my new job to pay the taxes and to hire a caretaker to look after it. Now that Niki has passed away, I'm free to be wherever you are. I want to be wherever you are."

"Whew," Amar said in relief, "I was afraid things might change when we got here."

That wicked Katya look he was beginning to know so well stole into her eyes. A sock-covered foot inched its way up his thigh under the table.

"Nothing has changed *dusha moya*, that is, so long as you hold up your end of the bargain."

Amar grinned, "My end of the bargain may prevent me from getting up from the table for a little while!"

The food arrived, and the foot disappeared. The Stroganoff was the best Amar had ever tasted: Russian home cooking at its finest.

Amar's phone rang; he took the call. It was Jan Meyer. "Hi Amar, we managed to get hold of the caretaker at Baikonur cemetery. There is room for Nikolai's urn in the plot with his parents. He'll prepare for your arrival for tomorrow. Is that still on your schedule?"

"It is Jan. It's about a three-hour flight, so we should be there before noon local time. Thanks so much for making that happen."

"All I did was find the phone numbers. Dr. Chatterjee did all the talking since I can't speak Russian. He also ordered a headstone with the inscription that Katya wanted. What a treasure he is."

"That he is, Jan, thank you so much."

"Is there anything else I can do for you?"

"Is Robby making any progress?"

"He received a truckload of instruments at the warehouse the other day. I looked over the invoice; there were some oscilloscopes, a mass spectrometer, a particle size analyzer, and some computer equipment. It's kind of a hefty bill."

"No worries, Jan, I told him to get whatever he needed."

"You're the boss, Amar, just like your father. When will you be back?"

"My guess is about four days. We'll see you then."

Amar and Katya finished their meal.

Amar, noting that the Stolichnaya was still half-full asked,

"Are we allowed to bring the bottle with us?"

"Of course, we can. I might need it tomorrow," she said.

Once again, arm in arm, they walked back down the street to Katya's *dacha* for the evening.

Amar's Citation X touched down at Krayniy Airport on the out-skirts of the decaying Baikonur Cosmodrome late the following morning. Amar was surprised to note that the famous launch facility of the Russian space program was located in a rather barren desert at only 300 ft. above sea level. They rented a car for the day. It was only about a fifteen-minute drive to the cemetery.

The caretaker had dug a modest hole for Nikolai's urn. He greeted them and told them to take as much time as they needed. He was aware that a headstone was being made and would install it when it was available. Evan had sent the obituary to the local paper, but no one else arrived for the burial. Amar carefully placed the urn into the hole. They stood before the graves of Katya's grandparents.

"They raised me until I was fourteen years old." She said wistfully. "It was a difficult place to grow up. It's not beautiful like Seattle." Amar asked, and Katya told the story of her youth in the adjoining town of Tyuratam. When she was done, Amar pulled the half bottle of Stoly and two glasses from the jet's galley out of his duffel bag. He poured a glass for each of them.

Katya held up her glass. "To Nikolai Chubukin," she toasted.

Amar clinked glasses. "To Nikolai," he agreed. "I am so glad to have met him."

She motioned for the caretaker to come over and fill in the grave, which he did.

"Do you want to look around the town?" Amar asked.

"Not really," she said. "It's all different than it was twenty-five years ago. Besides *dusha moya*, thanks to the Royal Historian of the Court of Vandalay, we have a mission to perform. Let's go home and start to change the world."

CHAPTER FIFTY-NINE

Seattle; Five days later

Ted Lockhart made a smooth landing on runway 14R at Boeing Field and taxied up to the PCI hangar. Amar and Katya deplaned and made a beeline for the warehouse and a meeting with Robby Harris. Gary Renfro had installed a new high-security front door with a surveillance camera while they were in Russia. Alice buzzed them in.

"Hi Alice, good to see you," Amar said. "Nice setup at the front door."

Alice shook hands with both of them. "Hi to both of you. I hope your trip went well. Gary did a complete security assessment of the building while you were gone. The new entry setup was his idea."

"Are Robby and Gary here?"

"Robby's in his new lair in the gym. He's expecting you. Gary is in the apartment on the phone. I'll send him down as soon as he's done."

"Is Dr. Chatterjee around?"

"Yes, he's staying at his hotel. Robby needed him to be around to translate markings inside the device. He's been running his business remotely from the hotel."

Amar and Katya entered the gym. The floor mats and exercise machines had all been moved to one side of the room. The other side was bristling with flat screen monitors, various kinds of instruments, a mass spectrometer, and an electron microscope. Robby was seated at a workbench toiling away with his back toward them. Computers were beeping and LEDs were blinking on and off all around him. The free energy machine from the ancient city of Vandalay sat on the bench to his right. He heard them come in and swiveled around on his chair.

"Hi guys, boy am I glad you're back! How was your trip?"

Katya took the lead since the trip had been primarily for her.

"It was fine, Robby; we'll tell you all about it later. What we both want to know right now is, can we reproduce the machine?"

Amar seconded Katya's question, "That's what I want to know Robby—can it be done?"

"The short answer is yes. We can reproduce the machine!"

Katya was jubilant. "That is, how do you say in America? Awesome!"

"Can it be adapted to produce house current?" Amar asked.

Robby held up two small devices, one in each hand. Pigtails with plugs on the end dangled in the air.

"Yes, using these translators, I've managed to pull both 120 and 240 volt AC along with 12 volt DC from the power source. This thing is amazing, boss; it's universally adaptable. All you have to do is plug it into an outlet, and it runs the house. It only produces power when a load is connected. Then it responds by generating enough power to meet the need. The physics is a little complicated, though."

"You can save that part for later, Robby."

Just then, Renfro walked in. He gave Katya a hug and embraced Amar. "Has wonder boy told you the news?"

"He has, Gary. This is exciting," Amar replied. "I would've checked in a few days ago, but my Greenstone phone went dead on the way back."

"You don't know?" Renfro asked.

"Know what, Gary?"

None of us have service anymore. Warburg closed escrow about a week ago and shut off all Greenstone phones owned by anyone at PCI."

"That figures. After all, Warburg is the enemy!"

"That he is, boss. But just like Dragan, he'll get his sooner or later." Renfro opined.

"Getting back to the project. Tell me this, Robby; you were instrumental in developing the Greenstone satellite design and the robotic factory to make them. Can we use similar technology to set up a factory to produce these units?"

"Yes, we can, boss," Robby affirmed. "I understand we want to make units that serve ordinary homes. How many units do we want to produce?"

"Use by common people everywhere is the target. I'd like to start with 1.2 million, at the rate of 100,000 units per month, and move up from there. How big would the facility need to be, and what size staff would you require to do it?"

"Do you want to make it all in-house?" Robby asked.

"You do realize that by making this machine available to everyone, we'll be painting a bulls-eye on our backs?" Gary said. "This generator is going to be a major disrupter. It's going to disrupt all fossil fuel businesses. In fact, it's going to deal a heavy blow to Warburg's oil empire. When that happens, the media will be rabid to know who's doing this and where they are. So, secrecy and security are mandatory. We have to remain anonymous, at least in the short term. I don't see outsourcing as a possibility. I believe we'll have to make all of the components ourselves."

"How big of a plant will we need to make everything from raw materials?" Amar asked.

Robby kept silent for a moment. Amar could see the wheels turning in his head. I'll have to complete the design work before I can be sure, but if we go fully robotic, I'd say we'll need 10,000 square feet and five technicians, including myself."

Amar fiddled with his laptop and pulled up photos of the ranch in Montana. Both Robby and Renfro looked on with interest.

"This is where I want to build the facility," Amar declared.

"When did you have time to find this place?" Renfro wanted to know.

"We made the purchase on our way to Russia. The ranch will be ours in two weeks."

"Why am I not surprised, boss?" Renfro exclaimed.

"On the surface, we'll pretend this is a rich man's corporate retreat. That'll explain the comings and goings. I've been doing some research, and indoor riding arenas are about 100' x 200' or 20,000 square feet. We'll have to bring in some horses to make it plausible. The ranch already has pastures and can support a horse operation. Indoor arenas like this are very common in Montana. We'll build a metal building with an underground basement. The floor in the arena will be dirt. Nobody will suspect there's anything underneath it.

The house has five master suites. If they double up, it will support ten staff. I'll hire a chef to feed everybody. The guest house will be for Katya, Gary, Evan, and me when we're there. There's even a grass strip and hangar for a small plane. We can disguise material deliveries one way or another. We'll buy our own delivery truck and send it out to procure raw materials from various sources. We can make deliveries at night, so we don't arouse the neighbors' curiosity. There are only a few homes on the road, some of which are seasonal residences. I doubt we'll attract much attention from the locals."

"This is totally cool!" Robby approved. "Twenty thousand square feet should be more than enough."

Katya initiated the horse ranch conversation with Amar during the flight back. "I've always wanted to learn how to ride," she said.

"I'll make sure you have that opportunity," Amar promised.

"We have to name the devices, boss," Robby said, "But whatever we call them, they can be used to power electric vehicles. Unlike diesel-powered vehicles, our delivery trucks will be absolutely silent. That should help us get in and out without annoying the neighbors."

"On that note, can we power the factory with the device as well? We don't want to attract attention by racking up high power bills that would be a dead giveaway that something is going on."

"Yes, sir, not only can we power the machinery with our devices, we can heat the place as well, so nobody will be tipped off," Robby said.

Amar inquired, "Gary, can you bring in some of our PCI operators to manage construction of the building?"

Gary thought for a moment, "Yeah, I can. Two guys come to mind. They've already signed non-disclosure agreements and have proven their loyalty to PCI. They might even be good candidates to help run the factory for Robby. There are a couple of tricky moves we'll want to use to keep this all quiet. I can hire one of our structural engineers in Germany to draw the plans. They won't know or care where or what the building is for. The only part we'll need to keep secret is the basement.

I can bring in some concrete people from overseas. They can buy or rent the equipment they need. We'll pay the concrete truck drivers to surrender their trucks at the gate and have our people drive them in for the pour. Once the basement is covered over, we should have a local construction company come in and build the steel-framed arena. We'll already have the footings in place, and they can erect the steel building just like they would anywhere else. Having locals build the building will give the impression that it's just another rich man's horse toy."

"Okay, great, please put that in motion." Amar said. "Robby, once you have the product designed, I'd like to set up the robotic manufacturing line somewhere off premises. Once the basic bugs are worked out, we'll covertly deliver and move the equipment into our new building. Can you arrange for that?"

"No problem, boss. The robotics guy I used for the satellite factory is a friend of mine. He's single and looking for something to do. He may come onboard not only to design and build the manufacturing line, but he could be one of our line operators too."

Lastly, I'm appointing Al Hemmings to take over the day-to-day operations of PCI as its new president. I'm confident he'll be able to keep things running smoothly while we get this project completed. The funds from the sale of GES to Warburg have been transferred to my personal accounts. I'll have a whopping tax bill to pay, but there should be plenty left for the near future. I'll be paying the bills on this project personally to avoid outside scrutiny. Last but not least, what name will we use to brand our new generators?"

They all sat puzzled for a few minutes.

Renfro said, "You realize this isn't just a product; it's a movement?" Everyone nodded.

Finally, Katya said, "How about Ularian Power or UP for an acronym?"

"Perfect," Amar said.

It was so clear and easy; they all laughed.

CHAPTER SIXTY

Aboard the Zoltan at Sea

After closing the purchase of both TaiwanCom and Greenstone Executive Security, Warburg no longer needed to be in Seattle. He placed some of his best people in charge of SatCom and the Greenstone satellite factory. He ramped up satellite production and made arrangements for launch capability. He did indeed hire Bob Alford to consult with his people. But Alford was a traitor, and his usefulness would be short lived, literally. Warburg's last act before steaming away from the area was to cancel Greenstone phone service to anyone related to Tom Parish or PCI Communications. The Zoltan was cruising to the west of San Diego when Julie Barton entered Warburg's office, two small cardboard boxes in hand.

"Mr. Warburg, I have news of Mr. Dragan."

"Tell me, Julie."

"I had one of our operatives in Iceland interview a man by the name of Harvey Kline. Mr. Kline was a member of the crew aboard the ship that Parish leased for his recent adventure in Greenland. After the application of suitable incentives, the man reported that our AW609 aircraft and everyone aboard were lost in a fiery explosion on top of a glacier at the end of some fjord in the area. Apparently, the explosion released a lake of ice melt on top of the glacier, and what was left of the aircraft and everyone aboard were washed into the bottom of the fjord. The fjord there is 500 feet deep. He said there were no survivors and no debris from the crash. Mr. Dragan and his crew are just gone."

"This is Parish's doing," Warburg seethed. "I'll have that little pissant put out of his misery for this. Call Lloyd's of London and have their investigator interview this man Kline. I want the insurance payoff for the aircraft. Where are we on the redesign of the Greenstone phone?"

Julie placed the two cardboard boxes on Warburg's desk and opened them. "The prototype just arrived from Taiwan-Com on the helicopter."

Warburg reached in and pulled the phone from the first box. It was a thing of true beauty. It was made of emerald green carbon fiber with silver titanium trim and a black glass screen. It was slightly larger than the original and the two orange extraction buttons had been removed. The new ZolaPhone logo was engraved on the back in the form of a red "Z". Just above the logo was a small solar cell capable of keeping the phone charged at all times. Warburg turned it on, admiring the home screen layout. In addition to the usual application buttons, this phone had buttons marked, "Buy," "Bill Pay," "Accounts," and "Market." It was set up to pay bills, check account balances, monitor investments, and buy whatever was available in the worldwide marketplace, all with one click. Multiple passwords were replaced by facial recognition.

Warburg handled the phone as if it were a sacred object. Julie was pleased that it seemed to put him in a good mood.

"This is perfect. They did a good job on the design work," he said.

Warburg reached into the second box which contained a point of sale card reader also manufactured by TaiwanCom. He held it up for Julie to admire.

"How does it work?" she asked.

"These terminals will be installed at every checkout counter in the same way that the way that chip readers once came online. In the beginning, we'll still accept credit and debit cards in the old manner. Let's use the grocery store for an example. You're a ZolaPhone subscriber; when you walk within two feet of the reader, it will greet you by name. The merchant can choose between either an audio or text greeting on the screen. You won't even have to pull out your phone. You won't have to enter a PIN. The system uses the best encryption software on the planet, so security isn't an issue. In the beginning, the clerk will scan your products in the old way. When the clerk is done, you simply press the "Buy" button and go on your way.

Eventually we'll introduce the next generation of RF bar codes. Your shopping cart will be fitted with bag holders. When you pick each item off of the shelf, you put it right in the bag. When you roll up to the checkout stand, the phone reader will read all the RF codes from each product simultaneously, add up everything in your cart in one second, and display the total. The "Buy" button will light up. You press the button on the reader or on your phone and head for your car all bagged and ready to go. This system will be so fast, it will make checkout lines and clerks, for that matter, obsolete.

The system will record all of your repetitive buying habits. Eventually, you'll be able to program your phone to buy a predetermined list of groceries which will be delivered to your door the same day with one click. The phone has its own built-in social media platform and internet browser, as well. We'll be developing app after app, so you'll never have to leave the ZolaPhone universe.

Then we'll roll out the new virtual currency. It's going to be called the Zoltan or the "Z" for short. In the beginning we'll peg it to the dollar. New subscribers will be given the choice to transact business in "Z's" or in dollars. We'll give them a discount on their monthly phone bill if they adopt the "Z" as their payment currency. The dollar and the "Z" will be interchangeable, but only temporarily. The dollar is dying; once we phase it out, the "Z" will then become the world's reserve currency.

We'll have a complete history for each user, and we'll know exactly how to target product advertising to that individual. Just the thing for the modern high-speed lifestyle."

"Wow, that's amazing, sir. Speaking of ads, the advertising guys came in on the helicopter. They're waiting in the salon for you."

Warburg actually smiled; he was acting like a kid in a candy shop. "Well, let's go see what they've come up with."

They entered the Zoltan's opulent salon. Todd and Allison Lethbridge were a husband and wife team who owned a San Diego based advertising and demographic research agency. They had willingly accepted Warburg's offer to be paid in cash, leaving no evidence of a financial relationship between them. Warburg greeted the couple, who appeared to be slightly nervous, "Todd and Allison, what do you have to show me?"

They had interfaced a laptop with the salon's large flat screen TV. Allison took the lead, unsuccessfully trying to convey that it was normal for them to be picked up by one of the world's most expensive helicopters and ferried out to a half-billion-dollar yacht to give a presentation.

"Nice to see you again, Mr. Warburg. As you know, we've spent quite a bit of time studying cell phone demographics. Our research indicates that millennials are the target market that will provide the fastest absorption rate for the new satellite phone system. As a group, this demographic is the fastest-growing segment of the population and is much more likely to embrace new technology, just because it's new.

For reasons that are not yet fully understood, millennials are willing to trust big government. As a group, they are much more likely to lean toward socialism. They're willing to trust big businesses like Facebook, Microsoft, and Apple. They will embrace a new company like

ZolaPhone, no matter how big it gets, as long as it appears to be the next technological step."

"What have we learned about the product's price point?" Warburg asked.

"We're recommending an introductory price of $995.00 along with a $100.00 trade-in credit for their old phone with no money down and easy monthly payments deducted from their ZolaPhone account upon approved credit. The system will be configured to accept their paychecks by direct deposit and convert any currency to "Z's" at the daily rate as it does so. We believe that once the millennials have purchased their phones and have demonstrated how convenient the new system is, the other demographic groups will follow very quickly."

"What do your studies tell us about the proposed transaction fee?"

"Our focus group research is indicating that a one percent transaction fee will not impede absorption of the system by the general public. In fact, a one percent transaction fee on the merchant side will be seen as a significant discount from the three to four percent most retailers must pay to accept credit cards. As a result, most merchants will be motivated to purchase the new point-of-sale terminals from you.

"Tell me about the ad campaign," Warburg commanded.

Allison clicked her presenter, and the first slide came up.

"We've identified four basic thrusts for our first campaign targeting millennials. In order of potency, they are technology, fashion, convenience, and safety. We're proposing a campaign based upon the modern equivalent of the old Marlboro Man. This rugged individualist now travels the world, engaging in one adventure after another without ever losing touch."

Allison brought up a short video showing a happy couple, in full mountaineering gear, climbing the slopes of a snow-covered mountain. The man holds up his phone and takes a selfie of them, which is immediately transmitted to their circle of friends who happen to be in other exotic locations. Some are at the beach, some rafting down a river, some on a sailboat.

All of the happy friends transmit selfies and comments, back and forth, sharing their wonderful adventures. In the next scene, the couple are sitting around a campfire on the side of the mountain. The camera looks over the woman's shoulder while she pays their bills in Z's, surfs the internet, communicates with her co-workers, and checks the security cameras at their home, which is thousands of miles away. The next scene cuts to a satellite orbiting over the blue form of the earth. The narrator says, "In touch, everywhere on earth twenty-four/seven."

Back on the mountain top, the woman finishes what she's doing; they click glasses and toast themselves under a starry sky.

Allison continued, "We've played this video to several focus groups. The feedback is ninety-five percent positive. If you like this approach, we can produce several different versions along the same lines."

She waited nervously for Warburg to respond. He sat in silence for nearly a minute. The silence was growing uncomfortable.

Finally, Warburg said, "I like it. I'd also like to see a version where the customer uses our video chat feature to interview for and get his or her dream job while using the phone."

"Great idea," Todd said. "We'll get right on that."

Warburg stood, ending the meeting. "Thanks very much. As you know, time is of the essence. The helicopter will take you back to the mainland. Let me know when the next versions are ready. We'll be cruising in the area for two weeks or so."

After they left, Warburg remained seated in the salon. He smiled to himself. He was about to achieve a level of control over the world-wide population of human sheep that was unprecedented in the history of humanity. Or so he thought.

CHAPTER SIXTY-ONE

Swan Valley, Montana

Amar Parish thought long and hard about his new role as a covert disrupter of the status quo. His first mission in life had been to investigate the possibility that humanity was much older than its limited perception of history implied. The discovery of the Imbrium Codex on the moon, the chamber at Persepolis, and the ruins of the city of Vandalay had proven his theories beyond a shadow of a doubt. His intent was to take advantage of whatever wisdom could be gleaned from the study of ancient civilizations to help save our own. His second mission had become more focused—to apply Ularian free energy technology to help liberate humanity from its self-imposed prison of debt. Free household power wouldn't accomplish that in the beginning, but it was a great start.

Men like Warburg had hatched one scheme after another to drain value from the currency systems of the world, all day every day. That license to steal helped them to accumulate vast fortunes which they had then used to acquire control over every free market on the planet. The principle of self-regulating free markets was still sound. The problem was that free, unrigged markets no longer existed. Men like Warburg had willfully achieved an unfair economic advantage over anyone who had to use their fake currency. Their scheme had grown exponentially since the 1970s and now included most of the world-wide financial system. The result was that the rich had become much richer, the middle class was dying, and the poor were teetering on the brink of destitution.

A single day listening to social media told the story—the common people were growing restless around the world. They knew something was wrong. Every year, they had to work harder and harder to keep from going backward financially. They had no idea whom to blame or what to do about it, except to borrow more money and work harder. Their anger was directed at every politician and political structure on the planet. Every day the talking heads wasted untold quantum's of energy debating whether the right system was capitalism, socialism, or communism.

For reasons Amar Parish couldn't fathom, most people still believed that the politicians would save them if only the right people were put in power. The truth was, the political class of every "ism" had been bought by the Warburgs of the world. The bickering was accelerating, and nothing ever seemed to change for the better.

Amar knew he was about to cause major changes in the viability of the fossil fuel energy business. He understood that the magnitude of what he was about to unleash would hurt some people financially. However, in the long run, the end of the fossil fuel era and the introduction of free energy could be nothing but good for all human beings and the planet. He knew there would be a transition period. People who owned homes heated by gas would want to convert to electricity. Electric cars would come to dominate the automotive industry. New all-electric self-powered homes could be located in more remote areas without the cost of utility line extensions.

Amar could see a massive entrepreneurial surge to develop applications for the new power source. The transition would be expensive in some ways, but well worth it in other ways. In his mind, the common good of humanity out-weighed the profit-taking needs of the investor class. Some provisions would have to be made for displaced workers. He could see it coming and was prepared to tackle that problem as well.

As Renfro had emphasized, disrupting the status quo at the level Amar was contemplating would paint a bulls-eye on all of their backs. In the beginning, they would have to lay low. Very low. One thing Amar Parish didn't want to give up was his ability to move around without the kind of scrutiny that might compromise his revolutionary activities. While he didn't want to be in the eye of the media, newly minted billionaires don't just disappear.

The sale of the Greenstone Satellite System hadn't gone unnoticed by the press. After a lengthy conversation with his teammates, it was decided that rather than trying to disappear, the best place to hide would be in plain sight. Amar already had a media presence as the young playboy heir of tech billionaire, Tom Parish.

Collectively, they decided the best storyline to feed the press was that the fledgling billionaire had found the love of his life. He then decided to retire to a ranch in Montana to enjoy his newfound wealth and loving relationship. As was the custom of the uber wealthy, his need for privacy was a foregone conclusion. He and Katya released some carefully crafted photos of them riding horses on the ranch and boarding the jet for far off adventures. A single page in People Magazine now and then seemed to mollify the media's appetite for news of the couple.

During their regular briefings, Renfro had insisted on the need for absolute security. He built a gravel road and eight-foot elk fence around the entire property. A complete surveillance system with full camera coverage and infrared sensors had been installed and was monitored in the gatehouse at the entry to the ranch. Many reporters were turned away at the front gate. Robby set up a virtual private network for internal communications. Since they no longer had access to the Greenstone Satellite System, all critical information between team members would be transmitted by encrypted email. Conversations that appeared to be normal would be conducted using regular cell phones to promote the legend they were creating for anyone who might be listening.

Gary Renfro had done a masterful job designing and building the new riding arena. Plans for the steel-framed free-span structure had been drawn by the German firm who neither knew nor cared where the structure would be built. Renfro brought two of his best PCI operators in from overseas to set the concrete forms and manage pouring the walls and floor for the underground factory. Prestressed concrete panels formed the ceiling of the factory as well as the subfloor under the arena. A tunnel had been constructed to the basement of the main house to allow the crew to go back and forth to the factory without being seen by prying eyes. The whole structure had been buried under two feet of dirt leaving only the footings for the metal building exposed.

When the metal building contractors arrived, all they saw were footings that had been poured correctly by others. The 100-foot-by 200-foot arena consisting of sixteen horse stalls, an office, tack room, and the remainder in indoor riding space, had been completed in less than two months. It was ready for horses just after the first significant snow fell on the Swan Valley that fall. A separate metal hay barn was added as well.

Task one for Robby Harris was to get the factory up and running. That first winter, he concentrated on completing the design work for the Ularian Power product line. The first product prototype was a 200 amp residential unit. A twelve-inch cube, it was the same size as the original Ularian unit. It was self-regulating and would produce enough power on demand to run the average 3,000 square-foot home. It was boxed with several adapters, the most common of which, was a four-pronged dryer-type plug. Installation was simple. You unplugged your dryer, plugged in the adapter, and then plugged the dryer cord into the back of the adapter plug. Then you turned off your main breaker, cutting off all power from the electric company, and voila, self-powered home.

The second product was designed to interface with any electric car or truck. Amar bought a Freightliner eCascadia electric tractor-trailer and a fifty-three-foot-long Featherlite Country Estate horse trailer. With Robby's generator on board, the unit could be driven forever with no fuel or recharging required. The horse trailer would serve to back up the legend they were creating about a gentleman's horse ranch. In reality, it would be used mostly to acquire and bring in the materials needed to produce the new line of free energy generators.

The trailer had a complete apartment on board, so the drivers wouldn't have to pay for accommodations anywhere they went. With no need to pay for fuel or lodging, the trailer crew could travel the United States without leaving an electronic trail behind them. The following spring, the trailer would be also be used to purchase and ship each individually selected horse for the new herd, further supporting the gentleman's horse ranch legend.

There were two ways into the factory. A large swing-away storage shelf was fabricated in the utility room located in the basement of the main house. When closed, it completely concealed the entrance to the tunnel leading to the underground factory fifty yards to the north of the house. A similar swinging wall, covered in saddle racks and horse tack, was built in the arena's tack room. When opened, it revealed a stairway and a conveyor belt which was used to move raw materials into the basement and bring finished products up from below. The large tack room had roll-up garage doors on two sides. With the horse trailer backed up to the outside door, horses could be unloaded directly into the arena. Materials could also be unloaded, safe from prying eyes, and conveyed down onto the factory floor.

Robby Harris, ever the mechanical genius, surpassed all of the accomplishments of a stellar career with the design and completion of the Ularian Power robotic factory. The assembly line had been fabricated under the strictest security in an empty warehouse in Everett, Washington where it went unnoticed alongside similar activities being conducted by the Boeing Corporation. It was then disassembled and covertly shipped to the ranch. The process of re-assembling and tuning the manufacturing line had taken the better part of a year.

When entering the mechanical marvel, one was greeted by a forest of bright red robotic arms bobbing up and down. Every robotic station was connected by CNC controlled conveyors that moved each Ularian

Power unit through the successive stages of its fabrication. Every operation that generated noise was completed inside of sound-insulated compartments that slid open to accept the next part and slid shut while the operation took place. A conversation in a normal tone of voice could be carried out anywhere on the floor. The background noise was a symphony of low whirring and clicking sounds. The whole manufacturing area was lit with full spectrum daylight LEDs producing the same light level one would experience anywhere on the ranch during daylight hours.

The robotic factory required a crew of only two people working in three shifts around the clock to feed materials into the line and box up completed units coming out the other side. Enough space had been left in the facility for storing only 10,000 units. Fortunately, a boat storage warehouse with a fenced-in yard had come up for sale in nearby Seeley Lake. It had failed as a business because it was surrounded by forest and had no street presence. It was perfect for Amar's intended use. He had snapped it up and was beginning to fill it with completed and boxed Ularian Power units.

CHAPTER SIXTY-TWO

London

Dr. Evan Chatterjee began the process of revealing the discovery of the Imbrium Codex, the chamber at Persepolis, and the ruins of the ancient city of Vandalay by approaching the BBC World News Organization. Being a British citizen, whose professional reputation was well known, Evan was granted a meeting immediately. He had carefully removed all references to the Ularian Power generator from his translations of the codex and the archived footage taken at Vandalay. The existence of the Ularian Power generator had to be kept secret, at least for a while. Once the BBC executives saw the unedited images from all three discoveries, they were anxious to help produce a documentary film as quickly as possible.

There was so much more to do. Denmark granted home rule to Greenland in 1979 but still retains responsibility for the foreign affairs and defense of the country. Evan asked for and was granted a meeting with the Queen of Denmark. Upon seeing the images from Vandalay, she contacted key people from the government of Greenland and brought them up to speed. The ruins of the city had been buried under fresh snow immediately upon the departure of the Aurora Star. Danish troops were dispatched the following spring to protect the site and prepare for the onslaught of visitors that would surely occur once the story was told. Access to the site would be strictly limited to an approved list of qualified archaeologists.

Dr. Chatterjee and the Queen visited UNESCO World Headquarters in Paris. Vandalay only needed to meet one out of ten criteria to be granted World Heritage status. It met nine out of ten of the criteria and World Heritage Site status was immediately granted. The BBC documentary was released the summer after the voyage of the Aurora Star. It began with a tour through the PCI museum narrated by Rachael Parish. The late Tom Parish was cast as the hero, which he indeed was. Rachael traced the history of Tom's career, the creation of the museum, and the acquisition of Lunokhod 1. Rachael presented the discovery of the Imbrium Codex and Evan narrated his translations of the material.

The BBC developed animations to illustrate the action of our solar system's binary orbit which sent astronomers and astrophysicists all over the world scrambling to verify or oppose the theory. Evan presented the discovery of the chamber at Persepolis and outlined how the location of Vandalay had been determined using the Greenstone Satellite System.

The documentary ended with the onsite footage of Vandalay and a call to action for all scientists and archaeologists to thoroughly investigate the new information. Amar's participation in the discoveries was downplayed to help protect his fake legend. No mention was ever made of Harry Warburg or Viktor Dragan and his evil band of mercenaries. The documentary opened in movie theaters around the world and quickly became the highest-grossing documentary film ever released. In the short span of four months, the names Vandalay and Ularia were in common usage.

The Iranians and other religious sects around the world came out in direct opposition to a discovery that upset their creation stories. Strangely enough, a progressive Pope embraced the tales of Vandalay and called for a thorough review by the Vatican.

All the nuts who believed the moon landings were fake, swore that this was just another attempt to defraud the people. But there was just too much evidence that everything in the documentary was true, and the protests never gained any traction. The people of Earth were ready for something new, something that changed the game. The ruins of Vandalay were real and would be in the news for years to come.

CHAPTER SIXTY-THREE

Aboard the Zoltan at Sea.

When Viktor Dragan and his crew hadn't returned, Warburg's interest in Amar Parish and his activities dwindled. He watched the documentary and when no mention had been made regarding the discovery of a new technology, he let the matter fall from his radar. Warburg was much too busy rolling out his new scheme for world dominance. The ZolaPhone was introduced to critical acclaim during the Christmas shopping season after the voyage of the Aurora Star. It quickly became known as the Z-Phone.

The major international telecom companies had invested hundreds of billions of dollars in the infrastructure of the new 5G network, which required the upgrading of cell towers all over the United States and most of the developed world. Warburg commissioned a study showing that bombarding the population with uniformly intense high-frequency electromagnetic radiation, broadcast by the 5G system, was detrimental to the health of both humans and animals. His study conveniently showed that the longer, weaker, and more efficient wavelength of the Zoltan Satellite System had no such side effects.

Warburg's ad campaign was accepted en masse by the millennial demographic. Z-Phone purchasers cited the looming health hazard of 5G as one reason for buying the new satellite phones. 5G wasn't green, but the Z-Phone was. They loved the high tech look of the device and the promise of every form of financial convenience. Many were infatuated with the slogan, "In touch, everywhere on earth 24/7."

Christmas sales soared into the hundreds of millions of units. The Z-Phone was accepted en masse in developing countries because there were no infrastructure costs. All you had to do was buy the phone, and you were connected. No cell towers, infrastructure, or terrestrial switchgear were required. Because of the solar cell, you didn't even need to be in the proximity of electrical power to keep your phone charged. People in developing countries could now stay in touch and surf the web without ever buying a computer. As Warburg had predicted, the one percent transaction fee was considered inconsequential. Money was rolling into his coffers by the trainload.

Warburg implemented data mining on a scale never contemplated by Amazon or Google. Retailers were scrambling to pay for an opportunity to buy targeted ads on the new network. Browsing histories were analyzed at an unheard of level. Few people understood that the Z-Phone was always listening. If you discussed buying something with a friend, a targeted ad with a one-click buy button appeared on your phone a few minutes later.

The entire system was privately owned and controlled by one man who had no national loyalty. Harrison Warburg was loyal only to himself and well on his way to establishing the template for a total surveillance society. Warburg already possessed one of the largest fortunes on planet Earth, yet few people had ever heard of him. He was beyond caring about money; he wanted control—total control. The subterfuge was almost complete.

While the Z-Phone was being touted as one of the greatest technological developments of all time, it also had the potential to become one of the most demonic inventions ever conceived. Its demonic potential didn't exist because of the technology itself. It existed because of the intent of its owner.

The new 5G network suffered acutely from bad press. The major telecoms were losing market share at an incredible rate. Billions of dollars in infrastructure investments were going down the drain. Having been told directly by Warburg what was coming, Amar Parish had avoided the 5G investment mania. Nevertheless, PCI suffered a loss of market share along with the rest of the big telecoms. Parish didn't care. He was focused on releasing Ularian Power for the benefit of mankind.

CHAPTER SIXTY-FOUR

Swan Valley, Montana

The second winter since the voyage of the Aurora Star had come and gone. Amar and Katya fell in love with the quiet winter season in Montana. Three feet of snow covered the pastures that winter. The evergreens were flocked in a lacey covering of snowflakes. They had fully embraced the horse ranch lifestyle, taking a real interest in building the herd. Amar acquired a twelve-year-old Belgian that was used to pulling a wagon. The gentle giant easily transitioned to pulling a sleigh, and the couple had spent many happy hours circling the ranch on the perimeter road, reins in one hand and hot toddy in the other.

Once again, springtime had come to the Swan Mountains. The ranch was surrounded by snowcapped peaks. At 48 degrees north latitude, the days were quickly getting longer. After the equinox, the extra daylight caused the pastures in the valley to green up in the short span of two weeks. The Tamaracks were re-growing their needles. Elk were in the meadows, and the bears were emerging from their dens.

Robby Harris had managed the factory all winter long, and the warehouse in Seeley Lake was nearing capacity. Renfro had spent the winter traveling back and forth to Seattle to spend time with his family and to keep an eye on Al Hemmings. It had fallen to Gary to make sure that PCI was functioning properly. Evan and Rachael traveled the world, giving presentations on the discovery of Vandalay. While they hadn't declared any significant developments in their relationship, Amar could see they were becoming increasingly fond of one another. Everyone had arrived at the ranch the previous evening to discuss the release of Ularian Power. They all gathered in the living room of the big house for a planning session.

Amar began, "It feels so good to be all together once again."

Katya added her greeting, "Yes, we are both so pleased to have you all close once more."

Everyone expressed similar sentiments.

Amar continued, "After all we've been through in the last couple of years, it's clear to me that we are family. But we're no ordinary family.

We're a family with a mission, and it's no ordinary mission. We're sitting on the greatest profit-making opportunity in recorded history. We're also sitting on the greatest freedom generator ever conceived. I have to ask one more time, are you still committed to foregoing all profits from this endeavor in favor of turning over the technology for the benefit of all mankind?"

Robby Harris said, "I'm in, boss."

Gary Renfro seconded, "Me too, for better or worse."

Evan and Rachael said in unison, "We're committed."

Amar put an arm around Katya's shoulders. "As are we. Gary, would you bring us up to speed on the legal issues?"

"I'd be happy to," Gary said. "There are several problems associated with dropping this technology onto the world at no cost. First, everyone will recognize that this tech has enormous value. They will all want to own and control it. We can't file a patent on the devices without revealing how they work. Once that cat is out of the bag, anyone with the resources could reverse engineer the technology and attempt to file their own patents, shutting us out. If successful, they could possibly take away our ability to make the tech available for free. That would defeat the point of the whole endeavor. There's also the problem of countries like China that have no respect for the intellectual property of others. Robby has perfected a solution to the problem."

Robby took his cue, "We discussed this idea before, and I've been able to make it work. The cases on our devices are TIG-welded shut. They can't be opened without cutting them apart. The critical components are kept in a vacuum chamber. If the vacuum is broken, a chemical compound is released, dissolving the guts of the device in a couple of seconds. I have also installed sensors that will do the same thing if they try to open the device inside of a vacuum chamber."

Renfro picked up the narrative, "We think we've solved that problem, at least temporarily. The second issue is that a black market for the devices will appear the day after we release the first batch to the public. We don't see any way around it. If we give a unit to a family who plugs it in and uses it, they'll receive a monetary benefit of a few hundred dollars per month in utility savings and possibly a few hundred more if they have an electric car which they can charge at home. If they decide to forego those savings and cash in by selling their unit to someone else, there's not much we can do to stop them. We also can't predict what kind of a price each unit will command, but it could be substantial. We've decided to let it roll and see what happens.

The third issue is the loss of jobs in the energy sector. That will happen gradually as the units become widely available. The impact could be significant, and the question becomes—how can we compensate people who've lost their jobs? A simple answer is we give them a second unit to sell. Depending on the black market value, that could more than compensate them for the changes in their livelihood. We also expect a new job sector to emerge as a full-on industry arises, adapting homes and vehicles for the new technology. Some of the displaced workers might be able to move into those new positions. Unfortunately, you can't make an omelet without breaking some eggs."

"Thanks for all of your hard work, Gary," Amar said. "Let's move on to the release of the technology. Katya and I have spent the winter trying to come up with the best idea to make a splash with the first release without revealing our identities. We have approximately 1.5 million units in inventory. So far, no one outside of the ranch knows what we're doing. Katya and I have come to love and respect the people of Montana. They make up a friendly, industrious, and family-oriented society. For the most part, they're not wed to the materialism that is so prevalent elsewhere in the country. They prefer the wealth of the natural beauty that surrounds them. We keep hearing and seeing the slogan that Montana is the 'Last Best Place,' and we're starting to understand why they say that."

Amar laughed, "You have to be willing to survive winter, though. My proposal is this: there are just under a million people in the whole state, living in approximately 338,000 households. Katya and I have discussed this idea at length. Let's make the entire state of Montana our test case. Let's give one unit to every household in the state. Without revealing what we're up to, we've met with UPS officials and discussed the idea of a massive delivery to every home in the state. They estimate it can be accomplished in three days. We'll still have over a million units in inventory for whatever comes next. We could also do the same thing in Wyoming in short order. I'd like to hear what you all think about this idea."

"That's a bold move, Amar," Evan said. "Montana is ranked 46th in the United States in income per capita. That kind of a move could cause enormous capital inflows and increase the fortunes of everyone in the state. Frankly, I'm completely in favor of the idea."

Rachael had an idea as well, "If we do this, Montana could not only become energy independent, but the state could also use its existing power-generating capacity to become a net exporter of energy resources in the short term. Making an entire state into a free energy zone will definitely create a huge media splash. How do we keep our identities secret in the middle of all of that?"

Renfro, ever the security expert, had already worked that out. "The only way we can be detected is if we leave a financial trail. The total shipping bill from UPS will be around 3.1 million dollars. We've set up a number of interlocking LLC's and offshore holding companies to funnel the UPS payments through. It'll take years for them to un-scramble the money trail. By then, the world will have changed.

The second way they could find us would be by tracing the move-ment of the units from our warehouse to various UPS distribution hubs around the state. I have a friend who owns a trucking company in Billings. For an additional million, he has agreed to provide trucking services to ship the units to UPS. His people have signed non-disclosure agreements and have been more than well compensated to keep their mouths shut. It's a risk, but one that can't be avoided."

Amar said, "One more thing—Robby has set up the each of the de-vices with a remote access chip. The chip will allow us to activate all of the units at the same moment in time. Robby tells me the activation will have to be done from the jet at about 50,000 feet over central Montana in order to turn the units on all at once. I'm sure you'll all want to be on that flight. Are there any more questions? So, we're all in agreement to proceed?"

Everyone nodded their approval.

"Okay then," Amar proclaimed. "there's still a lot to do; so let's get to it."

Epilogue

CHAPTER SIXTY-FIVE

The United States

By April of 2021, the Z-Phone had broken all the telephone sales records ever achieved. Even Apple was feeling the pain. An army of lawyers retained by the major telecom companies, and everyone else whose business was disrupted, descended upon Washington to voice their client's extreme indignation for the new satellite system.

Z-Phone sales were off the charts, but the adoption of the "Z" as a virtual currency was lagging behind Warburg's projections. That spring, in a fit of pure greed, Warburg unilaterally tripled the transaction fee from one percent to three percent for all phone holders who had not opted to transact their business in "Z's". Some Z-Phone subscribers took the additional charges in stride. Many converted to "Z's" to keep their low transaction rate. A significant number of them complained to the FTC. The press had a field day chewing on the unfolding story of the mystery man behind the new satellite phone system. It was the "who created Bitcoin" story all over again.

The satellite system was under private ownership. The Federal Trade Commission and the Department of Justice immediately formed a task force to determine who owned the Z-Phone system. Due to political pressure, a dedicated team of forensic accountants and investigators were assembled to follow every possible lead. They were unsure of the legal grounds upon which they were basing their investigation. There were no offices in the United States. The company wasn't traded on the stock exchange. The owner or owners of the Z-Phone system hadn't violated any securities law.

The lawyers for the major telecoms claimed that the Z-Phone was a coercive monopoly. A lower court judge ruled against them on three principles. First, disrupting a market through technological innovation is not illegal. Second, the Z-Phone system could not be classified as a coercive monopoly. True, it was the most well-developed satellite phone system ever conceived, but there were other competitors to choose from, and land-based cell communications were still available.

Third, no collusion between companies to corner the market could be found. The owners of the Z-Phone system appeared to be acting alone.

The lawyers then attacked the "Z" as a virtual currency, claiming that it was an illegal form of money. However, the Justice Department was way behind all of the new developments in the field of crypto-currency, and laws regulating it hadn't even been conceived of yet. That effort would take many years to adjudicate.

The major telecoms felt they were owed reparations for the disruption of their businesses. Despite all myths to the contrary, justice in the legal world is not based upon the principles of jurisprudence. It's a contest to see who will win, available to those who can afford the best legal gladiators needed to play the game. The owners of all the land-based cellular systems were well-connected politically. Such enormous pressure was brought to bear that the Justice Department convened a grand jury to investigate the Z-Phone.

The team of forensic accountants and investigators scoured the world for leads to the identity of the mystery man. Many months of digging through one offshore shell company after another produced no results. Finally, they decided to swim up the advertising stream to see who was responsible for the Z-Phone's ad campaign. Ultimately, the electronic clues led them to the Lethbridge Advertising Agency.

Todd and Allison Lethbridge were brought to the Federal Building in downtown San Diego where they were suitably intimidated and questioned mercilessly for two days under the guise of national security. Finally, with a guarantee of immunity, they revealed not only Harry Warburg's name, but the name of his yacht, the Zoltan. The Feds were beginning to get the picture. As one of the wealthiest oligarchs on the planet, Warburg had been on their radar for years, but had never committed a legal misstep that they knew of.

Surveillance of the Zoltan and both Warburg's jet and helicopter were set up. The Zoltan was currently cruising in international waters off of the coast of Mexico, just south of San Diego. The United States had no jurisdiction in that area. His jet was temporarily parked at San Diego's Lindbergh field. The Feds had no probable cause to arrest Warburg, but they could and would subpoena him to appear before a grand jury for questioning. They monitored control tower communications until the call sign of his helicopter came up. Warburg was on his way somewhere and would be coming into Lindberg Field to transfer to his jet for the trip.

The FBI waited until he stepped down from the chopper to cross the tarmac toward the Gulfstream. Suddenly, he was surrounded by black SUVs blocking his access to the jet. Several agents, accompanied by a news reporter and camera man, piled out. The lead FBI agent approached him and handed him an envelope. "Harrison Warburg, you have been served."

Warburg was so dumbfounded that he accepted the envelope. He had never been personally served in his life. The episode was being filmed and would be leaked to the press. The headline would read, "Mystery Man Identified!"

The FBI man went on, "Your appearance is required at the San Diego Federal Building at the date and time specified. If you do not appear, you will be held in contempt and a warrant will be issued for your arrest."

Warburg couldn't give the summons back. He sneered at the agent. "You have no idea who you're dealing with!" He turned and went back to the helicopter, growling at his pilot as he clambered on board. "Cancel my flight. Have the jet moved to Puerto Vallarta. Take me back to the Zoltan."

Upon seeing the clip of Warburg being served, the press went into action. They pulled out every picture of him, the Zoltan, the jet, and the helicopter that had ever been taken. They searched all financial records having anything to do with him. They listed his oil holdings and estimated his net worth. They dug into his personal life in a journalistic feeding frenzy. Despite the fact that Warburg's ownership of the Z-Phone network hadn't been proved, the headlines started to appear—*The mystery man behind the Z-Phone is a Romanian oligarch by the name of Harrison Warburg.*

Two weeks later a series of rolling electrical blackouts surged across the United States. No one knew when and if power would go out, whether it would be restored, or for how long. The blackouts were intermittent, allowing people access to news feeds part of the time. The press reported that the United States power grid had been hacked by cyber terrorists. Images of people dying in car wrecks when traffic lights went down, and every other kind of death or injury that could be attributed to the power failure, dominated the news cycle. When it was all over, 100,000 people would pass away as a direct result of the power failure.

Banks closed, and the New York Stock Exchange suspended trading. The internet went down, came back up, and went down, again and again. Everyone's life was disrupted. In a classic example of overspecialization, all businesses relying on the internet for daily operations couldn't function.

Ads were appearing on the internet, radio, TV, and print media touting that the only system remaining completely independent from the electrical grid was the Z-Phone satellite system. If you had a Z-Phone, you could still access the internet and communicate with any telephone that was still active. Since the Z-phone could be charged by its solar cell, access to the power grid was not needed to stay in touch. Z-Phone sales soared during the crisis.

The failure of the power grid was a national security crisis of epic proportions. Homeland Security, the NSA, CIA, FBI, and the US Cyber Command all went into action trying to find out who was behind the hacking and where they were located. They cast a very wide net. The hackers had concealed their identities well by bouncing the source signals of their electronic intrusion into the U.S. power grid all over the globe. They appeared to be attacking the system from multiple locations.

After two weeks with no control over the flow of electric power, the U. S. Government was homing in on the hacker's location.

Amar Parish and his crew were at the ranch in the Swan Valley when the power grid went down the first time. They all gathered in the main room of the big house. To keep up appearances, the compound was running on its propane-powered emergency generator.

Amar addressed the group, "I've never been so sure of anything in my life. This is Warburg's doing. He told me as much the last time I saw him. It's time to release the devices."

The Ularian Power Team executed their mission. A steady stream of semi-trucks pulled into the secluded warehouse in Seeley Lake, loaded up, and began their journeys to each of the major UPS hubs in Montana. Amar had recently acquired Iridium satellite phones for all members of the Ularian Power team so they could stay in touch.

Amar placed a call to Chris Taft, Tom Parish's mentor and boss from the early days of the Apollo Program. Taft was in his nineties but still sharp as a tack. When Taft was told that Amar Parish was on the line, he took the call immediately. After suitable greetings, Amar explained that a significant technological development was about to be revealed.

He told the former director of the Johnson Space Center that in three days' time Montana would become energy independent. Taft had seen the BBC documentary on Vandalay and connected the dots right away as the younger Parish told his story. Amar explained what was about to happen and stressed the need for secrecy in the short term. Taft was familiar with the unintended consequences of rapid technological development and listened with great interest.

Amar asked if Taft still had influence within NASA. If so, could he alert the operators of the International Space Station that the lights were about to come on in Montana? Could they video the event from orbit and broadcast it live? Taft assured him that he still had the pull to make that happen. He explained that the space station made fifteen orbits per day, and that the activation of Ularian Power would need to be coordinated according to very specific timing for the event to come off as planned. He would make the calls and let Amar know exactly when to push the button.

It was on a Tuesday and Wednesday that 338,000 households in Montana all received a package from UPS. Each package contained one bronze-colored Ularian Power Generator which bore the logo "UP" and was decorated with the double oval symbol of Vandalay, that symbol being the only clue to its origins. A smaller carton within the box held the power cords and an instruction sheet telling what the unit was for and how to hook it up. It also mentioned that every household in Montana had received the same package. All of the units would be activated that Wednesday evening by remote signal.

Montana was still experiencing electrical grid blackouts, and news coverage of the deliveries was spotty. Quite a few people thought the whole thing was a hoax. As they talked with their neighbors, the people of Montana discovered that every household had received a device. Local radio shows were passing on the information. Some people plugged in their devices immediately. Others waited for more information. As word began to spread that nothing bad had happened from installing the devices, more and more people plugged in their units. The media had been notified and reported that something of import was about to happen.

Early that evening, Amar, Katya, Gary, Evan, Rachael, and Robby boarded the Citation X at Glacier International Airport. Ted Lockhart and Jason Hall were in the cockpit. Responding to handheld light signals from the tower, they were cleared for takeoff. The tower reported light winds from the northwest, visibility unlimited. The Milky Way Galaxy glistened overhead as they taxied to runway 20 and began their acceleration.

At 150 knots, Ted rotated the aircraft and the Citation rose gracefully into the air. They all felt the thump as the gear doors clamped shut. About twenty minutes later, they were cruising east at 49,500 feet over central Montana. The members of the Ularian Power Team each had a window seat and were gazing down over a blacked-out state.

At an orbital altitude of 254 miles above the earth, the International Space Station was approaching the same location over the black landscape at 17,000 miles per hour. The window of opportunity was small and precise. A radio link had been set up by Chris Taft so Amar could communicate directly with the astronauts aboard the space station. The astronauts reported that they were five minutes away from their position and ready to film the event.

CHAPTER SIXTY-SIX

Aboard the Zoltan at Sea

Harry Warburg ignored the summons he had received from the FBI. He was seated in front of a high tech command and control console, two decks below the waterline in the bowels of the Zoltan, off the coast of Mexico. Five high-definition flat screen monitors were arrayed in a semi-circle in front of him. At the moment, he was using the surveillance cameras aboard several of the original Greenstone satellites to monitor the rolling blackouts that were sweeping across the United States.

Warburg, wearing a headset, was using his own unhackable satellite telephone system to direct the attack against the U.S. power grid that was emanating from a war room located in a chateau, deep in the mountains near Brasov, Romania. In return for the promise of millions of dollars, Warburg had assembled a squad of the most accomplished cyber terrorists on the planet for this mission. It was ironic that the true genius, Tom Parish, had made Warburg's method of communicating with his band of cyber terrorists safe and secure.

Marko Dragan was seated at another console nearby. One of the satellite cameras feeding Marko's screens was focused on the chateau that had once belonged to the Dragan family. The other screen showed a hidden camera view of the hacker's war room inside the estate. He was carefully monitoring the actions of the hackers at their computers.

Dragan sat up straight as he noticed activity on the overwatch screen. "Harry, there's a convoy of military vehicles closing in on the compound."

Warburg stabbed a button bringing the same image up on one of his monitors. Five MRAP military assault trucks were speeding up the road toward the chateau leaving a rooster tail of dust behind them.

"Damn," Warburg said. "I didn't think they would find us so quickly."

"Do you want me to end it?" Marko inquired.

"Hold for a minute," Warburg said. A tone of disgust evident in his voice.

They watched the monitor as the five assault vehicles surrounded the chateau. All at once, the doors on the vehicles flew open, and dozens of men in full combat gear poured out on a dead run toward the old building.

"Okay, now," Warburg pronounced.

Marko pressed a button, and the chateau, along with five assault vehicles, some of the best computer talent in the world, and every other person in the vicinity, erupted in a giant fireball. Warburg stared at his screens. Where there were once carefully controlled rolling black outs across the United States, now there was nothing. The entire country went dark.

Warburg threw down his headset. "Serves the bastards right. Let them figure out how to unscramble this!"

Aboard the Citation X:

Amar Parish turned to his colleagues, "We all know there will be unintended consequences for what we're about to do. Are you all content with the risks involved?"

Katya replied first, "I don't know where what I'm about to say comes from, Amar, but you know from your memories of Vandalay, you are not allowed to take direct personal action against Warburg and men like him. What we are about to do is both indirect and evolutionary. I, for one, am content that what we are doing is well worth the risks we face."

Amar flashed back to the events in Vandalay. He knew she was right. Although he hadn't fully come to grips with the rules of engagement in what was fast becoming his life's mission, he was starting to feel the presence of guidance from within.

Dr. Evan Chatterjee, who had often provided wisdom and counsel to his young protégé weighed in. "I'm reminded of something Sanjay said in the Imbrium Codex. He said that during the lower ages, humankind believes it is right and natural that the many be ruled by the few. All of our social and financial structures are based upon that premise. So far, the alternatives we've come up with to manage the affairs of humanity are capitalism, communism, socialism, and fascism. All of the "isms" have one thing in common. Despite what they say in the beginning, eventually, they all place an elite ruling class at the top of their societies.

"The ruling class believes it occupies the high moral ground. By right, they exempt themselves from all of the rules that everyone else must obey. As corruption from the top down accelerates, each of these methods of organization departs from its original inspiration and ultimately exists only to serve the interests of the ruling elite. When the people have had enough, they rise up and each "ism" finally destroys itself in a convulsion of violence. Then we switch systems and start the whole idiotic process all over again. We need to invent something new, and it must be based upon the principle of freedom from the bottom up.

Sanjay says there will come a time during the ascending cycle when we must both acknowledge and understand that the true nature of humanity is for all humans to live in freedom. If we don't take the actions necessary to manifest that destiny, a major extinction event may be in store for humanity.

Ularian Power is one of the first technological steps along the path to individual freedom. All of the generators are independent. If you take one or dozens, or even hundreds of them offline, the rest are unaffected. That's the antithesis of overspecialization. It's power from the bottom up. It's both evolutionary and sustainable. It's nothing less than the dawning of the understanding that there will finally be enough for everyone. The trick will be to make sure that no person, cartel, or government entity ever takes control of the generators. That will be the main battle we have to fight from here on out."

In turn, Amar locked eyes with Rachael, Gary, and Robby. They all nodded their agreement.

Just then, the radio crackled to life, "Mr. Parish, this is the International Space Station. We are in position. I doubt you can see this from your vantage point, but the entire continental United States just went completely black."

Robby Harris was buckled into his seat, holding a black box on his lap. Amar looked at Robby, "Well then, Robby, let's change the world."

Robby pressed a button on the black box. Amar's small band of revolutionaries looked out the windows of the jet. The deep darkness below began to twinkle as the lights came on in Kalispell, Helena, Butte, Great Falls, Bozeman, Missoula, and Billings, along with every farmhouse and village in the great state of Montana.

The last revolution has begun.

ABOUT THE AUTHOR

Willam O. Joseph is a craftsman, inventor and author. He enjoys the great outdoors and loves to kayak the pristine waters of the northwest. He has spent many years exploring the Rocky Mountains on horse-back and is a former Men's Senior Montana State Champion Cowboy Action Shooter. He loves the old west and currently lives and writes in Montana.

Aknowledgements:

First and foremost, this story is the result of a 32 year conversation with my wife Marshelle, for which nothing in writing could ever express my gratitude adequately.

I'd like to thank Mary Craig and Debby Swanson for their enthusiasm toward the end when inspiration is sorely needed to cross the finish line.

I'd especially like to thank Shannon Krzyzewski for her eagle eye and mastery of the English language. Thank you Shannon, I learned a lot on this one.

CPSIA information can be obtained
at www.ICGtesting.com
Printed in the USA
FSHW011519010420
68707FS